Dragon in Chains

Moshui

THE BOOKS OF STONE AND WATER

Dragon in Chains

BOOK ONE

DANIEL FOX

BALLANTINE BOOKS
New York

A Del Rey Trade Paperback Original

Copyright © 2009 by Daniel Fox

All rights reserved.

Published in the United States by Del Rey,
an imprint of The Random House Publishing Group,
a division of Random House, Inc., New York.

DEL REY is a registered trademark and the Del Rey colophon
is a trademark of Random House, Inc.

LIBRARY OF CONGRESS CATALOGING-IN-PUBLICATION DATA
Fox, Daniel.
Dragon in chains / Daniel Fox.
p. cm.
ISBN 978-0-345-50305-3 (pbk.)
1. Dragons—Fiction. 2. Magic—Fiction. I. Title.
PR6106.O96D73 2009
823'.92—dc22   2008044790

Printed in the United States of America

www.delreybooks.com

2 4 6 8 9 7 5 3 1

Book design by Mary A. Wirth

*This book is dedicated to
the one I love.*

Sort it out between yourselves.

*W*HEN DRAGONS BLEED,
THEY BLEED IN GOLD.
WHEN THEY WEEP,
THEY WEEP IN JADE.

ONE

Dragon's Breath

one

They called the fog her breath, the Dragon-in-Chains'.

They were peasants, of course, both sides of the strait. Superstitious and ignorant, they were apt to see traces of her in everything they feared.

Also, they were right.

UP HIGH on the Forge, he could look down and see it exactly, how she breathed. How the first wisps hung like trails of smoke, silk floss in the last of the day's sun; how they reached for one another, how they clung. How they drank moonlight when the sun was gone, how they thickened and spread. How her breath spilled across the strait to cloak the sea that held her, to brush two rocky shores with an inverted shadow of white.

From above, it didn't seem so dangerous: like bales of silk wadding that gleamed in the chill of the light, that stirred in waves and eddies like the waters that they hid. In truth, he knew, it was a banner of war flung down.

At his back was heat and noise and light, the boom of the mighty hammer striking a solemn toll, a sudden flare from the fire sending his own stark shadow rushing after.

Below—all the miles of living water from the mainland to Taishu-island, the farthest fringe of empire—was blank and silent, cold.

He shuddered, and turned away. It would be a hard night, a cruel night down there, in the dragon's breath. The fog swallowed sound and moon and starlight, it swallowed lives. He could be glad her breath didn't reach this high.

He hoped he could be glad.

two

*H*an would kill, or he would die tonight. On the water, in the fog.

If there was a choice, he couldn't see it. There would be a body, a dead boy pitched over the side into that dense white chill that hid the dark sea from the deck. It would be him, or else it would be Yerli. His new friend, Yerli. They didn't get to choose, only to fight.

He had seen death already: executed criminals and starveling children, an old woman in a ditch. A magician paraded on a board in the pomp of his magisterial robes, for all his townsfolk to wonder at the fact that he could die.

Han's own mother, dead in the family bed, with the babe that had ripped her lifeless in her arms and the copper reek of so much blood in the room.

He had seen death more closely, this day gone. His recent master, the scribe Han's father had sold him to: Master Doshu had died a scribe's death, brutal and swift and meaningless, and the brushes of his trade adorned his killer's topknot.

They'd been on their way from one village to the next, the endless circuit of the wandering craftsman. Master Doshu rode his donkey, his pride, while Han trotted in the dust of its heels carrying all his master's packs and baggages, his folded writing-desk, his shoes. The donkey was more useful, more valuable than Han; that was simply so, and he was used to it. He was happy enough: fetching and carrying, crying his master's skill in the marketplace, buying or begging his master's supper and bed, his own if he was lucky. Learning his characters. Learning to carry his bruises, his hunger, his other pains in the quiet of his heart. It was a boy's life, and one to be content with.

Their road kept them a cautious mile from the coast, the ingrained wisdom of travelers. It wasn't enough.

A bridge, that crossed a stream tumbling over itself in its eagerness for the sea. Three men, emerging late and swift from the shadows beneath, where they must have stood a long time waiting thigh-deep in bitter water. They were bitter too, to find a threadbare scribe and a boy where the clipping of hooves must have had them hoping for a magistrate.

Still, one seized the donkey's bridle, while another dropped a neat loop of cord over Master Doshu's head. Han saw that noose drawn tight, snaring his master's beard as it went, tugging the long hairs back beneath his chin so that he looked ridiculously unlike himself as he mouthed fish-like at air he couldn't reach, as his fingers scrabbled for a thong sunk too deep into his wattles.

Han screamed, and was cuffed aside. He scrambled up, knife in hand, and was seized and bound and beaten while all the time Master Doshu's face darkened, his legs slowly ceased their kicking, his hands fell slackly to the ground.

Han was let see that, all of that. Strong callused hands quieted the donkey, slapped its rump. Dizzily, Han heard a rough voice, "We eat well tonight." Those same hands checked his bonds, slapped him with the same casual dispatch. Someone chuckled.

Master Doshu's body was stripped of everything that might have use or value, which meant apparently everything he wore, down to his smallclothes. His ivory rings were grunted over; the poverty of his purse earned Han another slap, less contented. All the bundles and bags were divided up smartly, between donkey and boy; once burdened—more lightly than before, both of them, if fear and doom have no weight—donkey and boy were led away, each on a halter of rope.

THEY FOLLOWED the stream to an inlet below a promontory. In the shadows there, a high junk rode at anchor. Pirates, then—but

Han had been sure of that already. Regular bandits wouldn't be so swift to dispose of a donkey.

They slaughtered it right there on the stony beach, butchered it crudely and made mocking play with its head. A boat brought more men ashore; the bags were picked over while the meat roasted over a hasty bamboo fire. Han was poked and prodded, cuffed, discussed, not spoken to.

Another raiding-party brought another boy and three women besides, tearful and gagged with rags. Tossed down beside Han, the boy—Yerli—hissed questions at him until they were both kicked silent. Han watched the men, listened to their talk, tried to understand what he—and, yes, now Yerli—were here for.

What the women were for had been clear from the start, and the pirates made no attempt to hide it. They ate, they leered, they gambled and squabbled among themselves; mostly, Han thought, they waited. As he did, and the other boy beside him, and the women who were pawed at but nothing worse. Not yet.

An hour before sunset came their captain. Broad and squat, gray-bearded in a profession that should not run to age, he gazed down at the boys and smiled thinly.

"Two of them, is it? We only want the one. One will learn obedience, and it may only cost him a finger or two; two boys together is a hatch of trouble. Well. They can fight for it, hmm? Lads? One of you can be one of us in the morning, tagged as crew," and he reached out a hand, drew the nearest man close and showed them the heavy iron ring that pierced his left ear. "Tagged for the *Shalla*," and his fingers flicked the ring so that late sun picked out scratches on the metal, "not for me. If it makes any difference, if either of you can read."

"I can read, sir." To his own astonishment, that was Han, struggling awkwardly up onto his knees. "And write too."

The captain barked a laugh. "It's not a qualification, boy. My crew takes my word for it, that their tags tie them to my ship. So can you. Or your little friend here," the toe of his boot digging into Yerli's ribs. "Or are you a reader too, shall I be amazed?"

"I can read futures," Yerli said. "My master, that your men killed? He was a magician. He taught me."

The men muttered among themselves: *Wizard's pup? Worth the keeping . . . worth the selling . . . worth the killing, do it now . . .*

"Can you make spells?" the captain demanded, his face entirely not saying what the proper answer was, what might lead to keeping, or selling, or killing.

"No, sir. But I can show you what I see—and I can see some of what lies before you, where your blood will take you."

The captain grunted and turned away. "Leave him bound. I say where our future lies. And his, too. One knife between them, and we'll have one boy before morning. Get that meat cooked, and all of this aboard," what poor loot they'd gleaned, and their captives too, loot too. "Tide is turning, and I want to be stood well off by sunset, in case the wind shifts. After dark, lads, after dinner. You'll have your fight."

THEY TOOK the women first, trussed and gagged. One at least had some spirit left, trying to kick a man out of the boat; the way that man used his bamboo after, she must have regretted it.

That same long bamboo that poled the boat to and from the junk, he put to yet another use when it was the boys' turn. Half his teeth had been knocked out by whatever mighty blow it was with whatever weapon that twisted his lips into a pattern of scars; he grinned gappily down at where they lay in the ribs of the boat and slurred, "Boys don't need to read. Boys scrub and sew and carry water. And fight, when they are told to. And try to please the captain. Here is our last boy, see?"

And he reached out that long bamboo and nudged something black where it swung on a chain from the foredeck, half in and half out of the water. It erupted into a seething, swarming mass of flies. What they'd cloaked must have been a boy once, bound to the chain. His face was blackly empty, and Han couldn't tell whether he'd lost his eyes before or after he was dangled there.

Below the waist, below the waterline, he was barely more than half a boy, so much of him had been eaten away. His legs were bones, held together by rags of flesh and tendon.

"He lived three days on the chain," Half-Mouth said. "The captain had him pulled up every day, to see. Yesterday he was dead, so we came ashore for you. For one of you. You," a poke of the pole at Yerli, "tell my fortune. Before you fight."

"I'll need your blood," Yerli said. Half-Mouth hissed, and poked again before he punted to the well of the junk.

THE FOG overtook them after sunset, chilling the soul and the skin. By then the boys were sat untied, more or less unwatched in a corner of the foredeck. They'd been fed, even, one hunk of half-burned, half-raw donkey meat that they chewed at, bite and bite about.

"If you can see futures," Han muttered, "why are you here?" Why let himself be ambushed, his master slain?

"I can't see my own," softly back at him. "It's always other people. And it does take blood."

See mine, then, see who wins between us. I'll bite my lip . . .

Instead he bit that back. How could they fight, knowing already who would win? And if they didn't fight, these men would kill them both. That was apparent. The fight was a test as much as an entertainment.

Still, they were talking now, and it was hard to stop. "If your master was such a magician, how could common pirates slay him?"

What came back to him was a snort, almost a laugh aloud. "Rafen was no magician."

"But you said—"

"Yes, and so did he say. He was a fraud, a cheat. He gulled the stupid for cash."

"You said he taught you."

"I lied. He *found* me. He was a cheat already, but a poor one; I made him good."

"Because you are a better cheat?"

"No. Because I am not a cheat. Shhh . . ."

. . .

THE WOMEN had no chance to fight. They did scream, each of them, for a while. That much came up from the junk's hold, where the men had taken them.

One by one, a while after, they were brought out on deck and flung over the side.

The last, at least, was still alive. Han thought she was the one who had kicked earlier, and he wanted to applaud. She struggled again now, when she saw the fog; she begged to be killed first, before they gave her to the sea tonight.

The men ignored her. Swung and flung, as they had her unfortunate sisters.

She screamed her terror, all the way to the splash. Han could hear how the fog embraced her, how it drank her voice, he thought her terror too.

It wasn't the fall, he thought, or the water that scared her so. Nor the dying. It was what fell between here and there, what waited in that hesitation between the last breath and the ending.

The dragon, he thought she was saying, *the Dragon-in-Chains.*

HAN, AND Yerli. And a knife.

And a rope, to be sure they faced and fought each other.

The men cleared the well-deck, heaving out coiled cables, barrels of salt meat, gash timber. They made a pit, a theater for blood.

They dropped the boys into it, tied waist-to-waist with enough slack that one could jump back out of reach—but only just. Try to scramble farther, he would only draw the other after. With the knife. Turn to run, and he was dead already with the blade in his back.

The *Shalla*'s crew crowded on the upper decks to watch. They were laying wagers, of course; most seemed to be betting on Han. Those who didn't think that Yerli had a magic he'd kept hidden, something learned or stolen from his master. They'd both been searched again by pinching fingers, and they had nothing on them but the patched shirts and ragged trousers of apprentice boys—

but magic could be a word, a gesture, anything. Some of the men did not trust Yerli, and so they bet on him.

The captain shouldered his way through to stand above the well:

"You fight to be ship's boy, to belong to the *Shalla*. Loser goes over the side, living or dead. If you listen to the women, dead is better. If the other's hurt too bad to be useful, he goes too. That's all."

And then he threw the knife, a hard flick of his wrist to set it thrumming upright in the planking.

IT WAS a good throw, and a good plain knife. Handle wrapped in sharkskin for the grip of it; blade the length of a man's hand, worn hollow with years of sharpening; point—well, point sharp enough to drive thumb's-knuckle-deep into an old ship's stone-hard planking.

Han hurled himself full-length, Yerli too, the rope a slack tangle between them. Han's fingers found the knife's hilt, and seized it; a moment after, the other boy's hand closed around his wrist.

For that moment they were still, snatching a breath, organizing themselves, almost organizing each other for what must surely follow: the tumbling struggle for possession, elbows and teeth and desperate straining arms, rolling across the deck and slamming into the bulkheads, lucky not to roll right under the rail and down into the fog together, into the water, into the dragon's ken . . .

That didn't happen, though, none of that: because Yerli yelled and jerked away to the limit of the rope, all the distance that he could. He stared at Han through the torchlight and the icy drifts of fog. Han felt the burn of Yerli's grip still around his wrist, the press of fingers at the pulse-point where his blood rose.

And shook his head, shook his wrist, pulled the knife from the decking; rose to a crouch, while the men hooted down at them. It'd be so much easier if Yerli came back at him, made him use the knife, one swift blow and done . . .

Yerli wouldn't do that. He shook his head, straightened slowly, held one hand out in quiet request. "No," he said, too soft for the howling men to hear. "No, we won't fight. Give me the knife."

"Do what?"

"The knife. Give it to me." And then, impossibly, "Trust me."

If this was a trick, if it was a trap, it was too blatant for Han to see it. He said, "Is this your magic?"

"Yes," Yerli said. "I want you to see what I see. But I need more of your blood than I can feel through your skin. Give me the knife, and your hand."

There was fury above them, and the captain's voice bellowing; but Han held out his hand, open, with the knife flat on his palm. At the time or later, he never could have said why he did that.

Yerli took the knife and might have killed him then, one swift blow and done.

And didn't, he only opened the ball of Han's thumb till the blood ran; and then did the same to himself, and held them thumb to thumb, blood to blood. Now there was almost a silence on the upper decks as the prospect of magic ran like a whisper from man to man, like a shiver through the crew. The captain called for harpoons—"or a whip," he cried, "who has a whip?"—to goad these disappointing boys, but he didn't sound compelling and for sure nobody moved.

Han heard, but only distantly. For that little time he stood flesh to flesh, blood to blood with Yerli and felt his world shatter and fall.

See what I see.

What he saw, then, was himself. But not here, or not only here, blood-smeared and wide-eyed in a blur of fog. Here and somewhere else, on a journey he had not taken.

Yet.

He saw himself in tears, watching while a giant screamed.

He saw himself in chains and beaten, no surprise.

He saw a dragon reflected in his eyes.

He saw himself try to write a single simple character, and fumble it as a child might, or a man who could not read.

He saw himself as if in a mirror, do the same.

He saw himself in a dragon's shadow, sheltering.

No, sheltering from the dragon, trying to.

No—

"No."

That was Yerli, stepping away, taking his hands away, taking his blood and the beat of it and the vision of it, leaving Han bereft.

Han stared at him, seeing nothing but the boy, bewildered by him, lost. Yerli said, "Not like that, not when I look at you. See what I see . . ."

And then he used the knife again, but only to cut the rope that bound them waist-to-waist. He even smiled, a little, as he tossed the knife to Han's bare feet.

Han bent to pick it up. By the time he'd straightened there were half a dozen men in the well with him, and none of them mattered, because Yerli was already over the rail.

Over the rail and holding on one-handed, terrified, as though one glimpse into fog had cut through courage and inevitability and all; but he looked back at Han and said it again, shrieked it rather, "See what I see!"—and then he let go.

He lacked the nerve to jump, but he did force his fingers to unlock themselves one by one. And so he fell, before the men could reach him.

There was a rush to the rail none the less, but there would be nothing to see. Nothing even to hear bar the fog-drowned splash, because he fell in silence. The men turned away, frustrated, and would have fallen on Han surely if he'd flinched or whimpered, pleaded, fallen to his knees and begged.

Instead he stood there and looked at them, and perhaps he shrugged a little; and then he looked past them, to the shifting banks of fog that cloaked the water where his abrupt new friend had gone; and then he closed his eyes.

Perhaps it was that which held the men, that residual hint of magic. Perhaps it was the echo of Yerli's cry, perhaps they heard it as he did, endlessly, *see what I see . . . !*

Perhaps they looked at him and saw him doing that, looking through a lost boy's eyes, a fog-bound body falling.

Perhaps they thought that magic was infectious.

Perhaps they were right.

SEE WHAT I SEE.

Han closed his eyes, and saw the fog.

He saw it from below, like clouds iridescent with the moon they hid; he saw the *Shalla* like a darkness in the clouds, like a giant body's shadow in the sky, like a dragon free to fly.

He saw clouds and dragon rise, retreat as he fell into his own darkness, as the bitter chill of the water gripped his bones, as the sea's suck—

No.

See what I see. No more than that.

Yerli had gifted him that, blood to blood, but no more than that; Han had no right to share his death.

The moon on the fog was a suffusing glow, a lamp behind paper but higher, farther, fading now. The water was an enfolding darkness.

Han tried to open his eyes, and realized that they were open; he stood on the deck of the *Shalla* and there were men all about him, and he still saw nothing but the deep-sea dark where no light reached, only a boy, falling.

Falling toward something, a gleam, a hint of light below: a richness, all colors caught in a single point.

Not a point. A focus. Bigger than it seemed and drawing everything toward it, everything that fell . . .

Not shining, nothing so bright: all its brightness was wrapped within, and it only seemed to glow because the dark in which it lay was so intense. It gleamed like a charcoal heap at night, like a jewel mired in mud; all its light, all its colors were murky and dulled and indistinct.

All her light, all her colors.

See what I see.

What he saw, what Han saw: they saw a dragon.

They saw her, the Dragon-in-Chains where she lay sprawled on the seafloor, shackled in the strait that was her queendom, the empire's long prisoner. By her own dim bare light, they could see the chains that held her fast to the rock. Crusted and rusted, great works of spell and iron, unless they were spell entirely and only seemed to take the form of chains, just as perhaps she was spell entirely and only seemed to take the form of dragon.

Neither one of the boys could see enough to know that. Han saw only what Yerli saw, and Yerli was at the end of his seeing now, falling toward her, giving himself to what had scared him most.

At the end, at the last, did she open her mouth to take him? Or was it just her eye?

three

When she breathed, she fogged the mirror of the world.

It would come with the sunset, those evenings when the sea was kind and quiet, brassy in the late low sun, mirror-still; those nights when there was least breeze, and the men were most eager to fish. Eager till she breathed. Her breath would fill the strait: salt air suddenly as wet as the sea, beading like pearls on old men's eyebrows, dripping like rain from the sails, filling throats and lungs, drowning voices. Cloudy as rice-water, chill as spring-water, it would lie like a dense white quilt between dark and dark, the sea and the sky, her native elements. They said it was all she could do now, exhale one deep terrible nightlong breath to remind her people where she lay, under what burdens and how cruelly bound.

The fog was heavy but fickle, thinning here and parting there, roiling unpredictably on no wind that any sail could find. It was dangerous past measure, concealing rocks and shoals and whirl-pools, stealing all those signs—the stars, the lie of land in moon-light, the cries of birds, the swirls of muddy current—that men could steer by. It drew boats into uncertain waters, men into un-certain futures. It lapped at the solidity of land, changeable and deadly. How could her people help but be reminded of herself?

IN THE fog, even the bright red eye of the Forge was a sleepy smear. Even the hard hammer of the monksmith's work, which normally Old Yen felt like a bell in his bones: even that sound was flat and dull and not to be trusted, echoing off walls of white, walls of wet.

The Forge was a beacon, the hammer was a guarantee: the dragon was still chained. The monksmith worked night and day at his fires to keep that promise burning. Night and day, Old Yen was grateful. He had taught his children and now his grandchildren to deliver what was proper to the island in return, thanks with fish.

Only, not in the fog. Nights like this, let the monks pray hungry till tomorrow. Ships had grounded in the risky channels around the Forge; smaller boats had broken apart and been lost entirely. People, of course, had died.

Nights like this, as often as not he would let tide and current carry him all across the strait. He could sell his catch at Santung-quay as readily as he did at home; he could garner news to carry back with him. He could buy meat and cloth and incense. He could pray and make offerings to mainland gods, whom he would not ordinarily trouble.

Nights like this—as every night—his own Li-goddess would see him safe. Sometimes, he knew, shipmasters forgot to be devout. He never did. He took food to her temples; he paid cash to her nuns; he scattered rice and wine from his prow whenever he left safe harbor, and she always brought him safe home again. It wasn't only the tugs of current against his oar, the smells on the breeze that told him where in the strait he was. He felt her cool strong hand govern his as he steered, he heard her voice—liquid, lyrical—singing him a pathway through the fog. Where it cleared long enough to show him stars, he felt her breath in his face, to countermand the dragon's.

A man needed such a trust, such a goddess, when he took a great boat out into deep waters with only his eldest grandchild for crew. A great boat, and a fleet besides. If Old Yen glanced over his shoulder now, he would see the lights of half the village boats, pale blurs in his wake. He burned a brighter lantern from his stern, for anyone to follow who dared risk fog and sea together. For some, the chance of a good haul was always worth the toss;

they would fill their nets and let him do the worrying. As though he hadn't enough to worry about already, sailing this clumsy lee-tending hog of a hybrid with a crew of one. A willing crew, to be sure, but never enough; and young, so young . . .

A squint forward showed him two buttocks and a breechclout, where Mei Feng bent hazardously over the rail to haul a net aboard.

"Mei Feng! Take care . . . !"

Mei Feng lost overboard in this fallen cloud, this weight of fog, would be Mei Feng lost to the mortal world, a ghost fit to wander a world of water. Looking over the side, Old Yen couldn't even see the water.

Mei Feng waved and hauled, and the net came up: a shadow against the bow-light, fat and heavy and ready to spill, like a drop of water held pendulous on a hair. He turned to call across the sternboards, a low hooting wordless cry, fog-talk: little to it, because there was little enough to say. *Take in your sails; we will work these waters.* Tide would drift them slowly to the coast; wind and the river's push would hold them off until first light.

He heard his call picked up and passed along, a fading series of echoes. And then the silence after, fog-silence, with only the far faint pounding of the monksmith's terrible hammer to puncture it; and then not even that, true silence, the white wet weight of it, as though the dragon's breath could smother any sound in time, any sound at all . . .

AND THEN another sound, a new sound: a rolling, grunting chant. It took Old Yen a moment to understand it as voices, working to a rhythm, somewhere in that fog-choked moonlight.

For a moment he thought they must be far closer landward than he'd reckoned, maybe in the rivermouth already, and these were prayers from the temple on the headland. But his Li-goddess would have warned him if he'd led the fleet into danger. Unless her voice was drowned out by the dragon's laughter, and even then he would have known by the feel of the water against his oar, river silt fighting tidal salt.

So no, not that. Nor could this be the monks from the Forge. Close enough to hear their prayers, the fire's eye would be directly above him, searing . . .

No, no. This was something on the water, where there could be nothing on the water that had not come from men; which meant—

Which meant this: a sudden looming shadow in the white wall ahead, where the fog flung back the lamplight in a dazzle. A shadow that broke through the wall and was a boat; of course it was a boat. A boat that Old Yen knew, of course, he knew every boat on this coast. But so too did young Mei Feng know this one, and knew it had no business here: "A dragon boat! Grandfather, a dragon boat out of Santung . . . !"

"I see it." It and more. This one had a light burning in the prow, and he could see others now, dim and diffuse but definitely lights. He could hear them too, those other boats, the paddlers chanting at their work. And to meet one dragon boat out in the strait in the deadest hour of a fog-bound night was clearly impossible, so why not two, why not half a dozen?

Long and lean, this one was pulling alongside already, low in the water so that he could look down into her belly and see how many men were crouching there. Four dozen with paddles, and as many more as could be crowded onto the thwarts between them. Dragon boats were playthings, raced at festival for the crowd's pleasure and the profit of the fortunate; it had never struck Old Yen before, how well they could be used to carry pirates.

But they would need to know these waters very well to find their way, to find their prey in fog. And the men standing at the back, beside the steersman: they looked stern, dressed in a frightening authority, but not lawless. The opposite, surely, in those caps and robes. And, also surely, not at all men of the sea.

There was another in the bows, calling up: "You, there! Throw me a rope!"

Not a man moved, but Old Yen was anxiously aware of how they were armed, swords and bows to hand. Pirates or otherwise, he was their capture of the night. Their first capture: fog-talk said the other dragon boats were corralling the fleet around him.

"A rope, lord? Yes, yes, of course . . ."

He had ladders, more suited to a lord in his robes; but a rope had been demanded and a rope he sent, letting it uncoil in a swift fall to the lord's waiting hand.

That man climbed swift and sure, walking his booted feet up the planking, pulling himself easily over the rail. He stood half a head taller than Old Yen and broader in the chest, stronger in the shoulders, better fed by far. His glossy hair, his rings, his heavy skirts—even his mustaches spoke of rank and wealth and power. Old Yen might have kowtowed sooner than meet such a man eye-to-eye. If this hadn't been his own boat they stood on, in his own waters, in a fog where he was master.

He was thoroughly fogged now, bewildered, fallen out of his proper story: as though the fog had misled him into some stranger tale, where to be a fisherman and a grandfather was not enough for one man's life.

"You are not Santung men."

"No, lord. We are from Szechao."

"I am General Gao Ming; I serve the Son of Heaven. Where is Szechao?"

"A village, lord. General. On Taishu. That is an island—"

"I know what it is, fool," though there was no heat in the word, nor anywhere in him; more than the fog had chilled him, Old Yen thought. He seemed infinitely weary, beneath a superficial vigor. "Taishu is our purpose, if we can get there. Could you find it, in this fog?"

"Of course, lord." By the time they came there, the fog would have burned away; the dragon's breath never long outlasted dawn. He saw no point in saying so.

"Very well. Where is your crew?"

"Here." A single gesture to the single figure standing as mazed as himself, half naked as Mei Feng always was to handle the net and the haul, untroubled by the fog's chill, and—

"A *girl*?"

Very obviously a girl in breast-bands and breechclout, despite her hair cropped short and the lean muscles gleaming wet in lamp-light.

"She is all I need, lord," though he might as well have said, *She is all I have.*

The general grunted. "She had better dress. My men will be aboard."

Old Yen nodded and Mei Feng vanished into the cabin, where she kept shirts and trousers clean and dry until the fish were in their baskets and the boat had turned for home.

Then, "Your men, lord?"

"Those in the boat here, before it turns for more. The same for the rest of your fleet; you will take as many as you can convey on one trip."

"One—?"

The general smiled, and that was chilly too. "There will be many trips, man. Your boat will be more busy than you know, back and forth across the strait; you have an army to transport. An army, an empire. And its master."

When Mei Feng came up—barefoot as always but dressed otherwise, and a scarf bound about her head, and still she could be mistaken for nothing but the girl she was—he sent her for the ladders. This man might swarm comfortably up a rope, but not every man. He understood that; he thought he had understood everything, except why an army was coming to Taishu.

And then the first who came up the first ladder was barely a man at all, still a boy by Old Yen's biased reckoning; and his robes were yellow and his rings were jade, and so Old Yen found himself kowtowing on his own deck after all, because the general's hand cuffed him to it as the general's voice hissingly explained that this, this was the Son of Heaven, the emperor himself, here, now, standing with wet slippers among the spilled fish from the baskets.

four

The captain loomed over Han while some of his men were still leaning over the side, presumably seeing nothing but fog. *See what I see,* but for Han too that meant nothing now.

Briefly, he thought he might be following Yerli, following the women, down to see the dragon in his own flesh. The captain did not look happy.

He said, "I promised my men a boy, so I suppose we'd best keep you. For now. I also promised them a fight, and you defied me."

"I, I would have fought, sir," and he did think that was true, he was almost sure of it, "it was Yerli who—"

"I saw what he did. And I saw you give him the knife."

"I didn't know . . ."

"No. Which is what saves your life tonight. But you did stand still to let him cut you. That will cost you a finger in the morning. For now—"

He had a slim fillet of iron between his fingers, cut with a few dashed lines. Han tried to read it, but, "I'm sorry, sir, I don't know that character . . ."

"It says SHALLA. Learn it. By this token, you belong to the ship. To her, not to me; but she belongs to me. Remember that."

"Yes, sir."

The captain nodded, and held out his hand. When Han didn't respond, that same hand cuffed him hard across the ear, then reached and took what it wanted: the knife, from Han's unresisting grip. Han hadn't even remembered that he was holding it.

The captain used its hilt as a hammer, pounding soft iron against the rail until it curled back on itself, almost made a ring.

The captain's fingers, then, gripping Han's ear; that knife again, huge beside his eye; a sudden jab—and all the ringing and numbness in his head, all the dreadful fascination of the night, all the fog in him couldn't obscure that sharp point of pain.

Still, he didn't cry out. Not then, and not when the captain pushed the iron fillet through the flesh of his ear, tearing a hole that the knife had only started.

The captain closed the ring up with the simple strength of his fingers, and said, "What's your name, boy?"

"Han, sir."

"Han. You are ship's boy now, the *Shalla*'s boy; her men will teach you her ways, and I will teach you mine, and perhaps you will live. If you please me. I am called Li Ton. Draw up a bucket of water and wash that ear; then clean the deck here."

"Yes, sir."

WITH HIS ear and his cut thumb stinging from salt-burn and the well-deck scrubbed of blood, he was set to work restoring its former order: shown how to stack and tie loose timber, how to shift a barrel that he couldn't lift, how to coil a rope. Mostly the lesson came in shoves and kicks, close watch and rough hands. Half-Mouth tugged him about by the earring, making his eyes smart and the piercing ooze afresh.

The work was hard and strange to him, the blows were hard but familiar. Together, at least they kept him warm.

And at least he was able for the work. Tonight, he was able. He wondered how he'd manage it, a finger short in the morning. Several of the crew were missing fingers or fingertips, some more than one; he might have thought this a boat cursed by carelessness, if he hadn't been told otherwise. The thought of Li Ton's knife made him shiver despite the sweat of the work. It was a different kind of chill, but he thought it still belonged to the fog, or to the dragon.

· · ·

THERE WAS a lookout in the bows, shrieking about a dragon's eye in the fog, up high. It wasn't true. Han was sure of that, even before he looked.

Something was there, to be sure: a smoky red glow, fitful in the fog. Not any kind of eye, though, let alone a dragon's. Hers were green and wet, and down below. This looked more like firelight to Han. And it had a sound to accompany it, a dull repetitive booming. He didn't know what song she might sing if ever she rose against her weight of chains, but it wasn't this.

Li Ton was just as certain. He went up into the bows to fling curses at the man on watch; then he flung a coin after and called for less sail, for oars, for extra eyes.

Even Han was sent to the rail, one more lookout.

"Listen too," the captain said, clipping him smartly on the side of the head. "Your ears may serve us better. Listen through the hammer; listen for waves on rocks, for voices. Whatever you see, whatever you hear, cry out. If it's nothing, I won't be angry."

Angry or not, he would be rough. That big hand smacked Han again, on the back of the neck. Han muttered his obedience, gripped the rail and turned eyes and ears, all his attention outward.

IT WASN'T only dread of pirates that drove people inland from the coast. Simply knowing the dragon was there, chained or not, asleep or otherwise; that was enough to make folk wary. She hadn't risen for centuries, but the Forge was a constant reminder.

Han had never seen the sea, but he knew about the Forge. An island like a mountain peak, forbidden to anyone but monks. Smoking by day, a constant pall cast from the furnace at the peak; glowing by night, from the same cause. The sound of the great hammer he knew by repute, he knew it when he heard it.

Just as he knew the jetty, sight unseen, that they felt for in the fog: a long finger of old wood, reaching out over rocks to offer safe mooring. Boats would bring food to the monks, cloth, raw iron and charcoal. In return they would take blessings away with them, and worked iron goods: nails and wheel rims, axles, hinges. Locks and chains.

Chains, especially. They were the Forge's fame, even far from the coast where no one cared about the dragon, no one spoke of her, perhaps no one believed in her at all. Chains made here carried anchors for the greatest ships of the empire; they defended harbors up and down the coast; they were traded far inland, along the broad slow rivers, to bring security to mines and mints, to docks and workyards, to prisons and to treasure-houses.

People forgot, perhaps, that they were only symbols; no one forgot that the best chains came from the Forge. Other ironsmiths had lost hands or tongues for claiming that their own were Forge work. That was why the fire burned, why the hammer rang day and night; demand was insatiable. Unless it was the other way around: that the fire and the hammer had to work day and night to keep the dragon subdued, to refresh her chains with every blast of heat and every blow, and therefore the monks had much to trade away.

It was said that the monksmith slept no more than his fires or his hammer. The Forge had one master, it was said, and his eye, his craft, his skill were as crucial to its work as his prayers were crucial to its greater purpose, keeping the Dragon-in-Chains.

Han had heard this all his life, this and more, wild stories, fancies given life in words. He was a river rat until his father sold him, and stories ran up and down the water as goods did, as news did, with every oar and sail.

He'd heard the stories and shrugged at them, as he did tales of the emperor. Han was a river rat, and then he was a scribe's boy, grinding ink for his master and following his own footprints in the dust and mud of the road, around a long circuit of scattered villages and market towns. What did he care for dragons, or the Jade Throne?

And tonight he had seen the dragon in her chains, and now he was looking at the Forge. He knew it, and he thought Li Ton knew it too, though not what it meant or why it mattered. Neither the

Shalla's captain nor her crew were local men. He wasn't even sure they were the emperor's men. Master Doshu had shown him a map once, the whole breadth of empire on a single span of paper. He knew it was a true picture because it showed the Dragon-in-Chains just where she ought to be, just where she was, between the mainland and Taishu. His eye had been caught by other islands, though, not marked with names. They were the abodes of pirates, Master Doshu had said, wild men not even the emperor could tame.

Li Ton's crew seemed wild enough to qualify. Their accents were thick and strange to Han, though he'd heard many on the river as a boy. He could well believe they came from some island beyond the empire's reach, perhaps even beyond reach of her stories.

Not Li Ton; his speech was oddly cultured for a man so brutal. He was still not local, though, not from this province. Not if he was looking for the Forge. Any wise shipmaster would be holding off in this weather; no ship should call in any weather, except to trade at the jetty. Even pirates ought to understand that if they knew anything about the empire's long history, its magicians, its endless greed for beauty.

If they didn't—well, this, then. A junk sidling through the fog, lookouts posted at bow and beam; the captain looming with a breathy murmur, "Not many get their second chance to kill under my eye. You still owe me a finger, but stay close and do good work, do what I tell you, and perhaps I may not take it this time."

"Sir, sir, you can't kill the monks! This is the Forge, it's a, a place of magic . . ."

"Then we'll see what their magic is worth, won't we? And we'll see you blooded, if you want to keep that ring in your ear and your place on my boat."

"They will have no gold, no silver, sir. Their deaths will gain you nothing."

"Then they will die in vain. No loss. And perhaps I will gain a ship's boy, if he's wise."

"Sir—"

"What, *more*?"

"Sir," determinedly, "there is a dragon under the water," *I have seen her,* "and the monks' prayers, their work, everything they do on the Forge helps to keep her there . . ."

His determination was lost in the face of Li Ton's laughter. "A dragon, is it? Boy, I have spent long years at sea and never seen a dragon. I think I might like that."

"No, sir."

"No?"

"The Dragon-in-Chains, she's not a pretty mystery to be wondered at. She's, there's a *reason* they put her in chains and cast her into the strait. She's *terrible* . . ."

"Then we will hope the fog lifts," Li Ton said, "and the wind sets fair, so that we sail away before she rises. Enough, boy. I had a magician cast a luck-spell on my first boat, paid him for it, and she broke apart on a reef. I killed him for that, and haven't listened to another since. I'd have had that other boy's tongue out, if he'd tried telling futures on my ship. I don't care a spit for your dragon, if she's there. Keep careful watch, now—and here," the knife again, its handle slapped smartly into his palm, "edge this on your sole, you'll want it sharp. Give your precious monks a swifter ending."

"Sir, *please*, you don't need to kill them! Take their goods, their ironwork, their chains; take whatever you want, only leave them living . . ."

"One more word," Li Ton said, "it'll be your tongue I'm taking. You hear me?"

Han nodded, carefully silent. Li Ton grunted, and walked off.

This was a killing fog. Death was everywhere: before him and behind him, all around. There was nothing he could do. He propped himself one-legged against the rail and honed the blade of the knife against the hard leather of his heel, while he watched the blanket of the shifting fog, while his ears strained for any sound beyond the slap of water against the hull, the creaks of bamboo and timber and wet rope under strain.

· · ·

IT WASN'T he who first cried out for rocks, or for the shadow of the island looming, or for the jetty. He wished they could have been more lost, or the monks more careful. Likely they had never imagined raids. Anyone sailing these waters must know what they did here, how they kept the dragon subdued; who could wish them harm?

Almost, Han wished the ship had found the rocks before the lookout saw them. Splinter the hull and sink: they could all go down to join the women, join Yerli and the dragon. Almost, he'd prefer that.

Almost.

Weak, uncertain wishing has no power. He couldn't forget the last woman's terror, nor Yerli's, how frightened he was of the dragon he went to seek. Han had seen her as he did, and no, did not want to meet death in her embrace.

Did not want to meet death at all, and so he jumped with the crew from deck to jetty. Li Ton had told him to stay close, and he shouldn't make the captain look for him.

A quick squirm between hard bodies hot in the fog, the narrow boards of the jetty slippery underfoot: accumulating curses as he went, trying to skip the blows, he found Li Ton where he expected to find him, leading the men.

Han had the knife, and could do nothing. If he killed the captain, if he could, that was still nothing; the men would kill him and riot after, slaying every monk on the island.

They would do that anyway, he thought. He could survive it, or he could be dead himself.

He wasn't even going to think about running, hiding somewhere until the *Shalla* left. This fog would be like the night's dark, gone with the dawn, and the Forge was a rock; Li Ton would linger to find him in the morning, he was sure.

He followed his captain, as a good ship's boy ought. Born to be a river rat, he had learned to be an inkboy, an obedient apprentice; he could learn to be a pirate brat and a wicked killer. If he survived this night, if they all survived the dragon.

· · ·

A MONK met them with a lamp at the jetty-head. "Have you brought us fish? In this weather? If you only want to tie up till the fog lifts, you should know this is not the place—"

Li Ton said, "Han, take his light."

Han stepped off the end of the jetty, onto the cold damp stony path. The monk handed him the lamp without a word. Han didn't like the way it threw men's shadows onto fog; the *Shalla*'s crew seemed twice as many and twice as menacing, a crew of ghost-marauders.

Li Ton said, "Hold him," and two of the men stepped up to do that, long broad-bladed tao knives swinging loose. Just as their free hands reached to seize him, the monk was moving, screaming. Not running, not trying to lose himself in fog; not screaming for his fellows, or his god. Leaping, rather, leaping high, and screaming some kind of rage or exultation as he climbed the air; and then his feet, bare feet lashing out from beneath his robe, and each catching one of the uselessly clutching men so that both fell in a sprawl: one on the jetty at Li Ton's feet, the other tumbling off onto rocks below. Cursing as he fell, screaming when he struck.

Li Ton swore abruptly, kicked his man aside and swung his arm.

The knife he'd held in that hand caught the lamplight briefly, as it flew.

It struck the monk before he could sway entirely out of the way, though he made a fair effort; from only three paces' distance, it caught him in the shoulder, not the heart.

The sheer force of it sent him staggering backwards, off the jetty and close to Han. Too close, for a boy who had a lamp in his hands and a good sharp knife of his own unreachable in his belt.

They stared at each other, Han and the monk. Han couldn't read futures, but he could read a man's desires in his eyes. The monk came one brisk step toward him, and Han threw the lamp.

There are lamps and lamps, but this was the simplest: a bowl of whale oil, and a wick in flame.

Han only threw it because it was in his hands, and he wanted his knife there. Maybe he could die like a man, or at least like a pirate brat. The monk went to bat the bowl aside with the back of his hand, but it broke on contact; the oil spilled all over his robe, and then the flame found it.

Light erupted, from him and about him. So too did a noise, short and explosive, hard to understand how it could derive from a human voice.

Ablaze, then, a human torch, he still kept coming. Han hurled himself aside onto the stony steep slope of the island and the monk ignored him utterly, just running past. Running and scream-ing now, screaming again: he was a man of noises, and this time his scream was all turned inward. It spoke of searing agony, but he was talking to himself.

They could see his path quite clearly by the light of his own flame, until the fog ate him.

Small hope now of surprise; Li Ton sent men back to the *Shalla* for torches.

"If they want to burn," he said, "we can burn them all."

And then he came to where Han was still sprawled on the ground. Hauled him up by the scruff of his shirt, and nodded; and said, "Count your fingers, and be grateful. And stay close."

Han felt like a thief, under the warmth and weight of an ap-proval that he had not deserved and did not want, and needed.

THE PATH led—well, into the fog. After a while the fog brought them to a settlement. Scrubby soil, trees clinging to the slope, huts in array around a spring.

A line of monks was waiting for them, some with torches of their own. The pirates freed hands for fighting by tossing theirs into the nearest of the huts, or onto the dry reed roofs. That gave light in plenty, a hiss and a roar of light, driving back the fog.

The monks had no weapons except those torches. The crew was still confident against unarmed men; Han saw some charge for-ward screaming, waving swords and taos and dagger-axes, while others followed, vicious but cautious. Hotheads and wiser heads. Dogs and cats.

The monks were patient, waiting. Han remembered how the monk at the jetty had leaped and kicked; he thought of that same man running far enough on fire to warn his brothers. And flinched.

His brothers stood very still, very quiet until the pirates reached them. Then, like him, they were a blur of movement. Arms and legs that struck like weapons, torches too; and their voices the same, shrieks like blows that rattled Han's brains even at this distance, that all but silenced the pirates, that . . .

That made him notice suddenly how much of a distance there was between captain and crew. Li Ton had led the men here, but let them rush ahead into the fight.

And was turning away now, stumping toward a narrow path that led on up into fog and darkness.

"Sir—?"

"Fetch a torch and follow me."

"Sir, shouldn't we go to help them?" He cared nothing for these men, who had killed his master and stolen him—but it was hard to remember that, with an iron ring in his ear. Ship's loyalty was an infection, swift to grip. Unless it was just a measure of his loss, that he could see no other future in this fog.

He saw one pirate with his bare barrel chest stove in; he heard another's scream cut off by a faceful of flame. To keep the dragon chained, the pirates had to be stopped. Like that, by death, there was no other way. And there were more monks than pirates, and—

And Li Ton was laughing in his ear.

"Help? That pack of scum? They'd split you for it if they heard you ask, and play dice with your bones. Leave them to have their fun, they'll get bored soon enough. And fetch a light, I'm tripping over my own shadow here."

Choiceless, Han did as he was told, snatching up a discarded torch and relighting it from a blazing hut, feeling the scorch even at full stretch with his face turned away. Backwards glances as they climbed told him only that the noisiest pirates were noisy about their dying too, while quieter comrades seemed to find ways to meet flying hands and feet with blades more often than with bodies.

. . .

THE PATH was rough and stony, rocks jutting through sparse soil, sharp and damp and bitter cold. Han kept his eyes on his feet, and more importantly the captain's. He was barely aware of it when they rose above the fog; barely aware even when they topped the crest.

The hammer's massive beat had called them all the way, and it was that which actually startled him into looking up, more than the sudden red-cast shadows. Here it wasn't a sound at all, not even the terrible booming they'd been climbing into. Here it was a blow, like the monks' fighting shriek; he felt the strike of it all through his flesh, its echo in the marrow of his bones.

His hand shook, that held the torch; he needed the other to steady it.

A great open furnace topped the peak, with a rain-shelter roof of sheet metal raised on poles above. This was the dragon's eye, which peered into the fog below; the furnace was heaped high with fierce charcoal. That roof gathered all the sullen glow of it and cast it out to shine all across the strait, to let its glare reach to the mainland, and to Taishu.

It glared at Han, searing against the chill wet vision of the dragon that he held in his own eye. He might have stared at it all night, except for the people.

People. There were four of them, three monks with shaven heads and one other; and one of the monks was coming toward the captain now, and the others—

The others were in a wheel. Side by side two young men worked a treadmill, bare feet on relentless slats, round and around. The wheel worked chains that lifted the greatest hammer Han had ever seen and sent it slamming down onto an anvil, the impact slamming through his chest and jarring every bone he had.

As the hammer's head rose again, as the gasping monks stepped and stepped in unison to raise it, Han saw the hot iron that it was beating slowly into shape. A vivid twist, the thickness of his arm: meant surely to be one link in a chain, but it would be a chain no man could hope to lift. One man was sweating to work this single link, turning it with tongs on the anvil for one more stroke before it went back to the fire.

That one man was not a monk. He boasted a thick black thatch of hair, and his vast naked torso was muscled as though he had himself been beaten out on an anvil. His wrists were cuffed with iron, and a long chain swung between the two. Nothing symbolic, it was a solid heavy chain of many links that the slave would never break without a chisel.

He had chisels, on a rack beside the forge. Perhaps he was never left alone for long enough to use them? Or else it was this island that kept him, a rock in a bitter sea; if he broke his chains, he would have nowhere to run to. Easier to be obedient, be fed, not be beaten . . .

Even now he kept his eyes on his work, when even the young monks in the wheel were staring at these new arrivals, treading and staring, wordless only because they had no air.

The fourth man, the last of the monks, the one who was approaching: he looked the least of any, short and elderly and frail. Han wasn't fooled. He was here, he was coming toward them. That must mean he was the one to be most wary of, the monksmith himself. Who else could be so easy, smiling at raiders in the predawn chill?

Now, finally, Li Ton drew his sword.

"What can you offer me," he said, "old man, to spare your life?"

"Well," the monksmith said mildly, "I have three strong fellows at my back, where you have only a boy."

A boy with a torch in his hand, lowering it now in the light from the forge; a boy watching as the young men tumbled from their wheel, as the smithy slave left his anvil, as they gathered behind the monksmith; a boy wondering, perhaps, just where he chose to stand.

"But I have my sword," Li Ton said, "at your throat."

Literally he did, the broad curved blade of it sliding under the old man's chin.

"My blood will buy you nothing," the monksmith said.

"Your men's obedience, perhaps?"

"Oh, that you may have, if you will spare their lives and mine." The smallest gesture from him put the two monks on their knees, in a token submission. It was too subtle, perhaps, for the slave. "If I am dead," the monksmith went on, "they owe me nothing, and you less."

For a moment, Han thought that might be a saving argument. But there was a rush of feet on the path behind them, an eruption of figures into the light. Li Ton didn't even turn to look, he knew already whose men they would be; he always had known. Han didn't need to look either, even that one swift sorry glance he couldn't keep from taking.

Pirates, crewmates: streaked with blood, one or two running with it, gasping, laughing with it, eyebright in the forgelight, delighted not to be among the bodies left below.

"Captain?" If any man stood second to Li Ton, this was he: taller than his captain, lean as a rib-bone and scarred like bullock-hide, all his skin marked with nicks and gashes.

"Jorgan. How many dead down there?"

"Seven now. A few more, likely, by the time we go back."

How many of ours? was clearly what the question meant, and the answer too. Which meant that all the monks were dead, despite their skills. Han might have been impressed, if he hadn't felt so regretful. There was a whole different story of his life lost here: a rush of victorious monks up the path and the briefest of struggles to overcome Li Ton, a moment's generosity to spare the boy and a new future found for him, shaving his head and teaching him to fight bare-handed to defend the Forge. Han could have lived such a life, in the shadow of the monksmith, the eternal echo of that hammer.

The hammer was still now and its silence must be reaching across the strait, pulsing through the fog, an absence fit to trouble any boat on the water.

Li Ton grunted. "Spare the slave, so long as this one," his own turn to make a small and subtle gesture, a twitch of the sword that had the monksmith lifting his chin in a sudden shy from the edge of it, "doesn't move or speak."

That was all the instruction Jorgan needed. Han thought the monksmith would rebel, cry an order, something; but he stood stiffly silent, and his discipline kept the two young monks on their knees, at least for that moment too long.

Then they had men all about them, the chill of steel to hold them down. Jorgan strode over, his own long straight sword in his hand. There was no ceremony to it, no formality at all, just a high swift lift of the blade and its sudden fall, the hiss of its edge through the air and a more solid sound to follow, then the dull thud of a weight falling onto rock.

The second monk did struggle, despite his obedience. He was too late, helpless; the men gripped his arms and mocked him, and Jorgan's sword took his head too.

The monksmith twitched again, at the sound of it.

"Just you, then," Li Ton said. "One more time, and for your life: what do you have, that would allow me to let you keep it?"

"You have left me nothing that matters," the monksmith said, "except my slave's loyalty, here. I would give you that, if I thought I could trust you with it."

"No matter," Li Ton said. "I can take that for myself. And anything else I find here. You waste my time, old man."

And he drew his sword up for the lethal swing of it, and the monksmith only stood there when he should have been punching, kicking, anything, trying to run; and it was Han who startled himself and his captain both, dropping the torch and reaching for Li Ton's wrist, screaming at the visions of the dragon in his head.

"Captain, no! You must not . . . !"

His hand never reached his captain. His own wrist was seized as he grabbed, and that was Jorgan, strong as a storm-tree, immovable; and Li Ton looked at him, and for a moment the whole universe was very still.

Then Li Ton's sword swung with a casual strength, and took the monksmith's throat out so that the old man fell choking, drowning on his own blood. The smithy slave moaned and tried to go to him, but the pirates held him back. It took three of them to do it; they forced him down onto his knees and wrapped his wrist chain around the horn of the anvil. A hand in his hair and a knife in his ear and he subsided, muttering wretchedly in some broken language from far away.

The dragon was loud in Han's ears, which was why he tried to listen to the slave. Li Ton had a hard glitter in his eyes and Jorgan's grip was still unbreakable, and none of that boded well.

"Bring him over here," Li Ton said: toward the forge, the anvil, the slave.

Jorgan tugged on Han's wrist, and he went. Obediently, dispiritedly, already broken. The monksmith was dead, all the monks were dead, the dragon would be stirring under the water; what did it matter if Li Ton took a finger from him now?

"Put his hand there."

Jorgan slammed it down, onto the surface of the anvil. The iron was hot; Han hadn't thought, but of course it was hot. It stood in the eye of the furnace, and even the air here was hot. Besides, it had red-hot metal hammered on it all day, all night.

Hot was good, hot was welcome. Except for Jorgan's hand on his wrist, that was hot and tight and not at all welcome.

Li Ton went to the rack of tools, picked out a mallet and a chisel.

Han might have wept, he might have pleaded, but the glare of the forge was burning his eyes dry and it was useless to plead with the captain. He'd lose a finger, and live with it. Live without it. He could do that, of course he could. A moment's agony, a day or two of pain, a little clumsiness thereafter . . .

He spread his fingers wide to make it easier, to seem obedient.

Li Ton came back, and set the broad chisel's edge against his skin.

Against the ball of his thumb. His right thumb, and he was right-handed.

Han was screaming even before the mallet struck.

· · ·

ACTUALLY IT wasn't pain, immediately. There was a rush of heat, as if that were all leaving his body with his blood, leaving him shaking with the chill of it; and the fog seemed to be coming back, clouding his sight, but he did see Jorgan scoop something off the anvil and toss it into the furnace.

Then Jorgan dragged Han the same way, toward the fiery glow; he felt all his skin tighten against it, though he was too dizzy to care and he couldn't stop the shivering.

When Jorgan thrust the raw wound of his hand hard against the searing iron of the hearth, Han heard the sizzle, saw the smoke rise up.

Then he felt it, and his whole body jerked and made a sound like the monk had, down by the jetty when Han set him on fire.

AND THEN, yes, then there was pain; and Jorgan still wasn't finished, he pulled Han over to a quenching trough and thrust his hand in there, and the icy bite of the water didn't make the pain any the less.

Jorgan let go of him at last, and he could inch away from all these people and curl up around his maimed hand and shudder alone. But he couldn't quite faint, and he couldn't crawl too far, and he couldn't close his eyes or his ears to what else still had to happen.

They unwrapped the slave's chains from the anvil's beak, but still held him there; and Li Ton spoke to him a little, and the slave shook his head massively, but that would make no difference, Han knew; and then they held the big man's hands down on the anvil one by one, and Li Ton struck his chains off.

And the slave babbled desperately and fought against them, until the chain fell loose away; and then he howled, like a man in utmost desolation.

five

At first she thought he was just one more of the soldiers. Younger than most, perhaps—the ones she'd seen up close were scarred veterans, and this was a boy with clean skin and a clean chin—but still, only a soldier.

There were a great many soldiers crowding the deck, squatting by the masts or standing at the rail, peering into the fog. Calling in harsh voices across the water, to other boats equally invaded.

She would have sent them all below, but the hold was full of nets and boxes and bamboo and flotsam that her grandfather fished out of the water because it was interesting or beautiful or might prove useful sometime, and the cabin was full of the emperor.

It had been full of the emperor and his generals. The old men had come flustering out after an hour, though, saying that the Son of Heaven wanted to sleep. Mei Feng thought he would probably find that easier if his men weren't hooting from boat to boat, but they were bored and anxious in the fog, anxious on the water. They needed work and there was none, so they made noise instead.

With Old Yen on the steering-oar and so little wind in the sails, Mei Feng could reasonably claim to be best use on the foredeck, keeping watch. There were little boats about that might stray into their path; there were always ill chances at sea, other than the rocks and shallows she could trust her grandfather to avoid. Besides, if she kept her eyes fixed forward, she didn't have to see her beloved boat so swamped by strangers. She didn't have to catch their eyes or know herself caught, examined, desired . . .

She did still have to hear them, since their stupid generals hadn't the sense or discipline to silence the troops while the emperor slept. They seemed to be saying impossible things: war all through the empire, even in the Hidden City; the imperial army defeated, the Son of Heaven in flight with everything he owned except his empire, which he had to leave behind. It sounded as though he was coming into exile, right here on Taishu. And bringing his army with him, and his court too. They said the Jade Throne itself was in his baggage-train. And his mother, his staff, his treasures. All waiting in Santung, except for them; and what had they done to deserve this, adrift in a fog off a dangerous coast . . . ?

We're not adrift, she wanted to say, except that she was not going to speak to them; and *My grandfather will see us safe home,* with a little help perhaps from herself, if these stupid soldiers didn't get too much in the way; and *Don't come to Taishu if you don't want to, we'll happily sail you back to the mainland instead . . .*

But of course they weren't free to make those choices. Choice belonged to the emperor, who was sleeping in the cabin.

So did she belong to him, she supposed, in some big imperial manner. All the world belonged to the Son of Heaven. It had never seemed to matter, until now. And still wouldn't, of course, unless he wanted a fish for his supper and came down to the quay to collect it.

She could giggle at such a wonderful, impossible image—how would he ever choose, when all the fish were his? and were they his already, or did they become his only when she netted them, because she and her net both belonged to him?—and try to swallow the giggle and so choke over it, and so attract the attention of the boy stretched over the rail beside her.

Actually she thought she had his attention already, only that her choking gave him the excuse to make it obvious.

And so she could return it, and so see just how young he was, how clean and how unscarred, all of it made obvious by how little he was wearing: just a loose pair of trousers that hung barely below his knees and a rough shirt, as casual as she was about the chilly kiss of fog against his skin . . .

Her own shirt, she realized suddenly, and her trousers too, which was why they seemed quite so short on him: the spare set she always kept in case of an unexpected soaking. Old Yen could sail wet all night and take no harm, despite her most dire prognostications, but she hated sodden cloth chafing her skin.

He was a young man, startlingly young in this company. No, not even that: he was a boy yet, only trying to be a man. And he had taken her clothes, which meant that he must have come aboard in others and found hers in the cabin, and preferred them for some reason she could not immediately see; and—

—AND THE only boy who had gone into the cabin was supposed to be in there still, asleep.

She would have tumbled to her knees and hit her head on the deck, except that his hand on her arm prevented her. It stopped her moving altogether, as a spell's touch might. She barely managed to breathe, under the dreadful impact of that touch.

"Don't," he murmured, almost pleading, which was odd in a boy who owned the world. The world and her. "Don't make a fuss."

With a monumental effort, she made no fuss at all: only a little sound, a littler gesture, a tremulous shake of the head that he took for a promise, as it was meant.

He smiled at her. "Thank you. I can't get away with this long. Soon someone will spot my face, or one of those officious old men will go into the cabin and find me gone, and discover the hatch behind the cot and panic the whole ship in his terror. That will come. Until it does, let me have this little time out here," with his back to his inheritance and his face to the fog, to the future. She did understand, or she thought she did.

Then she thought it was rank impertinence, even to imagine that the Son of Heaven might have an impulse she could share.

Either way, her obedience demanded her silence, so she gave him that, until he asked a question.

"You live on the Tear of the Dragon?"

Or the Tear of Jade, or *we call it Taishu,* but, "All my life, lord," that would do. If *lord* was good enough, from peasant girl to emperor. She didn't know.

After a moment, he said, "My name is Chien Hua," as if she might not have known. He surely didn't think that she would *use* it?

After another moment, she said, "I am called Mei Feng, lord," as if he could conceivably care. *And those are my clothes you are wearing,* but she didn't say so.

"Mei Feng. I think these must be your clothes."

"Uh, yes, lord . . ."

"I suppose I have to thank you again, then. For the use of them." He was stiff and awkward in his gratitude, not used to it; and he knew too well how he sounded, she saw him hear himself and wince. Still, he pressed on, against his nature and his training: "In the people's sight, the emperor must wear imperial yellow. Just this once, I am glad of the chance of dressing to be overlooked. Tell me something about the Dragon's Tear, Mei Feng."

He wanted to dress in her knowledge, as well as her clothes. "We call it Taishu, lord."

"Do you?" He blinked, at this being almost contradicted. "Why?"

Because there is a dragon under the sea, and we prefer not to remind ourselves. "Because yours is, is a high-court name for it, lord, and we are simple people."

"I don't think you're simple," he said. "Some of the country we've passed through—well, never mind. They are mine also. But this ship would be a wonder to people who harness their own women to the plow."

"Landsmen never understand boats, my grandfather says."

And you are a landsman too, lord, or you wouldn't be calling her a ship. "And he calls this a bastard boat, and refuses to give her a name." And then—while she was doing this, visibly startling him, responding with more than a grovel of agreement—she asked her emperor a question. It was appallingly bold, perhaps ruinously so. But it was there on her tongue like a live coal, burning . . .

"Lord? Why did you leave the Hidden City, and come all this far?"

"We ran away," and if it was her tongue that carried the live coal, it was his that blistered. "They were meant to be my troops, my generals, serving me. But there were rebels in the hills, coming down; and the generals listened to my mother, not to me. And so they fled, and took me with them," and that was the bitterest thing, that they'd snatched him up and swept him away as though he had no voice in his own fate.

Once they started to run, they'd find nowhere to stand and no one to shelter them. Mei Feng knew about that, from a lifetime of listening to stories. Whole dynasties had foundered because one army had broken and run from a battle, and who then could ever trust them to stand?

So this boy had crossed all the breadth of his empire, chafing all the way, no doubt, furious and helpless; and afraid, most likely, learning at first hand how vast the empire was, how small himself. And harried all the way, dragging bands of rebels at his back while his own army must have raided like locusts as they went, stripping green valleys bare, inciting local lords to forswear their oaths and revolt in desperation. From that to this, her grandfather's boat; and at her side, now, and talking to her . . .

Not talking to her. He had fallen silent again, too soon; she thought perhaps he needed to be talking.

"Lord?"

"Hmm?"

"Why are you coming to Taishu?"

Was that the same question, only another way around? It didn't matter; he gave her a different answer. She thought perhaps Grandfather had lost them in the fog after all, sailed them to another world where the emperor stood in her clothes and answered her questions. She couldn't see how they would ever find their way back home from here.

He said, "Why? Because it is the Dragon's Tear, the Tear of Jade. No man can hold the empire who doesn't hold the Tear. The throne itself was made here, did you know? Mined and cut and carved. I suppose we're bringing it home. My mother says, on the Dragon's Tear we can rebuild our strength, before we reclaim the empire."

Mei Feng wondered how they would live, so many men squeezed in among her own people. There was precious little space, between the villages on the coast and the paddies and tea bushes inland. She supposed they could go farther in, and camp on the mountains with the miners. There must be food in the forests; perhaps each man could find enough to feed himself . . .

Perhaps not. She thought she and her grandfather would do a lot of fishing hereafter. If soldiers from so far inland could actually eat fish. If emperors could.

"Lord?"

"Mmm?"

One more time, and it could still sound like the same question, and it still wasn't: "Why was it you on the dragon boat, first out of Santung?" *Trying to cross the strait in the fog,* she meant, *like a boatload of idiot drunken boys only looking for a rock to break apart on?*

"Well," he said, "it wasn't foggy when we left."

And he was smiling, as though he had read her thought entirely; and at the same time he sounded a little shamefaced, as though he agreed with her, and he didn't seem to be angry at all, so she was bold enough to push.

"Even so, lord. You have an army of men to go ahead, to find the way and prepare a house for you. You have your lady mother the empress with you," whose name and reputation were better known than his own, because she was so much older and had sat the throne so long at her husband's side, "and all the court besides. You could have stayed safe in Santung with them, till all was ready."

"An emperor's place is at the head of his men," he said, sounding suddenly younger than ever. Younger than herself, even. She knew nothing of the court, but she knew that wasn't true. Emperors stayed in the Hidden City, and sent their armies forth with a finger's gesture and a word of command. Even generals sat behind the battle, planning.

On the other hand, a boy who had gone thousands of miles with his mother, closeted in a wagon all the way, never let ride free—such a boy might see the surge and splash of a dragon boat as an escape, however brief; the salt wind and far reaches of the strait as a gift to be treasured. He must have demanded his place in the boat, his right to be a man, to lead his people. To be first across the water.

She was still astonished that the court had countenanced it, let alone his mother. But then, they didn't know these waters. Perhaps they had stood on the headland and seen Taishu lying low on the horizon and not realized quite how far it was, or how much peril lingered in the strait. And the fishing fleet must have been at sea but they had the dragon boats right there, and the men to paddle them, and—

"Santung has no walls," he said, "and all the men were afraid . . ." Of course they were afraid. They had been running so long, and now suddenly there was a wall of water ahead and no way to cross it, fear building at their backs and no way to defend against it. They might have risen in revolt themselves, they might simply have scattered. Perhaps it was no bad generalship after all, to let the young emperor play hero and lead chosen men in the first crossing, while the army garrisoned the town around the dowager empress and waited for more boats.

"I thought it would be a jaunt," he confessed in a whisper that held all of his inexpressible fear, the fog closing in and his little fleet losing its bearings, losing its way; and then, brightening, "and then we found you."

"My lord was lucky," she said bluntly.

"Of course we were lucky, we had prayed for good fortune," and received it, apparently, eventually. Mei Feng didn't think they would have prayed to her grandfather's beloved Li-goddess; they wouldn't know her name. Li was of the strait, and would not willingly venture far from water. Li it was who had bound the dragon, perhaps.

Some god had blessed him, though, and all his men. If it was a blessing for an emperor to squat in the bows of a boat and shiver in the chill of the fog and have an impertinent fish-girl ask him questions. It seemed to be what he wanted, but his time was out. There was a desperate cry from the cabin; he sighed and came slowly to his feet, no hiding now, no making them search for him. She liked that.

A rush of shoes across the planking, and she liked this too, that he dropped his protection like a mantle across her shoulders. "This is Mei Feng, and I believe the gods led her to us on the water. See, these are her clothes that I found, like a token of how we will be welcome on the Tear of the Dragon; it is her eyes and her grandfather's that will find us the true path through this fog."

After that, they couldn't even beat her for not showing proper respect, although she was carefully on her knees now, with her head down to the deck.

She could see nothing but his feet, as bare as hers and almost as dirty. His voice was still clear, though, sharply determined as he said, "I want to keep her with me, at my side. See to it, before we land. Pay the old man whatever he wants for her."

TWO

The Weight of Jade

one

*D*own in the dark there, in the deeps: was she dreaming?

After so long, crushed under such weights and so far from light, it would be a wonder if there was any dream of sky left in her, any memory of freedom.

And yet she was herself a wonder, she who had been all heat and speed, all reach, all rapture. There in the cold clench of the ocean—her waters, *hers,* that were her jailer now—she was still wonderful.

Perhaps she did dream, lost though she was; perhaps some thread of her great mind still reached back to this world of pain.

Perhaps she dreamed that there was movement, change.

A shift, a slackening in that dread weight of chains.

Broken links.

Perhaps.

PERHAPS, IF she could think of it, she might dare to shift herself: to touch one leg, perhaps, with the notion of a motion, see what came . . .

two

The heart of the world is stone. That is known.

The heart of Taishu-island, that is stone too, which is why Taishu sits at the heart of empire, despite standing heart-deep in the sea and as far as it could be from the Hidden City. Taishu is called the Tear of Jade—which is to say the Tear of the Dragon—because its shape is pendulous and its heart is clear, its sorrows and its value known; it could as easily be called the Heart of Jade, because tears and hearts hold the same shape and they can sing alike.

The heart of empire is jade; the emperor is the Man of Jade. Without jade, he cannot hold the throne. Which is to say, he cannot hold the throne unless he holds Taishu.

The heart of Taishu is jade; which is to say that here at the heart of Taishu are the mountains, and here in the mountains where the dragon wept are the veins, the mines where jade is dug from other stone.

At the heart of Taishu, then, at the heart of empire are these who have never seen the emperor, whose work brings them closest to him: these who live and work and die in narrow valleys and dark holes, these who dig the jade.

EVERY VALLEY in the mountains has its failed digs, its hopes betrayed. Overgrown they are now, and the paths are lost; trees and creepers reclaim the ground, streams cut new ways down to old courses, rock remains under all.

Some valleys are pitted, mined, more deeply marked, where

veins have been worked out and the clans moved on. Again the forests and the rains have hidden or destroyed whatever was built aboveground, hutments and whole villages. Below are writhes of emptiness, narrow squeezes through gnawed stone, little enough to show for the work of generations. No gleam of green in those walls of rock, no chips or splinters on the rough-hewn floor. Where miners glean—for the emperor, yet!—there is no need to follow. Even their dust is swept and sifted, for any grains of jade.

Dead valleys, old tracks can still carry life: the grunts of burdened men and women, the stamp of bare feet on beaten earth. Twin baskets hang from bamboo yokes across their shoulders. Each basket is filled with slabs and nuggets, bags of chippings, jade dug from higher in the mountains. It takes skill to balance them, and simple strength to carry them. These people have both. This is their life, their journey; they live long but their journey's short, from the high mines to the wagon-road and back again.

Follow them back, old tracks and newer, climb and climb. Now, through the dense damp of the forest, through shade so thick the weight of it lies like silk against the skin, muffled sounds of wood on steel can be heard, steel on stone, the workings of a mine.

The clans hold the valleys; families hold the mines.

Buildings cluster at the foot of a rock face, one of those sudden upthrusts that break the forest time and again, like rude stairs for the gods. If the mine is new, the family small, there might be only one or two rough huts of wood and woven palm leaves. More likely it will be well established, for veins are rare and hard to find. The compound of a long-worked mine might be a village, near enough: stone-built with channeled water and crop gardens, a scatter of naked children, that sense of generations settled in.

The mine itself will be nothing from the outside, only a crack in the rock face. There's a long history of clan warfare, raids coming over the ridge; no wise miner ever made the mouth of his workings wider than one man could defend, with his family sheltered at his back.

Nowhere inside the mine will be much more spacious, unless

the seam is broken by a sudden cavern. That happens; these mountains are half hollow, blown with bubbles like a bad bronze casting. The rock that holds them can be hard as bronze, and harder to work. The miners cut nothing they do not have to cut, following the winding course that jade delights in.

The work is slow and awkward; a skilled man can work all day and have only a handful of chippings to show for it. From valley to valley, mine to mine, families chase ever-narrower veins ever deeper into the dark, because they are frugal, and because they are poor, and because it is not theirs. All jade is imperial jade, it belongs to the emperor and must go to him. Meanwhile they send their boldest ever higher in search of new seams, while the oldlings scour old ground for whatever starveling vein of stone they might have missed before.

Once in a long lifetime, perhaps, a seam that seems worked out entirely will swell suddenly to life again and yield marvelous stone. Perhaps a single miraculous nugget, perhaps a whole new vein; they cannot know until they work it. In bad light and bad air, cramped and twisted, half crushed beneath a massive weight of mountain, they dig—slowly, slowly!—to find their futures, loss or wonder.

Maybe both.

three

Old Yen had been a fisherman all his life.

Now, in his old age, he was a ferryman: back and forth across the strait, wastefully empty one way and dangerously overcrowded the other.

What was worse, he was the emperor's ferryman, touched by grace. Touched and burned. No one comes that close to glory and escapes unscathed.

Mei Feng was gone. "He wants her," a functionary had said, "he offers to buy her from you; he is the Son of Heaven, and generosity is native to him. However, he is your lord. It would be—politic—in you to make a gift of her, to welcome greatness to Taishu."

They had learned quickly to say Taishu; they had learned it from the emperor, who had learned it from Mei Feng. Old Yen supposed it was wise to be quick of study, when you lived and served at court. Even when—no, especially when—that court was a battlefield, or a dusty road. Or a bastard junk sailed by an old man in a fog, or—

He didn't know where the emperor was now. Where Mei Feng had gone. Perhaps he ought to learn. They had been slow of study for a long time on Taishu, where there was no need to hurry, where nothing ever changed. It was a new world now; this was its first lesson.

HE BARELY knew where he was himself: on his boat day and night, Santung or Taishu-port or somewhere between the two, like every other vessel on the strait. Even the jademasters' junks had been pressed into service, to bring the emperor's mother across the water together with all the court and all the treasures of the Hidden City.

Himself, he mostly carried soldiers. Even clerks and errand-boys had learned to be soldiers during the long months of their marching; now it was hard to know the difference, except that some of them could read. They were all equally drawn, equally hungry; foul of mouth and foul of skin, pocked and scarred by hardship and battle and disease. Hard men and hopeless, making this last move because that was what they did now, they kept moving.

What would happen exactly once they stopped, Old Yen did not want to see. He feared that. These men on his island, in his village, in his house. In everyone's houses.

"Hoi! Tie that off, or you'll lose it . . . !" Lose the rope and lose the wind, see the sail rip free, lose headway in this rising sea . . .

The boy he yelled at dived back to where his rope was unwinding itself, tied it off properly and glanced up with a gesture of apology.

Old Yen made his own gesture in response, impatience tightly controlled. The boy wasn't hopeless, and he was learning fast. Just, he was not Mei Feng . . .

His new crew was the boy, Pao, and another called Kang who thought himself a man and wore mustaches to prove it. They were both of them children, by his own biased reckoning. He had asked for men and been given these shallow, callow youths. They would both be trainable, in time—but the emperor had eaten time, it seemed, and spat out hurry.

TODAY, NOT even his Li-goddess would be generous. It had been foggy again in the early morning, but that was long burned off; the sky had been clear and the strait quiet, just enough wind to take a boat smartly on her way. Everything Old Yen knew about weather had promised an easy sailing day, ideal to tutor two youngsters in the habits of the boat.

And now he was bellowing instructions against the roar and snap of a storm wind, and the boat was tossing and jibing in a heavy sea. She could take it, and so could he; he wasn't sure about the crew. In a way, he supposed this too made for a good day's training, but . . .

"Kang! Stow those barrels, or they'll be over the side!"

The barrels were roped already, but ropes break under the sea's strain. So too do boys' nerves break, under the strain of their first storm. Kang would be better with something simple and physical to do. Old Yen didn't at all understand it, but he knew how to sail this weather, wherever it had come from; his crew's morale was a captain's responsibility, as much as bringing his boat safe to port.

Almost as much. The boat came first. Crew could be replaced; a boat was invaluable. Especially now. Even after this mad evacuation, there would be embassies and parleys, rice boats and raiding boats, an endless passage of men and goods to and fro across the strait.

So long as the strait—or his goddess—allowed it. There was a dark cast to the sky that he did not like at all. All his instincts, all his weather lore had nothing to say about a storm like this, unseasonal and unforeseen.

He worked the steering-oar with a strong, determined stroke against the tug of water. Even the currents here were suddenly awry; he could feel a massive confusion in the sea beneath him. He'd turn the boat and they could scud for home, there would still be—

THERE SHOULD still have been time. Even a storm that blows up without warning needs time to build its full strength, gifts that gave time to sailors. No storm that Old Yen had ever met could do this:

throw a veil across the sky that was not cloud or smoke but only darkness, like the finest sheer silk that would still let the sun shine through it but steal all its fire, to leave it moon-like and insipid;

still the wind as abruptly as it had risen, to leave this whole shadow-world breathless, anticipatory, in dread;

hurl the sea at him, from nowhere, all of it.

· · ·

A WALL, a brute hammer of a wall.

A wall of water, black and dreadful, as though dredged up from far, far down and solid with seabed-stuff; a wall that rose up too close, not even coming from the far horizon, gifting them no time at all.

OLD YEN screamed what might have been a warning. It might only have been an animal scream, terror or rage or simple disbelief. It might have been a denial of all gods, even his Li-goddess, if there had been time enough to shape such furious blasphemy.

There was not. There was no time even to understand himself. He screamed, and wrapped his arms and legs about the sternpost and hid his face, couldn't even see his crew, even before the wall hit them.

IMPACT: HE felt how the boat shuddered, how it was held suddenly and massively still in the turgid water.

He felt, heard, ropes and timbers snapping in that moment, and thought the boat herself would break, stem and stern.

Then the wall hit him and he thought he would break also, he couldn't believe he hadn't broken yet.

It was a wall of movement, solid and yet rushing; it struck like iron and engulfed him utterly, ripped the breath from his lungs and the thoughts from his head. He was a rag, tied around a pole; there was nothing left of him except the will to hold on, because that was what he did. An old man in a hard world, what else was there to do . . . ?

AND THEN the wall was gone and there was only wind and water and motion, a long slide down a curve of black-green glaze.

His boat, his bastard boat had met that wall, that wave, and survived it.

It had broken all around her, swallowed her seemingly, swallowed them all; and she'd saved herself somehow, thrust up and out, climbed and crested the wave and was slipping now down the eerie back face of it—

—INTO A pale sunlight that grew stronger by the moment and a wind that failed, as though that storm had been just a black frown, a moment of temper from his Li-goddess . . .

His goddess didn't behave like that, and neither did the sea, the wind, the sky.

And yet, it had happened; there had been a squall, a tsunami, something. A freak of weather and a monster wave, and his boat had brought them through, saved them all . . .

All?

He lifted his head for the first time, to look the length of his boat. He saw snapped rigging, absent sails, the broken stump of a mast. No matter. The boat was hurt, but she floated; she was a survivor. So was he.

He saw the boy, Pao, facedown and sodden on the streaming foredeck, his arms wound round and round with dank dark cable. Smart boy, he'd clung to the anchor rope, sure that if one thing on this boat did not break, that would be it. Old Yen saw that written in the boy's fevered stillness, the way he lay so pressed against the planking, as though his very bones and skin could cling that little harder.

It took him a moment longer to see that the boy was naked, that all his clothes had been ripped from him in that collision of water.

No matter. There were clothes below, just as there was bamboo and wood, rope and sail, whatever they would need for makeshift repairs and a return to Taishu. Mei Feng mocked him for all the junk he carried in the hold; she would not mock now. Any more than he would mock her chest of spare clothes in the cabin. If she were here.

Mei Feng was lost to him, lost to herself; likely the emperor had given her another name by now. He wished he could let her go, as easily as she had been taken from him.

He saw—

. . .

He did not see Kang.

Pao was a river rat before he was a kitchen boy, before he was a soldier. If there was one thing he knew, it was how to hold on. Kang had been in the imperial guards, tall and eager; he had once sailed a sampan on a lake in the Hidden City . . .

Old Yen and Pao scoured the boat, which took barely any time. They called helplessly, pointlessly across wide empty waters.

He said, "The Li-goddess took a sacrifice, perhaps, a price to save the boat and us . . ."

He didn't believe that, it was not her way, but he had to say something. Pao looked at him with the deep cynicism of the very young, and said, "What happened?"

"I don't know, I didn't see; the wave must have taken him before he found a solid grip to cling to." The barrels were gone, along with the fishing gear and whatever else had strewn the decks. Perhaps Kang had his arms around a barrel when the wave struck, and it took both of them together.

Perhaps he was still clinging to the barrel, perhaps he might float and kick his way to safety . . .

No. That was too foolish to hope for. He was gone. And Pao was a realist; he was saying, "No, not that. I mean, how did it happen, that wave, where did it come from?"

From the goddess, but no, he couldn't lie again; he said, "I do not know. I have never seen anything like it. We will ask at the temple, and at the docks."

"If we can get there," Pao said.

Old Yen smiled. "She brought us through the wave, through the storm; she will take us home," without saying, perhaps without knowing whether he meant the goddess or the boat.

The boat was wallowing in the swell, though, lying low, sluggish in response to the oar. He sent Pao down into the hold, and the boy came back wide-eyed, shaking his head, afraid.

"I stood, I stood this deep," and his hand touched his hip, "*this* deep in water . . ."

She would have shipped some when the wave broke over her, but not so much as that; her hatches were as tight as her hull. Old Yen remembered the sounds of breaking, the shudder in her when she met that wall of water, how it brought her to such an abrupt stop.

"She must have sprung her timbers, in the shock; she'll be leaking, down below the waterline. Nothing we can do about that here, like this," with so much water in her belly already. He wouldn't send a boy where he wouldn't go himself, to fumble for sprung planking in the dark.

He said, "We can patch a sail together, and get her under way—but this heavy already and taking on water, she won't make it back to Taishu. Nor to Santung." They were caught too neatly, in between the two.

How far had that freak wave flung them? He gazed all around, and saw nothing to break the skyline; and so gestured the boy to the surviving mast.

"Shin up, and tell me what you see. Quickly."

The boy swarmed up the mast like the river rat he'd been, and peered with the sharp eyes of youth, and shrilled down with youth's own sharp voice: "There is! There's something, westerly there! I don't know what, I can't see, just a jag on the horizon . . . !"

It was easterly that he pointed, but he was excited and frightened, and wasn't sure whether to be hopeful. There was a shiver in his voice, likely a dizziness in his head. Old Yen could be generous; he knew what that jag must be. There was no land between Taishu and the mainland except the one jutting rock, the monks' island, the Forge. If they could persuade, compel, inveigle the boat so far, he knew a way to put her where they could work at need.

If the boy could see the Forge from the masthead, Old Yen was sure his boat would bring them in. His Li-goddess would see them safe, the two of them. Young Kang she had already, safe another way.

SLOWLY, THEN, with just enough help from wind and tide, with old worn sails on the solitary mast—sails sodden wet from the hold, but that helped to hold the air—they made their easterly.

They came up abreast of the Forge, where Old Yen had often and often left a gift of fish on the jetty after a good trip or else after a bad one, because if his fishing was bad then so was everyone's, and the monks should not go hungry.

The jetty was gone utterly, leaving a scant handful of old posts like fingers jutting from the sea. No surprise. The monks would work hard to rebuild it. He could bring them timbers from his sons' boatyard and men to help, as many as were asked for; their sergeants would be glad of the request. Idle men made trouble, while labor would sweat them to a standstill.

Perhaps the monks would find new recruits among them. He had fetched more than one soldier to the Forge before this, run from some far mandarin's service.

There was still no booming hammer-sound coming from the island, as there had not been since the night he met the emperor in the fog. He did not, did *not* like this silence. Even through the breakers' roar, it rang in his head like a great bell broken.

Grimly, then, but still with the due care of a sailor for his vessel, he brought the boat—gently, gently!—in to where surf ground on rock, where it flung spume high. He knew just where two boulders lay like broken teeth, just a boat's width apart. Time it right, catch the wave and ride her in, she would lift and lay the boat neatly between them, lightly in their grip: enough to hold her in this ebbing tide, not enough to stop her floating free when the waters rose again.

With Mei Feng, he could have approached this carefully but confidently, even with the boat in such a state, rolling against the surge as the great mass of water sloshed in her belly. Without Mei Feng, with only this willing and inexperienced lad to help him— well, he had half a notion they might both end up under the rollers, slamming against the rocks, while all the broken timbers of his boat slammed around them.

They were survivors, yes—but everyone's a survivor, until they meet that moment they don't survive.

He looked at the island, the great rocky shadow of it looming above him, and was sorry almost to have such faith in his goddess.

It meant he had faith in premonitions too, he was obliged to. The hammer's stillness was like another kind of shadow, cast far across the future; he thought of the tsunami, of wind and water stirred to a reckless savagery, of a veil cast across the sky like the shadow of a dark, dark thought.

He thought, he could not help but think of a dragon.

A dragon stirring, waking. Not so chained.

four

Mei Feng had never imagined such a life, such a change. How could she?

She had never needed to imagine any kind of life. Her life had always been clear: she would marry a fisherman and bear him sons. She was a bold girl; she might look beyond the village for her man. For certain sure, she had not been much impressed by the boys she'd grown up with. She wouldn't let her grandfather take any of them as apprentice crew, so long as she was better. Which she was: not stronger, perhaps, but harder-working, smarter, swifter. She was not inclined to choose a husband from boys she had rejected as shipmates.

When she said such things, her grandfather laughed at her. *Wait and see,* he'd say. Thinking perhaps that she'd develop an affection despite herself, and so find one fit to crew the boat after all, fit to inherit it when he was too old to sail, as his own sons didn't want it.

That was her life, her future. Then there was an hour in the fog, and now—

WELL, NOW there was this. She had a boy, a man, a master.

What did he have? She thought she was a servant. The court thought she was a concubine. He thought—

She had no idea what he thought. It was not her place to ask; he was the Son of Heaven. Her place was in his bed, when he chose to find her there. Otherwise, it was a mystery to her. Even to be at his feet seemed presumptuous.

One thing she was sure of, her place was not here, at his side, in his business. Except that he wanted her here, and he was master, and she had no way to tell him he was wrong.

Proper palace servants, privileged by age and long service, they would have a way. Those who had known him as a baby, washed his body and treated his little hurts; those who had shared the hardships of these last months, crossing the empire with him. It was the task, more, the honor of good servants to help their master understand his own mistakes. But none of those was here in the hall; this was not their place and they knew it.

His generals, his advisers hinted and scowled, they coughed into their hands, their eyes threatened trouble for her but none of them had the authority—or, perhaps, the courage—to protest.

There was only his mother who could be direct.

Could be, and was. "Why is the girl here?"

"Because I want her," the emperor said, sounding for a moment like a sulky boy; then, more firmly, "She knows this island and its people."

"She's a peasant. She knows nothing and no one."

Nothing and no one that could possibly matter, she meant, to the emperor and his court. Mei Feng believed her, agreed with her, ached to go. And stayed just where she was, stilled by his hand on her shoulder.

"She knows the waters between here and Santung; she knows the coast."

"Oh, and you would make your military dispositions according to the word of a girl, would you? Your generals will be glad of that, I am certain. Send her away, Chien Hua. You may have your little flowers, but keep them in your gardens or your rooms."

"She knows the gods," he said, "whom we should pray to, to defend this island."

"Again, you would trust a fish-girl? If you want to pray, send for a priest."

Oddly, Mei Feng was angry now. She rose to her feet, surprising the emperor, surprising everyone; and looked to him and said, "My lord would like some tea, perhaps?"

"Yes. Thank you, Mei Feng."

If the others wanted tea, they could summon it. The emperor did not share what was his, or drink what others shared. It was a blessing; it gave her something to do, for him alone. A reason, almost, to be here.

Everything was laid out ready in a corner. The teakettle was hot, above a little pot of glowing charcoal. There was tea in a bowl, and his favorite dragon pot with the tiger on the lid, and his cup shaped like a lotus flower. They might have been toys to amuse a child, but he was emperor so they must be significant of his grace and power. Except that he was penned in among his advisers, scolded publicly by his mother; all the lands of his birthright lay behind him, lost; how was he emperor of anything?

He was emperor of her, that was certain. However much his mother disapproved, his generals glared, his servants looked askance. Her hands trembled—see?—as she ladled tea into the pot. She had never seen, never smelled such tea: silver-tipped twists of leaf the length of her finger joints, floral and almost fruity to her nose even before she poured on water.

She had been instructed how to do this. *Leave it for so long as it takes you to count a hundred, slowly; do you know your numbers, girl? All the way to a hundred? Pour it into the cup, take the cup to his side then drink from it there where he can see you, where all the court can see you. Just a sip, and from the rim opposite to that you offer him.*

She did all of that, and nearly scorched her lip on the tea's heat; and he smiled just a little as he took the cup, because he'd seen it nearly happen and he knew just how it felt, and because she gave him something he could smile at. Just a little.

He had tea; she had done what she was allowed to do, played servant to her lord. Or else she had flaunted herself like a slap in his mother's face, a gesture of utter disrespect. She should rise now as gracefully as a peasant fishergirl could, and withdraw to that same corner with the tea things, and wait his later pleasure. But just the touch of his finger and a glance of his eyes held her here, kneeling on a cushion at his side.

A snort from the empress, the silky rustle of a shrug: expressions of dismissal, an army withdrawn but not surrendered, ground ceded only for this time. Then blessedly the empress's attention, the room's attention turned elsewhere, and she could breathe a little—softly, softly!—and shudder in her unaccustomed silks and try just for a little not to be afraid or angry, both.

START WITH the little things, the near things. What lay beneath her eyes, her hands, her body. These clothes she wore, that were not hers or anything like hers, just as this part she played—servant or concubine or lover—was not her or anything like her. They were worn and soft with age, these heavy silks, tired despite years of care. It was easy to see where broken threads had been replaced, faded colors refreshed.

The cushion she sat on, that too was old and luxurious and worn, embroidered and ornate and not quite so obviously loved, patched rather than darned, its tasseled fringes thin with picking.

The floor, too: she had an intimate view of that and it was older than anything, hundreds of years old. Heavy boards dark in their age, iron-hard, immaculately joined. This floor would satisfy— better, it would impress to silence—her father the boatbuilder and his brothers too.

She didn't know whose the clothes had been, nor whose the cushion; only that they belonged to the household here, this house with the wonderful floors, and the house had belonged to a jade-master before the emperor took it to be his palace.

It was by far the grandest house she'd ever seen. Three courtyards! One for the master, one for the mistress, one for public audience. She was surprised that it was lawful for a mere merchant to build so arrogantly; but then, a jademaster was never quite a merchant. A steward, rather. Jade belonged to the emperor, to the throne. It couldn't be sold or traded away. The jademasters oversaw the mining and the carving—all the finest workers of jade came to Taishu, to be as close as possible to the source-stone of their art—and then its transport to the Hidden City. They paid the miners and the carvers, the wagonmen and the guards. They were handsomely paid by the palace in their turn, but no, they were not truly merchants, they didn't deal in jade.

The emperor was called the Man of Jade, he sat on the Jade Throne. Literally he did, or could, here in the jademaster's hall; it was the first of his baggage to arrive. Great slabs of fine-carved stone, a deep-sea green with the sea's own enchantment to it: she could just stare and stare, where it sat on the dark old wood of the floor like a temple altar, like a seat for the gods. Which it was, of course, a seat for the Son of Heaven . . .

It was awesome, but the emperor seemed oblivious to its majesty or his own. Just now he was sitting on the floor himself, the better to hunch over a map where it was spread between his generals. His mother had a chair, and loomed above them.

Stubborn as she was, Mei Feng couldn't keep her eyes permanently on her own folded fingers, the fabric they folded around, the floor she sat on. With so much else so close—edgy voices, fingers jabbing, all the signs of men working up to temper because they were uncertain, because they were afraid—she had to sneak glances sideways, she had to listen in.

She had heard of maps, of course, but never seen one. At first, she didn't understand it. The sea, the strait was in her, like salt in her blood; what could that paper mean, against the surging strength of tides, the brute blunt teeth of rocks, the welcome of safe harbor?

But she heard the men name places, points she knew; her mind made connections slowly, between the shapes drawn on the paper and the vivid realities in her mind.

Soon she'd decided that it wasn't a very good map, or else no map was good. It had nothing to say about where the currents sucked strangely, or where a natural harbor promised shelter in a storm; it couldn't map the winds or the seasons or the drifts of fish. Even the lie of the land it had wrongly: only in little ways, a tilt here and an angle there, but again and again until all those mistakes mounted up, until a headland could be drawn easterly when she knew it jutted north.

Grandfather would have mocked the map and disregarded it.

She might have said something herself, but she had caused the emperor embarrassment enough and they weren't trying to plot a course at sea, only choosing where to station men. Men and fleets. The boats of her own village they meant to move; Szechao was difficult to access by land. Here, on the other hand—a finger, stabbing down—was a creek closer to the town, wide enough to harbor a fishing fleet, and the men could cut a road . . .

"No!"

Surprisingly, amazingly, it was her own voice, despite all resolution: shrill but firm, determined, absolute. They should not, they could *not* . . . !

They were staring at her, glaring at her; and she couldn't simply say what was true, *You can't, that's sacred ground.* They'd never heard of the goddess, they wouldn't care, and the goddess had no powerful priests to defend her, no one they'd listen to . . .

She said, "Your clever map won't show it, lord," as though he was the only one who mattered here, "but there is a whirlpool, just at the mouth of the creek," which was also blessedly true. "That's why there is no village, no fleet, no anchorage. The old folk say there is a demon in the water," or at least some of them did. Her grandfather was old, and he said it was set there by the goddess, to guard her shrine. Mei Feng wasn't sure. Sometimes she thought that if rocks could just be rocks and a current just a current, then where a river's flow met rocks and sea together, a whirlpool could perhaps just be a whirlpool, an expression of the water's temper.

It didn't do to say as much to Grandfather. Here, it wouldn't do to say much more at all. She left her hand on the map, though, pointing, absolute. A general's was there already, and she marveled at the differences between them. There was hers, small and slender and yet callused grimly from the boat's work, one salty finger bent from where a slipping rope had broken it when she was nine years old; and there was his, massive in comparison and strong no doubt and yet soft-skinned from years of baths and oils and no labor. Even the hard march here had not toughened his skin, whatever it might have done to his soul.

And now here was one more hand, which was the emperor's

own; and it was smooth and long-fingered and had never had the chance to grow strong, but his voice was strong enough as he said, "Well, you have saved us time, then, and perhaps some few lives if the whirlpool is so wicked," and he didn't at all say *I told you she'd be useful,* but everything about him said it anyway. "General Hu, it is not impossible that the people of the island have already chosen the best harbors for their fleets. Perhaps you should send someone—or, better, go yourself—to ask questions and to listen to the answers before you make your dispositions. You can spare yourself the journey to Mei Feng's village. Leave that fleet where it is, and build a new road all the way. We have men enough, and to spare."

General Hu frowned and turned his head, looked up at the dowager empress, waited for her nod. When he had it, then he bowed across the map and said, "Highness, your wisdom exceeds your years, as your glory does the glory of your ancestors."

Mei Feng flinched at the clumsiness of that, resentful on the emperor's behalf. Was she the only person here he could command, was she his only friend?

Her mind was full of stories, of puppet emperors and scheming functionaries. That was what she wanted to see here, evil counselors plotting with his mother to disinherit him. Of course, it wasn't true. He had been barely out of childhood when his father died. Men of the imperial line traditionally lived long and had few children, but this was extravagant even for a Man of Jade, not to father a son until his extreme old age.

All through her own childhood, she had watched her family fighting over possession and use of the boat. Grandfather would not give it up, would not let his sons sail without him, insisted on his right to captain. One by one, Mei Feng had seen her father and her uncles walk away. By the time the youngest uncle left him, she had been—just—old enough to take her place as crew, his only crew.

She thought this was the same, or something like it: that the empress had sat a throne so long, she couldn't conceive of any need to give it up. The emperor was still her boy, young and callow and inexperienced; what could he know? How could a boy govern an empire—and why should he need to when he had advisers, generals, a mother above all . . . ?

Mei Feng watched them, she watched him sidelong; she liked it when he glanced at her, but she did try not to meet his gaze. That was the best help she could be just now, to be quiet, self-effacing, do no harm. No more harm.

SHE WAS still doing that, practicing harmlessness, when there was a flurry of feet and voices outside the hall, and then men coming in.

Two guards, alarmed and urgent. They ran, almost, into the hall. And met the sudden silence that greeted them, the impact of their betters' eyes, and lost their nerve along with their momentum. Caught like fish in a net, they dropped to their knees and hit their heads on the floor, and waited. Until the empress freed them, with a simple "Well?"

"Highness, mistress," and yes, she was the one they looked to. They were her men. Perhaps every man here was hers. Wisdom would assume so, at any rate. And would look for other men, to build loyalties of her own. "There is . . . something happening, mistress. Over the sea. Something strange, an enchantment, we don't know: a darkness, though, a veil across the sun . . ."

A storm, Wisdom thought, just one of those summer squalls that blew up and blew over: drenching and enervating if you were beneath it in a pitching boat, but no cause for alarm. She opened her mouth to say so, and was just wise enough to bite it back; and didn't need to nudge the emperor because he was already rising to say, "We will go up and see this . . . event. From the gatehouse roof," where there was a view over the harbor and the sea, to the Forge and farther. She would spend more time on the roof, if he would only let her.

Right now he reached down to help her up, which was unnecessary and adorable. They paraded out of the hall and across the public courtyard; and it really was a parade, because of course his mother and the generals and all the court had to follow him. But he held her hand all the way, and being first to the gatehouse roof the two of them could claim a corner and stand alone, as befitted his dignity and her desire.

And now she was clutching hard at his fingers, because that fine view across the strait was showing her something that was not a summer squall, no. It was a storm for sure, but she'd seen nothing like it, the dark sky and the pale sun and the fury at its heart.

And then the wave, that came punching out of that fury: the towering tsunami that outraced the wind, black and deadly. And she could do nothing, nothing but watch. No time to warn people at the harborside, let alone boats on the water. And there were so many boats, on the water and in the port; and the wave caught them and turned them over or hurled them against the harbor walls, and spat their wreckage high into the city along with all the people it had swallowed and everything else it had broken or dragged up from far below.

And this magnificent view meant that she could watch it all, in company with the mighty of the empire, who were just as helpless as herself; and it took long enough, she had time enough to watch herself as well, the numbing fear and the hidden rising heart of her.

What she saw in herself was the girl she had been all her life, sweeping aside this new Mei Feng, this servant or concubine or whatever she had become. The girl she truly was, child of her village, of her family, of the sea.

And the thought that came to her, the only thought that girl could have just now:

Grandfather . . . !

five

*N*ews travels inland like a wave from the sea. At the coast it is thunderous, monumental, it carries all before it. Where it finds a rivermouth it strikes upstream, far and far; its reach over land is shorter. Forests break it, dry plains soak it up.

What can reach the mountains, and the mines?

What they need, what is brought to them. Nothing of the rush, the impetuosity of news that rolls ahead of its authority. No one comes this far along the Jade Road except wagoners with their slow beasts under wary guard, bringing supplies and taking jade away. The wagoners are not loved in the high valleys: mean men, who take what is priceless and give little for it, less even than their masters would allow. These are not men to gossip with, nor to ask for news.

THE WAGON-ROAD is the only road, but not the only way to go. There are footpaths, private ways from valley to valley, ridge to ridge and so down to the lower hills and the paddies, tamed lands, farms and villages. The clans watch their own paths, of course. They share little and trust one another not at all, but some people are let pass from one to the next. Sometimes news is passed on for its own sake; sometimes it is traded, as though it were rice or cloth.

Sometimes, rarely, it is too important to trade for, too significant to delay. News can be like the typhoon, breaking down what it does not blast across.

. . .

As THIS, now: when the wagoners might not have brought it for a month or more and even then might not have passed it on, a girl has run with it in three days. There is something of the mountains in her—in her eyes, perhaps—and something clannish on her, a tattoo on her shoulder to say that she belonged here once, but she came from the town, barefoot and hot with it.

Bandits might have delayed her, dallied with her, kept her altogether, but she was too fast or too clever or too quiet to be caught. Any one of the clans might have kept her, might have killed her for not being one of their own; but they listened to her first and took her news for payment, let her run.

They let her run and so she did, higher and deeper into the mountains, every valley, every clan.

THE NEWS, of course, was that the emperor was on Taishu, and staying.

THEY COULD see why the jademasters might not have wanted them to know that.

"*S*ometimes," Li Ton acknowledged, "I make mistakes."

Even I, he meant, and he was looking at Han as he said it.

A MONSTROUS wave born of an unnatural storm had hurled the *Shalla* out of the strait, breaking spars and rigging, rolling her onto her beam, all but tipping her over entirely. They were saved by a sound hull and good seamanship, mostly Han thought by Li Ton's mastery of his vessel and his crew; and not, not at all by anything Han himself did or tried or was told to do.

He did try. The pain in his hand was savage but not overwhelming; he could use the fingers. And there was nothing wrong with his other hand, his legs, his back. He should have been some use, at least. One more body on the end of a rope.

He hauled himself through wind and water from one end of the tipping, twisting junk to the other. He seized hold as best he could, heaved when he was told to—and time and again he was cuffed or kicked away, as the rope or chain jerked free. He had no grip at all with his right hand, and no strength either in his left.

A broken spar trailed overside on tangled ropes, fouling their course; given a hatchet and sent to cut the wreckage free, he couldn't even manage that. It was Li Ton himself who snatched the hatchet from him, dealt with the ropes in two firm strokes, then backhanded Han across the streaming deck. No words, but none were needed.

. . .

THE STORM was as strange and hasty in its vanishing as it had been in its birth, leaving the *Shalla* to drag herself to safe harbor in a mainland creek. There was a village on the bluff, but the peasants kept their distance; when men climbed up in search of food and supplies, they found it deserted, far figures running through the paddy.

And took what they wanted, whatever they could find to help with the slow business of repair.

And now Li Ton was attending to the swift business of ship's discipline, on the strand in the shadow of the beached junk. A dozen of his men were within earshot, mildly interested, paying scant attention while they scarfed two planks together or whittled new pegs or caulked a sprung seam tight.

Behind him, Han could hear the steady pounding of the smithy slave's hammer, where he was remaking a shoe for a split mast. He'd set up a small forge on the beach, with an ingot of pig-iron on a rock to be an anvil. Han had tried to help, but he was small use even to find kindling for the charcoal furnace, when he could carry so little. Everything he turned his hand—his one hand—to, someone else could do it quicker and better.

Li Ton might as well kill him for all the use he was now, to himself or anyone.

LI TON was taking his time, playing to his audience just a little. He took so long, indeed—talking to Jorgan at his side, while his hands methodically stroked a stone along the heavy curve of his favorite blade—that there was time even for the slave Suo Lung to quit work, to come see. At least, the sound of his hammering stopped abruptly, and he was not a man who took rests. Han thought of him still as slave, even though his chains had been struck off; Han thought all the crew was slave. The ship owned them all, and Li Ton owned the ship.

Ready at last, Li Ton slipped the bladestone into a pocket and let the sun slide over the tao's edge so that it looked for a moment as though he cut the light itself. Then he glanced down to where Han knelt on the stony sand before him.

"It's a pity," he said. "I was angry; but I should have thought to take the left thumb, not the right. You're no good to me as you are."

With no more ceremony than that, the blade lifted in his hand—which was how it looked to Han, as though the tao worked the man—and the great thick curve of it caught the light again, just as it started to swing down.

Han wasn't going to move, not a muscle. Losing his thumb had been numbing, before it was appalling; this time there'd be no time for the numbness to pass into agony. One swift stroke would take his head and be done with it. He was almost grateful.

THE BLADE swung, and he felt the blow that laid him sideways on the earth; and for a while there was no pain, and he waited to feel his spirit drain into the wind as his blood must be draining into the sand, and he did feel dizzy and peculiar and detached, and . . .

but . . .

the pain came, delayed and atrocious, a bruising ache all down one side of his head; and there was a roaring in his ears but more, a stamping above him and a great shadow cast across him, shouting; and the shouting died away but he himself wasn't dead at all but only lying on the ground, sprawled on his side, still whole. And that was Suo Lung who stood above him, holding Li Ton's sword-hand in a rock-solid grasp that the captain could strain against all day and never shift.

Some of the shouting had been Suo Lung's and some had been Jorgan's, but Jorgan was now also lying on the ground, some little distance away. The men all around had likely been shouting too, but they were quiet now, because Li Ton was holding up his other hand for silence.

Li Ton, Han was sure, had not shouted. Even when the slave had stepped in, knocked Han aside and caught the blade-hand in its descent; even at the shock of that, Li Ton would not have shouted. If he wanted Suo Lung dead, he would say so, quite calmly, and his men would make it happen. Han thought he might well do that, and then return to unfinished business.

First, though, Li Ton said, "Why?"

The slave—well, the slave said something. Han had always found him hard to understand, and this ringing in his ears made it harder. He thought Suo Lung was pleading for—no, *demanding* Han's life.

Li Ton considered for a moment, then glanced deliberately down at his hand, his sword-hand, where the slave was still gripping it.

After a moment, Suo Lung let it go.

Li Ton nodded, hefted his blade briefly and slid it into his belt. Han didn't quite dare to feel reprieved.

Li Ton said, "Why not?"

"Give him to me," Suo Lung said, thick and slow and labored; which was no kind of answer, but even dizzy Han could understand him now.

Li Ton's eyes moved: not to Han lying on the sand there, but beyond him, toward the slave's improvised forge. Han thought he could follow what lay in the captain's mind:

The boy is useless to me, but perhaps not to Suo Lung.

The boy is useless, but Suo Lung is not. If Suo Lung wants him—for his forge, for his bed, for whatever—what does it cost me, to keep my new smith happy?

It costs me in discipline, in reputation among my men; this is the third time I should have killed this boy. Can I afford to let him live again?

After a moment, he nodded once, sharply. "Very well. He is yours."

HAN LAY where he was. His head pounded, and so did his heart; dizzy and sick, he felt easier—a little—if he could just close his eyes and be still. Great fingers gripped his arm, though, and yanked him to his feet. Here was the newest truth of his life, this vast man, naked to the waist and greasy with sweat, reeking of hot iron, his skin pocked with countless tiny scars and bubbled here and there with long ones. A smith, a slave, his master.

A smith, a slave, a stranger. His speech was slow, and not because his mind was slow, or not only that. The tongue was as foreign to him as he was to these lands, these waters. That showed simply in the size of him, in a country that did not run to big men; it showed in the shape of his face, too broad and heavy-boned. Even his skin was alien, the wrong shades, the wrong texture, too thick. Even his smell: below the sharp salt of his sweat and the iron of his work, there was still something that smelled of the stranger.

Something of that, and more. His smell, his touch, the look of him: everything about him said this man was afraid. Han couldn't help but remember how he had screamed on the Forge, at the anvil there, when his chains were struck off. He thought perhaps Suo Lung had been afraid then and ever since.

At this anvil here, he thrust Han a couple of steps onward, to where he had built a crude forge from the stones of the beach. The firebed was raised an arm's length above the ground, and two matched bellows pushed air in below.

A grunt, a gesture: Han dropped to his knees, took hold of the bellows' handles and began to work them alternately up and down.

His left hand could do that much, until the work exhausted him; his right—well, he had no pull in the hand, he had to kneel high above his work and drive down, haul up from the shoulder. Every movement awoke the sear of pain in the burn-scar of his missing thumb.

He didn't want to weep, but it happened anyway. Pain or fear or hopelessness, perhaps all three; together they were too much for him, they ate all his resistance. He worked the bellows, and sobbed at every stroke; and Suo Lung set aside the mast shoe he'd been forging, took a fillet of low-grade iron and set it to heat in the furnace.

And took it out when it glowed red, and hammered, and put it back; took it out and hammered again, while he sweated and Han sweated and Han thought that he perhaps was sweating blood, as pain ran like fire through the fibers of his body. A boy ought to bleed, he thought, who was hurting so terribly much.

He pumped air, Suo Lung hammered. And quenched what had

become a broader, thinner strip of iron, and heated it and hammered it into a crescent curve and quenched it again; and then called Han blessedly away from the bellows.

And took his left wrist and laid it on the anvil there, where the bent strip of metal fitted it quite neatly; and three swift blows of the hammer closed it around Han's wrist like a cuff.

Then the smith took up a steel scribing-tool and scratched uncertainly at the iron, as though he was trying to write.

And looked at Han, a question that the boy couldn't answer; the hesitant marks meant nothing to him.

Suo Lung looked, scratched one more tentative stroke and, strugglingly, said, "Stillness."

It cost him in memory, Han thought, as much as speech; he stared into the far distance and forced the word out as though he dragged it up from some almost-unreachable depth.

And then he jabbed his tool at the shape he'd marked on the iron cuff, and then Han understood it.

It wasn't the character for "stillness," but it might have been. It needed this stroke more, and that—and Han couldn't make those strokes. If he took the tool from Suo Lung, he couldn't hold it; if he held it, he couldn't hold it steady; if somehow he held it steady, he couldn't press hard enough to make even the lightest scratches.

If he'd understood why the smith wanted to write the character for "stillness" on an iron cuff on his wrist, he might have felt more inclined to try.

Instead he shrugged, and the smith hit him.

And then dragged Han up again from where he lay sprawled beside the anvil, took his wrist and turned it so that the light caught those awkward scratches.

"Scribe's boy," Suo Lung said, in that slow and difficult voice of his. He must have heard that from the crew and held on to it; it seemed to be important. *It's why he saved you,* Han told himself silently, *because you can write.*

Used to be able to write.

Because of that, and because he could have an iron cuff hammered around his wrist and then be beaten until he helped to make words to decorate it. Apparently.

"Stillness," the smith said, and shook him.

His head ached and pounded, both sides now. Shaking made it worse. He tried to shrug the smith's hand off his shoulder, tried to squirm free; and might as well have tried to shrug against an avalanche, to squirm free of his own tomb once he was dead and buried. This was rock's grip, an eternity of holding.

He said, "Yes, yes! Stillness! I understand . . . !"

Suo Lung did at least stop shaking him. One massive finger jabbed at the cuff. "Not good."

Well, no. Not good in any way, awkward and ugly, but he only meant "not right." Han said, "No, not good. Look—"

He reached down to the sand, and swept a patch clear of stones. With his free hand, his right, his maimed hand where pain flared like living fire when he did that.

And slowly, with the forefinger of that same hand—because it was the one he knew how to use, and because Suo Lung still held the other vastly by the cuff and what did he need hammers for when he could simply have squeezed that iron on?—Han wrote the character for "stillness" in the sand.

He wrote it large and clear, as if pain were an ink and his bones and flesh the brush.

Suo Lung looked worriedly from the character in the sand to the character on the cuff, back and forth between them, once and twice and again; and touched the scribing-tool to the iron, traced the path of a missing stroke, looked to Han for confirmation.

"Yes, that's right, like that . . ."

The tool cut into the iron, made the mark. And then again: the next stroke, the same consultation. This hesitancy would have earned Han a beating from his old master. It had, time and time again, when he was first learning his characters.

At last, though, the smith was finished. The character was lopsided and so badly written it was worth another beating, but it said what he meant, whyever he wanted to say it.

"Stillness," Suo Lung said, with just the hint of a question in his voice.

"Stillness," Han agreed firmly, nodding his aching head for emphasis.

The smith grunted and knocked the boy away from the anvil, pointed him back to the bellows.

Took another small piece of iron, and tossed it into the furnace to heat.

HAN'S SECOND cuff—eventually—said SLEEP.

THEN HE worked the bellows while Suo Lung heated and hammered at the mast shoe. Han tried to pretend that the weights of iron on his wrists helped him to drive down the bamboo grips and so force air into the furnace; but then he had to drag them up again, of course, and his hands soon felt impossibly heavy, when he could feel anything besides the pain. Thrusting and hauling, both hurt like molten iron in his bones.

Dizzy, then, and racked with pain, he pumped air and went on pumping. Sweating, sobbing, he worked his arms up and down, up and down. His clothes were sodden and great shudders seized him, and he still went on.

There was an explosion, an eruption of steam from the vast iron bowl that Suo Lung had heaved out of the lower hold, that he was using as a quenching trough. That was the work done, the shoe finished, and still Han pumped, until the smith's hand fell on his shoulder to prevent him.

It was his right shoulder, which the pain inhabited like a coiled living thing. The weight of that hand was enough to draw a thin scream out of Han as fire lashed beneath his skin.

Suo Lung grunted, lifted the boy's right hand up into full sun and looked at it; then he pulled a knife from his belt and laid the tip of it on a hot coal at the furnace-edge.

When the steel was smoking-hot, he thrust it clean through the seared scab where the second joint of Han's thumb used to be.

Han screamed again.

When the smith drew the blade out, there was a spurt of pus to follow. He squeezed the wound between his own two thumbs, until no more liquid came; then he heated the blade again, and seared it again.

Han had no breath left for screaming. All he could do was hurt, cleanly and deeply. His hand wanted to pull itself away from the blade, but the smith's grip held it easily, wrist and cuff both engulfed in fingers like steel bands.

When he was done, finally, the smith let go; and no, Han wasn't going to pump anymore. Not for his life, even. He huddled on his knees, breathing, cradling his hand against his chest, not quite letting it touch anything; even his breath was too much contact.

WHEN HE had done that for a while, he heard voices nearby, and one of them was Li Ton. He sounded pleased. Han didn't really care.

The voices went away, and when Han finally lifted his head the shoe was gone too, so presumably Li Ton or his men had taken it. Probably they were aboard the *Shalla* right now, shipping a new mast. He didn't look; he didn't care.

The smith had collected a great heap of iron makings: broken castings and rusting tools, unidentifiable objects of many weights and sorts. Some had come from the hold, some from the ballast in the bilges. All of it was for melting down, for reworking into what the junk most needed or her captain most demanded.

Suo Lung rummaged in that heap, and came up with a length of chain.

He laid that on a stone at the furnace-edge, so that the two broken end links were set in the fire to heat.

Then he beckoned Han over to the anvil once again.

seven

he feels—

WHAT DOES she feel?

She doesn't know. It's been an age since she felt anything.

For a little there, she felt free. Loosed chains, the suck of tide and current, the possibilities of movement. She stretched, she flexed; she felt free.

Now, thinking to stretch again—beginning to wonder if perhaps she dares to rise—she feels something that inhibits her.

She thought the chains were broken. Perhaps not. Perhaps she only dreamed it.

Perhaps she should just lie still, perhaps she should sleep again.

Sleep strikes at her like a rolling wave, and her body cramps into stillness.

But she still has the bitter tang of waking in her mind, an awareness of her self, her power, her loss. How much she has lost, movement and time and authority.

There is no authority here, in this grip of stillness, the lure to sleep. It is nothing that has any power over her; she will not admit it.

She will rouse, and move, and be herself again.

She will—

eight

The emperor was here, on Taishu.

No one really understood why—word spoke of rebellion and flight, but he was emperor, the Son of Heaven, the Man of Jade: how could he flee? and whom?—but the fact of it was certain. He was here.

All up and down the valley people had been excited for days, in that way people were when there were rumors of distant great events. They talked, they dreamed, they wove wonderful stories out of the nothing that they knew. Wonderful and dreadful: the emperor come, and war soon to follow.

It meant nothing. What difference could it possibly make, here in the mountains? There was jade to be mined and food to be gathered or grown; water to be fetched, roofs repaired, cloth woven. Nothing changed, simply because the emperor had come to the island.

So Yu Shan thought, at least. He had his own, his family's reason to be excited. He was young yet, but his grandfather was not; and his grandfather had never seen such a stone as they had found, in what seemed to be the last of this exhausted vein.

Yu Shan hadn't been let near it, except to see and marvel at the beauty, the purity, the simple size of what they'd found. His father and uncle were taking turns to work their way around it, chipping away the mother-rock flake by cautious flake.

There were days of waiting, hunting, gleaning, brewing—all the normal occupations for those not underground, all overlaid with a breathless expectation. Yu Shan spent as much time as possible in the forest. Ostensibly setting snares and gathering shoots while he prospected for possible new veins, in truth he wanted distance. Tired of speculation, tired of doomsaying—"We'll be paid for the weight of it, as always, it's worth no more to us than chippings"—he was glad just to be away from the sound of voices.

And so of course he met a friend, a clan-friend, a cousin among the trees, and had to talk to her. Ordinarily that was a pleasure, even if they only sat and talked. Some days, some nights they found other pleasures, and his mother meant to offer for her at the next clanmoot. Right now, she was almost the last person he wanted to see. She wasn't family yet, so he couldn't talk about the wonder-stone; but they knew already that he was hopeless at lying to her, she saw his secret heart.

When she cared to look. Today, he could be glad of the valley's wider excitement:

"If the emperor's on Taishu," she said, after they'd greeted each other and touched a little, "why do we need the jademasters anymore?"

Oof. She was like that, bold and direct and impossible. He said, "Hush," out of immediate instinct: not because he thought anyone was listening here, but she might so easily say the same thing somewhere else, where people were.

She shrugged. "It's true, though. Everyone's thinking it. We find the stone, we dig the stone. All the jademasters ever did was take it to the emperor. We can do that ourselves now. Take it to the road, take it along the road, and there he is at the end of the road." She smiled and shrugged, well satisfied at how easy it would all be.

He said, "And what then, he makes us rich, as the jademasters are?"

"I suppose. If he chooses to. It's his stone."

"Why do you want to be rich?" There would still be the valley, the mines, the forest; he wasn't sure what money would add to any of that.

A different manner of shrug, irritated, because she had no answer. "Maybe I only want to take their money away from them." And then—because she was honest and clear-sighted, and knew when she was being foolish—yet another kind, to shrug away her temper and the whole conversation. "Let's not talk about it. That stream we were exploring, last month? I went higher and found a new pool. We could go up, I could show you . . ."

Relieved, he was also stupid. He said, "Why—?"

"Be*cause,* Yu *Shan,* you might want to check it yourself . . ."

A pool in a stream was always worth diving, because there might be pebbles of jade gathered on the bed. If there were, it meant that the stream cut a vein, somewhere higher. If she had found a new pool, she had dived it; and she had found no jade, because if she had she wouldn't be offering to take him there. She wasn't his family yet.

If she had dived it, there was no point his doing the same. They both knew that.

But diving a pool meant taking his clothes off, and hers too. It meant swimming together, diving together.

Getting warm, getting dry together after. Getting hot, getting sticky, needing to swim again . . .

He took her hand, said, "Show me."

SHE WAS the first but not the last to say such things in his hearing. He heard it at the family fire, murmured in the darkness; he heard it in the family mine, murmured in the deeper dark, when he thought his uncle had only taken him in there to let him see the broad smooth glimmering green flank of the wonder-stone.

He felt it, all unsaid, day and night around him. Now particularly, when they had a stone of such majesty, a stone that could be cut into a famous piece, an imperial treasure; now, with the emperor on Taishu, why should they simply hand their discovery over to a common wagoner in exchange for his reckoning of its value by weight, paid in coarse fabrics and tea . . . ?

nine

This, after all, was what a girl was for. If it did not gratify his mother, it should at least content her.

Standing where she had been told to stand, Mei Feng waited as she had been told to wait. She had been sent for, summoned by her absent lord; groomed and fussed at by his servants; left here in the innermost of his rooms, his private bed. In his absence.

SHE WAITED, and he came.

Eventually.

Extraordinarily, apologetically, he came; the master of the world, of her world, hers, and he was flustered as he came through the door, "Mei Feng, I'm sorry, my mother kept me, have they had you waiting here long? Sit, sit . . ."

Which neatly prevented her from dropping to her knees and knocking her head on the floor, as his servants had told her that she must. He dropped onto the bed and patted the mattress at his side; she disobeyed him willfully, settling on the floor at his feet and putting one daring hand on his leg. Making her careful, urgent confession. "Lord, I, I don't know how to please you . . ."

She wasn't made or trained for these tender, courtly arts. She could be perfumed and powdered, yes, and dressed in rustling luxury. He already found her good to look at, to talk to, to listen to. She knew all that, and of course what that implied. It wasn't his body or his bed that frightened her; she had never had cause or opportunity to be shy. Sea-children worked together, washed together, played together: in and out of the water, in and out of their clothes. When her grandfather took her on as crew, she'd kept the same casual habits from simple common sense. If she was to be wet half the time, wet and fishy, why trouble with clothes? It did her no harm to be looked at as they left port, as they landed; one of those quayside boys might be a husband to her one day, so let them look. And she did love to use her body, the feel and stretch and effort, the achievement of it . . .

But all her uses were practical. She could fetch and carry, run and swim, sail and fish; none of that was any use to her here. He was the emperor and she had been sent to him, summoned finally to her proper duty, what everyone assumed she was here for; and she didn't know what to do.

Well, no doubt he could tell her, show her . . .

Except that his fingers trembled as he touched her hair, as he fiddled with the jeweled crane pin that his servants had struggled to affix there. Scandalized, they'd been, that her head was cropped as short as a boy's; how could a woman please her master, they had demanded, without a long heavy fall of hair to be her pride and beauty, his plaything?

With eyes and skin, perhaps, she had wanted to reply, *with talk, with tongue, with touch?* But she knew nothing of what would please the emperor, or any man. She'd kept quiet and let them fuss at her, with all this absurd decoration. Perhaps it would please him, she didn't know. To her, it seemed likely only to get in the way.

To him too, perhaps. He drew the pretty thing out and tossed it aside. Then his fingers seemed to want it, as they came back to her head again; they wanted something at least to fidget with, and seemed shy of tangling with the hair itself.

He said, "I'm pleased just to have you here. To be alone with you, Mei Feng."

Another man, touching her like this—finding her ear now, and running his thumb around the curve of it—might have made her angry, made her feel like stock being examined at the market or soothed in the stable. But he was so eager and yet so tentative, he had the same hesitation in his voice as in his fingers; she felt an impossible suspicion arising.

And couldn't express it, of course—*Lord, are you a virgin, too?*—and so just leaned her cheek into his palm and breathed the scents of him, perfume and sweat and boy-musk, until astonishingly he said it himself: "I don't know how to please you either, here," and his spare hand touched the covers on the bed and he sounded more nervous than she was, more afraid of shame.

She sat back on her heels, took his hand and held it, felt the butterfly pulse and said, "Truly, lord? No girls . . . ?"

"No other girls." His fingers closed around hers. "Never yet. My mother . . ."

Ah yes, his mother. Too close and watching him too carefully in the Hidden City, closer and more watchful yet on the road. Fearing rivals, perhaps, or simply determined to choose his pillow-girls herself when the time was ripe.

Even so, another boy would have found a way, she thought. Even on the march. She said, "But my lord has so many women to serve him," young and pretty and entirely his to do with as he pleased, "he must have found opportunities . . ."

He sighed. "My mother's women, all of them. Bought and trained to be my body-slaves, her spies. And yes, no doubt they will come to my bed if I require it, but then they will report to her on my, on my demeanor here, and—"

And he was emperor, he had pride as his birthright; so he had slept alone until tonight, when he could be with a girl of his own choosing and—he knew, absolutely—not his mother's.

And she had pride too, the sea's pride she could call it, and she loved to disoblige his mother. "I will tell her nothing," she promised. And then, "How should we begin?"

In truth she thought they had begun already. But her wide-eyed question made him snort with soft laughter, and that seemed a good way to begin again.

He said, "Perhaps by taking off some of these heavy garments, do you think?"

She did think so, and reached down to ease the wonderful embroidered slippers from his feet, which were long and clean and soft-soled, nothing like the hard leather of her own. Then there were all the difficulties of robes not meant to be unlaced by the wearer, and the awkward fumblings of two people not accustomed to such things: one who had never dressed himself, and one who had never worn such clothes before. Their efforts in the slippery lamplight led to tight, desperate giggles, and, "I think I have jerked this knot too tight to loosen now. Ah, I could summon my servants . . . ?"

And have it reported to his mother, that he and his little courtesan could not even manage to undress each other. She heard his despair, even through the laughter. "No, lord. Not them, not here, now. You and I can manage each other's, if not our own. Even if these cursed buttons never ever went through these buttonholes, I swear it . . . Does my lord have a little knife, at all . . . ?"

Her lord did have a little knife. Not one of the useful blades that every boy she knew would carry, as she used to do herself; his was ornate and perilous, a blade no longer than his fingernail, fine enough to take an eye out and no good, no good at all for gutting fish.

Buttons and ties went swiftly then, and let his women retrieve them all, on hands and knees in the morning.

Silk slid over warm and shivery skin, and was gone.

There was him, there was her; and he was not so much emperor now and very much more boy, urgent and clumsy and almost afraid. Of himself, of her. And she was—

Well, what was she? Here, at least: that much was certain. Very much here. Under his eye, because he wouldn't look away from her; perhaps he thought he might lose her yet, in this uncertain light. Under his hand, that too. Hands, plural, because he couldn't stop touching her, apparently.

If they were under his mother's eye also, if her women were watching through spy-holes, no matter. This was certainly what the empress thought Mei Feng was for. Let the old woman be satisfied, then, so long as her son was also.

And don't think about her now. Now was not for tomorrow, or for worry, or for herself. Now was for him, and whatever she had to give him, and whatever she could bring herself to take.

"LORD?"

"Mei Feng."

"Forgive me, I am clumsy and stupid, and . . ."

"I think that was me, wasn't it? I think you'll wear the bruises."

That was true. He was stronger than she'd thought, unless all men were strong when they were rutting. Confusion and awkwardness, a little pain: it had not been an occasion of joy for either one of them. There had been moments, though, glimpses of something other, something that waited, something that could be learned. "I think it will be better, lord. Next time." Better for both, she meant; but, nestling a little against his withdrawal, "I think my lord should practice more. With other women."

"I want to—practice—with you."

"Other women *too,* I meant, lord," laughing, kissing his shoulder. "Girls who know better how to please you. Then you could teach me."

"My mother—"

"Despite your mother. I am sure we can find a way." Now that this particular veil was torn down, she thought his mother might be less obstructive. Better to occupy the boy than have him bored and restless and prone to interfere; better a dozen women than one. Enough women could eat his time entirely, demanding treats and attentions, engaging him in affairs that mattered not at all beyond the palace wall. If she were empress, that would be her plan.

His hand was on her hip now, anxious, hopeful: "You should practice too, then, Mei Feng. Just, not with any man but me."

"As you say, lord."

"LORD?"

"Mei Feng."

"Tell me how you came here."

"You asked me that before, on the boat."

Three times, in different ways; but this was yet one more. She wanted to learn him, this boy she held in the dark. She wanted more than his lean body.

"My lord told me why he came, but tell me how. Tell me about the journey." She liked stories, and she thought he liked to talk. Already she was learning how to make him happy. He liked to be touched—perhaps because he was emperor, because nobody ever dared to touch him. He liked this, how she lay sprawled full-length against his side, with her head in the curve of his shoulder and even so her toes barely reaching to his ankle.

He liked how she lay with one leg cocked over his, some of her weight on him. It had made her nervous, a little, but his hand on her thigh said *No, that's good, stay there.*

He liked it, she thought, that her body was not soft and oily and almost unused: that she had muscles, she had scars, she had calluses and strength. He certainly liked it that he was stronger. She hadn't expected that, neither his strength nor the way he took pleasure in it, as though it had surprised him too. As though he had thought himself weak before tonight, and she had helped him to see that wasn't true.

"Aren't you sleepy?"

She couldn't help it, she laughed at him, before she remembered who he was. He seemed to like that too.

"Forgive me, lord, I didn't mean . . ."

"Shh. Laughing's good, don't be sorry for laughing. No one ever laughs around me. What did I say, that was funny?"

She had so many answers, she could count them off against his ribs: her rough and damaged fingers pressing on smooth unblemished imperial skin. She thought he might like that. Sticky as his skin was, salty beneath her mouth as she enumerated, not lifting her head, speaking truth directly to his heart.

"I have been crew on a fishing boat, lord, since I was nine years old. All the crew there was. When we were fishing, I didn't sleep all night. Or when we have festival, there are fireworks and dancing on the beach, all night long."

"You're used to staying awake, you mean."

"Yes, lord," but she hadn't finished counting yet. "And tonight not at all sleepy. Tonight I am in his bed with my emperor," and still frightened by the scale of it, the impossibility, although no longer frightened by this boy, "and I don't think I could sleep if I wanted to." Maybe *awed* was a better word than *frightened*. Maybe she should be awed at herself, just for being here. Surviving this. Finding that she could be this girl, as well as the other. Differently bold. "And," last point, one more finger, "I don't want to go to sleep. I like this."

"All of it?"

"I like to please my lord," which might be politic but had the grace of being true also. He might not be the man of her choice, but who ever got to choose? Her father would have married her sooner or later to some boatyard apprentice; he'd have done it years ago, if her grandfather hadn't been so determined to keep her on his boat.

No one could ever choose the emperor, but he had chosen her. She did like that. And she would always be his first now, which seemed to matter; and she did like the simple physical intimacy of being in bed with a boy, with purpose, their slow and mutual discovery of what was possible and what was good; and this, she liked this best, she thought: just lying together and talking softly in the darkness, telling stories.

Not another count for her fingers but the whole hand, flat on the solidity of his chest, "My lord was going to tell me how it was, coming here. And I think he keeps ducking the question."

"Do I?" His fingers played with hers, distractingly. "Perhaps I do. I hated it, you see. Every day of it."

Which to a wiser girl on another day might have been a way to say *No, don't ask, I am your emperor and I don't have to tell you.*

But he said it tonight, and to her; and she tightened her hand around his and said, "Tell me."

And, for a wonder, he did.

In a way.

· · ·

HE SAID, "I've been up on the gatehouse roof again, watching the bay below. Watching the boats come in."

"Yes, lord." She knew that, of course. Everyone knew.

"When a ship comes in with the wind in its sails, there's a wave of water that rises before it, as though the water knows the boat is coming . . ."

Yes, lord. We call that the wash, and you don't have to be up high to see it. She was learning courtly tact quickly in this strange palace, even more so in this strange curtained bed; she didn't speak her thought. She was pleased with herself, and baffled to know what he was talking about. She knew about boats, but he didn't.

"It was like that," he said. "*We* were like that, we were the water that came before the boat, the news before the event. We were our own news. No one knew there was a rebellion until we arrived, fleeing ahead of it. No one was prepared, no one could afford to give us food or shelter, so we fed ourselves anyway from all their careful stores and made more enemies at every stop. And so had to keep on moving, on and on . . ."

And at last they had come here, and there were so many reasons for that, she could see them all; and she still thought it was hopeless, because this was an island and could not feed them all.

"Lord? How will we live now, all of you and all of us, together?"

"Mmm? We will hold out, of course." He almost said it in someone else's voice, pronounced it like a banner, We Will Hold Out; he must have heard it so often when he asked the same question of his mother, of his generals, *What will we do in Taishu?* "It will be hard, but we have to. There is nowhere else to go; the jade is here."

"Perhaps, now that they have all the mainland empire to, to squabble over, to ruin," because that was an article of faith, that the empire without its lord must go to rack and ruin, "they will leave you to sit here, unmolested . . ."

She said that badly, baldly, not so practiced after all at this diplomacy, not so quick to learn. She felt the sudden chill in him, the sudden emperor, offended.

"Oh, will they let me do that? Do you think? Should I be grateful, if they let me cling to this last crumb of my own lands?"

"Lord, forgive me. I—"

She was a careless fool with words sometimes, but she was also a girl, his girl, his first; he couldn't keep hold of his offense, apparently, so long as he had warm hold of her.

He said, "Hush, no. I'm too late to be proud, after they've hounded me so far."

"It was your generals who fled, lord . . ."

". . . And took me with them. Yes. And my mother; I came because she said I must. But they were right, I expect. What did I know of war, then?" He knew more now, and that was still his story, and he was still not telling it. Never mind. "They were right then, and you're wrong now. The rebels will come after us, they must."

"Why so, lord?"

"Because the jade is here."

There was a world of truth in that, and a world of threat. They would come.

She didn't want to think about that, war and death in her own Taishu. Or in his, she didn't want to think about that either. She could allow herself just a little cowardice, just for tonight. She said, "Lord? How will I live now, what will you do with me?"

A lewd boy might have answered her otherwise, with his hands. He was emperor, and not accustomed to being coarse. He did smile, she felt that in her hair; and his hands did move, but only to hold her closer against him. "You will live with me, in these rooms here; and I will use you as my shield against the day, you will be my joy and my regard, my hidden city. What more would you have me do?"

"Lord, one thing. Send to my home village, see how they are after the tsunami. Help them if you can. And—"

"And ask for a list of names, who lives, who died?"

"Yes, lord. Please." *Grandfather . . . !*

"Of course. I should do that all around the coast, all across the island. A census would be useful: what boats are where, who mans them. What stores of food your people have, where soldiers can be billeted . . ."

"And where they can be used, lord, where they can help rebuild the people's homes."

"Yes, of course. That too. We have men enough, clerks as well as soldiers; we can ask these questions in every village on Taishu. And map the island at the same time, better than we have. The generals should be doing this already. You see? I said that we would use you, and we will. There will be another council meeting in the morning. I want you there."

"Yes, lord," sinkingly, determined. She knew nothing, but she would learn. If she wanted influence, then having been his first would never be enough.

She couldn't ask his mother what she needed to learn in the bedroom; but she could ask his servants, and that would get back to his mother. That would satisfy the old woman, she thought. It was proper, that his girl should want to please him.

What she needed to learn in the council chamber, she would have to discover by herself. And hope the old woman didn't notice, until it was too late to drive her out.

ten

Finally, Yu Shan was allowed to help. The great weight of jade had been freed from the mother-rock, but easing it out through the narrow, winding ways of an old mine needed ropes and patience, hard work in cramped conditions.

The way the stone lay now, there was barely squirm-room enough for one body to get by. One slender and flexible body, not yet limited by scar tissue and stiffened joints, all the damage a long miner's life could do even to their hard-used, hard-wearing flesh and bone.

Here was Yu Shan, then, stripped and oiled; and here was the jade, already wrapped and roped. That was common practice. They called it veiling the green, and did it for protection. Smaller pieces too were bagged as soon as cut. Even the chippings, even the shards and dust were sewn into pouches before they saw the light, while a wise miner spent no more time underground than he had to, and kept a scrupulous distance from jade when he could. It was the emperor's stone, not his to touch and treasure.

Uncle Yeng was less strict than Yu Shan's father; he did understand that a boy needed at least a glance, at least a secret stroke of a wonder-stone. But then, Uncle Yeng still thought that his nephew was a good boy, a careful boy, his father's son . . .

No matter. Yu Shan was careful enough, when anyone was looking. With his father at his shoulder and his uncle behind, he was very careful indeed.

He crouched low and reached into his own shadow, where it

stretched across the veiled stone. His arm first, and then his head: there was room, just, between the stone and the mother-rock.

It was a matter of faith, that where the head can go the body can follow. Eventually.

Rough sacking against his chest, hard-edged rock biting at his back—but it was his chest that was more deeply bitten, by the shrouded stone.

Jade miners have their reasons to be careful.

Clad as it was, he felt it sing to him, that wonder-stone; he felt its call deep in his bones, like an ache and a summoning bell.

He kicked and wriggled into darkness, his father's hard hands on his buttocks to impel him. Rock scraped the skin from his back, but that was commonplace; he expected to bleed belowground, and to heal swiftly after. He expected the world to sting.

The squeeze beyond the stone was wretched, all angles, a crude-hewn hollow barely big enough for a man to crouch in while he worked. Yu Shan fitted himself in as best he could, and waited for his father's order.

At last it came, in a hiss because one does not shout in the presence of jade; it would be like shouting in the presence of the emperor. Yu Shan laid his hands against the near edges of the stone, began to apply a steady pressure.

Gently, gently, one coaxes stone from darkness. Impossible to lift and carry through these awkward channels, where a man may be crawling at one time and then slithering on his belly and then sidling through a vertical crack. A large stone must be dragged, slid, rolled, inveigled on its way. Never coerced. Flesh can be crushed and stretched and scraped, but stone is immutable.

Lay hands on jade—even through sacking, through layers of sacking—and there is never any hurry but there is a surging urgency, a riptide in the blood, a brightening. Yu Shan had known it all his life. This stone made his skin shiver and his bones yearn; he wanted to rear up and break the hill apart above his head, to raise the stone to the sky and roar its wonder.

Instead he twitched it a finger's width this way, a finger's width that way, as his father directed. It shifted forward fractionally, a fraction more; it gave him a fraction more room to work in, and he could do a fraction more to help it move.

Something was grinding beneath the slab. It should have been nothing more than spoil, a stray splinter of the mother-rock. Yu Shan gave it no thought until the stone had slid its own length along the uneven floor; then he felt for that spoil in the dark, only to avoid putting his bare knee down on something hard and sharp and unexpected.

His fingers found it, and yes, it was hard and sharp and unexpected; and no, it was not spoil.

He knew it as soon as he touched it: a shard of jade, knocked accidentally from the wonder-stone or else a last glimmer, a ghost of the original seam, lurking in the mother-rock and not noticed as it was cut away to give access to its magnificent cousin.

Near-naked as he was, Yu Shan had no pouch, no pocket to hold the fragment, so he slipped it into his mouth.

THERE SHOULD have been cramps and pains as they worked the great stone up from the mine's depths, taking far better care of their burden than they did or could of themselves.

Yu Shan didn't notice. He did what was needed, when it was called for; his only effort was not to do more, not to float himself and the stone through worlds of wonder, through rock and earth and all on their way to the light. He felt as if he could do that; he felt it more and more as the hours passed, as the stone's song encompassed all his body, skin and bones and blood, while the sliver in his mouth set first his tongue and teeth atingle, then his throat and belly and all his softer inner workings.

At last, the grunts and mutters and sharp instructions ebbed into sighs of relief, contentment, a minute of rest. Then the stone was pulled away from him, lifted out of his sight. He scrambled after, into the open mouth of the mine. He thought he might be glowing green, but his father and Uncle Yeng were interested only in the stone as they carried it up into the air, into the family compound.

It was twilight, and again he thought he was brighter, he thought it must be visible to all. His family clustered around the stone, though, leaving Yu Shan entirely alone, so that he could slip that illicit sliver of jade from his mouth and knot it quickly into a loincloth. He ought to take it directly to the chippings-bag; he ought to confess it to his father.

He did neither, but only kept it close, while he washed off the dirt and blood and sweat of the last hours.

WAS IT fear of discovery that kept him away from the family circle, the fire-council that burned all night? Or was it hope of discovery, the sweet tang of confession that drew him into the forest, to the streams and pools where he and his clan-cousin were prone to meet? Certainly he still had the shard close against his skin, where she was sure to find it, if only he found her.

He didn't, though, despite his lingering by the waters till the rain came. He turned then and made for home, less tired than he deserved to be; and found when he reached the compound that a momentous decision had been made in his absence.

They would not take the wonder-stone down to the wagon-road, to trade it weight-as-value for their common needs. Instead they would breach all law, bypass the jademasters and take the stone directly to the emperor.

"It is his," Yu Shan's father said; "he may as well receive it from us. Maybe he will pay us a true value for the stone. Maybe he will look to us for the future, and not to the jademasters at all. Maybe he will call us his jademasters now. Maybe not. It is his, and it should go to him; that's all."

All except the one thing, how to take it there. The jademasters' guards watched the road; the clans had their own ways through the mountains, but those too were watched, clan by clan.

Except at clanmoot, when travel from valley to valley was free and disregarded.

"We will be going the wrong way," his father said, "against the flow; still, we should be let pass. That is the law. We will go in numbers, in case of trouble. As far as the plains, we will all go. Then one of us must carry the stone alone. We can't spare more; we have to find a new vein and make our claim to it."

One of us he said, but his eyes said *you*.

eleven

Han was chained now, and as afraid as ever; and he was bewildered also, dizzy with something that he couldn't understand.

One of his iron cuffs said SLEEP, but if that was meant to be magic it didn't cast its spell on him. He had been awake so long, he knew how far the stars had turned across the bitter sky. Exactly how far. More than that, he sensed the power and motives of their moving; he remembered that each of them had a name and a significance.

He didn't know their names just now, but he was afraid he might remember them soon. If anything was sleeping in him, that was it: a knowledge that was not his, an alien reach.

Suo Lung had chained him, and suddenly he felt unlimited.

No, not that. He was still a boy, down one thumb and slave to a pirate's slave. It was only in his head that something had opened, or stirred, or broken. Perhaps he had gone mad. He had teetered on the rim of horror for days now; if he ran mad, he thought no one could blame him.

If he ran mad, Suo Lung would restrain him. Chain him, he supposed. If Li Ton didn't kill him first.

Better not to run, then. Even mad, he understood that.

Too much else he understood, for a scribe's boy who had barely mastered his characters. He had never seen the sea, until these last days; and yet there was so much that he sensed now in the tide's suck and the salt whisper, the stir of current, the grim endurance of rock against the simple weight of water. And the sky that was like an inversion of the sea, one bowl turned upon another with mortal men squeezed into a narrow plane between them; he knew—how could he know?—that there were things to understand about the toss of wind where it hurls upward from a cliff face, the fling of a storm and the ease above it, the rain that was coming though it was not here yet . . .

He felt like a lone watchman, a guard with a great army slumbering at his back, waiting his call to waken; it promised a deluge that would defend him and destroy him, sweep him away utterly, never to be found again. Or else he felt as though he stood before a palace gate, and that gate was shut, but it only needed his willful knock to open it; and then—well, then there would be a palace, but it would not be his, he would be swallowed up inside it, just one more neglected servant.

Or else he was going mad, lying here awake in darkness staring at the stars.

Feeling the chafe of iron on his wrists, the weight of chains on his mind, the bafflement of magic. To Suo Lung, at least, there was something magic here: Suo Lung who had worn chains himself and screamed when they were struck off, fought to keep them; who was trying to recreate them now, struggling to remember words he barely knew, so that Han could write them for him with hands that barely worked, so that he could copy them onto Han's chains.

If there was madness here, perhaps it was not Han's.

And yet he felt another world at his back, another kind of mind; sometimes, he thought he saw through other eyes than his.

Madness or magic, there was a stranger in his head, wise and terrible, asleep. If it woke, it would be worse. If he named it, her—

No. He did not, he could not understand.

He didn't dare.

THREE

The Jaws of the Dragon

one

*T*unghai Wang stood on a height with the empire behind him, every standard mile of it written on his bootsoles.

Well, his own soles and his horse's shoes. And the horse had been reshod at need, and there had been, what, three other horses ridden to death between the Hidden City and here; and he had changed his boots too, more than once; but still, every mile of that journey had passed beneath his feet one way or another.

He might have made the journey in a single night, with a dragon to ride. In his mind, though, in his own tale he was the dragon: he soared, he stretched, he encompassed and possessed the empire.

He had earned it. His own feet had claimed it. He had mustered and led the army that followed him; he had kept its various commanders from one another's throats and his own; he had harried the boy-emperor's rearguard every day, every mile of the march, never letting him stop, summon breath and strength, look anything like an emperor. Every city on the road had closed its gates against him. That was Tunghai's triumph.

Even so, his quarry had reached the coast a few short days before him, just time enough. The emperor was on Taishu. That was Tunghai's failure.

And, of course, the emperor had taken every boat his men could find, and every man those boats could hold. Tunghai could see them from here: specks on the water tacking to and fro, taking more men, more treasures, more supplies to the island. Taishu was a smudge on the horizon, out of his reach for now; and no man had the empire who did not hold Taishu.

That did not mean that he who held Taishu still had the empire. Jade was essential; the Jade Throne was essential, and the boy had that; but that was all. Tunghai had the land.

And half the emperor's army, maybe more than half was still in Santung, watching the hills and waiting for a boat.

Tunghai wanted those men, even more than he wanted boats. He could build boats. Stranded on Taishu, the emperor could not build another army.

Santung lay in the rivermouth below. He could see the city clearly; he could see how it teemed with men, how the docks and the piers and the beaches too were crowded.

How the city had no walls: a trading port dependent on the empire's good order, banking on wealth and patronage and law.

A dragon has two jaws. He turned to the men who stood behind him and said, "Two wings, to close on the city from this height and the other." He had forces already on the opposite bank of the river; they could speak across the valley by means of giant flags where horn-song could not carry. "Kill as many as you capture; kill them all. No man escapes."

"And the civilians?"

"I have said. No man escapes." They had given shelter to his enemy; they had gifted escape to the emperor, where they might have trapped him. There would be a price.

The women—well. He had an army at his back, hungry and filthy, exhausted, frustrated. Santung was theirs, a prize, respite. So were its women.

"General Dochan, General Ma—take your men east and west. You will find splinters of the emperor's army, looking for boats," yet more boats; they could never have enough. "Do with them as you will, but leave their bodies exposed. Let the peasants be. We will need their harvests and their labor. I want you to outreach the emperor; however far his men have spilled, go farther. There are other cities on this coast, other fleets. Take them, by whatever means you need to. Bring those boats to me. Large or small, cargo junks or sampans, anything that can survive the strait. And crews, those too, whoever knows these waters."

"We'll need to build more than we can seize." That was General Ma, who was no strategist but a natural gleaner.

"Yes. Boatbuilders too. Bring them." Every beach, every inlet would be a boatyard; he would strip the cities of their iron, the land of its trees. He would do anything, everything he had to. His eyes went back to the island, and to the strait that lay between.

He could besiege cities and defeat armies, any man's armies, if he could only bring his own to land. It was the sea, though, that he must master first.

"Fetch me a fleet," he said. "Find it, build it, buy it." That mattered more than Santung. The city would fall, his men would sack it; there would be blood, as much as any man could want. More. There would be rape and looting and more blood, sobbing women and dead children and prisoners digging the pits for their own bodies; and through it all he would keep his eyes and mind on the island, because that was all that mattered. Santung was nothing, only a place to be, a winter camp out of season. There was no jade in Santung.

two

After seeing, hearing, smelling so many men in their deaths, she was almost ready when it came to be her own man who died.

Almost.

She and her children too, her daughters, almost ready.

IT WAS a good day, not to have sons.

IT HAD been a bad day from the beginning. In the early morning, that first light before the sun, Ma Lin was roused by her husband, Tojo. He was dressed already, smelling of smoke.

"What is it, why . . . ?"

"It's started," he said.

Actually she thought it had started days ago, when the first weary soldiers made their way down the valley road. The city had been filling with them since, an endless trail: men in squads, men with donkeys and ox-wagons and women, children too. Throng-ing the streets and sleeping in doorways, camping in the parks and gardens, occupying all the space there was. It was like another city overlaid across Santung. It was another city, more or less: the Hid-den City, chased down out of the north. They said the emperor himself had been among the men, with all his great lords and all his treasures too. He had hurried down to the docks and taken ship. And now every ship, every boat ferried men across the strait in his wake. Women and children had to wait; it was the emperor's army that he wanted.

There was another army coming. Those same rebels who drove

the emperor out of the Hidden City had chased him all the way down here, and they had no reason to stop outside Santung. A determined army ranked against them might have been a reason; but the emperor's army was sailing away, one boatload following another however much the citizens pleaded, whatever the governor demanded.

Yesterday, she'd heard, the governor had gone himself, with all his household: not the first of Santung to flee, but perhaps the last. Soldiers—new soldiers, the vanguard of the rebel army—had been seen on the headlands either side of the city. Now more than ever, boats were reserved for the emperor's men; the people had no way to leave.

Nor any way to keep the rebels out, no walls and gates to make a siege of it. The soldiers could come down from the hills or along the river, into the city when they chose to.

Which was now, apparently. Ma Lin stood on the roof in the cool half-light and heard distant sounds of catastrophe: shouts, screams, the helpless clash of metal. It was the river-wind that brought those, flowing down the valley, heavy with that same smoke that had breathed on Tojo.

"Where are they?"

Tojo shrugged, which meant they were everywhere, east and west and north. South lay the sea. The docks and the beaches and the sea, which should have meant escape but not today. She might have cursed the emperor, except that her every breath was rank with smoky warning and she didn't have the time to waste.

He said, "What shall we do?"

She said, "I will wake and dress the children. You pack food," what food there was, little enough after a week of an army's depredations. Every day she had scoured the city, just one among thousands on the same hopeless errand; the markets were barren, deserted. Every day she had cooked rice from the family jar and kept it, using yesterday's to make congee for the children. That way there would always be a day's food ready for the taking, when the time came to leave. If there was anywhere to go to, or any way to get there.

The time was now, utterly now; there were sounds of running in the lanes all around them, sounds of metal hacking at wood or softer stuff. Yelling, screams.

East and west and north, the rebels had been seen; from east and west and north they came. One brigade was marching along the river. The rest poured over the valley ridges, through the ranks of terraced plots and into the huddled mass of housing.

They were in the lanes all around, but not in this lane yet. The courtyard was frantic suddenly, a dozen families erupting from their rooms. Grizzling babies and stumbling children; half the adults no better, stupid from sleep and terror together. Ma Lin watched for a moment, to see if any one of them would take charge. She almost wanted to push her way into the mass and be that one.

She had her own children, though, her own man to protect. Smaller groups were best. She didn't suppose that anyone could save fifty, but she could perhaps save five.

She went to wake her babies, and found that her eldest daughter Jin had done it for her. Two little girls and a big one—husband-high, Jin was, if that could mean anything anymore—dressed and ready to follow where she led.

Tojo would do the same. It had always been understood between them, that he might be the man but the family was hers. If there had been a son, his father might have wanted charge of him, but a run of daughters justified her. What could he say, to so many girls?

He did well, in fact, he always had: a good provider who lived on easy terms with his womenfolk and let all four of them order him about except when it mattered, when he would listen only to one.

He listened now, they all did, solemn and afraid; then—leaving the rice, no time to fetch it now, no time to pack anything, no *time*—they filed out into the courtyard and squeezed through to the gate, herself leading and Tojo in the rear, everyone holding to the trousers of the one in front, tug-tug-tug as they walked.

The gate itself had been cracked open by two brothers who

shared a room across the yard. They were peering anxiously through the crack, not moving.

"What can you see?" Ma Lin demanded in a whisper.

"Nothing . . ."

"And what, do you plan to wait until you can see soldiers?"

"It's dark, Ma Lin . . . !"

Of course it was dark: high walls and narrow alleys, this predawn light couldn't reach down into them. "If you can't see them, they can't see you either. If they're there. Move now, fools, while you are still blessed with your nothing!"

When they still didn't move, she pushed them aside and opened the gate herself, forged forward into the lane without even looking.

She felt her family at her back, tug-tug-tug. Tojo would watch behind them; he was a cautious man.

The swift and easy way out of the city was uphill; but once outside the walls of their house, in this network of lanes and alleys that trapped and echoed sound, it was all the more clear what they'd meet that way, what was coming down. The damp beneath her feet was surely dew, but the screams of men so quickly cut off lent it a stickiness it didn't own, gave her visions of blood in streams like blind snakes nosing their way underfoot, down to the cobbles and gutters of the lower town.

The women's screams, the children's, those were not cut off so quickly. They were a chorus, a setting, the definition of the day.

Ma Lin led her family on and down. Into a trap, of course, she knew that. There could be no escape from the heart of the city, with soldiers closing in from all sides bar the sea. Up and out was the only way to freedom, but that was impossible; and to stay still was to court death, to wait for it, to count its coming house by house.

What she hoped—what she would pray for, if only they had time to stop at a corner temple, light a joss, linger for a word with the priest and another with the god—was that even men in a killing frenzy would tire before they had slaughtered all the city. Like all men they would start in earnest, thoroughly committed.

By now perhaps they would be weary of the stink of it, weary of the work. By the time they came near the river and met their brother killers who had followed the stream, saw how sodden with death those men were and so saw themselves reflected—perhaps by then they would walk past doorways, not search darkened go-downs, just not care.

Perhaps. It was a high hope to pin a future on; it was all they had. She led her family on and down.

SHE WAS hardly the first who had thought to flee. Where roads were wider, some must have thought to take their household with them. Perhaps she should not have been startled to tread on something soft, which was spilled fruit; then to stumble into something hard and obstructive, which was the tumbled cart that had spilled it; then to trip over something yielding but solid, which was the body of the carter.

She had lost her obedient tail of family; she could hear them—her teenage daughter and her husband, at least, while the little girls mewed at them—scrabbling for fruits in the shadows.

She had come down on all fours across the carter, and was learning how warm and wet a body is on the inside. How much blood it can spill, to gather in rank pools between the cobbles. Her mouth and nose were full of it, blood and the fouler odors of his dying, slashed as he was from throat to belly.

She had nothing but her clothes to wipe her hands on. Her trousers were filthy already so she used those, before remembering where her smallest daughter's hand should grip. She needed that clutch back, she needed to feel them all in line behind, tug-tug-tug.

She whispered back over her shoulder: "Leave that! How will you hold on to the little ones, when your hands are full of fruit?"

"We need food, Ma Lin." That was her husband, who should have known better.

"We need to keep together," she said. "And how much fruit can you eat, before your insides sour?"

"Better sour than empty," her daughter said. When did that girl grow so big, to argue with her mother?

There were the little girls to be corralled—too close to the stink of the body and starting to smell it even through the sweet crush of fruit, starting to ask piping little questions—and there were both ends of the street to watch, where any movement might mean anything, neighbors running or imperial soldiers coming up or rebel soldiers coming down.

If she didn't hate the carter for dying just here and just like this, she might yet hate the emperor's army for making no attempt at a stand, no effort to protect the city. For huddling on the beaches and quays, seizing every boat there was, stealing anyone else's chance of escape. Was that the proper duty of a soldier, to save his own life and let the weaker die?

Perhaps it was. Perhaps that was a lesson for the day.

But at last Tojo and Jin were satisfied with their haul, and Ma Lin could at least feel the tug-tug of the little girls on her trousers as they made their slow way forward.

HERE WAS a junction, where this street met another running up and down the hill. Red Stream Road they called it, for the color of the dirt that stained the run-off in typhoon season. After today they might have another reason. The stones really were sticky beneath her feet, and the air was dense with what had happened here. It was like walking into a wall of blood. And besides, there were the bodies heaped across the way like a wall, like a dam to block Red Stream Road entirely.

They were, she thought—she hoped!—the bodies of rebels, maybe all the rebels who had reached this far. The men who had slain the carter, perhaps. They'd been laid across the uphill arm of the junction, so that any more coming down would have to clamber over their own dead comrades. Opposite that, across the eastern arm was a proper barricade: tipped wagons with furniture heaped above and behind them, anything heavy and obstructive.

Behind that barricade—above and behind it, so they must be standing on something, more furniture, more barricade—were men with spears and no, she did not hate the emperor's army after all, not all of it, not these.

They weren't city men, the governor's guards, the hirelings who watched go-downs at the docks. These were lean, hard, with the dust of a thousand roads in their eyes, the dirt of those roads under their scarred skins. The men who had been occupying the city all week: not kindly men, not well disposed but focused, eyes across the water. Wanting nothing from Santung but boats and food, wanting to be gone. The men she had gone hungry for, almost willingly, if that was the price to see them go.

Their spears angled down at her; she was in the shadows here, while they were in the light. Even so, they could surely see that two of her party were tiny, only one a man.

She called up out of the gloom: "Soldiers of the emperor! Let us in, take us under your shadow." Not making a question of it, not gifting them the chance to refuse.

Her eldest daughter added her own voice, unexpectedly: "We have ripe fruits here, if your mouths are dry."

There was a mutter of voices, and then there was a basket on a rope that they tipped their fruits into: not enough to fill it even halfway, but enough. Because then there was a ladder of sorts, a bamboo pole with crosspieces lashed to it, that the little ones couldn't climb but they could at least cling monkey-like to her back and to Tojo's.

Her eldest daughter could manage, it seemed, a lot more than a tricky climb in the half-dark, up a rickety ladder. There were spear shafts to grip and then rough hands that gripped them one by one, to help them over the barricade. Ma Lin endured the hands but the girl did more, played up to them with a wriggle and a soft laugh. Ma Lin would have scolded her in public, slapped her in private, but the old rules were dead and left behind. The old city, she thought, was dying. Something new would rise, perhaps, with soldiers living in it. Soldiers always wanted women. Her daughter would not be one of those, she was determined; but in this hesitation between the old city and the new—well, if her daughter could manage soldiers of either side, that was a skill to be valued, yes, and no matter where she had learned it.

Here and now, it won back a gathered shirtful of those fruits; and the girl was right, of course, they were something to be grateful for.

And the soldier who heaped fruits into that shirt as she held it up, he might be leering at what he could see or what he could imagine, but he was also fumbling in his own bag to add a handful of dried fish, a pot of preserved greens, a length of cane for chewing. It was as much food as Ma Lin had seen in a day, for all of them together.

Her smallest daughter, breathlessly brave, "Mama? Are we safe now?"

And where Tojo would have said *Yes, precious, now we're safe, see the strong men to protect us?*, Ma Lin could give the little girl nothing but a perilous laugh. If there were barricades, it was because the emperor's army had nowhere left to run; soldiers fight when they have to, when there's nothing else to do. Nobody could be safe this side of the barricade—and here came a captain storming up the road to berate his troops for taking them, perhaps to send them back.

Her daughter—her big daughter, whom she was suddenly in this bewildering light discovering to be a woman—looked up at him and asked, "Please, where can we go that's out of your way?"

And—perhaps because she was not her exhausted defeated father, nor her ferociously determined mother, only young and fresh and hopeful—he said, "Come with me."

And, to one of his men, "Bring that ladder." And to Ma Lin, though he said it loud enough for all his men to hear, "I'll have no more soft bodies coming over, thanks to the soft hearts of these fools."

He led them just a little way down Red Stream Road, and through a broken gateway into a courtyard house. All the doors on this lower level were gone, there was a mess of torn fabric and splintered furniture in the center of the yard, but still it was a house much like their own, a sense of home in the dawnlight. Up to the gallery, where their own rooms had always been, and along to the far corner: to a broad square room that had kept its door, and had one small shuttered window that opened to the outer world.

To his man, he said, "Leave the ladder here," which meant *Go back*. To Ma Lin, "There's a temple down the street, dedicated to Tua Peh Kong." Ma Lin nodded; she knew it well, and never crossed its threshold. What had the god of wealth and authority to do with her or hers? "I have sent all the civilians there, together with my wounded. You could go there if you preferred it. There are priests and prayers and suchlike. We have made offerings." *For what little good they will do,* his voice implied. "But—well, I had meant to post a man here, only there seems little point. The enemy will be at our barricades soon enough, and I wouldn't trust any lookout stationed here, not to go out of that window as soon as he dared. Look—"

The window opened above that same street they'd come along. Almost directly below them was the angular shadow of the up-tilted cart, the slumped body of its owner. No man could jump this high, but it was only a ladder's reach down.

Beyond the cart was a mass of moving shadow: a huddle of newcomers—her former neighbors, some of them—on hands and knees, groping for spilled fruits. She thought they were fools, twice fools. Were they even keeping watch, did they realize how close the rebels had to be?

"When they come," the captain said, drawing the shutter closed again, ignoring those lost souls below, "they'll balk at our barricade and look for another way. Not this, it's too narrow and too high. They'll find all the lanes blocked, all the alleys. Then they'll be back. They have to break through somewhere, and here is most open to attack. They will break through, and then they will stream down the hill and kill us all; the temple will be no protection. But a few nimble folk could slip out of this window and away uphill after the flood, if they were lucky. You understand me?"

Oh yes, she understood him. He meant theirs would be five lives he was not responsible for; he would gift them a way out, and leave them to the gods.

More immediately, he meant they had to sit and listen while a howling mob of men ripped through the barricade, with death on every side; while they poured like brute red water down the road, howling for more blood. She and hers had to hold still, hold quiet, hold to hope. Hope that the men would glance into the courtyard and move on smartly, leave it in hopes of better slaughter farther down; hope that no one man came in to search here until all the men had already swarmed the barricade, so that none was left to see them scramble down.

This face of the house was in shadow. She could sit and watch the junction, and be confident that no one down there would see her. Tojo and Jin would keep the little ones quiet. The girls had barely made a sound so far, but that was not to be depended on.

Neither was her own courage. With urgency ebbing away, terror could build. She'd kept ahead of it so far; now she had to sit as still as her children and look back the way they'd come, wait for what they'd fled to catch them up.

It was a strange invasion that drove them from their home by its noise, that scattered its victims in their path, and yet she'd not yet seen a single rebel. Except those dead where they lay piled across the way, a taunt as much as a bulwark. Perhaps there were imperial troops in that same rampart, but she didn't think so; she thought the captain would treat his own dead with respect, if only to keep his living troops loyal.

Abruptly, men spilled into the street from some alley-mouth out of her view: men who had perhaps been balked by the rampart of bodies, because they were screaming, raging, with bare stained blades in their hands. Because the sight of people in the street here had brought them running, screaming, raging.

They were men of the same cast as the imperial soldiers: lean, exhausted, filthy. The flip side of the same defeat, and she didn't think that even they would call it victory.

Right now she, they, could only call it slaughter.

It was grimly shady down there, and hard to see through the cracked-open shutter. Even so, she saw enough. She saw the old man with bad teeth who had been a porter on the fish quays, tough as a root; she saw him hacked at, saw his arm hacked off when he tried to shield his head with it. Saw his head hacked open, saw what spilled out, saw him dead.

She saw another man, the young man who had been watching her eldest daughter recently in the courtyard; she saw him on his knees and begging.

She saw the man he pleaded with; saw the weapon that he carried, a heavy blade on a long handle. Saw that blade fall, saw it split the young man's spine. Saw him twist and writhe like a fish on a gaff, saw him die too slowly, in too much pain.

Heard him too, even above the noise of so much else. He screamed like the pain of it would tear his body open if he didn't; but he was torn already, his back gaping like a monstrous mouth, and he did die of it.

She was glad her daughter had not seen. Wished she was not watching this herself, but that was a wasted wish in a world too short of hope. She saw every man die below her, and the older women too. The younger women not, or not yet. They were pulled away by the arm or the hair, or else roughly stripped right there and dragged to a doorway or a corner, not far at all, not far enough. She thought the city's width would not be far enough.

She had to stay, if only to keep the others from the window. Tojo should not see this, any more than the children should; he would be afraid for her, too shocked to move. And they must move soon, if their chance came.

They couldn't avoid the bodies, but they could hide up, perhaps, till nightfall: see less, be less seen. Then creep through the lanes to the city's edge and out into the terraces, over the ridge and away. Where to, she couldn't imagine. There must be somewhere beyond this madness, where men didn't die for simply being men, where women could scratch for food and not be raped first and killed after, as those women down there were dying now . . .

IT HAS been said that time is a kindness of the gods, a gift to those who could not endure immortality. It may be true. There was timelessness in that shadowed room, no time at all; even the sun ceased to track its own progress in lines of shadow on the floor while they waited for the screams to end, the fight to start. Between the two there was an endlessness, all hush, like a glass string that must shatter when it's plucked.

The rebels gathered, man by man, in the street below: quiet now, knowing there was work ahead. One glanced up at Ma Lin's window. She sat icy-still, not daring even to draw back. Shadow should hide her, and the window was too high, out of reach. Too narrow also, too easily guarded: too obviously a trap. He turned away, she breathed again. They waited.

At last there was movement behind the dam of bodies, more rebels coming down from the ridge. What these had been waiting for.

Voices hurled across the junction as they dragged the bodies aside. Another day, an earlier day, Ma Lin would have covered her little girls' ears sooner than let them hear such things. Today she was numb to it, heedless. They had heard worse already, from the street below the window.

If Ma Lin had thought about war before, about men fighting battles over ground, it had never been like this, so close they could spit on each other. They were spitting. And cursing, promising terrible deaths to come. Just, not yet: as the captain had foreseen, there was yet more waiting, while rebels ran right and left to test for weakness in the barricade.

They ran, they came back. Santung might have no walls, but there were so many soldiers here, simple numbers must have fortified the streets. Men in every alley and on every roof, armed and vicious, knowing that nothing stood behind them but the sea.

The rebels would die and die, Ma Lin thought, trying to swarm the barricade. But there were so many of them, too; eventually the barricade must fail, and death's face turn the other way. Every man behind it would die, she thought, and every woman want to.

SHE HEARD the charge before she saw it, the rush of men like a single mass down Red Stream Road. They ran with long poles thrusting out before them, meant to break the barricade apart;

they ran howling, meant to break the will of those who faced
them.

The barricade was sturdier than it looked. It was their poles
that broke, and perhaps a few bones with them. But the men came
on, because they could not stop; and broke in their turn, not so
much like a wave of water but like wet bodies against a wall of
spikes, yes, very much like that. Ma Lin could see spears work
from above like darting needles, death writ like stitches in the air.
Those not pierced were crushed by the weight of their own friends
behind; or else they scrambled up over the bodies of their friends
ahead to meet brute steel in the hands of desperate men, and die.

But there were more and more of them, always more; and the
wall of their own dead before the barricade made a softer, kinder
rampart, easier to breach. They were beaten back but just came on
again, and yet again. At last they were too many, too stubborn, too
strong. They must have overwhelmed the defenses; Ma Lin saw
them pour across the junction and over their fallen, not pausing to
drag the dead away.

She heard screams and the clash of weapons, many weapons,
far too close. Spilling from Red Stream Road, pouring into the
courtyard of this house, even, she could hear the grunt and effort
of men's bodies just below . . .

She watched the street and saw it empty like a draining pool as
all those rebels pushed forward for their own chance to fight, to
kill, to wreak a savage recompense for this long and deadly balk.
She waited, and waited; as soon as she dared, she pushed the shutter wide and turned back into the room, "Quickly now, the
ladder—"

—AND THAT was the moment that the door banged open and a
man tumbled in.

For a moment she wasn't even sure if he was an imperial soldier
come to defend them or a rebel come to slaughter them all. But the
first thing he did was slam the door behind him; then he surged
across the room while they were still staring. He pushed Ma Lin
aside, and thrust his own head out to check the street.

By then, she'd decided that she knew him. She thought he was the man who had carried the ladder up at his captain's order. Indeed he was looking for it now, beckoning to Tojo, *Bring it, bring it!*

What could she do but nod, when Tojo looked to her? If one of the captain's men chose to desert sooner than die, it was a choice filled with good sense to her mind. Besides, the man was armed. Who knew how useful that would be, below . . . ?

Tojo carried the ladder to the window, and the two men eased it out.

"Now listen, little ones. Never mind the noises in the courtyard, those bad men aren't coming up here till we're gone. That's why we need to go now. Meuti, I want you to ride on Jin's back," and she hoisted the smallest girl and handed her to the eldest, "while Shola rides on mine. Hold really tight. We'll soon be down on the ground and you can run again. Quietly! You've been very good so far, both of you, but you must keep quiet still. Understand me?"

Two little nods, from nervous faces. She kissed them both, made sure Meuti was settled, lifted Shola as soon as she saw Tojo out of the window and the soldier following.

She made an awkward exit, kneeling on the sill and reaching a leg down blindly, with the weight of the tot on her back to unbalance her. The ladder had felt none too stable when she climbed up at the barricade; as she climbed down now, every rung seemed to shift beneath her feet. She clung to the main pole as tightly as Shola clung to her, like a monkey on a stick. At last she felt Tojo's hands on her waist, his voice in her ear, guiding her the last two cautious steps to solid ground.

She stepped back, shifted Shola onto her hip and watched the last two girls. Now she could really see how unstable that ladder was, but Jin managed it until she was within a man's reach. Then, before Tojo could, the soldier stepped forward and lifted her down.

And held the girl longer than he needed to, until Meuti twisted around to stare up at him, uncomfortably caught between Jin's body and his. The little girl's piping voice asked to be set down, please; and he did that, and then Jin was gripping her hand and the two of them came scurrying to Ma Lin.

"Quickly now, quickly . . . !"

She meant to head for their own house if it was possible. Give the children something familiar; hold there all day and slip out when the sun was gone. Hundreds, maybe thousands of others would be doing the same. That was good, she thought. The vulnerable flock together in the presence of predators. There were all manner of ways in which her small family should be safer, if there were many on the move.

She led them swiftly away before another burst of troops could come down Red Stream Road. Behind her, she heard Tojo and Jin ushering the little ones; she heard a *chok-chok!* too and looked back to see the soldier hacking at the ladder with his tao, cutting all those rungs away.

Well, the time was his to waste if he chose to. She saw him cut that long pole in two, and turned away, and heard him running after.

The tao was in his belt again; in each hand was a bamboo staff, a man's height or a little more. He thrust one of those at Tojo. "Here. You can fight with this, at least a little. Fend men off if they come at you."

Tojo blinked, and took the staff in both hands. Weighed it, tested the balance, swung it experimentally back and forth; nodded, and grunted a word of thanks.

Her husband, the fighting man. Another day she might have smiled, she might have made a joke for the girls to share. Today she wanted to believe it wasn't funny; she wanted to believe in him, as she wanted to be grateful to the soldier.

SHE THREADED a way through bodies, through pools of blood, all these dead people who had been their neighbors. Without looking back, she knew the solemn stare of her little girls; she felt it in herself. She too wanted to stare and be bewildered, wanted not to understand. Wanted to be afraid, even, if she could do it in unfathomable innocence.

Lacking that, she was afraid in ways she did not want to be; and was relieved to turn away from the bodies, away from the street, into the broken shadow of an alley.

There was a constant urge to scuttle from dark to dark, to hide in every jutting gateway, to look for shelter behind every door. The doors had all been kicked ajar already; that was no guarantee that they would not be kicked again. She headed onward, directly up the hill.

She was bold and brave, for her children; they couldn't see and need never know how her eyes darted, how she flinched from every bird-cry and every skulking cat. How desperately relieved she was to come to their own lane, their own house unchallenged.

In then, through the gate they'd left so recently, though now it hung broken on its hinges. Into the courtyard, which was a place of ruin: water-jars overturned, clothes and pots torn and broken and strewn all over. Fat Muoti's handcart that he used to haul his noodles around the streets, that was in pieces, the wheels jerked from the axle. Surely a looting soldiery could have found uses for a handcart, tomorrow if not today? Wrecked, it was no use to anyone.

No use to Muoti anymore, in any case. He was one who had died beneath that window, scrabbling for fruit.

Others had died here. Those who had lacked the wit or the courage to leave. They lay strewn among this ruin in a ruin of their own. Their faces were clear in the growing light, so were their deaths, and she hated for her little girls to see this. They were one on each hand now, tugging her toward the courtyard stairs.

"No," she had to say, "not that way." *Not home.* "Come through to the kitchen."

It was communal, of course, for all in the house to use. There might be food that had been her neighbors', that she could give to her family now and it wouldn't even count as stealing.

If not, if all the food had been taken or spilled, there was still the underfloor. A hatchway that was easy to overlook led to a cool space below. It was meant for anyone who had food to spare, which wasn't her or any of her neighbors and never had been, except for a sack of raw rice perhaps or an extra jar of preserved greens. There would be plenty of space down there in the dust; she meant them all to hide there. All except the soldier. She hadn't anticipated his coming this far at their tail; now she hoped to leave him on guard above.

She walked boldly up the three steps to the shattered kitchen door, and boldly in—

—AND THERE were men in there, two men, squatting very quietly with food spilled all around them and their hands on their weapons.

Rebel men, of course.

Hungry men, impulsive men, seizing this chance to eat instead of fight. Blood-spattered men, who must have done their share of slaughter; likely the blades they snatched up now were the same that had worked so grimly in the courtyard.

And were ready for more, men and blades both. She couldn't believe how swiftly they erupted from the floor; she barely had time to stagger back down the steps, no time at all to cry out before they were there.

Her little girls cried anyway, shrieked rather; after a morning of being so utterly good and quiet and terrified, this was one shock too many.

It was almost bizarre to see Tojo push forward, to stand like a warrior before his womenfolk. She felt an obscure pride and still thought it was hopeless, doomed. He had a length of bamboo pole, to face two rebels armed with blades. There was no future in him.

But he stood there, and she couldn't read but she thought the character for "defiance" should look like that, a silhouette of denial, *You shall not pass.* And then he wasn't alone, because the imperial soldier moved up to stand beside him. Perhaps the two of them together were just a little daunting; the rebels did seem to hesitate. Unless trickster time was playing that trick it had, to hold its own breath at vital moments, to make its victims believe that

nothing this bad actually could happen, some god was sure to in-
tervene, some dreamer wake, the world end, something . . .

No hint of gods, or other intervention; the world was what it
was, what she saw, her husband in dread peril and she behind him,
her children behind her.

Then, with a howl, the two rebels came plunging down the
steps.

Perhaps they just weren't very good soldiers. More interested in
food than loot, in loot than killing, in slaughtering innocents than
in real fighting at the barricade. Or all of that might be the absolute badge of the perfect soldier, how was she to know?

All she knew was that Tojo should be hacked to pieces in moments, trying to fend off a man with a tao; and yet, and yet . . .

TOJO USED his pole as he might have on the water, to fend off another man's barge. He rammed it into the one man's ribs, which
stopped that rebel where he stood. Sent him staggering back a
pace, even, half tripping over the step behind him. Which gave
Tojo a moment to be brilliant, to turn away from that man, to
swing his pole and clatter the other rebel on the back of the head.

Which sent that man also staggering, mazed and dropping his
guard, almost dropping his blade; which gave the soldier a chance
to clatter him also and then to drop his pole, to draw his tao and
move in fast. It was such a neat move, it almost looked rehearsed.

Except that of course it left the first rebel unwatched, while
both men were turned against the second; and all he had was
bruised ribs, maybe, and a rage born of humiliation. And a tao.

She might have lost Tojo then, she really thought she would.
She thought they'd see him cut down before their eyes. The girls
screamed; perhaps she did herself.

What he did, her sensible Tojo, he turned to run; but turning
brought him face-to-face with her and with her daughters, so that
he saw just who he'd be leaving in the tao's way if he did that, if he
ran.

And he turned again, horrified, belated, unexpected. He dug

his heel in and spun around it; and the rebel who was plunging after him—who already had his blade raised high for a triumphant vengeful slash at a fleeing foe—was caught instead, caught a second time by a wild flailing pole in the rib cage.

This time the man fell, screaming. And this time Tojo was screaming too, a voice she'd never thought to hear from this man of hers; and the pole rose and fell, rose and fell.

Eventually the rebel stopped twitching and kicking on the ground there, though Tojo went on pounding at his head.

What was left of his head.

Her eldest daughter had the little girls turned away, their faces buried in her trouser-legs. Ma Lin glanced beyond Tojo, to where their stray soldier was hacking the other rebel's head from his shoulders. It seemed to be all about heads, with these men; but at least she was free to step up to her husband, to put her hand on his arm, to still him.

To reach and take his bamboo away, splintered and sodden at one end as it was, one more ruin in this yard of ruin.

To hold that with one hand and his elbow with the other, to push and tug and inveigle him away from that thing he'd done, all across the yard to where he could sit very abruptly, very heavily on the gallery stairs.

The bodies would be best left lying as they were. Any more rebels coming this way, glancing inside, so many dead might prevent their coming in to poke about. The dead said, *This house has been despoiled already; it needs no more ghosts than us.*

Perhaps she should pose one of them on the kitchen steps. Brave was the man who would step past a staring, accusatory body, knowing that its ghost must still be lingering . . .

Perhaps: but later. Not till she had the little ones safely bedded down. She said, "Jin, take the girls up to our room and gather quilts and clothing. Bring them down."

Her eldest daughter nodded and hustled the little girls away, past their father and up the steps, giving them no time at all to gawp at what he had done. Or what the soldier was doing now, going from one rebel body to the other, picking whatever was lootable from their clothes and pouches, fingers, throats.

Tojo had discovered how splashed he was about the feet and legs. He would be no use to her until he had clean clothes, clean skin. His mind she could not wash.

She said, "Any man can prove a fighter, defending what is his. Come, we need you now," and stroked his head, and left him to think it through.

She still had his bamboo in her hand. She might ask the soldier to take the bottom span off with his tao, where Tojo had bloodied and splintered it. Clean, the pole would make a yoke to carry a few goods, an iron pot, their rations.

But the soldier was poking among her neighbors now, and she couldn't bear to speak to him above their molested corpses. She might find a cleaver in the kitchen, and do it herself. And arm herself, that too. It would be good to look . . .

She was heading to do that, completely on the wrong side of the courtyard when the little girls appeared on the steps again, distressed and crying out for her.

She called back to them, "Where is Jin?"

Meuti turned to look back over her shoulder, which was meant for some kind of answer. It was Shola who wept words: "We found Meimei, and she's hurt, and Jin said we should come for you . . ."

"Stay with your father," she said, but the soldier was ahead of her, running up past the girls, his tao unsheathed in his hand.

"No! You hold to your girls, I will see to this."

The girls clung to her legs, his little allies; she wasn't sure if this meant *Hold us!* or *Don't go up there!*

Either way, it stopped her. All she could do was follow the soldier with her eyes, up onto the gallery and along, in at the open door . . .

No. That wasn't all she could do. She could follow him with her mind, with her mind's eye; she could be ahead of him already, knowing what he'd find in that so-familiar room. Her own daughter and Meimei, almost one of her own, whom all the family knew by her milk-name: of an age with Jin, growing up in the same courtyard, even sometimes suckled by the same breast. These days she was a playmate, a nurse, a friend as needed to all the children.

Until today, she had been. Now she was one of the women missing from the corpse-count down in the yard here: probably just as dead by now, in the shadows of a room not her own. Ma Lin could see that, before the soldier reached the door. And her own daughter kneeling beside her, the one girl broken in heart where the other was broken in body. And now the soldier, a silhouette, the wrong one come, unwelcome; and no sign of Ma Lin at his back, only the great looming shape of him and perhaps his voice, hot and breathy with that urgent lust Jin had felt before when he touched her, and it didn't matter what he said because he was reaching to touch her again, with Meimei's fate like a reflection in his eyes, like a poison in his blood, like an ambition—

—AND MA LIN heard her daughter scream, and that was a terrible thing, because it only guaranteed everything that she'd been seeing in her head—

—AND SHE was terribly hampered by the children on her legs, who only clung the tighter when they heard their sister scream. Tojo was the one who was free: free to stand, free to turn, free to run up the steps in a loping dread, unarmed and helpless because even his bamboo staff was on the other side of the yard where Ma Lin had dropped it.

And yet he went, running and cursing, his voice rising ahead of him so that the soldier came out to meet him on the gallery, because this was men's business and after all the girl could wait; and he came out with his tao in his hand, of course, and Tojo simply seemed to throw himself onto it, so that the soldier might never have looked so graceful in his kill.

That was all. As swift as that, and she was almost ready for it, but not quite; and her little girls, not looking, they knew none the less and had almost been expecting it. So many men dead, why should their father not be one among them?

Because he was their father, and that was never going to be enough. Not quite.

So Tojo died, horribly and messily, his lights spilled out on the gallery; and Ma Lin wailed his death because she absolutely could not help it, could not stop herself, although it was only one more death in a long doomed day.

And the soldier saluted her with that dark doomladen blade of his, unless he was making her a promise, *You too, you and all your little children, when I'm ready*—and then he went back into the room.

Back in to her daughter.

Who had screamed already and now screamed again, and would go on screaming, Ma Lin thought, until he silenced her.

Perhaps he liked the screaming.

Ma Lin took her little girls, one hand to each, and led them to the kitchen. Very quietly she opened the hatch to the underfloor and ushered them down. Apologized, even, for the lack of quilts to make it softer; apologized that she couldn't stay yet, but she had to go and fetch their big sister away from the nasty man who was making her cry.

Looked around the kitchen and no, of course, no cleavers left, no kind of knife at all. And the soldier had taken everything from the bodies outside, including all their weapons.

Well, she had a pair of long cooking chopsticks. Those would have to do.

She'd gnaw them both to points, but she didn't have the time.

Barefoot and lethal, Ma Lin scampered up the steps to the gallery. Almost deliberately, she trod in her husband's spillings, the bloody grease of his guts, as she hopped over his warm and leaking body.

The soldier must have been so sure that a woman would not do this, would not find a weapon or the courage to use it, or a way to pass her husband's ghost. He had barely bothered to close the door; he was keeping no eye out for her as he lay on her daughter, pumping.

She actually had to make a noise, to make him lift his head.

Then she slammed a chopstick into his eye and through his eye and deep, deep into his skull.

While he was still screeching, scrabbling, she did the same—holding his head still against all his struggles, the one hand ruthless in his hair—with the other chopstick and to his other eye.

As HE died—which was still a noisy, writhing process, far longer than she'd thought—she realized she didn't know his name.

Good. That might help to pin his ghost here, earthbound, cursed. None of those who knew him would know how or where he died; she who had killed him knew nothing of who he was or where he belonged. Those disjuncts ought to doom him, so she thought.

SHE TOOK her sobbing, shuddering daughter by the hand and led her out, across her husband's body and so down to join the other girls, to wait for dark.

three

What can measure the weight, the depth, the intensity of jade?

As well try to measure the sea, or the majesty of empire; as well hope to name the colors of a dragon.

Yu Shan had the weight, the depth, the intensity of jade on his shoulders; he had it in his mouth.

Wrapped and double-wrapped, cocooned in his sleeping-quilt and knotted into a bamboo frame under a cover of greased hide, harnessed to his back with ropes, the wonder-stone was a looming, massive drag; but where a boulder would have dragged him down, this uplifted him. He thought it might raise him from the path completely, leave him trying to swim in air.

Hidden and secret, kissed and untold, sharp as a whispered word, the slipped shard sparked in his mouth as though it flung off crystals of light that pierced and burned and left no damage, only a fierce bite like pepper in his blood.

Half his family had conducted him over the valley-heads, down paths blessed by ancient use and strange god-carven trees, past files of clansfolk headed the other way. In the foothills, out of clan territory at last, they left him. They turned back to clanmoot and then their own valley, to the search for mother-rock, a new mine, more jade. He kept his back to the sun and stepped onward into strangeness and shadow, strangeness and loss.

If he wasn't at the moot, his mother couldn't offer for his clan-cousin. That was a loss, immediate and lasting. By the time of the next moot, who knew? There might be other offers, better made. His family had a worked-out mine and hopes, and nothing more;

hers might look elsewhere. Even now, perhaps: at this moot, in his absence . . .

He hated being absent, where she would be looking for him. He hated that his parents would lie to her and that she would believe them, she would think scouting for a new vein more important to him than she was. He wanted to debate it with her, fiercely, face to face, skin to skin . . .

But jade possessed his skin now in her absence, inside and out. It possessed his thoughts, even more than she did. He walked in its shadow and drew strength from it; nothing could outface him now.

Even this long walk into the unknown could barely brush the surface of his mind with fear; even that fear was thin, childish, nothing to be afraid of.

He had barely left his own valley before this, except to go to clanmoot. He had never left the mountains. Now they were behind him, everything he knew was at his back. Ahead lay foothills, plains, a great township and the sea. Flat lands, strangers, a tale told of water. He should have been terrified, but none of it was reckonable now. Jade on his back, jade on his tongue: he could do anything, go anywhere.

He didn't know the way, but no one did. No one left the valleys. They said it would be easy; it was only far, not hard. *Follow the road,* they said, *don't use it but keep it in the corner of your eye. Stick to forest tracks, so long as there is forest; then make your own way through the paddy. Avoid villages, people. Walk at night, as much as you can. If you lose the road, go north. North and east will bring you to Taishu-port eventually; if the emperor is on Taishu, he will be there.*

The forest was thinner already, the slopes were gentler. Everything he knew was gone, and everything he thought he wanted. This was the world, and he was loose in it. With a fortune on his back—not for him, but possibly good fortune for his family, his clan, all the mountain people—and a splinter in his mouth, illicit, all for him.

The road lay easterly and below, following the turns and twists of a swift river that grew deeper, wider with every mile as it gathered in the run-off from the hills. Yu Shan kept to the height where he could. Where there was no path, he cut his way through virgin undergrowth. He and his blade both were used to that, except that today he had to sweep a little wider either side to keep the stone from snagging; its bamboo frame stood higher than his head, broader than his shoulders. No matter. His arm was relentless, as his legs were, knowing just how hard they worked and yet still working, inexhaustible.

WHERE HE found a path or the ridge briefly rose above the tree line, he could walk freely. Where a gully broke the ridge, he had to plunge down and scramble up and wade a fierce freshet at the bottom. Otherwise he stepped and cut, stepped and cut in a steady, familiar rhythm.

Stepped and cut, stepped and cut, while his mind went elsewhere entirely, sinking into jade, feeling jade sink into him.

Stepped and cut, stepped and cut—

—AND WAS brought back to himself, brought up short by the kiss of a blade against his neck.

"Well, look," a voice murmured, close to his ear. "It's a pretty boy, a mountain boy. What shall we do with the pretty mountain boy?"

"See what he's carrying." Another voice, farther off, not interested in playing games.

"Let's ask him. What are you carrying, pretty boy?"

"Jade," he said. There was no point lying, where they only had to look. As he spoke, he slipped the shard under his tongue, hoping to keep that at least.

If he could keep his life.

"Jade? Jade is for emperors, not for boys."

Yu Shan said nothing. There was a shadow to his left; it resolved itself into a man. He was short and gaunt, with joints like twisted knot-roots, but his blade held extremely steady at Yu Shan's throat. His head had been badly shaved, too long ago or else not long enough; tufts of wiry hair stuck out at angles between patches of stubble. Likely he'd done it himself, with this same heavy blade.

His eyes were green, which spoke of the mountains; so did his leanness, and his wiry strength. Strip him, Yu Shan thought, and chances were good there'd be a clan tattoo somewhere on his body.

An old one, faded, with nothing new to say. Nothing even recent.

Rumor had always said that there were bandits in the foothills, outcasts, strays who couldn't face the work of the mines or the discipline of their clans. Yu Shan had never troubled to believe it. He couldn't imagine exile and would certainly never need to leave clan lands, so why should he worry?

Here was a reason, perhaps. No, a pair of reasons. Here came this man's partner, cut and step, hacking his way now he didn't need to slither under cover of Yu Shan's own noise.

This one looked even more like a clansman, one who had himself mined jade; he carried himself with the stone's authority. He said, "Truly, jade?"—but he didn't need to, because he could see the truth of it in Yu Shan, even if he was too far away to feel the stone's own truth.

"Truly," Yu Shan said.

"The stone belongs to the emperor."

"I am taking it to him." And then, in response to baffled stares, "The emperor has come to Taishu. This stone is a gift to him, from all the clans," lying at last, just in case they might hesitate to steal from the god-on-earth, if not from their own people.

They might not. The first man still didn't move his blade a hairbreadth as he said, "Jade. What can we do with jade?"

"Sell it, of course. Down on the roadway, a wagoner will give us something."

"And him?"

"The same. He might even be worth more than jade. You said, Fuo, he is pretty . . ."

· · ·

HE COULDN'T run through thick brush with the stone on his back; however much it uplifted him, there was no path unless he cut one.

He couldn't move at all, against that blade at his throat.

They took his own blade from him, and tied his hands behind his back. Another rope made a halter for his neck. Yu Shan would have fought with his family, to defend their mine or their compound or their lives; he would have fought with his clan to defend the valley. Out here he had only his own freedom and the wonderstone to fight for. And one of those was beautiful, but didn't belong to him; the other was an illusion brought on by solitude and time. He belonged to his family, the stone belonged to the emperor. Those were still true, and not affected by a rope around his neck. When Fuo tugged, he followed.

Quietly, still sucking on his splinter.

THE SECOND man cut a path for them, but he wasn't carrying the stone; he cut too narrow, and Yu Shan kept getting snagged as branches tangled with the jutting frame.

He stumbled and twisted all the way downslope, earning Fuo's curses with every jerk on the halter. The wiry little man jerked back, again and again, with a venom that should have wrenched Yu Shan's neck out of true but somehow didn't; he thought the stone lent something of its weight to him, so that the rope might as well have been tied around a pillar of rock for all the harm it did.

DOWN AND down, from the ridge to the roadway. They were almost there, in the last of the bordering woodland, when the man who led held his hand up.

Fuo was instantly still, and a glance behind warned Yu Shan not to move or call out. That blade was bare in his hand again; one slashing sweep and the halter would not be needed any longer.

Yu Shan had small hope of help, whoever came. A wagoner wouldn't help him; nor would a guard patrol, watching out for the jademasters' interests. There might be others on the road, people living in these hills, but they were more likely to be victims than rescuers. How else should bandits live, if not from banditry . . . ?

When she did come, she was a single woman, gray showing in her long loose hair and a harsh song on her lips. She carried a bundle on her back, but nothing in it would have any value and neither did she, even to outlaws willing to steal and sell a boy. They could all just crouch here and let her pass by in her ignorance . . .

Except that of course she was a woman, and perhaps these men hadn't seen one in a while. She was suddenly a woman with a blade at her breast, a bandit urging her off the road.

She at least wasn't fool enough to do what he wanted. She stepped off the rutted dried mud of the road, in seeming obedience—and then just kept moving, spilling the bundle from her shoulders and running blindly into the forest. Sheer luck took her at an angle away from where Fuo waited with Yu Shan.

The other bandit gave chase. Fuo tied Yu Shan's halter around a tree branch to free up both his hands, and waited. So did Yu Shan, necessarily. Waited, listened; heard the sounds of frantic, difficult progress through the scrub, followed—patiently, relentlessly followed—by the methodical sounds of cutting.

After a while, they heard the woman scream. Then there were other noises, hard to distinguish, but they ended abruptly.

Fuo sighed, discontented. Yu Shan was glad for the woman. He thought he was. It was what she should have wanted.

The cutting resumed, coming steadily through the forest toward them. He wondered if the two men would argue, if Fuo was disappointed enough. How hard could it have been, after all, to bring her back on the end of a rope?

Perhaps they would fight. Perhaps they would kill each other.

Which would leave him, of course, bound to a tree; and there were creatures in the forest, always eager to feast on helpless boys. Not to mention the gods, any one of whom might wander by and take him, as casually as pick a fruit . . .

But he could break the ropes, perhaps. With time enough, he could rub them raw against the tree's rough bark and snap them thread by thread. Or, better, he had that shard of jade in his mouth, like the broken fragment of a blade; hold that between his teeth and he could nick the ropes apart. The emperor wouldn't mind . . .

But no. These men wouldn't fight. Over a woman astray on the road, and her not even beautiful? And dead? Of course they wouldn't fight . . .

Swing and slash, cut and step, the other came toward them. He saw the scrub move, like a presentiment; he saw branches fall, before he saw the blade that cut them. Then he saw the blade, and behind it the shadow of the one who swung it: tall and dark and stepping forward, cut and step, and—

—AND THE man whose name Yu Shan didn't know, that man had been shorter even than Fuo, and this figure was taller than either. As tall as Yu Shan, perhaps. And there were creatures in the forest, or it could always be one of the gods; but the gods don't use blades to cut a way through undergrowth, and nor do ghosts or demons.

But otherwise, there was only the woman, and—

—AND YES, astonishingly that was her, stepping through the shadows with a sword in her hand. If she'd had a sword before, he hadn't noticed it. It was a short-bladed tao, fit for forest work: much like his own blade and much like Fuo's, extremely much like the one the other man had carried except that it was darker now, streaked with dark.

She'd tied her loose hair up in a swift knot, and she moved with a quiet rangy confidence, no more shrieking and running. The blade looked right in her hand. And she'd cut her way directly to them, when he'd thought they were hidden; and—

—AND FUO was as startled as he was, but only for a moment. One moment to stare, to draw a breath; then a swift recovery. He looked suddenly as lethal as a mountain snake, crouched and swaying, passing his tao from hand to hand, drawing her gaze into the dance of it . . .

Trying to draw her gaze. She wasn't even watching his hands. Nor did she try to copy his stance. She came on bold and upright, and Yu Shan thought this would be over very quickly, and he would still be a bound prisoner at the end of it.

Prophecy is an unhappy gift in mortal men; it should be left to the gods, who understand its habits of betrayal.

They met, and the canopy had to swallow the ugly sound of steel scraping steel. Fuo swung his blade ferociously at her neck and she deflected it, just in time. And stabbed at him while he was overreached and awkward, but so was she; he made a leap back, graceless but effective, and so they began again.

He tried a darting thrust but she blocked it, the two blades edge to edge; and so again; and so again.

Except that last time, he swung from wide and the steel made a different, duller sound when she blocked it, because she'd used the back of her blade instead of the edge. She'd stopped his swing two-handed, numbingly; and now her own blade flung back at him with the strength of both those long arms and the whip of her shoulders and a twist of her back, and his body was still tipping forward from the effort he'd put into his own stroke, and—

—AND YU SHAN thought she'd take Fuo's throat out, and was wrong.

She took his head off, whole.

And meant to do it, knew just what she was doing. He could see all the work she put into the stroke, how it cleaved expertly through flesh and bone together.

Fuo's head didn't just fall. She had struck his neck at an angle, rising; the deep blade of the tao lifted his head entire and sent it tumbling through the air like a tossed ball, spraying leaves and mud and all the clearing before it fell into the undergrowth with a dense thud.

Yu Shan caught a spatter of blood across his face, and couldn't wipe it.

Fuo's body crumpled strangely, as though all its strings were cut, not just its neck-strings. The woman stood and watched it fall, breathing heavily now. Yu Shan could be patient; let her recover herself, before she recovered him. Meantime he offered silent thanks to whatever gods watched this hillside, this roadside, travelers astray. When his hands were free, he would make better offerings. It never hurt to be grateful.

She came to him sooner than he'd expected: sheened with sweat and wiping blood from the tao, she stood before him, looked him up and down.

"What are you," she said, "his mule?"

"I was his prisoner," with no emphasis at all, waiting for her to use that sharp blade and cut him free.

"What's in the pack, then? Mule?"

"Jade." Again, why lie? She need only look.

"One piece?"

"Yes."

"I didn't know it came so big. Or that one man could carry such a rock."

She shouldn't call it rock—but she'd called him a man, which made up for a lot. He smiled. "It's very special. And I'm stronger than I look."

"I think you must be. And I'm sure it is. What were you doing with it, mule?"

"Taking it to the emperor. And my name's Yu Shan."

"Is it?" She was amused, which made him angry. *Patience* . . . "Your name's Yu Shan and your eyes are green, and you carry a treasure to the emperor. Do you know the way?"

"If I go to the port city, I can find him."

"I'm sure. If people stop tying ropes around your neck."

"And my hands," he said, hinting.

"Yes. That too. Poor mule. What were those men meaning to do with you?"

"They said they'd sell me, on the road. The wagoners . . ."

". . . have orders not to deal with privateers, but I'm sure they do. In jade, and other goods. Fine healthy lads, for example. Well. I won't do that, I won't sell you to the wagoners," though she still wasn't cutting his bonds.

"Please," he said at last, "you could untie me?"

She just smiled. "We'll have this off your back in a minute," poking at the straps that held the stone. "You'll be more comfortable without, and I'm thinking we should camp up for the night. Hereabouts," with a glance at Fuo's sprawled body. "Not just here, but I don't want to be on the road after dark with creatures like this about. They're like ants; one alone may truly be alone, but two means there'll be a nest somewhere. What's inside the bamboo?"

She'd noticed, then, how the ends of the frame were capped. "Rice," he said, "and pickles." Enough to see him to his destination, if he wasn't delayed. If he didn't fall into the hands of bandits, say; or if he wasn't promptly rescued by a lean and curious woman, oddly dangerous and oddly on her own, who might well be hungry for rice and pickles.

"No knives, anything like that?"

"No. I had a tao, but he took it . . ."

"Yes. I don't suppose that was difficult," though she showed no signs of retrieving it from Fuo's body.

"Please," he said, "who are you?"

"My name's Jiao," and she was untying his rope at last—only the wrong end of it, the end that Fuo had tied around the tree.

"What are you, then?" Her name was no use, it didn't tell him anything. Which she knew perfectly well.

"Whatever I need to be. I thought I might find some land and be a farmer— Why are you laughing?"

"No reason," except that even on short and perilous acquaintance, he thought it unlikely that she could settle to the patience of earth and weather, plowing and planting and gathering in.

"Really? Is that something you do, you men from the mountains, you laugh suddenly for no reason at us simple plainsfolk?" She was not simple by any means, and he doubted that she was from the plains; he doubted that she was from Taishu at all. "Actually," she went on, "I did wonder about settling with your people, if they would make me welcome . . ."

Small chance of that, anywhere among the clans. He thought

she knew it; she was still not being serious. What she had said before, about one ant alone: she was very likely a solitary bandit, picking up whatever she could plunder. If she had thought at all about making her way into the mountains, it would be on a dream of stealing jade at source.

Which of course she need not do now, because she had a precious piece of it right here. Jade and him, both bound and ready, plunder for the picking.

four

She was still again, under the water; she was still again, in his head.

Others talked about her, so he didn't have to.

Not the crew, they knew nothing and would not learn; they sneered at every mention of her. Not Li Ton, he refused even to hear her mentioned in his presence.

Those who talked were local, from the village on the bluff. They were old, and like the old everywhere they thought that age was a byway into wisdom. They stretched the crew's patience; if they tried to stretch Li Ton's, likely he would stretch their necks for them. Or shorten them, by a swift head.

Han had seen this before, where a community sent its weakest and most easily spared to treat with soldiers or outlaws, so as not to lose too much if negotiations went badly. He had seen barren women sent into an army camp; he had heard of children carrying food to the forest, to keep bandits from raiding the village. He had not heard that all of them came back.

Here, once it was clear that the *Shalla* would not be lifting on any tide soon, the locals must have felt it a shame not to be dickering with her men. On the third day, the first of the old folk came warily down the steep cliff path. They went back up with a list of what was needed, from charcoal to good rice; the *Shalla*'s own lay salt-sodden in the hold. In exchange, they had their pick of whatever had been hauled equally sodden out of that same hold and laid out to dry on the beach.

Peasants lead harsh lives. Han knew it, had known it intimately; was reminded of it now, seeing how eagerly his late master's smallclothes were added to the pile.

For free, the old people gave their wisdom as they gleaned.

"That wave, that dreadful wave? That was the dragon, stirring in her place beneath the sea. How could you doubt it? The Forge has fallen silent. The dragon must be free. Why the monks betrayed us, we don't know. They swore to keep her chained, and now she's free.

"She stirred, she woke; and so the wave, the storm of it, the wrecking. There have been wrecks all up and down the coast, not so lucky as you. You should sail to safer waters. She will stir again. She will rise; and when she rises, oh, then will be a storm . . ."

And so on, and on. They talked of the dragon endlessly, so that Han need say nothing, even to himself. Especially to himself, perhaps. Suo Lung and he barely talked at all, except in single words that might be scratched in iron.

THE CHAINS he wore chafed his wrists; the dragon chafed his mind. He flinched away from her and padded his cuffs with ripped cotton rags, and tried to pad his mind much the same, tried not to feel, not to believe.

IT WAS the seventh day of their stranding. They were promised seven more before the high spring tides, before they could hope to float the *Shalla* free. In the meantime,

"You, boy: run aloft," which meant upslope to the village, "and try one more time to persuade those fools to send some women down. Tell them the men will run mad else, and burn their precious hutment to the ground. Say we will pay handsomely, in real silver. Oh, and take a basket. When they refuse you, which they will, go on into the forest and make believe you're picking mushrooms for tonight. Come back with something, anything, I don't care what. And while you're there, try to sniff out where they're hiding their women . . ."

Thus Jorgan, speaking in his master's voice; and therefore Han, not the first to climb the cliff on this futile errand. The pirate crew had done the same already, scouring the forest margin beyond the village paddy, threatening the old folk, getting nowhere.

Every village within striking distance of the sea must be familiar with raiders, and have its strategy for survival. That might be an uneasy, unequal contract with one particular boat. It might be constant watchfulness and a place to hide. Here, Han was willing to bet there was another cruder village deep in the forest, where everyone bar the old folk was sitting quiet, waiting. They would have weapons at hand; if the pirates found them, they would fight. And die, of course, the men more swiftly than the monks on the island, the women more slowly. The children might be taken off and sold, if they were lucky. If that was luck.

The pirates hadn't found them yet, and neither would Han. He was resolved on that.

Jorgan didn't expect him to. Han thought the *Shalla*'s mate simply wanted him out of sight. He'd been condemned to die, and saved, and saved again. He was so useless there wasn't even makework he could do, and yet he still wore the *Shalla*'s ring in his ear and Li Ton could still not kill him, because the smithy slave wanted him alive.

So this, now, an errand that offered the chance to run if he chose to. He thought Li Ton would like that, just to be free of him. He also thought that Suo Lung would despair. He thought he could live with that. But if he ran, he took the dragon with him. She was in his head now, as much as in his chains. And barely contained by either.

It was like a mirror, he understood that. His chains were an image of the dragon's; words, characters had meaning on both sides of the reflection, but on one they were potent beyond measure.

If they were well remembered and properly written and in the significant order.

None of that was true, here and now. Suo Lung sweated to remember the words, Han sweated to write the characters that Suo Lung struggled to copy. If this was magic, it was a threadbare broken-backed echo of a spell. The dragon lay still for now, but she was a pressure behind his eyes, a weight on his mind, a hunger and a calling and a need. He didn't think that she would sleep forever, now she'd woken once. He wasn't sure she was asleep at all.

So no, Han would not run. He needed more chains and better words, but Suo Lung was all he had. He would cleave to the smith, work with him, live with him; if that meant working with, living with Li Ton and Jorgan, all the crew of the *Shalla*—which it did, all too obviously—then he would do that too. For now.

If he ran, he'd have to take Suo Lung with him. Which would be the opposite of easy.

HE FOUND no one in the village except a scatter of the elderly, and asked his dutiful question about the women and accepted their sucks of air and shaking heads with a dutiful nod, and went on toward the forest's edge with his empty basket.

And didn't get so far, not half so far; had barely set foot on one of the raised paths that ran through the paddy before he saw movement ahead, figures coming out of the trees' shadow.

Not the villagers coming stupidly out of their hiding-place, no. This was a band of armed men, dark shadows and bright blades; men on horseback, men afoot. More men than crewed the *Shalla*, and better armed.

Han might hate Li Ton and all his crew—he might well do that, if he ever stopped to think about it—but Li Ton had the smithy slave, and Han's chains, the dragon's chains depended on Suo Lung. *Everything* depended on Suo Lung. Han couldn't trust that man's safety to some chance-met army, which would take him for just another pirate.

Back through the village, then, not even pausing to cry a warning to the old folk; down the path and plunging recklessly to the beach, wildly off-balance and grateful that Suo Lung had not—yet—chained his ankles; and he must have been seen coming, because Jorgan met him at the edge of the sand, and was angry.

Han barely had breath to give his message, but it was enough to see him dragged off to tell his tale to Li Ton. And at least he had the half-trained scribe's memory for what he'd seen, whether it was written characters or patterned flags on a distant hill or men moving slowly through the paddy. When Li Ton asked for numbers, he counted rapidly in his head. "A dozen officers on horseback. I saw sixty, seventy men on foot, but there were more. Every time I looked back, there were more coming out of the trees."

Li Ton scowled. "That's too many. They can't settle so many in the village, they can't camp in the paddy; they're coming for us. For the *Shalla*. They know she's here, and they know the size of her crew. One of the villagers has betrayed us."

It would be the headman, his decision. It would have cost him his village, but the soldiers would be there before Li Ton could be. The captain set his anger aside and went on, "They're coming in numbers, because they want her and they don't want a fight; but if it comes to that, they won't care how many lives they spend to get her."

He looked over his shoulder at where the junk lay beached, half her tackle dismounted and strewn across the sand. He was a realist, necessarily. If the thought of resistance crossed his mind, it didn't linger.

He said, "If we cost them lives, they won't spare any of us. Let them come down, and they'll want us. I never met a landsman yet who could double as a sailor. She needs her crew, the *Shalla* does; she'll be no use to them without. I can make them see that."

And later, his expression said, *when we're at sea, we can deal with however many soldiers they put aboard my vessel, mine . . .*

HAN HAD never seen the crew so disarmed, or so discomfited. The men stood about in awkward groupings, conspicuously doing nothing: which is of course the birthright of all sailors ashore, but here it was a lie, and not one they could sustain with any conviction.

What they were actually doing, they were watching the cliff path and waiting to surrender. Waiting not to fight, which was something they did extremely badly.

Suo Lung at least had work, filing down the rough edge of a casting. Han knelt at his feet, and the smith grunted words at him:

"Tight."

"Narrow? Constricting?"

"No. Being tight. Held."

"Bound?" But that was a character he had already written on his chains.

"No. Held tight in darkness."

It was like this constantly. Suo Lung struggled to remember words; he mispronounced or misunderstood what he did remember; everything he gave to Han was garbled, and had to be picked open, cleaned up, made comprehensible.

Han had the dragon in his head, just a little, as much as he was inside hers. She knew what they were doing, or trying to do. She muddled his thoughts her own way. It was hard to focus on the smith's words while his mind surged to the tugs of other forces, tide and wind and current. Hard to remember his own painful lessons in the art of writing when the weights on his wrists were a link to another life, another world, where chains were an abomination, a rank intrusion into what should be free and flowing and majestic, magnificent, untouchable . . .

It was almost a relief to see how the pirates were suddenly alert, silent, unnaturally still; to look up the cliff path himself and see the first soldiers coming down.

Soldiers killed pirates, wherever and whenever they could. That was imperial law, almost a law of nature. And yet the crew stood quiet and watched them come, disarmed already, surrendered already. Dead already, if Li Ton failed. All he had to save their lives was a presumption.

Han was one with the men in this at least, that he did very much want to live. He needed to, or more and many more than he would die, and the dragon would hold all dominion.

Sometimes he thought he wanted that, but actually it was her, inside his head.

He was one with the men another way too, that if Li Ton's hope failed, then he would die alongside them, one among them. That was guaranteed. From the captain to the cabin boy, they would all be given to the same cruel ending.

The simple soldiers came down first, spears and bows. They clumped cautiously together much like the pirates, just at the foot of the path. The two parties stared at each other, across the sands and stones of the beach; they were in shouting distance, but no one shouted. No one quite knew what to do, Han thought. The pirates had never offered a surrender before, the soldiers had never received one. The situation was clear enough—one side bristled with weapons, the other was empty-handed—but it needed someone to make a move. Slowly.

Li Ton stood in the shadow of the beached *Shalla,* and didn't stir.

At length the cluster of soldiers parted, as three men came pushing through. By their dress, by their urgently nervous manner, these were the officers. If this was a trap—if the pirates meant to make a fight of it after all, if they had weapons hidden behind their backs or beneath the sand—then they all knew who would be first to die.

Han watched Li Ton.

Who shifted his weight, stepped forward, went to meet them, with Jorgan as ever in his shadow.

It wasn't the first time Han should have kept silent; nor the first time he'd done the other thing, hurled himself in where he was not looked for, not wanted, not safe.

HE FELT the force of her intent, and tried to throw a wall against it. As well try to build against the typhoon, with only twigs and string.

TOO LATE, he flung his arms high and wide, as far as the chains allowed him; he bruised his wrists against their absolute forbiddal; he flung that resistance, the refusal of iron, back at her. He fought to subdue her, to suppress her, not to let her rise. He struggled to send her back, down, into the murk of the sea bottom.

SHE DID subside, but still it was coming, she had sent it on its way and nothing he nor she could do would stop it now.

. . .

So HE seized Suo Lung's wrist, and dragged him down the beach to where Li Ton and the army captains were speaking.

"WHAT ARE you doing, boy?"

That was Jorgan, inevitably: coming between him and the man he had to talk to.

"There's trouble," Han said urgently. "I have to tell the captain . . ."

"The captain has trouble already, it's here. Haven't you noticed?"

"Real trouble, I mean."

"These men could kill us all. And will, if he doesn't talk them out of it. Is that real enough for you?"

Han knew that, and no, it wasn't. "The dragon," he gasped, "there's a, another big wave coming, like the tsunami . . ."

Not much like the tsunami, in truth: he knew what she had done and there was a world of difference. That had been one vast and bewildered shrug, like a mountain remembering how to move; this was focused, deliberate, malign.

Aimed at him, at Han.

He could feel it, the weight of it as it surged through the ocean. He understood her, and it too: almost well enough to feel that he could turn it around and hurl it back at her.

But she was dragon, he was only boy. He sat like a little thing, an annoyance in her head, like a fly on a bull ox; the least little tendril of her mind lay across his thoughts like a yoke, too great a burden, he could not bear it. She could splinter him in a moment, if she weren't so chained.

So she sent her waters to do it on her behalf. She was all the sea and the sea-wind too, where he was negligible, flotsam bobbing on the waves. He couldn't touch her work. All he could do was anticipate it.

"The *dragon*?" Jorgan cursed his contempt. Han knew that because of the way the man's lip curled; he couldn't hear the actual words, because of the roar of waters at his back.

Jorgan saw them first. Han knew that because of the way the man's eyes bulged, his mouth worked, he turned to find Li Ton.

Han was ahead of him, almost: ducking under Jorgan's arm, diving forward to seize Li Ton's, so that in fact he was more or less last to see it, although he'd known it first.

IT WASN'T really a wave. Waves ride on the surface of the sea. This was a surge from deep, deep down: a careful toss of her head, as much as she could move against the chains he wore.

Hurling up from the seabed, this great mass of water met the mouth of the creek and was squeezed, thin and high and tight; and crashed through that rocky cleft like a wall of water, and broke like a brutal wave into the broader space beyond, and came crashing down on them all.

And Han was dragging at Li Ton and dragging at Suo Lung, hauling them to where the *Shalla* lay broadside to the flood, thinking that at least her bulk could break the force of the waters for them. Han had to live, to keep the dragon even so lightly chained; which meant Li Ton had to live, because he was Han's best chance of surviving after the wave; and Suo Lung of course had to live, because he was Han's only hope of making those chains heavier.

The wave found the *Shalla* and lifted her, and broke under as well as around as well as over her; and so she offered them no shelter at all and they were overwhelmed, tumbling end over end in the surf of the rising flood.

HAN WAS the chained one, first to sink. Weight of iron dragged him down just as weight of water crushed him, just as the weight of the dragon's mind came at him, leering.

And he had only that one last frantic moment to strike back at her; and he gave her the only thing he had, his own fear transmuted:

And what if I die, here, now? These are still your chains, still spelled to keep you bound; and they will lie on a dead boy somewhere under the sea here, and you can't reach them or me, you can't move, you're chained because I am. And if I'm dead, then what are you? A little of me is a little part of you now, and do you want death in your heart, in your mind, softly rotting? And my bones may rot but the chains will still hold you, the characters we cut will shine as bright as your eyes underwater . . .

. . . AND THERE was a stillness in the water then, as though what had been boiling could suddenly be chill, as though the sea and stars hung motionless for a moment, except for the stars exploding in his head.

And then there was a great sucking, a draining-away. The chains that had weighed him down made an anchor for him now, to hold him against that pull; and suddenly the water was gone and he was lying sprawled and empty on the smooth sands of the beach.

Empty of everything, air too. Like a newborn he had to learn, he had to choose to breathe; and when he tried, it was all coughing and spewing salty water, retching and gasping and pain in his throat, pain in his ribs and deep inside, pain everywhere.

He thought it was the soldiers who saved his life. Soldiers flooding down the cliff path, all those who had not been caught by the flood: looking for their own comrades, of course, and their officers, but pummeling survivors indiscriminately, forcing their bodies to work: making them strip, stand, move about under the hot sun, anything to fight off the wicked cold of the water.

Which was how Han, and Suo Lung, and perhaps all his crew except Jorgan—all his surviving crew, for there were men missing—first saw Li Ton naked, in his true form, as himself.

Exposed, his body was knotted with muscle and twisted with scars, but more, all his skin was a mass of tattoos. Not the crude images that half his crew favored, nor the intricate designs afforded by a few. These were brute block characters all over his chest and shoulders and belly and back, his thighs and buttocks and calves. Some of them Han could read, even in distant glances. They reminded him of nothing so much as his own chains; he thought they should have the same effect, they should make a spell of the truth.

They made words like *traitor, renegade, exile.* They spoke of disgrace, of banishment; they demanded his death and promised a price for his head if it were delivered to any of the Hidden City's gates, sent as a gift to the emperor.

His genitals had been taken in advance. That was almost more shocking than the stark tattoos, the dark absence between the captain's legs.

Castration and tattoos together meant imperial punishment. Han knew it; so did the soldiers. So did their surviving officers. Li Ton was put in chains, heavier than Han's; that was Han's first work, to rebuild and fire up the forge, for Suo Lung to make chains for their captain.

Meanwhile the *Shalla* floated, mockingly free in the creek's deep channel, ready to take them all upcoast to the captains' general, to face his summary justice.

five

The news of his own coming, he thought, would be all through the harbor, on every quay and dock.

It would follow hard on the morning's earlier news: not so significant or strange, perhaps, but fresher and easier to deal with and welcome.

That first news would have been the smoke, visible as soon as the sun rose: smoke rising from the Forge again, after days and days without.

There would have been small comfort in it, once the first wash of relief was past. This was no fine shimmer of forge-smoke. Rather it was a greasy black pillar that overhung the island like a tree's canopy, only nothing so sweet or hopeful. It was a sight of ill omen. When he was seen to follow it, crabbing slowly through the waves in this battered stew of a boat, those who knew him—which was everyone who belonged in the harbor, everyone with rope-scars on their hands and salt under their fingernails—would see him as a hopeful sign, the promise of survival: *see, not all is lost! Even those we gave up for dead can still come home . . . !*

Old Yen would be sorry to disappoint them, but his awkward progress was a worse omen even than the smoke, he bore worse news.

None the less, he expected a rush to hear it. He was looking for a sudden blossoming of sails, boats racing to greet him. One who had survived the tsunami against all odds, and of course it would be Old Yen in his bastard boat: dismasted and half-wrecked, rudely patched and leaking but see, she takes the waves as grimly determined as her master, she may wallow a little in the troughs but she rises every time, and . . .

AND SHE was close in now and there was no hint of movement in the docks or on the water. No sails, no boats rowing out, no figures running on the foreshore.

Nothing moored up, either, so far as he could see in glances snatched between the constant demands of coaxing his own boat this last little distance, as he had coaxed her all the way from the Forge. Tides had turned, the light had gone and come again; he was exhausted, and he dared not relax. Pao was all the help he could be, not enough; the boy had to spend half his time down in the hold, pumping out the bilges.

Old Yen missed his granddaughter more than ever. Nothing would be as dreadful if she were here. Even the news he carried, even the grim task that had left that column of smoke climbing into the sky: he'd have borne it all so much better for her company, and she'd have borne it because that's what she did, endurance came naturally to her.

And she was gone, not coming back; and he was bringing news of death and doom into an empty harbor, and he didn't understand that at all.

Until he docked, gingerly edging the heavy hog of a boat up to a quay, sending the boy leaping over the rail with a rope. She couldn't stay here; his first move was to look beyond the docks, to where a natural beach shelved gently down into deep water.

Which was when he realized that the harbor wasn't empty after all, of either boats or men. He'd never seen so many craft out of the water at once, or so many working on them. There were others coming down the quay now, hurrying. Still not the welcome-party he had looked for: two of these were soldiers, while the third had a paper in his hand. That made him a clerk of some kind, Old Yen supposed, but if so he was a clerk with authority.

"You—where have you come from?" Authority and an accent; he was no one from Taishu. "Why is there nobody aboard?"

"That boy's all the crew I have. We've been on the Forge, and I have news—"

"We don't need your gossip. Take your boat out again, sail to Santung. These men will come with you, to be sure you're not diverted."

"The tsunami—"

"We know all about the tsunami. It wrecked half the fleet. Which is why every other boat has to work harder. Untie, I say, and turn about."

"She'd sink before we made it out of the harbor. See how low she sits already? Her belly's filling with water while you watch. Stand here long enough—or keep me standing here—and you can see her go down."

"If it's in such a state, why have you brought it here at all? Old fool?"

"Because I need to speak to the harbormaster, about where best to beach her; and because I have an urgent message that cannot wait even while I do that; and—"

And his own impatience was threatening to betray him; he would knock this stupid functionary off the quay if the man wouldn't get out of his way.

If the man hadn't had soldiers to back him. If the man hadn't smiled thinly and said, "I am the harbormaster. I have General Ping Wen's warrant for it. If your boat's not fit to sail the strait, you must take it—"

"I'd take her to my sons, gladly, if I could get her there." No one knew this boat better than family. "I told you, though, she's not fit to sail farther. She'll have to keep here for now. I have an errand to run. Pao, quit staring and get back to the pumps."

"You cannot leave it there," the harbormaster insisted. "The fleet will be in before sundown, and I need every berth."

"The whole fleet at once? What's changed?" They had been back and forth like a chain, before the tsunami.

"Santung is under attack. The men are struggling to hold their lines, while we take as many as we can off the beaches. The port is lost already."

And they would go all together for safety's sake, because one boat alone was too easy to pick off, and they would not willingly lose one boat to the enemy. Old Yen understood that. He said, "If you need the berth, a boat can tie up to mine as easily as she can to the quay. If there are fit men aboard, they can help my boy pump. I have a message for the emperor."

"I do not see the banner that would make you an imperial messenger."

"I said I have a message," and his patience was straining at the cable again; but this man could maybe bring him closer to the emperor than he could come himself. He wasn't naïve, only urgent, and a lifetime at sea had taught him sometimes to be urgent slowly. "A thing we have seen, that he must be told about."

"Tell me, and I will see that—"

"No." Waste his news here, to promote some underling? Oh no. Never mind how urgent, he would use it for his own good too. "It must come from me to him, directly."

The harbormaster stared; if he could have made his eyes bulge, he would have done it. "You, *you*," *a common fisherman with a leaking boat,* "dare aspire to speak to his majesty? Himself? In person?"

"Why not?" Old Yen said. "I've done it before." And then, swiftly, "I am the man who brought the Son of Heaven to Taishu, in this very boat. I was twice blessed, because he chose to take my own granddaughter to be the companion of his heart, even as he chose my own boat to journey on. The gods don't arrange such matters for no purpose. Now I have news that is for his ears and from my mouth alone, and if you can help me to reach him then you should certainly do so, for your own benefit and the throne's," *in that order.*

Stunned by so much, the harbormaster took a moment to recover. Eventually, he nodded. "Of course. Forgive me, I did not know. See, I will take you myself to the general's own chamberlain, and if he cannot find a way to admit you to the august presence, then it cannot be done at all."

· · ·

So THEN there was leaving the boat in the care of the boy, with the soldiers to help him pump, and hurrying through the streets of Taishu-port. Climbing up from the docks and the dockside markets, which Old Yen knew well; hurrying through the lower town, the inns and brothels and doss-houses which Old Yen knew not quite so well, but well enough; hurrying in the harbormaster's wake, who did not know the town at all but knew perhaps the way to the emperor's ear, which Old Yen could not begin to fathom.

Nor did he know the upper town, the great houses behind their walls and guards. He'd never had cause to come up here, even when the great men living here were all native. Now the guards had strange armor and weapons and wore their hair in a queue as a sign of their devotion to the emperor. Even their faces were strange, long pale faces of the north.

Old Yen had fought warehouse fires in his time, passing buckets of water along a chain of hands. Today he felt like one of those buckets, raised just a little higher at every move. The harbormaster couldn't take him directly to the emperor, nor to the general from whom he claimed his own commission, nor actually— despite his boasts—to the general's chamberlain.

It was the general's gatekeeper who took him into the first courtyard of the general's palace, with the harbormaster left firmly outside. The gatekeeper passed him to the house steward, and the steward to the chamberlain; and Old Yen couldn't quite believe he'd come even this far. Nor apparently could his escorts, to judge by their increasingly bewildered glances as they were authorized to take him on and on again.

At last, inevitably, he did come to a stop. Not with the chamberlain, but with his master the general; and he thought it highly unlikely that he could inveigle or bluster his way any farther.

So, clearly, did the general.

"I am Ping Wen," he said, from behind a lacquered desk in a small dark room. Ping Wen was all too obviously a stranger here: too big for the room, almost too big for the house, nearly knocking his head as he entered, not quite comfortable in his chair.

Old Yen was standing before him, and the general's face suggested that he thought kneeling might be more suitable, knocking his head on the floor might be wise. Old Yen was too stubborn to do either. He would kowtow to his emperor, because that was the law, but he never had yet to any man else and would not start it now.

"They call me Old Yen," he said. "Excellence," he said, because good manners never hurt and he could respect a man without needing to fall on his face before him. "I have a message for the emperor."

"So I gather. You may give your message to me, and trust me to convey it. If I think it worth the emperor's time." If not, his tone suggested, there would be trouble all down the line, and someone could be depended on to see that Old Yen had his share of it.

"Excellence, I cannot. It is a matter for the emperor directly, and it needs to come from me."

"If the emperor feels any need to speak to you, once he has heard it," *if he does, if I judge it worth his while,* "no doubt you can be found. Perhaps my men will keep you close."

He was a fleshy man, this Ping Wen, with a beard he liked to toy with, stroking it through his fingers. His eyes were sharp, though, and there was nothing complacent in him. Even so, Old Yen said, "Forgive me, excellence, but it is mine to tell and his to hear. It touches on the Son of Heaven himself, and his throne. The gods were good, to let me find him in the fog and bring him here; now they have shown me something more, and I must give it to him."

"I am aware," the general said slowly, "of your early contact with his imperial majesty. It has won you great favor, fisherman, in fetching you this far. There is nowhere more for you to go. If you know anything, *anything* pertaining to the welfare of the Jade Throne, you will tell it to me now. Otherwise, I will find ways to extract it from you. These quarters may be makeshift, but no doubt we can make shift."

For the first time Old Yen felt a hesitation, a shadow's touch of dread. Had he overreached . . . ?

Undoubtedly he had, but his Li-goddess was apparently watch-

ing over him yet, even here on land, which was not strictly her do-
main.

In the silence, the short time the general allowed him to decide,
a servant came into the room. Ping Wen was annoyed at the interruption; Old Yen could tell by how still he sat, not a glance or a
gesture toward the incomer.

The man was one of his own, though, one of these northerners
with their shaven brows and pigtailed hair. He wouldn't have broken in on his master without good cause. He bent to murmur into
the general's unyielding ear, and the few words Old Yen could
make out were claggy with dialect, shifty of meaning; he couldn't
guess at the message.

Ping Wen had it at his fingertips. He dusted them together for a
moment, as if to brush off an unpleasantness. Then he spoke.

"Where a man may not rise, a god may yet stoop. It seems you
are more fortunate than I knew; the Son of Heaven has sent for
you. Come, I will escort you myself. It never hurts to show humil-
ity before the gods."

He meant—transparently—that it would do him no harm at all
to be apologetically present, and so hear this mysterious message
for himself. And, perhaps, learn how the emperor knew there was
a fisherman astray among the palaces, seeking an audience.

As to that, Old Yen could have told him—a goddess had
deigned to stoop: it was nothing more mysterious than that, or
less wonderful—but the general should learn it for himself. It
would be ill manners to bring a man face to face with a deity, all
uninvited.

He went meekly, then, with the general and all those other men
without whom it seemed the general could not move. The higher
he came in this world, the more people clustered around him.
Could the general never be alone? And if not him, then could the
emperor . . . ?

ANOTHER HOUSE, larger yet and better guarded; but they were all
immense, these palaces, he could barely register them as places

built, places to be. They were like the cliffs, the rivers, the ocean: on the wrong scale for humankind.

He followed the general who followed his own servants who followed those of the house here, through gates and courtyards and on into vast gardens. Down gravel paths, past ponds and pergolas, between sweet-scented banks of flowers to a pavilion where, yes, here was the emperor.

With his mother and being read to by a clerk, attended by half a dozen others.

Never mind them, or any of them. Kowtow. They all did it, the general too; Old Yen went down with the mass of them, and smote his forehead on the wood of the pavilion floor.

And they waited, all of them together, for the emperor to recognize the general; and what he said was, "Old Yen. Good. Walk with me."

It was perhaps starting to rain, but even so they walked a path to an ornate little bridge where carp blew bubbles among the lily-pads below. Just himself and the emperor: no mother, no general, no hangers-on. The two of them in the same world, step after step after step; and the emperor said, "So tell me, what is this news, that is quite so imperative?"

"Majesty," Old Yen said, "I have been to the Forge, and it is silent."

"I know. I have been told that already."

"Forgive me, majesty, but do you know why?"

"No. My generals sent a boat, because an eye on the Forge could watch all the strait at once. The sailors said the jetty was gone."

"It is, but there are other ways to land." Because there was no easy way to say this, he said it bluntly: "The monks of the island are dead, majesty. All of them."

The smoke he'd left behind had been their bodies, burning on a pyre. It had been as much as they could manage, he and Pao between them.

"Dead? How?"

"Killed. Cut down." That was the worst news, more cruel than their deaths.

"By whom?"

"Majesty, I do not know." There were pirates in the strait, of course—but even pirates should have known never to touch the Forge.

"They should be hunted down, whoever they were—but I can't spare the boats, nor the crews to sail them."

"No, majesty." Nor did it matter now. It was only the fact that mattered. "With the monks dead and the Forge cold, I think the dragon must be free."

"Ah. Yes. I have been hearing about your dragon." Of course he had; there was another fact that mattered, that they were not yet talking of. "You need to understand, Old Yen, we have mostly come down from the cold dry north, where dragons are not common. My people"—by whom he clearly meant his mother, his generals, facts that mattered—"do not quite believe in your dragon. I'm sorry."

"Majesty, the tsunami—"

"What, was that your dragon? We are inlanders; we saw a freak wave, nothing more. A tragedy, but not a myth. I think we expect the sea to do evil. I'm sure I do." He gazed across this more peaceable water, reflections broken a thousand times by the soft impacts of the rain. "If that was your dragon, unchained—where is she now? What prisoner lingers, once the door is open?"

"There was another stir in the water, majesty, just yesterday," not even a wave, nothing that he had ever seen before: just a sudden rise, enough to float his boat off the rocks sooner than expected and barely patched. It had seemed like water on a mission, water with intent. "I think we should not expect to understand the dragon. She is beyond us."

"Not beyond our prisoning, if your tales are true. A handful of monks kept her chained undersea, how long?"

"For centuries, majesty. Yes. Jade is beyond us, but not beyond our mining . . ."

The emperor smiled, and played with the rings he wore. "What do you know of jade, old man?"

"I know it is heaven-sent, and so sent back to the Son of Heaven." There was a rhyme that said so, that all the children of Taishu chanted in their games. "I had never seen it till now. But I never doubted its beauty."

"No. They told you it was true, and you believed it, and you were right. I'm not a fool, Old Yen, I understand the lesson. But you'll need more than dead monks and a freak wave to help my mother and all those tired soldiers believe in a dragon. We have crossed the empire and heard ten thousand stories on the way, and not seen the truth in any of them."

"Nevertheless, majesty. Some of them must be true. The dragon—"

"—is something we can't deal with, true or otherwise. If she rises, she could wash us all off this island on a whim, and we could not resist her. If she chooses not to—well, let your dragon lie, and your dead monks too.

"Talk to me about the coast. With the enemy in Santung, we're taking as many men as we can off the beaches, but it won't be enough. A lot of them will die. Some will get away into the hills. They'll find places to hide, and we need ways to contact them; it's useful, crucial, to keep men on the mainland. I won't abandon the empire, and Taishu can't feed all the men we've brought across already. Can it?"

"Not for long, majesty. If we make farmers and hunters of them, turn more land over to paddy and hunt out the forests, if we fish the seas dry, we can feed them for a season. Perhaps through the winter, if we all go hungry. In the spring, though? When the dried stores are gone, before the new crops come in? We go hungry as it is, some years. With this many to feed, we will all starve."

"Which is why I need men on the mainland, to gather supplies. And men with boats, to bring them. In the dark, secretly back and forth, with my enemies looking for them . . ."

"Of course, majesty. I can do that; I can find others who will do it with me."

"Good. This is your task, then. Whatever you need—men, supplies, repairs—it is yours, but you'll need something to show, a sign of my authority . . ."

The emperor pulled a ring from his finger. Old Yen almost shrieked, shying away from it, hands helplessly refusing.

"Majesty, that's jade!"

"Of course." The emperor frowned, which should have sent Old Yen to his knees, to his face, in an ecstasy of terror. "I said, something you could show."

For a commoner to keep a piece of jade . . . even in the raw, in the rock, let alone an imperial ring . . . "No, majesty. Not that." The boy had no idea, clearly, of the enormity of it. He might have crossed the empire, but he had never stood the other side of the wall. Old Yen tried to be reasonable, to scale the offense down to something an innocent would understand. "If any man of yours saw me with that, they would say I had stolen it, and send you my head with it when they returned the ring. It was a good thought, but give me your chop on a scrap of paper . . ."

The imperial seal would have been like a ring of jade, too much to hope for, too much to accept. The emperor's own chop, though, his own name stamped in red on something short-lived and wastrel: that could only have come fresh from his own hand. It couldn't be mistaken or misused.

"Do you have paper?"

"No, majesty."

"Pity. I have my chop," of course he did: in a pouch that hung from the complex weavings of his belt. "I could ink it on a leaf, I suppose . . ."

A leaf would last a day or two, enough to win what he most needed for his boat; not enough to recruit a team, men suited to hard and secret work in guarded lands. Old Yen was still trying to find a tactful way of saying *Think again* when the emperor chuckled, bent over, lifted the hem of his own robes.

Ripped out a hand's breadth of the lining.

He said, "Hold out your palm," and Old Yen did that. The emperor laid that stretch of silk across it, the lightest softest thing

Old Yen had ever touched or held. The emperor's own hand pressed the carved face of his soapstone seal into a little pot of cinnabar paste that he carried with the chop; with his other hand beneath Old Yen's to steady it—skin on skin, and would he ever get used to this?—the emperor stamped his chop onto the silk.

Pressed it down hard, rocked it a little to and fro; separated the soapstone carefully from the silk, looked and grunted.

"Anyone who knows my chop will know that."

"Majesty, anyone who can read will know that. Who else would dare?"

"Well. Keep the rain off, if you can."

Old Yen was already sheltering with one long hand what the other so cautiously held: already wondering what he could do with it, more than he had promised.

The emperor turned to go back to his mother and his generals, his war and other troubles. It was Old Yen's place to follow him, but the emperor glanced over his shoulder. "Don't come with me. Go that way," a nod of the head, a narrow path that wound between rhododendron bushes in the wet, "it'll bring you to a gate where the guards will let you out."

"Uh, majesty, I came with the general . . ."

"I will tell him I have sent you away. And I will tell him what you told me, so that he doesn't feel too wounded by your absence. You, Old Yen? You just go. That way."

And the emperor was almost beaming as he pointed, bubbling like a child with secrets that he's determined not to tell, that he can't help but give away.

OLD YEN couldn't move until the emperor had gone his way; no man may turn his back on god-on-earth and hope to live.

Besides, he hoped for more than life. He couldn't move.

Until he was alone, and then—slowly, uncertainly—he did make his way off the bridge and along the path. Awkwardly, with the frail silk in his hands, shielding it from any fall of water as he shouldered through the bushes, head down to watch his hands, his feet, not to trip or stumble at this crucial time, in this critical place. Hopeful.

Head down, he could only watch the path, his hands, his feet. He couldn't see what waited.

"GRANDFATHER!"

It was all he'd hoped for, more.

He stood quite still, to be sure of his footing; and lifted his head to see her plunging toward him, and fended her off with his elbows, crying, "Careful! This is precious . . ."

"Oh, what is it? What do you have?"

He had her voice in his ears, her body just a reach away. That was precious beyond measure. What he held only meant a few lives saved, perhaps the difference between starving and not starving come the spring. What did any of that matter, against a hug from her?

He said, "This is the emperor's chop, that I can use for all manner of good, if I don't let it smudge. You hold back."

She snorted, "I could get you a dozen of those," but held back like the girl she was, occasionally and briefly obedient until she could find her own way to what she wanted. On this occasion, that was a glance behind her, a swift gesture, someone coming forward to take the chop from him. Old Yen was reluctant to let it go, but he needed his hands. He surrendered it, with only the vaguest notion of who this person was who took it—a man in queue and cap, embroidered yellow: an imperial servant, then—and she said, "Hui will keep it till it's dry. That shouldn't be long, the silk soaks up the oil. Then he'll find a bamboo to roll it up in, safer than your sleeve, Grandfather," which was of course exactly where he would have kept it.

And then she seized his wrists and kissed his palms and smiled up at him, and said, "How are you? Tell me all the news, all of it . . ."

Well, he would do that; but first, "Was it you, then, who had the emperor send for me?"

"Of course!"

"How did you know, to do that?"

"Grandfather, all these palaces were full of our own people, Taishu people, before the emperor came. All his generals and councilors brought their own servants, but those are almost as grand. They're not cooks and laundrywomen. So all these palaces are still full of our own people, where there's work to be done.

"And of course they're also full of incomers, all the clerks and soldiers. Those are scared and exhausted and a long way from home, and they don't understand Taishu. They hardly know how to talk to us.

"So I make it easy for everyone to talk to me. Our own people do it because I'm one of them but they think I have the ear of the emperor; the incomers do it because I'm not one of them and they think I have the ear of the people. I knew you were coming before you were let in at Ping Wen's gate. I already knew you would come, because I saw you limping into harbor earlier," which was to say *I've been watching for you, all these days,* "and why would you come to Taishu-port except to bring news? So sit down and tell me, 'fess, you, what have you done to our boat . . . ?"

There was a bench to sit on, under a sheltering roof. He sat, and she splayed herself and her voluminous skirts at his feet and tried to play at being Mei Feng of old. Her dress betrayed her, heavy and intricate, a robe from a painting more than real life; he had trouble picturing his lithe and vigorous granddaughter in such a dress, even when she was right here wearing it. But then, his granddaughter, his crew knew no more about courtly life than she did about courtly dress; what was a simple village girl, a fishergirl doing, setting spies and making alliances?

What was she doing, pumping her grandfather now for information?

"Aren't those clothes uncomfortable?" he asked gruffly, meaning, *Don't you find all of this impossible, unbearable, this new life of yours?* Meaning that he was unbearably uncomfortable himself with the setting, the spying, the servants, even with her.

"Yes, of course," she said, meaning, *Yes, of course, but what choice do I have?* "I'm learning how to wear them, but they don't bend where I do."

She was young, she was flexible; it would be she that bent, necessarily. She was bending already.

He was old and stiff, but he could still adjust to a changing world. If he had access to the Son of Heaven, he couldn't allow himself to waste it.

He said, "Mei Feng, whatever we do now, however things fall out, it will be a long winter and a hungry spring to follow. We are the emperor's people as we always were, but his own people will stand between us and the throne. Worse, they are soldiers mostly, used to taking what they need."

She shrugged slightly. "So is he." She didn't say it as though it were a grief, as though she'd rather still be a fishergirl. Her man will change a woman, regardless of who or what he is.

The same was true the other way, that his woman will change a man. Old Yen knew. He said, "Even so. There will be limited food, and too many people; and if we let them, the soldiers will take all we have. We need to ensure that Taishu folk have a fair share."

"Grandfather, what can I do?"

"Ask your lord the emperor—"

"My lord the emperor," and she sounded bitter about it, no longer caring who heard or whom they told, "has people of his own, between him and the throne. Oh, he may sit on it, he may wear the jade rings, but they take what they want from him," meaning his power, his authority, his command. "If I showed him the starving in the street, he would have nothing to give them except his useless pretty things," by which Old Yen guessed she meant herself.

*B*y the end of the first day, she'd taken the rope off his neck.

Halfway through the second day—bored, he thought, by his submissiveness—she loosed his other bonds and simply trusted him to follow.

On the third day, when a path needed cutting, she handed him a tao.

Even so, Yu Shan was still entirely Jiao's prisoner. She still meant to sell him: just, not to the wagoners on the road, and not as a common slave.

"That stone you're carrying," she'd said on the first day, still cheerfully tugging him along by the halter, "I know just the person. He'd kill for it, if it's as good as you say. Just the size of it, that's going to drive him demented. He's a jade carver: loves his work, hates the man he works for, like they all do. And can't do anything about it. The stone belongs to the emperor, the trade belongs to the jademasters. You'd know that. So do I; he never stops grumbling.

"If I bring him a piece of jade the masters don't know about, with the emperor right there on his doorstep, he can make something glorious and deliver it in person, do himself some good and do the jademasters down at the same time. And what I'm thinking, he could use a boy in the workshop. One who knows the stone already. You're a smart lad; work hard, maybe he'll train you up apprentice, let you buy your freedom, you'd like that. You'll like the city, too . . ."

. . .

YOU COULDN'T call it a conversation, because he said nothing, only worked his little jade splinter with his tongue; but after that Yu Shan became conspicuously cooperative, so that day by day Jiao relaxed her watchfulness and his bondage. Not her tongue. She talked on the march or sitting still, building a fire or washing in a stream or plucking a bird for supper. Presumably she hunted in silence, but Yu Shan didn't see that. When he saw her, she seemed always to be talking. He thought perhaps she'd been alone for a while now, wasn't used to it, didn't like it.

He hardly spoke at all himself. He had always been the quiet one among a quiet people. Right now, he felt as though he'd lost his words entirely. It didn't seem to matter. He let her talk wash over him, and concentrated on what was his own: his body, his burden. His little stolen sliver of the stone. His life, his future. *His* . . .

THAT THIRD night, she set him tasks at evening: gathering leafy branches to weave into makeshift shelters against inevitable rain, seeking out dry wood, gathering nuts and berries while she hunted.

He made their separate beds, little roofed nests not too close together in a clearing by a stream, where the burbling water should cover other noises in the night. She spitted and roasted a pair of squirrels; they scorched their fingers as they ate, and tossed bones into the fire to sizzle and pop. She talked about this city ahead, other cities, the life of a wanderer. Unusually he talked himself, a little: about his family, his valley, the life of a boy who had never thought to wander.

Then there was settling down in the dark, in the last of the fire-glow. In the rain, a fine mizzle as though a cloud had rolled down off the mountains simply to sit on them.

It was gloomy and chilling, and suited both Yu Shan's mood and his ambitions. He lay still, barely tired after a long day of hack and carry, a long long way from sleep; he listened to the brook and waited for Jiao's silence first, and then longer. He waited for her snoring, and a little longer yet. He waited till—he hoped!—she would be deep in dreams, whatever a pirate soul might dream about.

Then slowly, slowly he drew himself up, set his feet beneath him, rose from under his rain shelter; slowly, slowly he took one step, a second step, a little distance and then a little more, farther and farther from the sleeping Jiao.

There was all the forest and all the night to lose himself in. He didn't want to be sold to a jade carver who would know him just exactly for what he was, which Jiao did not.

He didn't want to abandon his family's future either, the wonder-stone. Nor would he. Tough as she was, muscled with rawhide, Jiao couldn't carry it. He'd be impressed if she could lift it. All he had to do was hole up somewhere, close but not obvious; if she searched for him, she wouldn't do it long.

HE HAD come perhaps a hundred paces into the density of the forest. The darkness had closed like a door at his back, but it didn't trouble him at all; he was just starting to feel safe when there was a cold steel edge at his throat, and a laughing murmur in his ear. "Don't be in such a hurry, we'll move on in the morning."

He might have fought, he might have tried to run. But she had a tao, and he didn't; and she was fast and quiet through the forest, even tracking in the dark. And more, she sapped his hope, just with her competence.

So he did as she told him, and came back to the clearing. They hunkered down by the last hissing ghost of the fire, and she said, "Where did you think you would go?"

He shrugged. "Not far. You couldn't move the stone."

"So you would retrieve it, once I'd given up and gone. Of course. And what then?"

"I would take it to the emperor," as he was meant to, because he had no ideas else.

"And did you think I wouldn't watch the road? There isn't much more forest, my poor dim mule. After these last slopes, it's plain and paddy all the way, and only the road to go by. If you had gotten away, you'd have found me waiting."

"Why, though? What's so important about me?"

"About you, nothing. That stone's worth a fortune."

"Not to you. Your friend the jade carver doesn't have a fortune."

Which was incontrovertible, but leanly shrugged aside. He wondered how an outlaw woman and a jade carver might be friends, where they could have met, what drew them together. All his answers were perilous. Jade belonged to the emperor, and yet . . .

People did steal it; he knew. He had a sliver under his tongue. It wouldn't need guards on the road if there weren't thieves and smugglers. There must be a market, wealthy people in the empire who would buy jade although they could never be seen with it. Perhaps she dealt with such people, smuggling the carver's work to them?

Now more than ever, there must be a market. With the emperor on Taishu, those who had chased him here must be hungry for whatever legitimacy they could snatch at, as they didn't have the throne. A magnificent piece of stone magnificently carved, that might make a symbol to rally the people, to declare an end to one dynasty and the birth of another . . .

Jiao must be thinking that, or something like it, whatever she said about letting her jade-carver friend take it to the emperor. There was nothing there for her. For the moment, though, she had it all. She had a stone that the wagoners had never seen or recorded, that the jademasters knew nothing of. She had a boy to carry it, a man to carve it. Then all she need do was take it—with the boy, perhaps, to carry it again?—and find a boat, and yes, then, find a fortune . . .

He gazed at her across the fire's ashes, nothing more to say. She sighed, and her face was all in shadow but he thought he could hear a smile in it; and then she came around to him and said, "What am I to do with you now, mule?"

That was exactly what he'd been wondering. He hadn't anticipated her rough hand lightly on his cheek, her body so close to his own, her voice like a teasing breath in his ear. "I can't have you sneaking off in the night, because you're right, of course, I couldn't carry that stone. I'm astonished that you can. I suppose I could tie you up again, keep you leashed and hobbled, but that's tiresome for both of us. There is another choice, though, another way for me to know exactly where you are all night long . . ."

And then her hand was in his hair and her mouth came seeking his, challenging, demanding.

OFF-BALANCE ALREADY, frightened by her ruthless competence and his own perilous insights, he was suddenly scrabbling on a cliff edge, falling, lost.

And clung to her, or his hands did: felt whipcord muscles moving under sticky-wet skin, felt her body twisting as she somehow discarded clothing without ever leaving go of him. She swung one leg across to straddle him, settled her weight—light but firm, solid, startling—on his legs and dealt swiftly with his tunic top.

Her fingers, her nails on his chest, on his back, dragging trails of fire . . .

He had no say in this, apparently; she saw no need of further words. Her mouth was too busy for talking: tasting, testing, lips and tongue together. Teeth, too, nipping at him now.

Her every touch made him gasp for air that seemed suddenly too thin and too warm. He felt his last resistance crumble even as his body stiffened; *yes* and *no* were both equally impossible, irrelevant. He was her prisoner, her possession. What was there to be said?

Her skin tasted salt, and rainy too; her mouth was like tea, freshly bitter. She chewed some herb as she walked, when she wasn't talking or singing. Often when she was.

All her body, her unhurried urgency was a life-lesson. Time with his clan-cousin had been—well, not like this. Jiao was rough when she wanted to be, enticing his own strength, roughness in response; or she was gentle but not tentative, teasing but not pleading. What she wanted, she knew how to make him give. Or not give, how to hold him back, delay him, make him sweat and grunt in sudden peril. She mocked him, he thought, but only a little, and no more than she mocked herself.

Just once she was puzzled, tumbled out of her certainty. She held his head still, and slipped a finger into his mouth where her tongue had been. Probed, and watched him flinch, and said, "What is that?"

"Just a sore," he said, "it's nothing."

"There's a hardness . . ."

"Yes," a splinter of stone, that he'd worked into the flesh to stop her finding it. "It's infected, I think. It'll swell and burst and be foul for a day, then it'll heal. Just a forest fever. It'll pass."

OR ELSE it wouldn't, nothing would. The night was timeless, a hiatus, without stars. The fire was dead, the rain eternal. There was nowhere to be but here.

seven

*W*ith their captain exposed, humiliated, chained, the crew of the *Shalla* had no instinct to rise up and fight their seasick overlords.

Nevertheless, a random two swung heavily dead from her mastheads, upsetting her balance and every man who sailed her. Every man of whom wore his own noose of wet rope as a collar now. The noose was a constant reminder that any or all of them could be as swiftly dead; the rope was wet because everything was wet, because a constant unseasonal storm was battering the strait.

Han had his own collar, although he was no sailor. He spent the storm hunched miserably belowdecks with Suo Lung, pumping out the bilges, feeling the *Shalla* toss and shudder as the sea churned, as she twisted under the weight and sway of water in her bilges. He thought she might tear herself apart before ever they made port. This was no natural storm, and there was no limit to the dragon's temper. Han had lost that brief link, where their minds had touched; contact now was distant and various and fearful, glimpses of vast dark furies and awesome dreams.

It would be more than hard, impossibly hard to hold a course up top, running under bare poles with the seams working and water everywhere and her captain in chains below, through the thunderous savagery of a dragon's rage.

Add that the crew worked under Jorgan, who had always been second on this ship and was utterly unused to command, distraught with it; add that Jorgan and all of them worked under

watch, from men with weapons drawn; add that those men's officers were spewing and wretched in the captain's cabin, keeping no
kind of watch on their men. Add too that the crew knew only that
their lives were in peril on the journey and in peril too at the end
of it, and Han was astonished that they sailed anywhere at all,
that the wind or the sea or the men's despair didn't just hurl them
onto the rocks of the lee shore.

Down in the hold there, he couldn't see their crawling crabwise
progress. He and Suo Lung could only see each other by the thin
dark glimmer of a lamp: pale exhausted faces, rocking back and
forth with the pump's long handle. They didn't talk. There was no
point in trying, above the riotous sounds of wind and water; besides, there was nothing to say. No one brought them news. They
were the forgotten of hell, neglected and alone, and the *Shalla*
might have been anywhere, any moment likely to be their last . . .

Except that he knew just exactly where they were, all the time.
The dragon knew it, and so did he. He knew where she was, without pausing to think; he could point, down through the hull and
through the waters, *there.*

He didn't think she meant to drown him now, where she still
couldn't reach him. This was a temper tantrum, a child kicking
against its reins, a prisoner railing against chains. But she might
break the boat anyway, regardless of intent. She might simply not
know how eggshell-fragile it was in her mind's grip, in her storm's
toss.

He pumped in hopes, and because he'd been told to, and because it kept him busy, kept him warm; and because Suo Lung had
to be doing something, and this was all there was; and because the
Shalla was a good ship and deserved kinder treatment than she'd
had. It was even possible that their pumping might keep her afloat,
if the dragon didn't tear her keel out, if the wind didn't overthrow
her.

He listened to the suck and swirl of water too close beneath his
feet, the relentless pounding of great waters on either side, the
frail creak of timbers in between; and tried to listen for the

dragon's thoughts behind and around all that noise, for the same real reason that he pumped, because it might after all make a difference.

Perhaps it did.

Perhaps they did both make a difference, the pumping and the listening. He heard the dragon strain against her chains, and tried to quiet her; he let her hear his own strain against the pump, its futile swoosh-and-gurgle against the pounding of the storm, the leaking of the vessel all around him, how the sea broke in between all the seams of her working timbers.

Slowly, slowly the waters stilled, the wind dropped, the junk ceased her dreadful heaving. Instead she wallowed, but Han and Suo Lung could help that now. Exhausted as they were, they flung the pump handle between them, heard the water spurt and knew that the *Shalla* grew imperceptibly lighter, higher in the water with every stroke. The sea was still oozing in, but she wasn't twisting against her stem any longer, her timbers didn't gape at every movement.

Jorgan could nurse her to safe harbor, governing sails and tiller in the post-storm quiet, governing her crew.

It took so many men, to keep her afloat and bring her home. She was a simple thing, this junk, against the ferocious complexity of the dragon below the sea; and to control the dragon there was only Han, with only Suo Lung to call on.

It wasn't, it could never be enough.

All they had, though.

It would have to do.

"BREATHE."

He was breathing. It was about all that he could manage. Finally fallen away from the pump, blistered hands and aching shuddering arms unable to push that handle one more time, he lay on his back on the deck with those jellyfish arms tossed up behind his head, weighted there by his chain, simply beyond him now.

He lay and breathed, as Suo Lung told him to.

No, he didn't.

"The dragon's word," Suo Lung said. Somewhere there was still a little lamplight, a little work to do. Here was dizziness and sparks and nothing: the cold wet greasy wood he lay on, words in his ears, breath in his body. Nothing. He felt as hollow as the air, and as useless. "Breathe," the big man said, his voice perhaps something to hold on to.

He wasn't sure his own voice held anything that Suo Lung could actually hear, but he said, "How can she breathe underwater?"

Suo Lung would be shrugging, massive and silent. He never could answer questions. Had his own chains ever actually said BREATHE? Han had no way to tell. The words he gave Han did something, every new word added to the link between boy and dragon, but Han didn't feel at all that he controlled her. They were chained together, mind to mind; all he could hope to do was persuade.

"Breathe," he said. "Yes. I can write that for you. Later . . ." When his hands could work, when there was light and time, when his thoughts weren't so giddy or his bones so empty. When they were in harbor, perhaps, wherever these soldiers meant to take them. If the soldiers had survived the storm, if the crew hadn't seized the ship and freed her captain, if Li Ton wasn't even now in command again . . .

LI TON was not free and not in command. Han proved that to himself, once he was sure that he could move and not pass out, not throw up, not have his legs suddenly fail beneath him.

The pump was in the well of the junk, deep belowdecks. The lower hold was in the bows. Han slung his chain around his neck, and left Suo Lung in the dark; with their little light cupped between his fingers, he made his way forward.

Even a short boy could crack his head down here. It was good to have a chain so heavy, shoulders so tired, to feel so utterly worn; he had such a stoop already, he barely needed to crouch under the brute-low beams. He might have crawled, if he'd thought his arms would hold him.

The upper holds had hatches, directly from the deck; this had a door. Which was bolted, but not watched. Perhaps the guard had fled the savage tossing solitude of his post, sought out company to drown with.

There was a hole rough-chopped into the wood of the door, big enough to pass food and water through, not big enough to pass a man. Plenty big enough to spy through.

Han lifted his light to the hole, and peered in.

There was the captain in his nakedness, in his tattoos, in his chains. He didn't move, except to look up at the light. He said, "Is my ship well?"

"Uh, yes, sir. I think so. She will be . . ."

"You, is it, boy? Are you the cause of my curse, should I have killed you before ever I let you aboard?"

"Yes, sir, I think so. But you shouldn't have killed the monks. You set the dragon free."

"Oh, damn your dragon. I've sailed all the coast from Pan Gut to the Holy Isles, and never seen a dragon. I have seen storms and tsunamis, and I've seen them both sink ships. It's only weather, boy. Will you leave me the light?"

"Yes, sir, if you want it."

Li Ton stirred, reached. "I'd like a little light, for a little while. Until they make up their minds to play emperor and kill me."

"They won't . . ."

"Why not? It's a way to assume his place, if they adopt his enemies as their own. But let me have light in the meantime; I will always have something to read," his own body, indicated by his own ironic hand.

His chains made the stretch difficult, spiked as they were into the floor of the hold, but his hand came close enough to take the lamp when Han reached it in through the hole.

"Thanks, lad. Now run away, before—"

Too late for that: there was a step behind him, a man in the gangway, a grip on his neck. A cold damp grip, and the man stank sourly of vomit. So much water in and around the ship, Han thought he might at least have washed.

"What do you want here, boy?"

"Sir, I came to see the captain. Is it forbidden? Ow!"

"He is not the captain. He is the prisoner, condemned. And you are a slave, and anything not ordered is forbidden to you. And you have given him a light, when the commander said that he could sit in darkness . . ."

Every accusation was punctuated with a blow. That didn't matter. Han was a seasoned hand at being manhandled; his yelps were more ritual than real.

When he was let go, he scuttled back to Suo Lung and found him waiting, the soul of focused patience. He had kept his tools beside him in the storm, not to lose what was most precious; in the dark, he had rummaged for and found his scribing-tool.

HIGH ON the foredeck, then, in light and air, he cut this new character with slow muddled concentration into Han's chains, seeking to bind the dragon with yet one more flimsy thread. The peak was a place to be fond of, a discreet vantage point; Han brought Suo Lung here often, to keep the big man out of the way of smaller men who might not see the point of him. He had done it under Li Ton's command and he did it now, with some kind of makework for their hands that might or might not cover their work on his chains.

The dragon's temper had scoured sea and air together, to leave a scrubbed blue sky and quiet, clear water. The junk was the only ugly thing abroad, straining to catch the breeze, rowdy with men and awkward to the eye.

Not running for the shore, though. That had been Han's expectation and the crew's too, that they would seek harbor and start the hard round of repairs again: caulking seams and patching sails, mending rigging and restowing jumbled stores.

Instead, the new commander ordered the *Shalla* westward, lying close in to the coast until they came to a great gathering of boats all together in a rivermouth.

There were river junks, such as Han hadn't seen since he was a child. There were seagoing junks much like the *Shalla*, only none so big. There were fishing boats and ferries, all kinds of craft, anything that floated. Some were roped together like prisoners or slaves in coffle; some were anchored separately or beached, but they were all clearly one fleet under one command.

Even now, the *Shalla* didn't turn her bows to land. Instead she flung out an anchor and hung a flag from a staff at the stern: a declaration, a message that caused flurry ashore and then a small flotilla of rowboats heading out toward them.

The decks were cleared of idlers, but not the peak where Han and Suo Lung sat in the shadow of a sail. They watched while tough men, important men, were hailed aboard, men before whom the *Shalla*'s new commander was quietly respectful. Those men stood in a knot on the well-deck and waited; and here came one man more, too splendidly dressed for the awkward transit from sampan to junk, too heavily fleshed among all those lean soldiers. He made the transit without awkwardness, though, a practiced strength in him that did not show through his silks and colors. Then he nodded to the commander, stamped on the deck and said, "Good. This will do for a flagship, to lead our squadron to Santung."

From their faces, Han wasn't the only one who thought she was ill chosen. Her current commander was bold enough to say it. "General, we have to pump her belly constantly, she's shipping so much water; and she is clumsy in any weather, and will be until we can restow her cargo—"

"What is her cargo?"

"Sir, I don't believe anybody knows. There is no manifest, and the holds are in chaos after these storms. It's pirate gleanings, but what's in there . . ."

"Throw it out," the general said decisively. "Keep timber, rope, chain, iron of any sort; everything else goes overboard. That should ease her belly. What more?"

"One thing more, General. Also in a hold, but not quite cargo. This you might want to keep . . ."

• • •

GENERALS DO not stoop below low beams, or peer by oil-light through bolted doors. Li Ton was dragged up on deck, still naked in his chains. If he relished sun on his skin and sweet salt air, it didn't show; all his effort was in standing when he was allowed to and holding himself pridefully erect when he wasn't, when the guards forced him to his knees.

Even at his most terrifying, Li Ton had always been impressive; he still was, even in his utter degradation. He was foul of skin and weak with hunger, dizzy in the glare and dry as a husk. Someone flung a bucket of seawater over him, to wash off the stink of the bilges. Even that he endured, in the bitter silence that he seemed to have fetched up with him like a shadow from his cell.

When the two men were brought to face each other, it was like an inversion of how Han had always seen the captain, alone but surrounded by others, the focus of all eyes. Nothing had changed, he was still alone and surrounded, but everything was different. Now he was on his knees, and they looked down on him.

The general was a soft-spoken man, and Li Ton was suddenly worse; his voice was a cracked whisper. Han really shouldn't have been able to hear. But Suo Lung had cut the character for "listen" into a link of his chain yesterday; and if they imposed a little of their will on the dragon, he thought perhaps he could borrow back a little of the dragon's strength or skill, a fraction of her magic.

"CAPTAIN MA. I told you, did I not, that your shadow would never grow slimmer? You were a hopeful young man, and I am gratified to see that you have achieved prosperity in your age."

"I am comfortable in my skin, thank you, and in my position—though I hope to grow fatter yet. I am General Ma now; we meet as equals, General Chu Lin."

"Not quite, alas," which might be the closest he could come to making an exhibition of his nakedness, his tattoos, his maiming and his chains. His captors had already made an exhibition of them, but that was beneath his notice. "I lost that name when I lost my rank; I am called Li Ton these days. And I am only a captain now. We have quite changed places, you and I. But this is my ship, the *Shalla,* and so I welcome you to her."

"My ship now, I fear. I must claim her from you."

"Well, perhaps. You may find that she makes up her own mind about that; she has always been a very independent vessel. Which you are not, General, or at least you never were. Unless the gods have rebuilt your character to match your waistline. Who commands?"

"There is a council . . ."

"I am sure, but who commands?"

"Tunghai Wang has chief voice among us."

"Tunghai, is it? Is he still alive? Funny, I was sure the old man would have his head."

"It would seem that even you can be wrong about men—Li Ton, is it, did you say?"

"I did, and it is. And yes, it would seem so. So is the old man really dead?"

"Emperor Chien Sung died three winters gone."

"Finally. How old was he?"

"It is said that the empire was blessed by his rule for a hundred perfect years."

"Damn them, they even take more time than they're entitled. Still only the one boy, though?"

"Indeed."

"Tragic. So long a life, and so little to show for it," though the sourness in his voice might itself have counted as one of the late emperor's achievements.

"His imperial majesty did leave a great and thriving empire for the young Chien Hua to inherit . . ."

". . . Which Tunghai promptly tried to seize for himself, is that right?"

"It was felt that the young emperor was—well, too young, and his mother too much of an influence. He needed governance, she needed shortening by a head. We proposed a council to advise him in her place; she fled, and took him with her."

"And you have harried her and him across the empire's breadth, and still not gotten what you wanted, or it would be Emperor Tunghai by now, with a boy's head rotting on his gates."

"Perhaps." General Ma seemed suddenly to realize that he was being interrogated here by his own prisoner. He waved all that matter aside and said, "What of your own life, Li Ton? You were exiled, your own body proclaims it, and I myself saw the sentence passed."

"And carried out."

"That too." The tattoos, he must mean, and the mutilation. "And yet, here you are . . ."

"Why didn't I crawl off into some far craven corner of the world and die, you mean, as I was meant to? Because if the old man lacked the nerve to order it done to me, I was damned if I'd do it to myself. He did . . . this . . . and I thought it was enough. Well, no. I didn't think that, I didn't think anything, I was out of my mind with pain and fever; I could go mad, but I was just a little too stubborn to let myself die. I begged and mumbled my way to the coast, lived off garbage and gutter-leavings, eventually found a place where the empire doesn't reach. I learned to be a fisherman first, and then a pirate. Not well enough, seemingly."

"Oh, as well as any pirate does, I fancy. It's written into the fate of every emperor to live a dangerously long time—unless he's a boy, of course, with the bad habit of listening to his mother—and it's written into the fate of every pirate to die quite soon, and quite unpleasantly. It must be thirty years since you were exiled. That's eminently respectable. It's almost unique. Would you care to share your secret with an old friend?"

"No secret. Just a good ship, a greedy crew, and no compunction in their captain. Hatred for the empire, that helps too—but only as a sweetener, I should have known not to let it drive me. With so many rumors abroad—rebellion, the emperor in flight— I thought the jade ships might be vulnerable, so I came west to try a little raiding. I never dreamed you'd let the boy come this far."

"Neither did we, but the gods were against us. Everywhere I look, people are living longer than they ought. I must have a word with the man who casts horoscopes for me; he neglected to mention that. But perhaps we should not run contrary to what the gods decree. There may be ways that you can continue to defy my expectations. It might be a pity to put an end to a man who hates the emperor quite as much as you do."

"Be careful, General. It's the empire I despise, not that runaway boy. I don't blame him for what his father did; I blame all of you. Especially you and those like you, those who were there and might have stopped it. Tunghai, he was there . . ."

"Oh, indeed. I understand that. But that boy is the empire, and so long as he lives, so does the Jade Throne and all that that implies. Including what was done to you, which none of us dared speak against. Bring him down and his dynasty dies with him; and then, who knows? Your exile would be revoked, that much is certain. Besides, you've said already that you find yourself unexpectedly tenacious of life. If the choice was to work with us or else to die a pirate's death, I think I know which one you would elect. The offer must come from Tunghai Wang, if it comes at all; but perhaps I can give you food for thought in the meantime. Which of your men has known of your condition?"

"What, that I was exiled and condemned? Only Jorgan. It was he who found me in the gutter, his boat that took me out of imperial reach."

"Indeed? Commander, pass the word for this man Jorgan."

JORGAN WAS found and fetched. Perhaps he came willingly, seeking recognition for his good work in holding ship and crew together. Perhaps he thought he was safe.

Even after he saw Li Ton on deck, perhaps he still thought he was safe. Perhaps he thought he'd been fetched to stand witness: the long-delayed execution of a traitor and its happy sequel, the elevation of ship's mate to ship's master . . .

If he thought any of that, he must have been quickly disabused. By the men who seized his arms, most likely, or else the one who ripped the *Shalla*'s iron ring from his ear.

The general spoke a few swift words of sentence, and Han tried not to listen further, but some stories are not so easily set aside.

They made no effort to silence Jorgan; his screams were a part of his punishment, Li Ton's lesson, a warning to the crew.

They twisted his arms behind his back and tied them with one end of a long rope, which they rove through a block on the mast-head, the same that had hanged Half-Mouth before the storm. This time it hanged a living man, for the time they took to work on him.

Because he wasn't watching except in glances, Han couldn't tell how soon Jorgan's shoulders broke, from being turned so wrongly against the joint with all his weight hung from them. Not soon, because he was writhing so much for so long; before the end, certainly, because he was trying to writhe and couldn't achieve it, could only scream every time his torso twisted and broken edges of bone bit hard against each other. And yet he did try to writhe, because hanging still was worse; the pain of what they did to him outweighed the pain of trying to escape it, as the mountain outweighs the rockfall.

They cut his clothes away, with careless clumsy knives that left him dripping blood onto the deck. That was nothing, except that Li Ton would want to see it scrubbed.

They fetched cords and boards and bamboo poles, and made him scream a dozen different ways. Han saw him beaten where he hung; he saw his feet and ankles bound with boards and crushed slowly together, till they were a broken bloody pulp; he saw the same thing done to his genitals.

He saw his eyes put out with a knife, his ears sliced away.

Not his tongue, or what would he have to scream with?

Finally, it might have been an hour after they began, the rope was cut and Jorgan was let fall. He was kicked and prodded to his knees—and again Han's hearing was too good for this, he could hear how the man's broken voice still made a bewildered, agonized kind of sense—and a gesture from General Ma brought an eventual mercy, far too late. One swift blow from a long sword and Jorgan's head fell away, rolling some distance from the spurting slump of his body as the deck swayed in the swell.

. . .

THEY WERE two more days in the rivermouth, while General Ma's squadron was gotten ready for a brief sail up the coast; and there were men enough to do what work they could, so Han and Suo Lung could still spend some time on the peak.

And, bizarrely, Li Ton could spend it with them. Still in his chains, still naked, but at least he could be washed and fed and watered, he could sit in the air and the light. He could talk, even, with the idlers of what was once his crew.

If not a changed man, he was at least a quiet one. Disarmed, he could afford to be disarming.

"Sir . . ."

"Who am I—or who was I, rather, to deserve all of this," his scars and other marks, his treatment past and present and to come, "that's what you want to ask me, is it, boy?"

"Sir, yes. Please . . ."

"When I was Chu Lin, I was a soldier in the emperor's service. The then-emperor, this boy's father. He was a great man, we thought he was eternal: centenarian already, and as robust as any of us. He'd have fought his own wars still, if the court had let him. Even emperors have to listen to their servants, though. You thought I was in command of the *Shalla*? Only by the crew's consent, with Jorgan to achieve it. My poor Jorgan . . .

"Well. I fought for the emperor, and did it too well; he raised me to general too young. And sent me to fight a war I couldn't win, and so I lost it. The Son of Heaven never overreaches, so it must have been my fault; and so. As you see. Does that satisfy you, boy?"

No, of course it didn't, though he said it did. Li Ton smiled, and told him stories; and eventually said, "I am sorry about your monks, on the island." Not *I am sorry about your thumb*, because of course he wasn't and he wouldn't lie about it. "I dislike killing for no purpose; sometimes I have a purpose and still dislike it. I had heard that the monks protected shipping in the strait. That's why I had them slain, to give me safe access to the jade ships."

He hadn't misheard, he'd only half heard and misunderstood. The monks protected shipping and more, all the people of the empire, because they kept the dragon chained. Until Li Ton came by to kill them all. Now Han had to do it, and he did it badly, with only the smithy slave to help; and there were armies on both sides of the strait and a great fleet building, and all that meant was more men to the slaughter, if the dragon rose.

When. When she rose.

FOUR

Links in the Chain

one

For Old Yen, the hard thing wasn't saying no to the soldiers, *no, you may not come back with us to Taïshu. We have orders that require you to stay.*

The hard thing was saying no to the civilians: the desperate women with their filthy starving children, the few—the very few—men who had escaped the horror that was Santung. *No, Taishu is over-full; we cannot feed the mouths we have. Stay here among the peasants, live as they do, grow rice and glean the forests.*

He was meant to say *grow rice for us, for your emperor, in secret; we will come to claim it when we can,* but he was too ashamed to do that. He thought the emperor would also be ashamed, if he could see these people.

He didn't imagine that would make any difference to the order, but he still thought the boy would feel shame.

He would have ignored the order, of course—an old man in his own boat, what did he know of orders or obedience, what did he need of an emperor?—but that he had soldiers aboard who would enforce it.

Soldiers he had picked himself from the hordes overwhelming his island, his village, his own house. Wherever he went now there were hard men, staring. Much of the time they stared across the sea, looking for boats, for danger coming, cruelty and terror. Otherwise they stared about them, looking for whatever they could take. Individually, perhaps, strangers on a shore, they might have looked for a way to live, for a home. But they were masses, locusts, rapacious; they would devastate Taishu before they knew it, before they had learned to care.

He was afraid of many things, and most of those came back to the soldiers.

Nevertheless, night after night, he and his sergeant and his dozen men slipped across the water. He taught the men to sail as they went, he taught them how to fish; he found quiet coves on the mainland shore to anchor in, and the sergeant led half his men away into the dark.

If he hadn't left the other half aboard, he'd have returned to find his transport gone. All up and down the coast, stray soldiers fled from Santung or cut off by her fall hid in caves and bamboo groves and watched the water with a desperate hunger. With armed men against them, they'd wait for the sergeant's return, listen to his orders. Listen, at least. Even a sight of the emperor's chop wouldn't guarantee their obedience now, after the emperor had abandoned them. But they were never enough or bold enough to overrun the boat; and the sergeant said that if they turned bandit now, they would be the rebels' problem and not the emperor's, and that was all to the good.

Old Yen didn't believe there was any good to be found in banditry, but he kept quiet. Stray or located, obedient or rebellious, the soldiers were not his concern.

The refugees, though, they absolutely were.

As now, here:

in the shelter of a creek, in the still of a warm wet night, where outflowing riverwater met incoming tidewater in a tussle that slapped against the flank of the boat;

where the men left behind were gathered in the stern, sitting in a circle on the deck, playing some idle game that involved tossing a knife over and over into the sternpost, which had already made him more angry than he could say;

where he was alone in the bows—missing Pao almost as much as he missed his granddaughter, but he didn't need the boy with all these men aboard, and preferred to leave him safe behind—when he saw them come, three figures of darkness moving down the slope, down the creek toward the boat, the soldiers, him.

Nervous, but determined: they could hear the soldiers, no doubt, but they could see the boat. The first might be a terror; the second might be salvation. On they came.

Eventually, because they would not stop, he went to meet them.

They were no threat. Sound travels, over water; their silence was eloquent. So were the sudden clutches, one to another. He could see when their courage left them, when they froze entirely together as the men laughed, as one stirred and stood and came to the rail to piss over the side.

They were women, women and girls. He was sure of that, and not afraid except for them; and wet enough already in the soft steady rain. He let a rope down and went over the side.

He hated to leave the boat like this, but the alternative was to let the women come to him, which would be to give them over to the soldiers, and that was no alternative at all.

Down the hanging rope, then, and swim slowly ashore, an aged huffing walrus in the water; pull himself out and shake his head, wring out his beard, find a rock on open ground and sit wetly on it; wait for the women to come to him. They'd come this far, they wouldn't balk now. And he couldn't make himself seem any safer, an old man conspicuously alone, foolishly dripping riverwater . . .

ONE WOMAN, two girls. The moon had just edged high enough to throw its light into this narrow creek. A mother and her daughters: and the one little girl reminded him cuttingly of Mei Feng when she first came to crew for him, wide-eyed and stubborn and protective; the other was older, too old for her own content or safety. She should have been like Mei Feng now, fierce and delightful and growing away from everyone who loved her. Instead she was closed in, hunched over, silent in her mother's wake. It was her little sister who held her hand, not, as it should have been, the other way around. Old Yen found it far too easy to guess what had happened to her.

Before any one of them had spoken, he said, "No. I am sorry, but I cannot take you to Taishu."

"You must," the woman said. "Take the girls, at least."

The little one made a movement of protest, *We won't go without you,* but it made no difference. He shook his head. "I *cannot.* We have no food, no roofs. My own house is full of soldiers, as my boat is," deliberately drawing her attention to them, and the steady *chunk!* of their knife in his sternpost. "The emperor forbids me to take any more across the strait."

"But my girls . . ."

"Will be safer on this side of the water. It is true," he said, believing it. "The emperor's men are no kinder than those you have met already. It makes no difference whom they serve, the Son of Heaven or the rebel lords; they are men adrift, out of their proper place, greedy for whatever they can grab. Would you put your girls within their reach? You would be sorry for it, before we were out of hearing."

"Ohh . . ." She was half persuaded, but, "What shall I do?"

She had fixed on this one thing, to cross the water to Taishu; she had found a way apparently to do it; now he had taken that away from her, and left her bereft.

He said, "Here," and pressed a package into her hand, cold rice pressed into a cake and tied in a palm leaf to keep dry. It should have been his supper. "Feed them tonight. And look up; see there," where the moon made a looming shadow of the cliff-head, "see that silhouette above the water?"

"Yes, I see. What is it?"

"An old temple to the Li-goddess." He knew it, twice over: he knew all the landmarks along this coast, and he knew all her particular places. "No one uses it now, the people hereabouts won't go there. Take your daughters; she will give you shelter."

"We give flowers and rice cakes to the Li-goddess." That was the little girl, the bold one. "For her festival day, at the big temple in the city."

"Yes." He wondered if anyone would, this year: if her temple

was still standing, if her nuns were still living, if anyone would remember or have the rice or the courage to spare. "Now you can
stay beneath her roof a little while, and fetch her flowers every day,
and eat your rice with her," and pray that she find them more rice
and somewhere else to live, because the goddess would not keep
them long. You couldn't play turn-and-turn-about with heaven.

"Why won't the people go there?"

Of course the mother had to ask; she was still helplessly, hope-
lessly trying to protect her children.

He said, "Because they think it's haunted."

"Is it so?" The little girl again, uncertain whether to be sneering-
brave or frightened.

He wouldn't lie to her; his words touched sacred things tonight,
and the Li-goddess would be listening. "They have seen lights
move in the night, and they think that was a ghost. Me, when I see
lights move in the night, on this coast, I usually think it is a sailor."
By which of course he meant a smuggler, but he could tell truth
without telling it all. "If I'm wrong, then I think it would be the
goddess herself, moving about in her house. She wouldn't let evil
spirits dwell."

The girl looked at him with a cynical eye, but seemed to see that
he at least believed it. She nodded, and looked up at the temple
again; and said, "It's on the wrong side of the creek," meaning
We're on the wrong side of the creek, "and the ford's a long way
back from here. Too far for my sister to walk."

He thought they were dealing in the same currency here; she
too was telling the truth, and not all of it. Her elder sister was
probably too distraught to walk so far, drifting internally, but her
mother was a consideration also.

As it happened, Old Yen agreed with her. The woman's hopes
had been invested in a boat and escape, absence, elsewhere. What
he'd proposed was the opposite, a fixed spot, staying. Small wonder if it didn't inspirit her.

No point suggesting they swim across the creek. But there was
his sampan on the bank, which the sergeant and his soldiers had

used to come ashore. He said, "I can take you across, if you will climb the bluff. There is a path," or there used to be. That was long ago, but there should still be a ghost of it through the rocks and scrub. The little girl would find it; the goddess would show it to her, or the moonlight would. Perhaps they were the same.

two

"Why won't you call me by my name?"

Sometimes he asked the stupidest questions.

Sometimes he liked to bring her to what he called the throne room, when the council wasn't meeting there. It was the mansion's audience hall, on the first great courtyard just beyond the house gate, and to her it was immense, profligate, the grandest human building she'd ever been inside. Of course they'd set the Jade Throne here, of course it was his throne room. But the eunuchs and generals and his mother too, they shrugged and sneered and called it by other names, as though it demeaned the Jade Throne to stand anywhere so mean and parochial.

He liked to sit on the throne and talk, just the two of them in this vast empty hollow echoing space. It unnerved her, but that wasn't why he brought her here. To him this really was a mockery; the throne did look absurd within its cramping walls, beneath its low and humiliating roof. Perhaps he liked it because that made him feel less magnificent, more human. Or perhaps it was because people would leave him alone in here, because they feared and respected the throne itself, even if they neither feared nor respected him.

She neither feared nor respected the throne, but that was down to her ignorance, she knew that. She'd had it explained to her, again and again.

Him, now, him she could both fear and respect. To a degree. Both were limited, a little, by how she'd heard him fart in bed. Still she would not, could not call him by his name.

She sat—uncomfortably at first, though she was getting used to it—on a little carved ivory stool at his feet, and said, "Because you are emperor, lord, and I am only a commoner." Even the great of the empire did not call him by his name. Even his mother should not, at least in public hearing. Mei Feng never did, even when she knew they were alone.

He said, "You don't act like a commoner. Nor a noble either."

She twisted her head upward and smiled at him. "No, lord. Not if you mean calling you majesty and banging my head on the floor. You wouldn't want me to do that."

"No. You might bloody your nose," and his fingers tweaked it gently, just to make her smile again. Then they lingered, rested on her cheek; she grunted, and let them steer her head to where it could rest against his leg, nestled into the stiff silks of his robe.

She'd called him lord at first because she was so ignorant. Now she did it because she liked it, and because she thought so did he.

His name, though—no. She would not call him by his name. There was always someone to hear.

Except in here, perhaps, if they spoke softly. She glowered suspiciously at the boards beneath her feet: ancient wood, the planks so darkly varnished, so tightly joined that she could barely see that they were planks at all. No mortal sound could find its way through those. She drummed her heels on the floor in any case, to avert unfriendly spirits. "Lord?"

He almost sighed, he almost laughed; he must have been expecting it. It wasn't proper to ask the emperor questions, still less to ask him favors, yet she did. And she talked to him, and told him what she heard; and listened to him, challenged him, argued when she thought he was wrong or weak or idle. She couldn't call him a coward afraid of his mother, or too lazy to stand up to his generals; but she could think it, and she could let him understand that she thought it, even while she stepped with ostentatious care from word to lily-pad word above the darker waters of her thoughts.

Sometimes that was enough to goad him into a sudden reversal, a pronouncement in public or in council that couldn't be opposed or ignored.

Sometimes, of course, he would just say no to her. Sometimes he thought she was wrong, and said so.

Sometimes, perhaps, he was right. What did she know of empires, politics, armies?

She knew her people, though, she knew her island; and she knew what was happening out there beyond the palace walls. She said, "Lord, Taishu welcomed you and all those who came with you, all your officials, all your troops. You are the Son of Heaven, and they want to love you. They will love you, if you will allow them. But it's hard, when your soldiers try so hard to make them hate you."

He frowned and said, "I don't understand you." Which was a lie, of course, because this was the same note on the same string that she had plucked and plucked for days and weeks on end. She might have been impatient with him for pretending, but he was a boy, and they did that. Besides which, he was emperor and she was a fishergirl, and it thrilled her beyond measure that he would stoop so far as to lie to her.

She pulled a face at him, only to see his smile; then she said, "Lord, you do. Every day there is news," and she knew that he heard it, because she made sure to tell him. Not the scrolls she couldn't read, but her own people's messages. "Women are raped or enslaved, men are killed for no reason, whole villages are driven from their homes and fields, everyone is hungry now and frightened all the time—and all of this in your name, so is it any wonder if the people hate you?"

"Not in my name, Mei Feng. Not all of it." He had spotted her lie. Of course he had; he was emperor, and trained to listen for the meanings in every word. Besides, he was a boy, and sensitive of honor. "Not rapes and slaves and killing."

"No, lord—but they are still your men who do it."

"Maybe so. There is little I can do, Mei Feng. I told my generals to keep better order among their men." *After the last time you complained, or the time before.* "I'm sure they've done all they could—"

"All they cared to do, you mean. Lord."

"Yes. That's what I mean, of course; and no, I don't suppose they do care. Much. They have other priorities; they can't always be watching the men for faults."

"Well, but they have commanders, captains, sergeants . . ."

". . . All of whom are watching the sea and waiting for invasion. That matters more."

"We are your people too, lord."

"Yes—and Taishu is mine, more than anywhere else in the empire it is mine; and if I have to keep here awhile then so does my army. You must learn to lie quiet beneath the sword, Mei Feng. Only for a while, until this danger passes."

She saw no prospect of its passing. The rebels wouldn't lose patience and go away; the emperor couldn't defeat them. Not after he had fled them so far, so long. He and his men were at bay here, and the more dangerous because of it, but not to the rebel army.

He spoke of invasion, but she thought Taishu had been invaded already.

And could not say so, because that little thought was treachery and heresy, both together. Besides, she didn't want to hurt him.

"Mei Feng? Why are you laughing?"

She wasn't, not really: only choking suddenly on a startling impossibility, and trying to hide it behind her hand.

He was the emperor, and she didn't want to hurt him.

She shook her head mutely and buried her face in his skirts again, because she was still simply overwhelmed sometimes. She wanted to be back with her grandfather on his bastard boat, hauling a netload of fish from a moonlit sea; and she could never do that again. Instead she had to do this, let the emperor stroke her hair for comfort, help him to misunderstand her. Now he thought it was a sob rather than a laugh that she'd been hiding. Well, she might have done that, wept for her people, if she'd been another kind of girl and differently helpless; and it was unthinkable, of course, to allow the Son of Heaven to discover he was wrong.

She sniffled, and rubbed her cheeks against his silk, and lifted her head into his caress; and was just wondering how she could urge or drive or bully him—bully! the emperor! but he was a boy, and hence vulnerable to bullying, and she was desperate—into confronting his generals one more time, when there was a sudden riot of sound outside the hall. Voices and running feet, men shouting, the grating clash of steel.

Her mind shrieked *Revolt! rebellion! assassins!*—but she knew that wasn't right. This whole palace was like Taishu in miniature: too many people packed too close, tensions breaking out in temper, quarrels resolving themselves in blood. It didn't need the war spilling across the strait—though that must come, she knew, and dread the day. Meantime, these stupid men would fight on their own account, nothing to do with the emperor.

Most of the palace servants were natives, gifted to the emperor with the rest of the jademaster's property. His own servitors had been lost or sold or left behind, somewhere on the march; the men he'd brought here were not all soldiers, but they might as well have been. Even the court officials, even the eunuchs carried blades and were all too willing to use them. When trouble broke out, as it too often did, it was usually between her people and the emperor's.

Mei Feng had to jump on a chest to peer out of a window too high for her, but she was sure already what she'd see. Nothing that might have started this particular quarrel, there was no obvious reason for it: only the fact itself, the fight itself, two young men bloodied and frantic in a rowdy circle of onlookers.

No: one young man bloodied and frantic. The other was only marked with his opponent's blood, a spray of it across his army tunic, smears on his knuckles. Knuckles were all he needed, apparently. He was calm, and utterly in control.

His opponent—barely more than a boy, she saw now—had a common kitchen cleaver in his hand, which confirmed her suspicion. Just a household servant, then. And he was trying to use the cleaver as a weapon, and didn't know how; which the other man, the soldier, must have seen. And had laughed, probably, before he handed off his sword to a friend and went to work on this boy just with his hands.

It might have been an act of generosity, a lesson taught and learned, not to fall into a fight with a soldier; except that such

lessons end in early blood and crowing, and this would go on and
on. The boy swung his cleaver, the soldier stepped casually aside,
a hard fist hammered into the boy's elbow. The cleaver dropped to
the ground; the boy gaped at his own arm, where it hung numb
and useless, and the soldier hit him again, and then again: in the
ribs, in the face, in the belly. Each blow calculated and deliberate
and opening the way to the next like steps in a dance, links in a
chain.

The soldier was a hand's breadth taller, as these northern men
tended to be; and he had the hard scarred leanness of a man who
had fought for his life and scavenged for his food, and starved
when there was no time to scavenge. The other was lean too—
there were few fat men on Taishu—but his was the leanness of
simple poverty. He didn't have muscles like cables beneath his
shirt, he didn't have skin like roughened hide on his hands or so
many thousand miles of march beneath his feet.

He didn't have a chance.

Even in a fair fight, one on one, he wouldn't have had a chance.
But all those men around him, they were soldiers too. Every time
he was punched into that wall of bodies, he was punched and
kicked some more before being pushed out into the clear circle
again.

There was movement behind Mei Feng, the emperor come to
see. Tall northerner, he didn't need to stand on the chest to look
out of the window. He probably didn't need to rest his hands on
her hips either, but he did. Her hair brushed his face as she turned,
as she said, "Please, go out and stop them . . ."

"I can't."

Oh, she was so tired of hearing that! He was emperor, he ruled
as much of the world as he could reach; he could surely reach from
here into the courtyard. "This much you can! They won't hurt him
any more if you—"

"Mei Feng, I *can't*. If an officer bothers to investigate, those
men will get a flogging, both of them, and maybe the bystanders
as well. If I go, they will die for it. The Son of Heaven, dragged

from his throne by a rowdy set of fools? They could never be permitted to survive that, to boast about it, the day the emperor came to see what they were doing. The best I can do for them is not to notice."

It was an odd throne he sat on, she thought, that left him so utterly helpless. Helpless and wrong too. She didn't think the servant would survive this.

As she watched, the man stumbled under one more blow, and fell to the ground. Picked himself up, and came back for more; and was punched in the head, kicked in the belly, fell again. This time he was slow, too slow to stand. Two men stepped out of the circle and seized him, dragged him up and held him, for the soldier to hit him again. And again.

It was too much for Mei Feng. She spun away from the window, glowered at the boy behind her—eye to eye, as they were sometimes in bed but never like this, it was outrageous and overmastering and probably illegal—and said, "You're not going to do anything?"

"Mei Feng, I *can't,* they'll lose their *heads* . . . !"

"Well, I can."

One short girl with a shorter temper, she jumped off the chest and ran, all ready to overawe a pack of hothead soldiers. As she hauled at the heavy door, she thought she heard him call her back—but quietly, so as not to be overheard by the guards outside. She could ignore him, then; and ignore the guards too, just run straight around the corner into the courtyard, elbow her way through that tangled knot of men—

—AND SHE only registered their unnatural stillness, their silence, their tension when it was already too late. She'd burst through into the circle at their heart, and there were more than the two fighting men here now, more even than the soldier and his two friends and their victim. Those four were here, yes, all of them facedown on the ground; and here too was one of the generals and some few of his retinue, with swift justice on their minds.

If it was death to disturb the emperor, all too clearly he felt that it should be death to disturb a general also; and he was entirely ready to deliver it, to see it done there and then.

Except that she had disturbed him, and he was briefly prepared to suspend their execution in order to diminish her in sight of his men. Why not? She wasn't even a concubine of rank, just trash the boy-emperor had picked up on the boat and refused to part with.

Mei Feng could see the contempt in his face, the way his lip twisted as he readied some remark; and he would pause for that little moment before delivering it because that's what bullies do, to make sure they have their audience's full attention; and so she could dive headlong into that narrow closing space, like leaping into the dragon's jaws to choke it.

"General Ping Wen," she cried, improvising wildly, almost joy-fully, this was suddenly such a mad endeavor—and loving the fact that she'd remembered, that she could greet him by his name in full view of his aides and officers—"were you also drawn to this exhibition? His imperial majesty has been watching from the throne room"—a wave of her hand toward the windows of the hall, where he might still be watching, if anyone should actually dare to look—"and was much taken by the skills of this man, fighting bare-handed and barefoot. It is an art he would like to see developed; as you know, steel for weapons is in short supply. It would please his majesty greatly if this man were instructed to teach others. Not our servant, though," poking the Taishu man with her toe, "alas, we have need of him just now."

With another significant glance toward the high windows, she nudged and hauled that young man up, all blood and dust; latched her hand about his wrist and hauled him off, leaving the general, his entourage, her entire audience gaping in her wake.

She might have saved the soldiers' lives; she hoped so, despite her rage. This one, the servant, she would make sure of.

Which meant taking him all the way into the throne room, be-cause she could feel the general's hot eyes on her every step.

Which meant, of course, bringing him before the emperor.

Well, she had survived that, when she was just as unready; no doubt he would survive it too. She could be ruthless when she needed to, in saving young men's lives.

The guards saw her coming, and dragged the door open for her and her reluctant companion. He shied violently, and would have pulled away—would have run, she thought, he had that tremble in him that said he was a runner—but her rough hands were very used to snatching live fish from a slippery deck. He'd break her fingers before he broke that grip.

Once into the high shadows of the throne room, he wasn't fit for breaking anything. He didn't struggle anymore, but she still had to drag him; and when his eyes had penetrated the gloom enough to be sure that, yes, that really was the Jade Throne in its solitary splendor, and yes, that tall boy by the window really was dressed in imperial yellow, and for the obvious reason—well, then there was no doing anything with him at all, he was dead weight on the floor, facedown and shuddering.

Mei Feng had let go his wrist when she felt him start to drop. Now—for appearance's sake, for the emperor's, not to disgrace him before a commoner—she dropped neatly to her knees and laid a hand on the trembling servant's neck. She'd done much the same with a dog once, that had attached itself to Old Yen in the Santung docks and wouldn't leave him. It hadn't apparently understood the concept of boats until they were out in the pitching sea. Then it had spread-eagled itself on deck in an ecstatic misery, and wouldn't even suffer itself to be hauled below; all she could do was sit with it, until they were close enough to Taishu that it could hurl itself into the surf, swim ashore and vanish.

If this young man chose to vanish as soon as this immediate terror was over, she wouldn't blame him. Nor miss him, to be honest, she could get by without more responsibility; but it was too late for that, she had saved his life and was responsible already.

Which the emperor acknowledged, even if she'd rather not. He said, "Well, and what are you going to do with him now?"

Clean him up, first off; she had blood on her fingers, and didn't

want to get it on her clothes. She'd wipe it off on his, but that was
too possessive, too contemptuous a gesture. The dowager empress
would do that, without a second thought.

The dowager empress, she thought, would never have put herself in this position. Once show sympathy for a servant, and they
were yours for life; and what did she want with another young
man . . . ?

She looked down at him, and remembered that this young man
would be a runner, if she only let him go.

She poked him lightly. "What's your name?"

A mumble, inaudible: swollen lips and terror and close contact
with the floorboards do not make for clarity of speech.

Mei Feng poked him again, heard him swallow; hoped he
wasn't swallowing blood, because she did after all have a use for
him now, and suddenly very much wanted to keep him.

"Say it again?"

"Chung, lady."

It was probably a monstrous breach of etiquette to hold conversation with another in the emperor's presence, but if the emperor
wanted to join in, no doubt he would.

"Can you run, Chung?"

"Now, lady?" There was a glimmer of humor in him, then, despite it all. She thought likely he'd survive.

"Not now, fool. When you're fit."

"Yes, lady. I can run."

"Good. Can you read?"

"No, lady."

"That's good too." She glanced up at the Son of Heaven, who
was watching, listening, with half a smile on his face: lofty amusement at whatever she was up to, she thought, awkwardly coupled
with an impossible desire to be involved. She made a rude face at
him and said, "Lord, can you make him an imperial messenger?"

"Yes, of course." At last something he actually could do, something he managed to say yes to. "Why, though? We have messengers . . ."

Yes, but this one would be hers. "He can run between us and my grandfather, lord," she said, graciously allowing him to share. The empress owned all the official messengers: some she'd brought with her, the remainder she'd bought or co-opted here, local men. It would be good to have one messenger of their own, reliable, untainted; one sworn to Mei Feng personally, who could run messages that even the emperor didn't need to know about. One more knot in her network, a way to reach out beyond the palace walls.

And a messenger's sash, a flash of imperial yellow would be good for Chung too. It was death to assault a messenger, death to delay him.

The emperor nodded. "My doctors should see him first, to be sure he isn't too hurt."

"Lord, your own doctors . . ." Would be outraged at being asked to examine a servant, a native, not even one of their own.

". . . Will do as I tell them," he said, and of course that was true too. They would be outraged, and obedient, and meticulous. Doctors held their own lives in their own hands, when they treated with the great.

"Well, let me clean him up first . . ."

"Mei Feng, no. We have servants to do that, to take care of our servants. I want you with me."

It wasn't often that he was absolute. When he was, she didn't trouble to argue. He was still emperor, and this was only a glimpse of what that meant, mostly a reminder of how seldom he remembered it when he was with her.

"Yes, lord."

three

Yu Shan had imagined the city a thousand times, ten thousand.

Of course he had. He was a boy who lived much of his life in the dark, all of it in the narrows of his valley, the narrows of his clan. Knowing that there was a sea somewhere—a sky's worth of water!—and buildings that clustered beside it, too many to be counted and the streets busy with more people daily than he might see in a lifetime, he had spent much of his dreamtime making pictures in his head, without ever wanting actually to go there.

Now he was there, he was here, this was it; and it was terrible and awe-demanding and utterly, utterly unlike anything he had ever imagined.

He kept stopping to stare at the way the buildings went up and up, or the way they crushed together, or the sea—the sea!—or the docks, the markets, the—

"Yu *Shan*! Keep up, or I swear I'm putting that rope around your neck again, I'll lead you about like a dog . . ."

"Yes, Jiao. I'm sorry. But, look, look at that ship just coming in, it's like a city itself, it's so tall . . ."

"It's a trader's junk, though it looks like a troop carrier now. I suppose they all are. You can come and stare tomorrow, they're as common as rats in a gutter. How stupid was I, bringing you this way? It'll be dark before we even reach Guangli, if you don't step up. I'd be better off selling you right here on the quayside, let someone make an oarsman of you. You're strong enough for the work, though the gods only know where you hide the muscles . . ."

She was grumbling for its own sake, he recognized that. It was about all he could recognize in the welter and storm that assailed him, the chaos that was apparently a city.

THE ROAD they'd been tracking all this time was still called the Jade Road, still watched by the jademasters' guards. From long miles out, though, it became such a way of common trade, there was no point in avoiding it any longer. Instead they let themselves be swallowed by the stream of farmers, traders, wagons, oxen and stray soldiers that infested the road like mites on a rocksnake. The occasional stand of guards troubled no one; they were there to guarantee the jade, Jiao said, not to police the peasants.

Yu Shan really couldn't have told when they entered the city proper. All day there had been more and more villages among the paddy, more and more huts and stalls along the roadside, more and more people. He was expecting a wall, a gate, perhaps an in-terrogation, but there was nothing. Only that the paddy disap-peared, and then the huts were backed by other huts, with other roads running parallel, more intersecting with this one. The huts grew to be houses, vast to his eyes; soon the only green was behind walls, gardens glimpsed through guarded gates. If he jumped, if he caught the top of a wall and hauled himself up, he could see houses that were grander yet, great palaces within the gardens. Jiao would only let him do that once. She said this was where the jademasters lived, and if the guards saw him, then they really would be interrogated. Which neither of them could afford.

And she asked him again if he understood how much that jade weighed, and he said yes, he knew exactly; and when she asked how he could possibly jump so high with such a burden on his back, he shrugged against the heft of it and said he was used to carrying stone, he'd been doing it all his life.

Then he walked sedately—more sedately, at least—at Jiao's side, and stared about him until the city's rising became altogether too much. He tried looking at the people instead, the crush they walked among; that was almost as difficult, almost as much.

Through his life, from one year's end to the next, he'd barely see a face he didn't recognize. There were strangers at clanmoot, yes, but they were at least all clan, he knew their dress and their habits, their lineage and skills. Here he could barely pick a rice farmer from a laborer from a high house servant, a trader from a soldier from a fisherman.

Jiao answered his questions as best she could—"What's that man? And that? That woman, what?"—but it didn't help much. He didn't understand how these people all fitted together, to make anything that worked. One by one he could see them, but he couldn't see the city in them.

Just as, when the road reached the docks—one great highway that birds must see scored like a brand from the mountains to the sea, from where the jade was dug to where it took to ships— he could almost not see the great ships where they floated on the water. They were too big for him, for his mind to encompass.

He would have stood all day in awe and bewilderment, if Jiao hadn't been there to seize his elbow and drag him on. He was almost grateful. He'd had too much of everything today, the city and the sea. She'd brought him here; he needed her now to take him away.

She didn't do that, she couldn't, but her mixture of hurry and caution closed it all down to glimpses, sudden snatches of this and that, which was better than staring and staring and being eaten by it all:

a boy with twisted legs, sprawled with a bowl in a doorway, and Jiao said that he was begging;

the sea again: he thought they'd left it behind at the dockside but he was getting all turned around now that they'd left the long straight of the Jade Road, and suddenly there it was at the end of an alley, the glitter of sun on so much water, so impossibly much;

a trader thrusting something into his face, a necklace like a string of dried fungus, and the man was gabbling about monkeys' ears and ill luck and how to curse an enemy;

soldiers, soldiers everywhere, standing or squatting or pushing through the crowds, and Jiao was almost too careful to keep out of their way, now that she was so close but still in peril of losing everything;

a house like so many in this city, a house that bewildered him because it seemed like no house at all, only a blank wall with a closed gate, a cave with its back turned to the world.

In his life, among his people, clan fought with clan, endless rain fought with bitter cold and brutal heat for the right to be king weather, and even so houses were built to be open, wide of door and generous of window. Here there were no clans, no one to fight; every house must shelter every other, against whatever strange city weather might come; and yet they were built to shut out, to say no.

Maybe it was because they were packed so close and not family, not even clan, maybe that was why they turned stiff shoulders, house to house. He couldn't imagine living so hard up against people who were not near kin.

He wouldn't need to imagine it, he was set to meet it. One way or another, Jiao meant to leave him here.

She thumped cheerfully on the closed gate. After a time—too long for her, too short, perhaps, for him—there was the sound of bolts being drawn. The gate swung out toward them, and a massive figure filled the frame.

He stood in shadow, with light behind him. Yu Shan was not entirely certain he was human. This could so easily be a city of demons; likely only demons could survive the size and noise and bustle of it all.

Jiao stood carefully in the sun and said, "Tong. How is it with you, and with your master? I've brought something for him to see."

Tong's massive head moved from her to Yu Shan, and back to her. "Jiao." The voice was slow and deep and shrewd, very possibly demonic. "He will be glad to see you."

"And what I have brought him. Trust me, he will be glad to see that too."

"Perhaps. What is the boy?"

"My pack mule. Nothing more, unless your master likes him better. He is not the pretty thing I bring," though her smile teased Yu Shan, saying *Pretty enough for me, mind, I can hardly bear to part with him.* Saying it with a mock, a kiss of the eyes that belied the dark intensity of their nights together.

He said nothing, aloud or otherwise; he had no idea what to say.
Tong grunted, and stepped aside.

WITHIN WAS an archway, high and square, walled with stone and
roofed with timbers; almost a tunnel. After a moment, Yu Shan
understood that it was a passage through the house, with rooms
above. He still hadn't adjusted to houses being built upward,
rooms on top of rooms.

The passage brought them back into sunlight, though they were
still within the house. There was house on all four sides of him,
doors and shutters, stairs rising to a gallery above. That was how
the house could be so closed off to the busy city: because it was
open to its heart, to this courtyard where small trees grew in pots,
where carp mouthed at the sun-warm skin of their lily pond,
where a man sat on a bench with a piece of jade in one hand and a
thin tool in the other. He was turning the stone in the light, looking and looking.

Yu Shan's heart turned and turned. Open doors in the gallery's
shade showed him benches and shelves and racks of tools; set in
the sun out here was a lathe with a stool beside it. Even with his
eyes closed—yes, and even with this great weight of stone on his
back—he would still have known that there was jade on every side
of him, a fine scatter of jade-dust on the spread cloth beneath the
lathe. He could see it now, a glitter of green in the sun, but he had
felt it first.

And, ah, that man on the bench. Stone in one hand, tool in the
other, only now pulling himself back from his work, lifting his
eyes to look at them instead—no, to look at Yu Shan, as a man
might look at the sun, blinkingly.

Yu Shan would always have known him for a man of jade, just
as the man seemingly knew him. A jademaster, he wanted to say,
without meaning anything remotely to do with those who lived in
palaces and accumulated fortunes. Not a miner, blatantly—this
was a fat man by mountain standards, which no miner ever was—
but he had the stone in his eye, in his blood, in his head and heart.
Yu Shan turned to the man as a needle turns to the north.

It needed Jiao to cough, quite loudly, to draw their eyes apart.

"Jiao. Forgive me, my mind was adrift. With my stones. Yes."

"I saw," she said, drily at Yu Shan's side.

"Yes, yes . . ." He rose to his feet, and showed himself to be tall as well as portly; and was still dwarfed by his doorman Tong.

And set stone and tool on a table nearby, where the jade was immaculately lit by sunlight reflecting off the water of the pool. Yu Shan could see now how it was half carved to show a demon struggling to free himself from the raw rock that bound him, unless it was the rock that made him, unless he needed such a tool to carve his own lineaments from the rock he was.

Yu Shan might have looked at that piece of work for an hour or a day or for many days together. But the man moved deliberately between him and it, so that he must look at its maker.

Jiao said, "Guangli, I have brought you—"

"A boy from the mountains, from the mines, I think; and a piece of stone. Yes," although the stone was so well wrapped that he couldn't conceivably see it. "I just don't understand how either of them came to be in your possession, Jiao?"

"Oh," she said, "that's a short tale simply told. Idiocy and banditry, neither one my own."

"Mmph. It wants something, perhaps, in the telling. Sit down," with a fond gesture toward a bench beside the pond, "and compose a longer version, while I make tea. You, boy—perhaps you should set that stone on the ground."

"I can manage it," Yu Shan said.

"I'm sure you can. Nevertheless. Over there, please," the farther side of the pond. "And then attend your mistress," to be sure, clearly, that he left the stone and came back.

Yu Shan hated even to shrug the harness from his back, let alone to step away. That was the moment—at last, much delayed—when he had to accept that he had failed his family and his clan. It didn't seem to matter too much now, what happened to the stone, or to him.

Except that the stone was a thing of beauty, and never mind its value; he should be glad to have delivered it into the hands of a man who would admire and appreciate it, in whose hands it could appreciate. Fresh-cut from the mountain, jade was a wonder. Carved by a master, it could be something more than wonderful. He understood that, just by looking at this demon struggling from his rock . . .

"Don't touch that!"

He hadn't meant to. He hadn't realized quite how close he'd come, bent right over the carving, close enough to smell the warmth of jade in sunlight. He gabbled an apology to Guangli, where the man had paused in a doorway, and scuttled around the pond to join Jiao on the bench, feeling the weight of his loss in the weight of the burden lifted from him.

Guangli had disappeared; there was a distant clatter and chime, the sounds of a man making tea. It seemed preposterous. He whispered, "Does he not have servants?"

Jiao snorted. "Look around you. Does this look like a house busy with people?"

No, it didn't; but the courtyard and workshops were neat and cared for. Things didn't sweep and tidy themselves, that was a lesson beaten into him early by his mother at the compound and his father at the mine. And a man so wealthy, a man who kept such a house should surely have money enough to keep a staff.

Yu Shan said that, or something like it. This time Jiao laughed aloud.

"You think he's rich? What, because he handles rich things? So do you. Are you rich?"

No, he had only ever had his due portion of his family's wealth, which meant a place in the compound, a share of the pot, work in the mine. Now he supposed he had nothing at all, if she did indeed mean to sell him here. But, this house! On two floors! So much space and privacy, a garden and a gallery and a man to guard the door, and . . .

Words embarrassed him, where anyone might be listening. He said what he could with a shrug, a shake of the head, a glance upward and around, a glance at Tong.

She said, "Oh, this house isn't his own. It's given to him, because he needs solitude and security to do his work. The jademaster supplies all of this. And Tong. It's why I thought Guangli might snatch at that," a nod to the wrapped stone, "give him the chance to be his own man, under the emperor's patronage. Why he might snatch at you too: someone to get up at dawn and do the housework, make the tea. The man keeps it orderly down here, because he loves his garden and he cares about his tools; domestically, he's not so dainty. First thing you do, you can scrub out his kitchen for him."

Yu Shan eyed her, eyed Tong, said nothing. Eyed his stone, too far away. Out of reach now, as he was himself, out of everyone's reach who loved him. He should have run away, before they came this far. Taken the wonder-stone and run. Why had he not run . . . ?

Because she stopped me, with a blade at my throat—but that was only the once. He might have tried again, but she seduced him and he lost all heart, all hope. Now—well, they could call this a house or a workshop, it was still a great stone box with a guarded gate. How could he run from here? And where could he go? He knew the route back to the valleys—follow the Jade Road, all the way—but not why he should take it, what he could take with him to earn a welcome home. Hope was the treasure they had sent him off with, and he had lost that.

Here there was at least stone, and a man who knew it: a man he could learn from, perhaps. If he had to play that man's slave, serve his tea and scrub his kitchen, he could do that. For a time.

Guangli came back with a steaming pot and three tiny cups: apparently Tong did not drink tea, or not with his master.

Apparently Yu Shan did, or was supposed to. It was hard. He was monstrously nervous suddenly, nervous of everything. He dreaded seeing Jiao leave, though he hated her for stealing him, possessing him, wanting now to sell him; he dreaded being left here, alone and bewildered; he dreaded being told to leave this place. Jade's tingle was in the gravel beneath his feet, the walls on every side, the air he breathed. He wanted never to walk out through that gate again. At the same time as he wanted not to be here, never to have been here, never to have left the mountains.

He lifted fine translucent porcelain to his lips, barely knowing what it was. He wanted to cup it cautiously between his fingers and just look at it. Partly for the thing itself, in its fragility and beauty; partly to stop him staring at the stone, or at the man Guangli who was master of the stone, might be his master too. The cup was brimful of scalding tea, though. He had to drink that first. If he could swallow. He wasn't sure. Breathing was hard enough just now, against all the tensions in his chest.

First was the perfume in the tea, he could simply sit here and sniff. That too was fragile and beautiful, floral and tender and un-expectedly refreshing. When at last he sipped, his mouth filled with an effusion of light and heat and water, the whole history of growth from the earth through root and branch to the budding leaf.

He heard, "Don't mock him, he's a hill-boy; he's never met any-thing like this before. Anything like you."

He heard, "I'm not mocking. Not at all. Tell me about him."

He heard, "I thought you'd be interested in the stone. You haven't even looked at it. This could be your freedom, damn you, and you haven't even *looked* . . ."

AND SO the bargaining began. Yu Shan tried to disappear back into his tea, into this unfolding of taste like a landscape, fore-ground and distance and hints of something far, far out of reach. He held worlds in his mouth, worlds unseen and truths unspoken.

And still couldn't block out what Jiao was saying, because she was talking about him and his, stealing the stone from him and himself from his family, a little more with every word. Never lying, quite—claiming them both by right of sword, which Guangli did not dispute and nor did he—but neither quite telling a story that he recognized.

The way she spoke about him, he didn't even recognize himself.

Hardworking, she called him, which she couldn't possibly know, and *quick,* which was obviously not true or she never would have caught him, that one night he ran. *Slow and stupid, ox-like* she did not say but it was how he felt, letting her sell him without protest, without a word.

Without a word until she spoke about the stone, when he lifted his head abruptly and said, "No."

She turned, she stared, she glowered at him furiously; it was Guangli who said, "No?"

"She doesn't know. She hasn't even seen it. You know more about it than she does."

"Perhaps—but you know more than I. Why don't you tell me?"

He laid down his cup—tiny, he'd thought that, but the tea was so immense—and walked around the pond, because talking about jade was like talking about fire or the forest at night or the mysteries of his clan-cousin. Talking failed, at every point.

Touching, though: touching made all things closer and more real.

He talked despite himself—how they'd found the stone, last spit of a failed seam; how it had been so obviously wonderful from the first moment, the first gleam of it through the mother-rock—but mostly he worked, untying the harness, stripping away the ropes and the bamboo frame.

Talking to no purpose, because the stone was the purpose and that was right here, in the light now as he lifted away the last of its wrappings. He fell silent, sat back on his heels, let them look.

The stone stood in the courtyard, in the sunshine like something lifted out of its proper inheritance, which it was; like something too beautiful to be contained within these drab walls, this apologetic garden, which it was; like something more alive than any of those who looked at it, and perhaps it was that too.

Like the tea, like the land it came in layers, in variations, many voices to sing one true song. The bulk of it, the heartstone was a deep dark green, the most common color for the stone, jade-green. But there were other greens in the slab, paler and creamier, and a

seam of black at one end to be its base; and a single streak of pure
ivory that struck down at an angle, no kind of flaw, just a change
of mood, a blaze of light.

Yu Shan sat back and let the jade carver look, resting only one
hand and that only lightly atop the stone, feeling its bite through
his fingers. The wrappings had muffled that, all these days it had
been on his back; now it was loosed, and he really didn't need even
this least of touches. He could feel it in the air and all through him
like a sonorous bass, underlying all the other jade-notes he had felt
already.

Guangli didn't need to be touching either, but here he came:
around the pond with the most delicate of treads, as though the
stone were a sleeping wild thing he was anxious not to wake. Even
his breathing was hushed and tentative.

For a long time he only looked, bending as close as he dared,
following each of the strata with his eyes. Then he sat back and
looked again: drinking in the colors, Yu Shan thought, bathing in
them.

Then—at last!—he reached to touch.

As Yu Shan had, as lightly as human flesh could bear to; and
even that fleeting finger was snatched away on a breathless word,
as from a man who has tested the heat of an iron and found it untouchable, but could only learn by touching.

There was more squatting, more looking; but now it was Yu
Shan that he looked at, with all the same measuring intensity. And
yes, when he was done, Guangli did reach out a wary finger and
brush it over Yu Shan's cheek, the very lightest and most fleeting of
touches.

Jiao snorted with laughter, across the water. "What, are you
seeing if you can carve him too? Not with any of your shiny tools.
He's stronger than he looks, stronger than he knows, or those
moron bandits could never have held him and neither could I. If
you want to shape him, you'll need subtler ways to do it. I think
you should, he's ripe for it and just what you need, only don't cut
into that pretty flesh, it's not what I brought him here for."

Guangli ignored her, and so did Yu Shan; they were turned totally on each other.

Guangli said, "Well, you don't sting as fiercely as the stone does—"

—no, he knew that; he wasn't made of jade—

"—but you do still sting. I can *feel* it in you, boy. What have you been doing to yourself?"

Yu Shan just looked at him and didn't answer. He'd said nothing for a lifetime, all his short life long; why should he speak now?

"Oh, don't tell me, then. I'll tell you. Jiao, too, I'll tell her what she's selling here. You're a miner, and a miner's son: you've spent your life in the mountains. And I do mean *in* the mountain, don't I? Down the mine, every minute that you could."

Yu Shan shook his head. "We're not allowed. Clan rules: no one goes down the mine except to dig, and children aren't let dig at all."

"And of course you break clan rules whenever you can. From the time you start to crawl, you kids are heading for the mine. Being forbidden only gives it more allure, and it has plenty to start with: it's dark and mysterious and scary, and there's treasure.

"If your parents are firm, if they keep a good watch at the minehead, perhaps the little ones don't get into the current workings; but the valley's riddled with old abandoned mines that are supposed to be sealed up, yes? Yes?"

"Jade belongs to the emperor," Yu Shan mumbled. "Even in a worked-out seam, there are always fragments we don't find or couldn't reach. So yes, old workings are forbidden, sealed . . ."

". . . and unsealed too, opened up by children for the reckless adventure of it, for the smell of rock and the being underground and maybe just the hint of a touch of jade, am I right?"

He shrugged, reluctantly.

Jiao said, "What's this about, Guangli?"

"I'll tell you. That's a normal childhood, for a miner's brat; that's what they all do. And they start to help in the current workings before they ought to, as soon as they can wheedle consent from an uncle, a cousin, anyone who might be glad to have a youngster on hand to fetch new oil for the lamps, sweep up the dust, whatever needs doing.

"But sometimes, every now and then, one kid will go farther, he'll do everything he shouldn't. Told to pack the new jade quickly into sacks, he'll linger, he'll play with the stones, turn them over and over in his hand. Sniff them, lick them. If he's bold, he'll steal a pebble and keep it in his bedding, sleep with it in his hand. He'll hide one somewhere at the mine-head, so that all the time he's underground, he has his own jade with him. By the time his family knows what he's been doing, by definition it's too late. If you can see the damage done, you can't undo it."

"I don't understand," Jiao said.

"No. You don't know the stone, and you're susceptible to charm. But you said yourself, he's stronger than he ought to be. How far has he carried that slab of jade?"

"From the mountains. On his back, all the way."

"Yes. Can you lift it?"

"I don't know. I haven't tried . . ."

". . . Because you knew you'd fail, and you didn't want to know that, it raised too many questions. Exactly. You're a strong woman, Jiao—but you could fetch me the strongest man in the emperor's army, and he wouldn't carry that stone fifty yards. Tong here would struggle to do it. But this boy carried it for fifty miles—"

"—and *jumped* with it still on his back, this morning. Jumped and pulled himself up to the top of a wall, just to see over."

"He's an idiot. I hope you explained that to him. So are you. What else has he done?"

She shook her head, bewildered. "I don't know. Nothing. He sees well in the dark, but I thought that was just practice. I don't understand, Guangli, what are you *saying*?"

Yu Shan wasn't saying anything: only sitting, huddled tightly in on himself, feeling all his secrets stripped away.

"I'm saying there's a reason why jade is reserved to the emperor alone. Well, there are many reasons, but this is prime. It's why common people aren't let near it, why the wagons are so carefully watched, why the wagoners sleep a long way from their cargoes. Why I live alone and keep what distance I can afford between me and the stone, and handle it as little as I may, and I'm still a stronger man at fifty than I ever was at twenty. Jade infects anyone who handles it, Jiao. It makes us more powerful, sharper in our senses, longer-lived. How old was the last emperor?"

"I don't know. Guangli, are you *serious*?"

"Utterly. Even the dust from the mines, the dust from my working here, all of that goes to the emperor. It's mixed into his food and he lives a long, long life. And has very few children, there's always a price; the late Chien Sung was a vigorous man for a century or more, and barely achieved one son. If you read any history, if you could read, you would know that all our great emperors have been notoriously unlucky in the number of their heirs. Do I need to say that all of this is secret, Jiao? If you tell anyone, it means the boy's life for certain and probably your own, perhaps mine too."

"Oh, what, because he's worked too hard, spent too much time with the stone, grown too strong? That's a benefit, a virtue, how is that a crime?"

"Because he's stolen from the emperor. What's your name, boy?"

Had she not said? Or had Guangli forgotten? He supposed it didn't matter. "Yu Shan," he mumbled.

"Yu Shan. Well, that's appropriate. What's the worst thing you've ever done, Yu Shan?"

He knew the answer to that, and would never confess it. Not the way he used to sneak into the mine when he was supposed to be watching at the mine-head, the way he slept in the mountain's heart with the stone pulsing in his blood and all around him, not that; not even the way he used to suck a pebble all the time he was underground. His tongue touched the shard where he'd hidden it inside himself, and he said, "I used to swallow the emperor's dust, when I'd been cutting out stone from the seam. I sucked it from my fingers . . ."

"You see?" Guangli demanded. "And you see what it's made of him?"

"I see the dangers, but I still don't see the harm."

"No. Well, he's likely the only jade-miner you ever will see. The clans don't leave the valleys. However careful they are, they're still exposed; the least of them is unusually strong, and they tend to live long and not have many children. They live in extended family groups, because individually they can't sustain a holding. Or protect it.

"Nor can they travel far from the source. Jade is addictive; they need to keep it close. Separate a miner from the stone and he'll sicken. All that strength and resilience is only borrowed, not possessed."

"Yu Shan has come this far," she protested.

"Jiao. Yu Shan had that boulder on his back," with a gesture at the great gleaming slab of jade. "With that, he could walk forever. Without it, if he tried to walk home, he'd never get there. Boy, why did you leave the valleys? With this? Did you steal it?"

"No!" Except from the jademasters—and this man worked for the jademasters, or one of them. But it was too late to be circumspect.

"Why, then?"

"To take it to the emperor, as a gift. And, and to show him that he is here now, his jade is only a walk away, he doesn't need jademasters to stand between us and him . . ."

"Yes, I thought it might be so, or something like it. What you people don't understand is that you do need the jademasters, or something like them. You can't leave the valleys; you've always needed someone else to take the jade away. It could be you that employs the wagoners, perhaps—but then, how can you trust them? By employing guards, of course, but that only doubles your problems, because how can you trust the guards? You can't watch anything from the mountains. Those closed little valleys, and your closed little society . . . No. You couldn't manage this trade. Not even from one end of Taishu to the other. Perhaps, now the court is here, the emperor can provide his own oversight. You could lose the jademasters that way, from the top. Not from underneath, your people can never cut them out."

"You could," Jiao said. "That's why I wanted to bring it to you. It's stupid being so dependent on them, when you could be independent, treat with the palace directly . . ."

". . . and share my profit with my friends, of course?"

"Of course."

They exchanged smiles of mutual and entire understanding, until Jiao undermined herself or felt his undermining coming; she said, "But?"

"But I am almost as much a prisoner as your boy here, and his people. I am as cautious as I can be, and infected none the less. I need the stone, a steady supply of it coming into my hands and going out. If I could, ah, negotiate my independence with the palace, I'd still be dependent on supply. The jademasters would only need to cut me off for a short time, and my rebellion would die just as shortly, as I groveled and sold myself back to them."

"But if the emperor controlled the trade . . . ?"

"Well, yes. If that, perhaps it would be possible. I could sell myself to him instead. He is a boy, much under his mother's hand by all reports; can I trust him? Or her? With my life?"

No one spoke; it was a question without an answer, unless and until he took the chance. Meantime, there was the stone in sunlight, and Guangli was reaching to touch it again; and caught himself at it, and stood, and put his hands firmly behind his back. And looked down at Yu Shan and said, "Come back to the table, boy. Drink more tea."

Jiao snorted. "Don't be giving him orders, he's not yours yet. Perhaps I'll take him and the stone to another carver, you're not the only one . . ."

"I'm the only one you trust enough for this. And he will be mine, you know that. We only need to settle terms." And then, looking at her with the same care he'd spent on Yu Shan, he said, "Jiao, you've been sleeping with him. I can see it."

Astoundingly, she blushed. "Your eyes aren't that good, old man."

"Better than you'd think. Where the stone is concerned, my eyes are immaculate; and the infection goes so deep in him, some little has, uh, rubbed off."

Jiao swore, blisteringly. "Are you saying I'm poisoned?" *Poisoned with strength, and extra years?* Her language was acid, but her body said she was more interested than angry.

"Not in the body, no. Not enough to harm. In the mind? Perhaps. Why did you?"

"It was the best way I could think of, to stop him sneaking off in the night."

"Only that?"

"Well, and he's young and robust, and those green eyes are very taking, and—damn it, Guangli, you know I'm no shivery little mouse of a girl . . ."

"Oh yes, I know that. I know the roster of your men, or some of it. Just as I know you're not ordinarily susceptible to a vivid pair of eyes and a shy smile. I know it's shy, I haven't seen it yet," with a mock scowl at Yu Shan. "The stone does that too, it draws people to its own. It gives the emperor his allure; a little of its own shine rubs off. It's hard to resist."

Jiao grunted, scowled, said, "So what drew him to me? It takes two, you know."

"Indeed. And he's a boy, and you're a woman grown. For him, that's all it takes. Be flattered. And name me a price."

four

Santung was full of ghosts, but not all of them were dead.

Yet.

Tunghai Wang's army encircled the abandoned city, but his soldiers were not allowed inside. There were ghosts to say so: their
abandoned heads on pikes at every roadway, eyeless and slowly
rotting, jaws hanging wider and wider in their own astonishment.

They were the men caught starting fires. Or those suspected of
it, or just unluckily found looting in a district where fires had been
set, their clothes smelling a little too strongly of smoke. That was
enough, in the face of the generalissimo's anger. Fire threatened
the docks he needed for his invasion fleet, the township he would
need after; fighting it drew men away from the real fighting, and
the pursuit of the emperor's stranded army up and down the
coast.

So firestarters proclaimed their own fate in thickets by the road,
their heads sundered—gross dark buds on high bamboo, a swaying perch for crows—and their bodies flung into the river, their
ghosts perpetually torn. They were the first ghosts, and least
worst: too small and high to stink, and more or less deserving.

For the first days, the city had mostly stunk of fire, smoke and
wet scorched wood, where it had not stunk of blood. Now the air
was sweeter and heavier and far more foul, and any soldier with a
nose was glad to be exiled from it.

Han had a nose, and thought perhaps he was a soldier now; but
he had license to pass the ghost-heads and go into the city, more
often than he could bear. He had a task, two tasks.

And hated them both, and was not good at either.

"Grab ahold there, slave boy. Cripple slave. Do your share . . ."

The city was full of bodies, and the commander couldn't wait even a season for weather and carrion birds to do their work. There were great pits being dug, wherever there was soil enough; elsewhere there were pyres, continually burning. Corpse-gangs scurried to feed both, dragging the dead on carts or carrying them on hurdles, cleansing the city body by putrefying body.

That was Han's first task, vile enough, made worse by his maltreated hand and by his chains; and by his companions who mocked and struck him in more or less equal measure, because they too hated the work and needed someone to blame for it and there was always him.

At least his team had a cart today, he didn't have to struggle with a hurdle. Once the cart was loaded, he could bend his back against the crossbar and help to tow it well enough.

And while he towed, he could keep watch both sides of the road in pursuit of his second task. All the corpse-gangs were told to fetch back fuel for the pyres—doors and shutters and screens, broken furniture, anything that would burn—but Han was a smith's boy also and his master wanted metal. Iron, steel, copper, any.

So he scouted as he towed and scavenged what he could, whatever could be tossed into the cart. His gangmates grumbled at the extra weight and wouldn't help, so he seldom had more than a scant armful to offer Suo Lung for his forge. Even that he was as like as not to lose, to another smith's boy with stronger hands for grabbing and swifter legs to run.

Every house offered something: pans or pot chains from the kitchen, hinges on a door frame, an old broken wheel-rim in the courtyard, something. It had been hard, though, to persuade his gangmates into the houses at all, while there were still bodies in the streets. All the city was rank with the smell of them, but the houses were the worst.

Street bodies became farther and farther to seek, with so many corpse-gangs working the same roadways. Han had argued for the houses, and won once; and then won often, until houses became what they did. They had smoke-sodden scarves to tie across their faces; they learned ways to search that took them in fast and brought them out soonest; they learned to hold their breath like divers, working without air.

Even so, houses were worse than streets, and not only for the stink and flies. Houses held ghosts, living as well as dead. Female, always, as the worst ghosts always are.

Han supposed that some men, some boys must have escaped the slaughter, but not by hiding up and waiting. Even the women weren't really hiding anymore; lurking, rather, clinging to this dreadful city for lack of any other where to go.

Lost to hope and unconvinced by death, they scuttled among the shadows or crouched in corners, unspeaking, unblinking even at the sudden incursion of a corpse-gang and the snatching-away of those bodies they had lingered over. That was what made them ghosts rather than survivors, how they didn't howl or clutch or try to follow, didn't plead or curse. They neither asked nor offered anything, trapped like spirits in the silence of the ghostworld.

Han had seen other wagons, other corpse-gangs with one or more than one of these ghost-women stumbling behind, a rope around their waists to drag them. Every day, he wondered if today one of his own gangmates would find a woman he thought worth keeping.

What he'd never wondered, what simply didn't occur to him, was what he would do if it happened to him.

IT WAS their last trip of the day. They all had other tasks, and not even the generalissimo would send them into the city in the mid-day swelter. They started early, at first light, and were gone by noon.

This trip was a rush, after they'd taken too long with the previous load—Han's fault, apparently, though he wasn't clear why—so they took the first house that lacked a sign scratched on the doorpost to say *We have searched here.* Every corpse-gang had its sign; theirs was linked circles, to represent chains. His gangboss thought that funny. Han didn't care.

The gate hung half off its hinges, so they chopped that free and flung it into the cart. Then they fixed their scarves and went inside.

Breaking away the gate had barely broken the crust of stillness inside. There was a body sprawled in the courtyard's sun, a man hacked half to pieces; and death carries its own lingering quiet that the stir and buzz of flies only accentuates, that comes hard to walk into.

It wasn't until they lifted that butchered corpse that they realized there was another body underneath, a boy still in diapers.

Well, they had seen many such already. The small body was tossed in with the first.

Like the bodies, everything in the courtyard was broken or hacked about. Much of it was salvageable, though, or at least flammable. While his gangmates seized splintered wood and ripped fabrics, Han went swiftly in and out of doorways. He was expert in scouring shadows: anything rotting, anything swiftly retrievable? If not, move on. No point in digging nails out of wooden beams; there was still plenty of loose metal to be turned up in the city.

One room, nothing.

One room, two more bodies: he yipped to warn the others, and moved on.

The kitchen, treasure: an iron cauldron broken in pieces, shattered by some great mindless hammer-blow. He could gather up the shards while the others saw to the bodies. He couldn't carry them all at once, but here were empty rice sacks . . .

The fragments were heavy, greasy, hard to manage. His crippled hand could hold a sack open, but his chains made it more than awkward, and he was tired already. Lifting the first sack, carrying it out to the cart took all his focus; coming back, he was shocked though not really surprised to see a ghost in one corner, that he'd completely overlooked before.

Seen or unseen, it made no difference to her. She sat and watched him, as though she would never do anything else; as though, when he was gone, she would sit and sit and do nothing at all. Perhaps she would. His mind held no hope for these living ghosts. They weren't survivors, they hadn't evaded their city's brutal end, they defined it. Ghost women in a ghost city, only waiting to be picked apart in the winds.

He had long ago, days ago stopped speaking to them. There was no point, and his words were precious to him. He seemed to have fewer with every day that passed, as though they were being stolen while he slept, when he did sleep. Perhaps the dragon hoarded them. At any rate, he had none to waste here.

And yet, and yet: this once, he said, "Mother, you should not stay. In the dark, when it is safe"—a lie, but she would excuse it— "you should leave this city. Someone will give you shelter." That too might be a lie; he couldn't tell. Neither could she.

If she understood him, she showed no sign of it. Perhaps she hadn't even heard. Perhaps her spirit was long gone, and her unattended body was the ghost.

Han shrugged and bent to his task. His maimed hand had no grip at all, and he had to carry the sack on his bent forearms. Out to the cart and dump it. His gangmates were snatching a breath of air, but still going back in for one more body. So must he, then: across the courtyard and into the kitchen and—

—AND THE ghost was standing right there, just inside the doorway. She had a long wrapped burden in her arms that she held out to him, and for a moment he thought it was iron, he thought she'd seen his pain and awkwardness and bundled it all up for him.

Then he took the bundle, or at least she thrust it at him and his arms came up to take it; and no, it was too bulky and too soft. And too heavy for him but he held it none the less, because he knew already what it was.

He'd held and handled too many of these already. Just never with the mother right there, wordless but holding his eye, telling him everything.

Her hands batted about her daughter's head, though there were hardly enough flies to notice. The child must be freshly dead; so many of them were, not quite survivors after all.

The stink was on her clothes, a crust of old rank blood. He had no interest in what lay beneath, what damage had been done. Her hurts might have killed her in the end, or it might have been her memories. It might have been her mother. Too many of the dead girls they'd found had been smothered, by desperate parents who couldn't bear to let them live.

It was perhaps one reason so many of those mothers were ghosts now, haunting the city of their shame. Waiting to keep company with their daughters' spirits, appalled perhaps by their own survival, the depths of a bitter endurance.

At least this ghost wasn't hoarding her daughter's body, hugging barren bones to a barren breast. She was giving it up, rather: to the wagon and the fire, the ashes—with their half-burned bones, half-burned bodies sometimes if it rained untimely—flung into the river for current and tide to disperse.

And then the little body turned its head, its eyes opened, it almost looked at Han; and Han so nearly screamed, so nearly dropped it.

HE RECOVERED his grip, at least, if not his senses. Once the impossibility had settled into his head—*this child is alive, maybe just another ghost but alive, in its own body*—then everything else seemed to follow by nature, by some inherent law.

He said, "Come with me," and the ghost-woman nodded her obedience.

He turned and walked out of there, the child rooted in his arms.

In the lane, his gangmates were loading the last of the corpses. They watched him go by, called after him; he ignored them entirely. They could do as they liked with his painfully gathered scrap: leave it or lug it back, trade it to another boy, whatever. He didn't even show them the living child as excuse. Let them think he'd found some tradeable treasure, bargained or seized it from the ghost-woman, was hurrying it back to his master. That should keep them from coming after him; Suo Lung was too big, too strong, too random. They called him Tai Feng, and were afraid of him.

Perhaps they were afraid of the ghost-woman too. For sure they would fear the child if they saw it: a corpse reanimated, an alien spirit investing a dead girl. They might throw it into the pyres regardless, just because its living would seem to them so wrong.

LIKE ALL ghosts, this one seemed to shrink in daylight. In the house she had loomed at him, but now she panted like a normal woman, hurrying to keep up.

She wasn't his priority. He ran where he could, while there were streets and space, despite his own aching exhaustion. Too soon he was out of the city and into the great encircling camp, with no room to run; he was squeezing between tents and stepping over ropes and there were men everywhere and women too, survivors of Santung or camp followers picked up on the march. The child in his arms weighed heavier with every step, his muscles burned but he was not going to drop her. Nor pass her off to her mother. There, there at last was what he sought, a large tent with a board outside it, characters painted on the wood, MEDICINES AND TREATMENT HERE.

He had brought the child to a doctor, the thing he could do that the mother could not. He didn't know what to do next. His corpse-gang would be on the way to the pyre, and angry with him. He could go to Suo Lung, empty-handed and worn out, useless; or . . .

Or he could stand here, so he did that.

THE DOCTOR'S was no makeshift tent flung together from whatever wood and fabric could be scavenged from not too far away. On the contrary: it was his place of business and his home too, it traveled with him where he went.

It barely needed the board outside to declare it. It declared itself: a high broad structure of pale heavy silk, an instance of order set among the chaos of its neighbors. Here was stillness, quiet, ease, like a pebble in turbulent water.

Even its furnishings were old and dark and heavy, speaking peace. There was a long table where patients might sit to speak to the doctor, where they might lie to be examined; there was a man, indeed, lying on it. There was a bench, where others might wait. Were waiting. There was a run of shelves, holding a succession of paper-labeled jars; there was a chest of many drawers, each one marked with a scrap of written silk.

There was a brazier set on a stone, a pot of fresh charcoal, water steaming in a kettle.

There was matting on the floor; there were lamps hung from the tent's supporting poles, along with texts of health and wisdom, images of beneficent gods.

There was a girl who radiated cleanly well-being as she greeted people, looked at their hurts and listened to their complaints. She might be the doctor's daughter, she might be his servant, she might be someone he had found on his journey and chosen to keep. Whoever she was, Han thought she likely did as much good as the doctor.

The doctor knew it, too. He called her over to give orders for the preparation of a medicine; halfway through, his eye was caught by these new arrivals, hesitating in the doorway of the tent. A slave in chains, a bundled child, a ghost: his gesture sent her hurrying to where she was more needed. He could assemble his prescriptions himself.

That was how Han read it, at least. Certainly the girl came; certainly the doctor fetched a bowl and went toward his jars.

"Hullo, I'm Tien. How may my uncle serve you?"

"This," Han held out the child, "this is her daughter," with a jerk of his head backwards to indicate the ghost-woman. "I—found them both, in the city. The child is, is, is not dead . . ."

Which was as much as he could say, except one thing more, as Tien went to peel back the wrappings from the child's face: "If you don't take her, truly, I am going to drop her. Now."

The girl was quick. He felt the child's weight lifted from his arms, in that precious last second that he had. His hands dropped, under the weight of their cuffs and chains; a moment later so did he, straight down onto his haunches.

That was better. The chains could puddle around his bare feet, let the earth take their weight. Some of it. The rest was still on his wrists, where they rested on his knees; on his neck, where his head was bowed.

His shoulders burned, his arms trembled cruelly. His head was dizzy and he wanted to lie down, but wouldn't do that. This was a place for the genuinely sick, not for giddy boys who were only tired and hungry and afraid, a little frantic deep inside.

There were voices above his head. One was resonantly male; it said, "What is the matter with the boy?"

Another was lighter, swifter, he'd heard it already. Tien said, "I don't know. He's filthy, he's exhausted, but there's more. His right thumb's gone; that looks recent, and I think it must hurt him. The chains, though—I don't know about the chains."

"No. Neither do I. Give me the child. You take the boy to the river. See that he washes, see what else he needs."

"Uncle, no! You need me here. See, this is the child's mother, she—"

"She will wait, while I tend her child. What can you do? See to the boy. I mislike those chains."

THE GIRL didn't—quite—take him by the chains and tug him to his feet, though her temper might have liked to. Her hands were cool on his arm, her words were crisp: "Can you stand up, boy?"

A moment ago the answer to that was a firm *no*. Now there was her voice, and that was impelling. There was her strength, as a counterweight to the chains. The two together were irresistible.

Once he was up, he found he could walk as well. One step after another, and if he was leaning on her more than a boy should lean on a girl, that was not such a terrible thing, as it turned out. She smelled pleasingly, astringently clean, and there was a firm resilience in her that he might have been interested in, curious to explore on another day, a better day, any other day than this.

DOWNSLOPE BEHIND the tent, clean water ran between the camp and the city. He wouldn't have called it a river, himself; give him a bamboo pole and he could vault it, without a second thought. Could have vaulted it before, when he was a river rat or a grubby little ink-boy. Now he was a crippled slave, and no: his hand wouldn't grip the pole properly, his weight of chain would drag him down, he'd likely end up in the water, even in this narrow little hop-over . . .

He ended up in the water anyway, barely needing her encouraging shove when they came to the bank; dressed as he was, he dropped straight into the icy bite of it.

The bed was stony and the stream was shallow; he had to crouch, to duck himself right under. By the bank he found he could sit and have water no higher than his chin. It was fiercely cold on a hot day, but all the more wonderful for that. He dropped his head back into scrubby grasses and closed his eyes against the sun and thought perhaps he'd never move again, he'd only sit and let the current slowly, slowly wear his skin away, pick his flesh and leave his bones white-polished, scattered, finally free of chains . . .

He didn't even notice when Tien went away: only when she came back, the soft swift rustle of bare feet in the grass, almost a giggle in her voice. "Are you asleep? Or dead?"

Reluctantly, distantly, he denied it. Denied them both.

"That's good. Uncle would have been cross with me if I'd let you drown. I brought you soap, and a brush to scrub with. And clean clothes, so take those off first." When he didn't move, she added, "Do I have to come in there and do it myself?"

Was that meant to be a threat, or a promise? Either way, he was too tired to be teased. He said, "No. Just let me, let me sit for a while . . ."

"No. The water's too cold, it'll sap your energy. It could steal you away altogether. Seriously, do you need help? Those chains can't make anything easy."

Indeed they didn't, but, "No," he said, "no, I don't need help. Thank you."

He wriggled out of shirt and trousers to prove it, reached to drop the sodden things on the bank behind him and found that too much effort, so just let them go on the current.

"What are those chains for, anyway?"

"I'm a slave," he said shortly, as he rubbed his chest vaguely with her soap.

"No," she said, "not that. Oh, maybe you are, but who chains their slaves? That heavily, I mean, to stop you working properly? Besides, whoever owned you before, you're with the army now. Tunghai Wang can be cruel, but he's not stupid. Any smith on the beach would strike you free for the asking. Or for the iron, more likely, but they'd do it, go and ask . . ."

"I belong to one of the smiths on the beach," he said, in denial of the evidence, with the *Shalla*'s ring still in his ear.

"Oh. Oh, do you? Then why—? And why was my uncle so—?" And then, after a moment, "You're not going to tell me, are you?"

He could say *Ask your uncle,* but that was three words and complications, politics, evasion. It was easier just to say "No," and be sorry.

"Why not?"

That was a question he couldn't answer. Anyone who grew up along this coast knew about the dragon, knew about the Forge. He'd tried to tell Li Ton, had told him and his crew over and over, and had never been believed. Now he was among an army of strangers, and what had always been open knowledge seemed to have become his secret, his and Suo Lung's, and he didn't know why. Except that he was tired of being laughed at.

Tired of everything, now. Tired of hurt, of work, of bodies, his own and the dead together. Tired of scrabbling for scraps of iron to feed a war he cared nothing about, of thinking back to the *Shalla* as somehow a better time than this; above all, tired of watching his own thoughts in a dread anticipation, waiting with that endless grim certainty for the dragon's next stirring, and her next, and . . .

"All right," Tien said behind his head, "but if you're not going to scrub harder than that you need to get out of that water now. Besides, I want to look at that thumb of yours."

He let her coax him up onto the bank, where the sun could dry him while she tutted over the raw scar and demanded to know how that had happened.

He was too tired even to keep refusing, apparently. He said, "Li Ton did that. With a chisel, on the Forge."

"Who is Li Ton?"

"He is—was—captain of the *Shalla*. The ship that I belong to." His fingers reached toward his ear, checked, fell back into his lap.

"I thought you said you belonged to a smith?"

"Yes. He, we," *everyone belongs to the Shalla*. Explaining was too much trouble. Like everything. He fell back on a shrug, a hunch of his shoulders against her and the world and its deaths and its dragon.

Except that she wouldn't or couldn't be shrugged at, apparently. She still held his maimed hand, lightly in her own. "This needs treatment; it'll go on hurting, else. Uncle should look at it. Why did your captain do this to you?"

"Because, because I disobeyed him." Was that right? He wasn't sure, quite, but it must be close enough. It made sense, at least. It had seemed quite simple at the time; his life had grown more complicated since.

He didn't want to think about the dragon. Nor did he want any more questions about his maiming, or his chains. Instead, desperately, he said, "Tell me about you, your uncle, why you're here . . ."

She smiled at him distractedly, not in the least deceived—except about the dragon—and pressed more deeply at his wound, until he yelped. "Uncle's a doctor, he comes where he's needed. I'm here because he's my uncle, and where he goes I go. It isn't complicated."

It wasn't his life, so no, it wasn't complicated. He said, "Why do you follow him?"

"Because otherwise I'd have to stay at home and work all day in the paddy, and wait to be married, and then work all day in the paddy. With Uncle I have the empire to travel and all the world to learn. There is his knowledge to borrow, and my own to find."

Han—who would have stayed a river rat all his life, if his father hadn't sold him on—shook his wet head and looked deliberately around at the army camp and the ruined city, the death and destruction and the utter loss of hope. "But this is appalling."

"Yes. Of course. It would be just as appalling if I were still at home, and I wouldn't be here to help make a few things better."

"Is this what you want, to be a doctor like your uncle?"

"Better than a peasant's wife and the mother of more peasants. Better than an ironsmith's slave, too," and she gave his chains a little shake.

That was the first time she had touched the links. She must have seen already how the cuffs were graved with characters, but now her fingers found the smaller ones cut into the links themselves. She frowned in puzzlement, looked at them more closely, read a few aloud.

"Submission, rest, consent . . . content . . . compliance, ease . . . Han, these are not the words I would give a slave to carry."

"No. They're not for me."

"What, you bear them for somebody else?"

Surprisingly, he could still smile. "It's a slave's task, to bear burdens for his master." *Or his mistress,* but he could still be misleading even while he spoke nothing but truth.

"I want to meet this smith," she said, in a tone that bore no goodwill toward Suo Lung. And when he shrugged, unwilling to expose the man to a sharp tongue and a sharper mind, "Well, if you don't take me, I can always come and find him. I only need to look for you. That's if you're at work, of course. Not running around saving random girls."

"Will your uncle save her?" If not, this had all been pointless; and he felt it now as dangerous somehow, or at any rate portentous, ready to topple into meaning like a stone into a pool, sending waves far and far. He resented that, hadn't bargained for it, blamed the gods hung in the tent there for playing games with him.

"I don't know. It depends how hurt she is. Uncle will discover. Shall we talk about your hurts now?"

"No. Tell me why your uncle follows the army," *with you in tow, running loose around the camp, all these men in their raw blood-hunger . . .*

"All right, but close your eyes." She waited for him to do it, then laid his crippled hand flat in her lap. He felt her leg under the silk of her trousers, heard soft sounds he couldn't identify, and peeked: saw her draw a fine tube from where she kept it tucked in her sash.

Saw her glance at him, scowling.

Closed his eyes swiftly, and heard her smile as she said, "My uncle thinks that no man is doing his duty in the world, unless he is being tested in a hard court. He hates war and cruelty; his work is to heal bodies and lives. So he follows the army because this is his work, and they need him so much, and he hates everything they do. This city, this work has tested him to his limits, and he is still here."

"And so are you."

"Of course. If I want to learn, I must be tested too. He says."

"What do you say?"

"I say, if I want to learn, I must stay with him; so yes, I must be tested too. Hush, now. Eyes closed, mouth closed. No more questions. Be still."

He felt it then, a cold fine touch on the back of his hand, the firm tap that sent it home into his flesh. Another one, two more into his wrist, slowly, her fingers finding the place to set the point of every needle. One in the crook of his elbow. One into his shoulder, and then one into his neck; she tutted, and he felt her finger's pressure there, and guessed that she was wiping blood away.

"Good. Now stay," as though he was an ill-trusted dog; and then, because she had promised, she told him stories about following her uncle, following the army. All her stories were lessons, he thought, and her needles were the point of them.

He had the sun on his skin, her needles in his flesh, her voice in his ear. Pain had ebbed; it was a distant thing, untroubling. The world was a still slow place, even the blurred noises of the brook were another kind of stillness, an expression of what was. He had so little that was still, ever, in his life, so little time to sit and not work, not hurry, not hurt, not be afraid . . .

· · ·

UNTIL THE dragon rolled over in his mind like a cat that rolls in the dust.

Reached out a leg, a long claw to pluck at him.

UNLESS THAT was the needles, doing more than push pain away. Unless it was her voice, doing more than tell him stories.

SOMETHING IT was, and she undid him, she cut all the strings that held him so tight and together; and whether she was the dragon or the girl he couldn't say.

It didn't seem to matter.

HE DIDN'T move, he couldn't; he sat as she had set him, with his hand still in her lap, and he wept.

When she asked what the trouble was, he said, "I have a dragon in my head, and I try, I do try to keep her chained . . ."

AND THEN of course there could be no more silence, no more secrets. He told her of the Forge, of Suo Lung, of the dragon and her chains.

At some point, the girl's uncle had come down to the water's edge. He was standing behind them now, out of Han's sight but within his ken, listening to his confession.

The doctor's own news came later, broke over them like water over rocks, too strange to do harm.

Tien had asked him how the little girl did, and how her mother. He said, "That . . . child . . . is not a little girl. Nor a boy, now."

FIVE

Breaking Faith

one

She said, "Chien Hua?"

He said, "Oof!"

She said, "Lord?"

He said, "You're heavy."

She said, "I am not."

He said, "You are. I think they've been feeding you. But that's not it, that's not why you knocked all the breath out of me. Mei Feng, you said my *name*."

She—who knew that perfectly well—said, "Oh! Oh, I did . . . !" and gazed fretfully about her.

He said, "What? I'm not angry, I liked it. It's what I want."

"Yes, lord, but—" She gestured at the walls, the screens, the perfect hush of his bedchamber. "Someone might have heard me, and you know they would make trouble. I dare not say the emperor's name, it is forbidden . . ."

It was properly forbidden to all his court, even his highest generals, even his mother. But it was Mei Feng on his bed, in his lap. "Hush," he said, nuzzling her neck cheerfully. "No one heard but me. You can say it when we're secret."

"Lord, we never are. You *know* they listen all the time." Every servant was a spy for someone; that was axiomatic. Some these days were spies for her.

"If they didn't listen, how would they know when they were wanted?"

He was being quite unreasonably reasonable, and she let him know it: pouting at him, shifting her weight, drawing a gasp in response. "I hate it, always having to be so careful what I say. And it's worse for you, it must be."

"I'm used to it."

"Not like this, lord. Not having them so close all the time, so that you can never have space for yourself, or for you and me, or you and anyone," graciously admitting that he might occasionally like to spend private time with someone else, because she knew just now that he was so obsessed with her. "It's this house," she said, glowering at all its walls, "it's so *small!*"

He was laughing at her, hugging her, almost bouncing beneath her. "Mei Feng, you told me you had never been in a building so huge. Huge, you said. You thought it was a palace. The throne room used to scare you, you said it was too big for people, it was like a temple and somewhere so big should only belong to the gods, you said . . ."

She had said that; she was quietly pleased that he remembered. And hid her face in his chest and muttered, "I know, I did. I was overwhelmed. You overwhelmed me, lord, but I blamed the house because I was so frightened of everything."

"You're not frightened now."

"Always, a little bit; you are emperor, and everyone here out-ranks me . . ."

"You quarreled with my mother, last week. You told her she was wrong. And she's scarier than I am."

That was true too, every part of it. She smiled, letting him feel it against his skin. "I did, didn't I? You lend me courage. But they still scare me, all these people, packed so close."

He sighed. "Mei Feng, I'm sorry, I cannot give you rank. I am emperor, but they would never let me marry you. *Because* I am emperor, they will never let me marry you."

"I know, lord. That doesn't matter. I just don't think it's safe for you to live like this. The guards are always fighting, and your mother and her women are so close," *too close,* "you can't get away from them or from the generals either. You need space, and you can't find it."

"There are no larger houses, sweet one. Anywhere on the island."

"I know." She took a breath, and said what she'd been working for. "I think you should build one."

LATER, RESPECTFULLY on her knees before his mother, she said, "Great lady, if the Son of Heaven"—which was flattery every time she used it, because of course he was his mother's son as well—"if he is to stay here on Taishu, he should have a palace proper to his majesty."

And so should you, her eyes said, delicately lowered to the dowager empress's slippers.

No danger that the empress would disagree with her on that. They were all so predictable, these clever courtly people: they were so trapped in their proper courtly roles, their feet followed ancient paths and they could only go exactly where they did.

The old woman said, "The proper palace for his majesty is the Hidden City; nothing else would remotely satisfy."

"Yes, great lady."

That brought her a black-eyed stare. "Girl, do you imagine you can rebuild the Hidden City? *Here?*"

"Yes, great lady." A moment, for that to strike home; then, swiftly, before it could be classed as insolence or ignorance or bluster, "I think we must, great lady. His majesty deserves no less; he cannot properly be accommodated in anything less." Those weren't her own words, she had heard them from a clerk and stole them shamelessly. "The true Hidden City is the emperor's heart, but we could build him a mirror of it. You only need to choose the site," passing her a map. "We have men to do the work; it would be good, to give them work to do."

The empress frowned. "The army watches the coast. The rebels are massed across the strait; we cannot spare one man to build a pleasure-palace."

"Of course, great lady, the emperor's safety must come first, before even his comfort," *before even your own,* which the empress was shrewd enough to hear. And perhaps to feel in her stiff joints, her own cramped quarters. "But you brought ten myriads of men with you, a mighty army." She had no actual idea of the numbers; she was gambling that neither did the empress. It was, she thought, the only gamble she made today. "It doesn't take so many to watch the sea. If the rebels come, we will see them from a distance, and this is a small island; there will be time enough to meet them with as many soldiers as you choose.

"Until that day," she went on, "idle men are dangerous. If they have no war, how long before they want one anyway, to rise up against their generals," she managed not quite to say *the emperor,* "and govern their own lives? Give them work, keep them busy, you will keep us all safe. And what better work, than to build a new house for the Jade Throne? Until he can reclaim his home in the north, his majesty has no home at all unless it is here. Let us build it for him, great lady. Please."

"Who will . . . plan, design this palace you dream about?"

Oh, she was sharp, she had spotted it already. "There are architects here at court, who know the Hidden City intimately; but it will be his home, great lady. It should be his to plan."

Idle men are dangerous, emperors no less than common soldiers. A scheme so great as this, it would possess him; it would leave the day-to-day governance of the island and the army where the empress most wanted it, in her hands and her generals'.

She nodded slowly, imperiously. And gestured at the map and said, "Where, then? Nowhere on Taishu is far"—indeed, nowhere could be far, to a woman who had crossed the world—"but it should be less than a day's journey from here." Close enough for her to interfere, she meant, while it was building.

Mei Feng intended it to be farther than that, and managed not to say so. She laid a finger on the map and said, "Here, I thought, great lady, on the Jade Road: between the mountains and the sea, and the road already there to make the journey easy," and her lying finger might lie satisfyingly close to Taishu-port but it was a long road, days of travel at old-lady pace, and she had in mind that the palace ought to find itself much closer to the hills. His strength at his back and all his vast empire spread before him, if he could only see so far.

That final choice, of course, would turn out to be his. That was her excuse, prepared in advance, for when the empress objected to it. In the meantime, they smiled at each other in perfect collusion, two women making plans in his absence for their man.

The empress said, "I will summon the council, to consider this. They may wish," meaning *I will tell them*, "to send men out on the road immediately, to discover possible sites and make sketches of them, to show to the Son of Heaven for his consideration."

Mei Feng bowed where she knelt.

THE COUNCIL was pleased—very pleased indeed—to approve the emperor's notion that another Hidden City should be built, and that he should have the planning of it. Why, the generals said, they could find him the finest woodcarvers on the island to make models of the buildings, all the palaces and pavilions as he planned them, all the barracks and administrative quarters, the treasure-houses and the temples, all that had been left and lost; he could lay out his models right here in this hall, arrange and rearrange till all was to his liking, on a map of the site that could be painted onto silk and laid out like a carpet . . .

The emperor was there, to watch them please themselves so very much. And Mei Feng was there too, sitting on her stool at his feet, smiling privately to see how they thought to contain him, a boy playing with his toys.

AND NOW, only as much later as it takes for orders to be given, here they were in the courtyard outside the hall; and here was a caravan in the making, and there was the gate out into the city, into the world. Just a notion, just a step ahead.

She was a fish-girl from a fishing village, though she had to pinch herself to remind herself of it sometimes. When you needed to go somewhere, you stepped onto a boat and cast her loose, and wind and water took you. Mostly.

Mostly, if she had imagined land-travel, she would probably

have seen it the same way. You sat on a horse and cast it loose, and it took you where you wanted to go. Mostly.

Reality, it turned out, was something else entirely. Of course it was. Everything about this new life was other than she had imagined it. Why should travel be any different? Besides, this was travel with the emperor. Of course it would be noisy and difficult and delayed.

The jademaster's ponies had to be conscripted from his stables, and his traveling wagon likewise. Their own preferred guards and servants had been forewarned, but were still not ready. She and the emperor stood on the throne-room steps—he on the top step, she just one below, where he could lay his hand conveniently, possessively on her shoulder, and she could lean lightly against his whippy strength and pretend that he ruled the world—and they watched chaos slowly resolve itself into some awkward kind of order, and waited with a dreadful patience for the council and his mother to descend upon them.

Which they did, fussing and scolding but not quite able to forbid, because after all he was the Son of Heaven and they were not; and he said—to his mother, ultimately, because she was ultimately the one who mattered—"Of course I am going. It is my project, it will be my palace; who else should choose where it will stand?"

The old eyes narrowed. "Majesty," his mother said, always a danger sign, "this is ridiculous. It's a giddy game, a child's prank . . ."

"Not at all. I have been mewed up here in this little house since the night we landed." So had Mei Feng, because he would not willingly part with her, and because imperial concubines did not run around free while their lord's attention was elsewhere. "The people are not used to us; we are a burden and a cause of fear. It may help them, to see their emperor abroad. It may serve to quell unrest, if we give them sight of us; and, yes, let us get at least a breath of air. When we have built the Hidden City—we'll call it the Autumn Palace, I think, they say that autumn is the best season on the island—we'll have parks and gardens, all the space we want. Till then, at least let us have the road between there and here."

That wasn't a plea, it was a commandment. And he was emperor and could not be gainsaid, not even by the dowager empress his mother, not in his servants' hearing. There was one more round of argument when a horse was brought for him—"The emperor does not ride like a common soldier!"—but apparently he did.

Mei Feng felt victorious—shaken and jolted, but still victorious—passing out under the great gateway, turning onto the Jade Road itself, leaving the empress and the generals and the stultifying court behind her. The emperor might ride like a common soldier, but of course she did not. Even if she were allowed she could not, she hadn't the first notion how to sit or steer a horse. She rode in what had been the jademaster's own carriage, attended by her favorite pair of maids. They were sweet and quiet and lightly scandalized by her insistence on leaning out the windows to see the world. If that meant the world could see her too, so be it. Why not? The world had had plenty of time to watch her, all her life until now.

Besides, what she could see of the world was flat on its face along the side of the road, carts and mules all abandoned as the people fell down before the emperor.

Indeed, here was the emperor, drawing rein right beside the carriage, laughing at her, just a little scandalized himself:

"Mei Feng, get back inside! You're like a child, trying to upset its nurses . . ."

"You're the one upsetting my nurses," she said, aware of the fluster behind her, the two maids not knowing what to do in the presence of the Son of Heaven, where they had no space to kowtow. "And if you want the people to see you abroad, as you told your mother, perhaps you should tell that man up front to stop bellowing your approach. Everyone who hears him is trying to dig themselves into the dirt, so no one gets to see you at all."

"Oh," he said easily, "the bold ones will peep. And the story will spread, everyone will know that I came this way. You told me that, this is your *idea*, Mei Feng . . ."

It was; she did. She lied.

She only lied a little. It just wouldn't make much difference, she thought, to the people of Taishu, where and whether the emperor came or went.

On the other hand, it would make a deal of difference to the pair of them once it was established as a habit, a thing they did and could do as they chose. His mother might be thinking of this as a singular event, one rebellious journey and hereafter he'd be content to play with maps and building-blocks in the jademaster's hall. If she did think that, she'd be swiftly disabused. The Autumn Palace was to be his project, his own; of course he'd need to spend time there, perhaps more there than in Taishu-port once the work began.

If there was a flaw in her plotting, she couldn't see it. The emperor would be happier, with the wind in his hair and work to do; her people would be happier, with so many soldiers isolated inland, less of a threat and less of a burden; even the empress ought to be happier, with her son distracted and out from underfoot.

And Mei Feng herself—well, she was here. There was wind in her own hair, and that was good, even if it had no salt in it. The bone-jarring progress of the wagon was nothing like the smooth toss of a boat under sail, and the seat was inadequately padded, but there was always another way to achieve a softer ride.

"Lord," she said, "you ride your horse like a hero, but even heroes get saddle-sore if they ride too long," and he was already shifting his weight from one buttock to the other, rising in the stirrups to relieve both at once. "Will you not give yourself and your noble animal a rest, come in with me where we can talk more comfortably?"

Where she at least could be more comfortable, she meant, cushioned against the jouncing within the firm resilience of his lap. Her maids would be so upset, she might have to make them walk.

She couldn't honestly be sure, until she asked; she didn't know what pleasures he took from horseriding. His breaking grin reassured her that the pleasures he took from her could still be paramount.

It couldn't last; sooner or later—and likely sooner—his mother must find other women for him, and one or more than one of those must catch the fire he still reserved for her. Not yet, though. For the moment, she had his heart and eyes.

Also, the new palace project would always be hers, hers and his together. All her plots were immediate. As immediate as might be, to move regiments of men as far down this road as she could contrive it; immediate today, to give the emperor this time free of his mother; immediate now, to ease her own sore buttocks by planting them firmly in his lap.

Sometimes she thought she used him, abused him as badly as his mother did. But she choked that thought with laughter, every time. However she schemed and manipulated, in the end she still gave him exactly what he wanted. She could do that exactly, in the way that his mother could exactly not, because at the moment what he wanted was exactly her.

two

*Y*u Shan was watched, and they wanted him to know it. Tong did it massively, gloweringly, standing foursquare in the gateway with his arms folded and a blank, blocking look on his face. Master Guangli was simply and openly curious, delighted to have a stone-addicted miner in his hands, full of ways to use him and not at all prepared to let him go.

Even so, he was stricter than Yu Shan's family had ever been.

"You have an affinity with the stone," he said, "and that's a precious thing. I'll teach you to carve, and we'll see if you have a gift in that direction also. The exposure you've had up till now, though, you will not enjoy again. There'll be no more sleeping with it, no more sucking it, no more swallowing dust. You will touch it as little as you must, and treat it as a poison. Which it is. Is that understood?"

"Yes, master."

"Good enough, then. You and I live and sleep upstairs; we eat up there or in the garden here. You go into the workshops only when I tell you. Again, understood?"

Again, "Yes, master." And then, "Uh, where does Tong sleep?"

"Tong sleeps by the gate, and guards the house. Never mind Tong."

YU SHAN didn't actually want to run away. Sometimes he did want never to have come here, always to have stayed with his family in the mountains. Now that he was here, though, he was content to stay. His clan-cousin always had said that he was too accepting.

She was probably right, but there was no point howling at the mountain, or fighting a river in flood. He had lost what he loved, including her; if he couldn't go back, then he should learn to love something other. He could sit at Master Guangli's feet and learn his art. That might be enough.

If he was allowed to do it. The first day, Master Guangli kept him away from jade altogether. Jiao had been right, Yu Shan did indeed scrub out the kitchen; that was a daily duty now. So was sweeping through the living quarters. And hauling buckets of charcoal, lighting the stove, cooking meals. He didn't really know how to cook, but he was learning. And washing his master's clothes and his own, and hanging them out on long bamboos from the gallery to dry in sunlight. A hard day's chores, and barely a glance at a distant piece of jade to season them.

By sunset on that first day, his head ached and his palms sweated, there was a shiver of fever under his skin. Master Guangli looked at him and grunted, told him to be glad it wasn't worse. "I didn't truly think you could manage all the day. Come on now."

Downstairs from the gallery, into the courtyard garden where Master Guangli had worked all afternoon. The piece was out of sight now, put away; but there was the length of oiled silk he spread to work on, still glittering with shards and dust of jade. Yu Shan could take a delicate squirrel-hair brush and sweep up all those leavings; he was allowed to gather it—with his hands, even!—gently, scrupulously into a pouch, which he might then watch Guangli weigh and seal in the workshop. Where now Yu Shan was allowed to look at some of the work, even to touch it as he cleaned and tidied, until the light was gone.

His headache ebbed from the moment he came close to jade; his skin calmed after the first touch. Even so, that little hour's work around the stone could never be enough. The headache had ebbed but not departed altogether, it lay like a threat on his horizon; his skin was cold and sticky yet, he wanted to rub it. Actually he wanted to rub jade-dust into it, but Guangli was watching him.

Guangli made him strip and wash, and gave him different clothes to wear. His own were checked carefully, the jademaster feeling all the way along the seams to see if there was hidden stone sewn into them.

Wet-haired, cool and damp and starting to shiver again, Yu Shan said, "Master?" entirely as though he did not understand.

Entirely as though he was not fooled at all, Guangli said, "I thought you would be sicker."

In truth, he was sicker. He had jade under his tongue, under his skin, where even Master Guangli hadn't thought to look for it, and he was still sicker than he seemed. That little sliver might keep him alive, if it was all he had to depend on, but it would be a poor, weak, desperate kind of life. It wouldn't see him home.

He wanted the wonder-stone, and wasn't allowed it. He asked if he could see it, and earned himself a cuff on the ear and not a glimpse.

"Not a glimpse," Master Guangli said, who had spent half the morning hovering over it, behind the privacy of a closed door. "Go to bed, and if you so much as dream in green I will know it, and beat you in the morning."

He was given a bowl of cold rice and pickled plums, though, to take to bed with him; Master Guangli's words and hands were rougher than his heart.

Bed was a pallet in a bare and dusty room upstairs, a terrible great space. He didn't mind the emptiness of things but it was empty of people and he didn't like that at all, he didn't know what to do with it. How to sleep.

When he was a child, he slept with the women, with the other children. Then they said he was a man and he slept with the other men, except some nights when he and his clan-cousin could find each other and sneak off to sleep in the forest, if they slept at all.

Or there were the nights he was on watch at the mine-head, when he was alone but did not sleep; and there was the couple of nights after he'd left the valley, when he slept on his own in the forest, until Jiao found him. Even then he hadn't felt alone, because he had the wonder-stone. He hadn't slept much, and when he did, yes, his dreams were full of green.

And then there was Jiao. Who was not his clan-cousin, but still.

She was good to sleep with, and consolatory, and he would have welcomed her just now.

He would have welcomed any company: Master Guangli, Tong, any breathing body. He missed the sounds of other people's breathing. His own breaths scared him, in such an emptiness: they were too loud, they said too much. He thought the room was hungry for him.

He ate his rice and pickles with his fingers, in the dark. And lay down, and pulled a cover over him, and had never felt farther away from sleep.

He wanted . . .

He wanted Jiao, yes, but only because she was nearer and more possible.

He wanted his clan-cousin, but only because he wanted to be somewhere else, someone else, that mountain mining boy who was already lost.

He wanted the wonder-stone, but only because it was unachievable, a glory beyond his reach, far beyond his deserving.

He wanted his old jade pebble, that he had sucked smooth through the years. He wanted to slip that into his cheek and play it gently with his tongue, roll it from one side to the other, tuck it behind his teeth, suck and swallow and suck again, feeling the little tingle in his mouth and all through his body as his blood carried it about.

He sucked his fingers, where there was still a lingering taste of black vinegar and star anise. That was all he had, and not at all what he wanted.

He found himself on his feet and in the doorway, stepping out onto the gallery: gritty, gappy wood beneath his soles. He should scrub these boards, perhaps. Tomorrow.

Below, across the courtyard was the workshop where the wonder-stone stood together with much more jade. Stones had all the company they could want, and he was alone.

Perhaps they would not mind, if he should join them . . .

But there was a soft guttering yellow glow breaking out of the

workshop, and then the door opening, and out came Master
Guangli with a lamp in hand. He paused, and looked up: looked
straight at Yu Shan.

And didn't speak or gesture, but turned and locked the workshop door behind him, very pointedly, before he went to speak to
Tong in the gateway.

By the time he mounted the gallery stairs, Yu Shan was back in
his room, back in his bed and shivering beneath the covers, sucking his fingers, alone.

IN THE morning he had to find fresh clothes and wash everything
from last night, clothes and bedding too, because they were sodden with a sour sweat.

Guangli saw him hang his quilt over the gallery rail to dry. The
jademaster looked Yu Shan over carefully, and his frown only
deepened.

"Did you sleep at all, lad? Truthfully?"

"Yes, master," though only fitfully and toward dawn, and then
he had been dreamracked and desperate.

"Mmm. Do I owe you a beating?" And then, after a moment,
"That was a joke, lad. Of sorts. There's no need to laugh. What I
mean is, tell me of your dreams. Whether or not you dreamed of
jade."

He tried, but it was hard: all shattered images, as though he'd
only ever seen the shards. Instead Guangli made him talk about
the long night when he hadn't been sleeping, how he'd sweated,
how he'd shivered, how he'd thought the darkness was a living
thing, close friend to the silence and the two of them conspiring to
engulf him.

Master Guangli made him a drink of herbs, and that did help,
at least to give his mouth a fresher flavor and to settle his roiling
stomach. It still wasn't what he needed.

The jademaster knew that too, and startled him by pressing a
key into his hand.

"This will open all the workshops," he said. "It will be your duty every morning to unlock the doors, open the shutters, let the stones have light and air. Don't linger, don't touch, don't try to steal more than I give you. Take what this is, and be grateful."

"Yes, master."

WITH THE jademaster's eyes on him, he went to the wonder-stone last. There were other workshops around the courtyard, some holding no jade at all; he deliberately unlocked those, went in, and threw their shutters wide. Simply knowing that the stone lay ahead of him—soon now, soon!—let him take his time toward it. Unless it was perversity. He knew people who would say so.

Had known people who would say so. He had a new life now; he knew no one.

Still, those who had known him would recognize this stubbornness, as he let what he most wanted linger in the corner of his eye, as he showed his new master that he did know how not to grab.

One by one he came to the doors that concealed treasure. Unlocked the first, and walked in; breathed air that jade had breathed all night and felt the hurt and harm of his own night judder back a step, two steps.

Opened the shutters, so that light fell in and the stone sang in his eyes; and walked smartly out with his back impossibly turned to all that jade, and went to the next door and opened that.

Last and best, he came to the door that hid the wonder-stone, and so to the stone itself. And didn't even think to trail his fingers across it as he passed, going in or coming back. His eyes were greedy for it but he still didn't falter, didn't stay. And if his tongue was pressed hard against the floor of his mouth, no blame to him for that. It was a dishonesty, but only a small one—a tiny one, a sliver—and he felt he'd earned the jademaster's approving nod regardless.

He held out the key, but Master Guangli said, "No, keep it. You can lock up again at sunset, once you've swept out the workshops, as an apprentice should."

You can lock yourself out, he was saying. *It's a test.*

· · ·

BEFORE THEN, though, he brought Yu Shan into one of the workshops and said, "I don't suppose you can read, lad, eh?"

"No, master."

"No. You'll need to learn, if you want to be a jade carver. I suppose I can have you taught. In the meantime, though, every boy
should know how to write his name. Sit here," on the floor, with
an old crate before him like a table. "Take these," a sheet of paper,
brushes, inkstone and a water dropper. "You know how to grind
ink?"

He did; he had seen that done. They weren't savages, in the
mountains. They wrote letters. His uncle could write. And offered
to teach him, but he hadn't seen the need for it.

He ground inkstone and mixed it with water. Sitting beside
him, Guangli took the brush and wrote two characters at the top
of the sheet. "Yu Shan. Jade Mountain: a strong clear name, with
strong clear characters. Is this the first time you've seen it written?"

Actually not, but he nodded anyway, to please the jademaster.

"Watch again, and pay close attention to the direction and
order of the strokes. It's important to make the characters just as I
do. Left to right, top to bottom, and close it out like so . . . Now
you. Take the brush, take ink, do as I did . . . No, these two and
then the vertical, and the bottom stroke to close it . . . Yes. Again."

And again, and again; and then he was left alone with a fresh
sheet of paper to do it more, until his strokes were straight and
clean. It wasn't really learning to write, he understood that, it was
a dog's trick, *see, I have trained my boy to write his name;* but still
there was a pride, an excitement in it, the making of marks that
meant himself.

Master Guangli came back into the workshop and all Yu Shan's
skin was alert suddenly. His eyes couldn't find it, but—

"Yes," Guangli said, almost sadly. "You know it's there, don't
you, boy?"

He reached into his sleeve and drew out a flat plaque of jade
with a crack that cut right across it.

"This is no use for anything but practice. You know how to

mine the stone, and how to abuse it; today you have your first lesson in how to carve it. You've learned to write your name in ink;
now you can learn to cut it into jade. You'd like that, wouldn't
you? To see what the stone says, and know it's saying you?"

He was teasing, apparently, and he was serious at the same
time. Yu Shan nodded seriously back because yes, of course he
would like that, it would sit in his head like a bright star in a clear
sky.

Guangli laid the plaque before him, and Yu Shan did not—
quite—touch it. He didn't need to. He could have closed his eyes
and traced out its dimensions exactly: its size, its weight, its damage. Its nearness seeped into him through the fingers that were not
quite touching, through the sweat on his skin and the water in his
eyes and the air that he wasn't actually sure that he was breathing.

"Feel better, don't you, lad?"

A nod. It didn't need words.

"All right. Take the brush, and write your name on the plaque."
Then, when he hesitated—"Yu Shan, it washes off. Even carving
can be smoothed away. The stone forgives the craftsman. But you
do have to begin. Nothing forgives the lazy man, or the coward
either."

Lazy he was not; coward—well, perhaps. Certainly he was
afraid of this. To make marks on jade and do it not well, that
seemed unforgivable. Heretical. Unbearable.

He lifted the brush and dipped it in ink. Wrote his first stroke
on the stone, and watched how the ink ran away from the brush,
to dribble across the plaque. Aghast, he raised his eyes to the jademaster's.

"I told you," Guangli said gently. "Wash it off, dry the stone,
begin again. And remember, stone does not absorb ink as the
paper does. Take less on your brush."

He did all that, and tried again. And again.

"Don't be so hesitant, Yu Shan. Art is bold, always. It can be
subtle; it cannot be shy. And don't try to write so small. You have
all the space of the plaque, a double palmful: two palms, two
characters. Use it all."

The longer he took in his lesson, the longer he could stay with the jade; but that would be stealing, cheating. He would not be deliberately awkward. Besides, he didn't need to.

Again and again, until he was satisfied and the master too.

Guangli took the brushes away, and gave him a slender tool with a bamboo handle and a glinting steel head.

"This is a scriber. Jade is a hard stone, but this is harder. Scratch away the ink, and you will find your name scratched into the stone beneath."

He gripped the plaque with his left hand, brought the scriber to it with his right.

"Yu Shan. If you pick at it that lightly, all you'll do is tickle the ink away and leave not a mark on the stone. Let the blade bite. You've spent your life chipping jade from the mother-rock; you can't tell me you're shy to scratch it now."

He chipped it raw from the mother-rock, and it felt like liberating something that needed to be free. This, though: this had been shaped and cut and polished already, even though it was flawed; hurting it further was . . . difficult for him. And besides, he was touching it; it lay in his hand, and his body was drinking that touch and it was doubly hard to cut at what sparked in his blood, what seared his skin like a hot spring pool, water too hot to move.

But. But Master Guangli would take this away from him, if he wouldn't or couldn't be a carver. Yu Shan didn't want to be a servant all his life, sweeping floors and washing clothes.

So. He set the blade of the scriber to the ink, where it lay upon the stone; he felt it like a blade against his own skin, and nevertheless he pressed as deep as he dared, dragging the blade along the stroke of the ink.

And stopped short, because he would have sworn that he was bleeding. Master Guangli scolded him twice, once for being tentative—when he was sure he'd been determined, even aggressive—and once for checking too soon, when he was barely well begun.

Yu Shan looked at the plaque and saw the brief scratch that he'd actually made, as against the deep score that he'd felt. And nodded and put the tool to the stone again, gritted his teeth and cut.

It wasn't—quite—pain. It was like an examination of his spirit. As when he was young and he caught a splinter under his skin and his mother would work it out with a needle, prying sharp steel into his tenderness and never quite hurting. In some fractional and divided sense, he was a part of the jade, and it a part of him; and this was not violation, quite, but it broke their proper border. The blade of the scriber wrote in him as much as it did in the jade.

If he could feel where the blade cut, he could guide it more truly: here and here, this way and that. He cut as he had written, left to right and top to bottom, closing off the characters and adding their final dashes, trying to copy the same swift confidence with the scriber that he had copied with the brush.

He worked, and then it was done; and then he stopped, laid down the scriber, looked to Master Guangli.

Who said, "Yes. Well. Not much I need to give you, is there? Beyond a lifetime's practice, I mean. Give me the plaque."

"Is it, is this well done?" He couldn't tell, he could barely see it; it was like trying to see himself, without any kind of mirror. The simple fact of it overwhelmed him.

And the plaque still lay in his hand there, the stone was singing to his blood and his blood was singing back, and—

"It is well enough done, for a first attempt," but the jademaster said it with a sense of something left unsaid, as though his pupil had surpassed his expectations and it was a struggle not to praise him for it. "Give the plaque to me now."

It was a weight in his hand, but not a burden: like the weight of a man's own bones, proper to carry. But a man's bones seemed dead in his body compared with this; the stone pulsed with its own life. He could feel the fracture, a falter in the pulse, but—

"Yu Shan."

Master Guangli sounded like the jade itself. He struggled to lift his eyes from the smooth green and the characters of his name, and saw that his master's eyes too had a green cast to them, as deep as the jade, although they could not sing so clearly.

"Yu Shan, give it to me."

Well, he could do that. He lifted the plaque in both hands, stood to face the jademaster, presented it with a low bow, an offering, as though it was his to give.

Master Guangli took it from him with the same respect, both hands, nothing mocking or dismissive.

And then it was gone, and he wanted it back, and couldn't have it.

He asked, "What will happen to it now?"

"You know that. Jade belongs to the emperor."

"Yes, yes, of course—but it is cracked, it cannot be a gift for him." *And it has my hand on it, it has my name on it; and I, I am also not a gift for him . . .*

"Indeed not, but it must go to him none the less. He has his own craftsmen in the palace, who make lesser things out of broken pieces. Or he may choose to keep it, as a record of his newest servant," with a dark and potent glower at Yu Shan, to say he was not worthy.

It wasn't about being worthy; he wasn't willing. "I am not the emperor's servant!"

"Servant to his servant," a touch at his breast to indicate himself, "so indeed you are. And how not, when you have set your hand to jade?"

Some child in Yu Shan had him wanting to put his hands behind his back, shuffle away from the crate with its giveaway scriber and its betraying dust, deny his name and his handiwork altogether.

"It's said," the jademaster went on, "that he has a list of every man who has ever carved a piece of jade for the throne, for any emperor."

Yu Shan gawped.

"Of course, he may have left his lists in the Hidden City. His caravans could only bring so much. If so, he will want to start anew; and from today, your name must needs be on it."

Master Guangli put the plaque away in his sleeve. Yu Shan folded his hands together, against any inclination in them to shake. Or snatch. Or reach to the crate, run his fingers through the inky jade-dust there, lift it to his lips.

There was a little dust, a very little under his nails, and in the creases of his hands, caught by the damp of his sweat. He could feel the faint tingle of it on his palms, in his fingers, as he could always feel the shard in his mouth.

Master Guangli was reading his mind again, unless it was his body that gave him away. "You don't need any more for now. You're not the same boy I brought in here an hour ago; you're bright, alert, like a plant in sunshine. That'll see you through the day, lad. Gather up this dust—every last grain of it, please—and wash your hands. Thoroughly. Then get to your chores. See if you can learn to be a houseboy, as swiftly as you learn to handle jade."

ACTUALLY, WHAT he was learning was not to handle jade. It came hard. Some days he was dizzy or sick, some days he sweated, some days his belly and bones gave him so much pain he could barely walk. And that was with the secret sliver still in his flesh, giving him at least some relief until he was allowed into the workshops again, to learn the use of another tool or to work the lathe or just to watch Master Guangli until it was time for him to sweep and tidy and lock up.

That was better, all of that was better: but then there was the night, and he had to endure that alone, except those nights that Jiao came.

MORE NIGHTS than not, Jiao did come. Sometimes it seemed that Master Guangli had bought her too, that day he bought Yu Shan.

The first time, Yu Shan thought the jademaster had sent for her. It was his third day in the house: after his second night of sweat and yearning, pain and twisting and no sleep. That day Master Guangli took him out of the house for the first time, to show him the way to market. And have him carry the basket—not that there was much to fill it with: he used to eat better in the mountains than he did in this teeming city—and then send him to carry the marketings home, to scrub and peel and chop vegetables, to pick over dried beans and soak dried fish for dinner.

When Jiao turned up in time to eat, the jademaster was not at all surprised. Yu Shan inferred that she had been invited. *To distract the boy* seemed to be inherent. When she stayed—when she stayed and stayed, after Tong and Guangli both had gone to bed, after even she had entirely run out of words and she still stayed—he was sure of it.

If he had to be wakeful and needy, far better to do it in wakeful and distracting company. When she gave him other reasons to sweat and grunt, to turn and reach on the pallet, he could almost forget the tooth of hunger in his soul, almost find that the sliver under his skin was enough jade to see him through the night.

Almost.

Master Guangli seemed to like the better look of him in the morning. And Jiao seemed to like to watch him work, whether he was cutting jade or scrubbing pots or sweeping. At any rate, she lingered late and came back early.

Perhaps it was only that she had no reason to be elsewhere. The courtyard was a pleasant place to sit. She and Guangli were old friends who could do business together when there was any, talk and laugh and eat when she had nothing to trade except her time, which she spent freely. When Guangli worked behind closed doors on the wonder-stone, she left him alone, happy enough to torment Yu Shan instead.

She tossed knives across the courtyard, to make them *thunk!* into one or another of the wooden columns that supported the gallery. She sprawled in the sun, lazily sharpening her sword or else, more often, lazily asleep. She slept a lot and called it a soldier's habit, being thrifty of herself, storing up what was needful for when it might be needed later.

Later perhaps meant the nights, when she could stay awake with him, keep up with all his lack of sleep. More nights than not, she stayed.

· · ·

"Yu Shan!"

"Yes, Jiao?"

"Leave that and come here. Sit, sit. I've brought you a present."

Sit, sit apparently meant *kneel, here in front of me, where I can adorn you.* She was still admirably possessive, forgetful perhaps that she had sold him on.

Guangli barely looked up from his workbench, met Yu Shan's gaze and shrugged at it, neither helped nor hindered. Left him to take this as he chose, which meant passively, easily; the easiest way to handle her was to let her handle him.

She'd brought an amulet, on a necklace of green stones. His heart missed no beats at all; they were sea-polished pebbles, nameless and meaningless.

She said, "The green goes with your eyes; I knew it would. The amulet is for some local goddess, you should know who . . ."

Not a valley goddess, not a mountain goddess; how would he know?

"I thought it'd give you something to suck," she said. "For those nights I'm not here, and you need something to do with your mouth."

He wasn't sure whether she deliberately made him blush, or whether she just did it without trying. She still grinned, every time she saw it.

"The man I had it from, he said she gave protection from dragons. I expect she does. Suck on this and I don't suppose you'll be bothered by dragons your whole life long."

She was mocking, which was the best way to say she was a stranger. Even Yu Shan knew about the dragon beneath the strait.

The man must have been a stranger too, to be parting with a dragon-ward at a time like this. He'd be one of the emperor's soldiers from the far north, most likely, where they knew nothing. Yu Shan could guess how it was: some woman struggling to the beaches, pleading for a place on a boat, offering whatever she had to trade. He'd be fast enough to trade it on again, why not? Knowing no better . . .

Jiao knew no better than he did; she said, "I like to see my men all pretty," and dropped the necklace over his head so that it lay bright and anomalous over his dull worn shirt. It didn't matter then how much she misunderstood it. Even his clothes weren't his own here, he wore what the jademaster gave him; the amulet and its necklace were instantly precious to him, because they were his, and because she gave them to him.

And she had long cool fingers and her own wiry wicked pirate strength, which she would use and use through the night, along with the wide mouth that seemed so much softer in the dark, the tongue and teeth that did not. And the lean body of her, slippery and forceful and insinuating, leaving him no space to be alone or needy, leaving him nothing that was his alone except what she chose to give him.

That saw him through the nights, those nights that she was there. When she wasn't, even then he had the image of her in his mind, the memory-touch of her on his skin—if she never left him bruised, it was not for lack of trying—and the taste of her in his mouth. She saturated him; he had that to set against the yearning jadesong. It was better, he thought, to be fought over than simply to be craving. It was always better not to be alone.

HE CLUNG to her, with a need she was too wise to read as passion. And when they were bodily exhausted and he still not sleeping, often she would not sleep herself, another gift she gave him; and so they were lying together and talking softly, sticky where they touched, when they both heard the first sounds from below.

Yu Shan's room was directly above the passage that led from the lane to the courtyard, his floor making its roof: *Servants' quarters* Jiao said, so that those who slept there would hear late arrivals. He didn't mind the implication, that he was only a servant here; it was true. The gate stayed locked from sundown to sunup, in any case. Tong was a guard more than a gatekeeper: a weapon of ward, not a welcome.

And yet, they both heard the creak of hinges and the shuffle of feet directly beneath the boards they lay on. A murmur of voices, too: heard clearly, because they'd both fallen entirely silent at the first creak of the gate. She by long-standing piratical instinct, he because her hand was on his mouth to silence him.

She counted men off as they passed, her fingers tapping the count against his lips: *One, two, three, four. Five* . . . And then a hesitance, an uncertainty, a shrug: *Call it five.*

Five, and there were two of them: but she was a rogue, a pirate, already swinging to her feet and reaching for the tao she always carried. Naked and unworried, she stood by the door and eased it open, glanced back to see him on his feet and as ready as she was. Unarmed, but ready nonetheless.

She sidled out and he followed, too big and too heavy to ape her lightfoot glide; the boards creaked beneath his feet. That didn't matter. There was sudden noise below, a lot of noise, sounds of chaos and destruction.

Yu Shan hoped the jademaster had sense enough to leave this to his household. Master Guangli had not been young for a while; he loved his garden and would want to defend it, and should not.

Definitely, he should not. Jiao was running around the gallery toward the courtyard stairs; Yu Shan looked over the rail, and counted. Yes, five men wreaking mayhem by torchlight. Breaking the walls of the pond, overturning the bench, smashing the image of the water god Gung; and this was only making noise. They meant worse than this. They meant harm. They reeked of intent; he did not like those torches, in this dry and wooden house.

They had seen Jiao: seen her sword and her nakedness, and welcomed both with a shout. They saw a fight coming, and a frolic after. He thought they were fools, on both counts.

She had the stairs, on the far side of the courtyard. He put both hands on the gallery rail and vaulted over.

Dropped twice his own height and landed barefoot on gravel, yelling to be sure the men would notice. Two turned and saw a boy, a naked boy, no more: less than the woman, even, as he didn't have a blade. One snorted, as if he was barely worth the killing. They both came forward, though, drawing steel as they came.

The first saw no need for anything subtle. Killing Yu Shan

would be like breaking the statue, overturning the table, just a gesture. He came with his tao raised and hacked like a man hacks at creepers in the forest, like a butcher hacks at a hanging carcass, a hard clean blow that should have divided Yu Shan's ribs from his belly.

Except that Yu Shan wasn't quite there, where the blade was cutting. Which meant of course that the man was off-balance, meeting nothing but air and toppling into it, so that Yu Shan could reach out with both hands, seize wrist and forearm and *twist,* as he sometimes twisted a grown bamboo to get at the pith inside . . .

The man screamed, as his bones splintered.

The tao fell to the ground, but Yu Shan didn't trouble with that. He had no fighting skill with a blade; all he could do was hack, and he'd just shown himself what a bad technique that was. He clubbed the man on the side of the head, just with his fist, and dropped him amid the ruin of the courtyard garden.

The second man was a swift learner, but still confident. No wild swings; he crouched low and jabbed the point of his blade at Yu Shan's belly, jabbed and jabbed, swift and hard and never over-reaching. Yu Shan had to back away, back and back, only barely dodging those darting thrusts.

There was something behind him, one of the wooden pillars that held up the gallery; there was movement high in the corner of his sight, Master Guangli in a robe, with a long sword in his hand, heading for the stairs.

Yu Shan wondered—briefly—where Tong was, in all this noise and disaster. Then he ducked behind the pillar and looked for Jiao instead. It was hard to see her clearly in snatched glimpses, with three men about her and everyone in motion, but he thought that at least one of the men was bleeding, and she was not.

The blade came slicing at him one more time, around the slender pillar. But the blade of a tao is sharp only at the point and along the leading edge. He snatched downward, his hand like a heron's beak, seizing. He had the heavy back of the blade between fingers and thumb, and shouldn't have been able to grip it that way; oiled steel thrust forward and jerked hard back, it should have slid away from him like a fish in bitter water.

It didn't. His fingers locked on it as though they were welded to the metal; when he pulled, he ripped it out of the man's hand like stripping creeper of its leaves, that easily.

Ripped it, looked at it, flung it aside.

Stepped out from behind his sheltering pillar, and it was the bandit's turn to back away now.

Not far, he was no coward; he just needed something in his hands to fight with. A length of bamboo that had been a pole for climbing plants became a stave instead, whirling in the space between them—until the man swung it savagely at Yu Shan's head, and he flung up a hand to catch it.

Caught it like a flung stone, and barely felt the sting; gripped it, tugged it away.

And flailed with it, inexpertly but too fast for the bandit. The bamboo slashed across his face, splintering as it went, tearing a thousand little channels of blood; then Yu Shan swung it back again while the man was howling blindly, caught him hard on the side of the head, felled him where he stood.

So now there were three—or there had been. One of those was on the ground, blood-swathed. Jiao had backed a few steps up the stairs again—deliberately, Yu Shan thought, to prevent Master Guangli from coming down—and was holding the surviving two at bay, at swordpoint.

Yu Shan ran across the courtyard, screaming, "I'll take the short one, Jiao! Leave him to me!"

He was quite proud of that. They were, distinctly, a tall one and a short one; and his yelling did make the short one check, step back, look around. Which meant that when Yu Shan drove his bamboo brutally into the back of the tall one, sending him sprawling across the stairs, Jiao could finish him with a single swift thrust to the neck, and then the two of them could turn together to face the short one.

Who snarled like an animal, but did not run. His gaze flicked toward the gate and then came back to them; after that single hopeful glance, he didn't look that way again.

He did still fight, and took a length out of Yu Shan's bamboo, which didn't matter; and held off Jiao through a brief frenzy of swordplay, which didn't matter either; and lost his feet then because Yu Shan swept them out from under him with one long-armed crouching swing of the bamboo, and so died, which presumably did matter, at least to him.

He died because Jiao thrust her blade through his belly and his spine as he lay tumbled before her. Swift and neat and savage, sprayed with blood that was not her own, she lifted her head and looked about her, as if she was disappointed not to find more men to kill.

Master Guangli came down and looked at the destruction; he looked at the fallen. He looked at the gate where it stood wide and said, "Where is Tong?"

And that, of course, changed everything. Three words remade the night.

The gate was open. Apart from the three of them, only Tong could have opened it without a deal of force and noise; Master Guangli had good locks.

In the room above the gate, both Jiao and Yu Shan had been confused by the numbers of men below, as though there might perhaps have been a sixth.

Before he died, that last bandit had given one desperate glance toward the gate; he might have been looking for help that did not come, rather than an escape he could not reach.

Tong was guard and gatekeeper, here precisely to defend his master's house. Tonight, when he was needed, somehow he was not here . . .

Yu Shan was already running. He heard Jiao call after him, but not Guangli; without his master's voice to halt him, he kept on.

Out through the gate and into the lane, and yes: there was Tong, unmistakable, his vast frame moving at the best speed he had.

Yu Shan was faster, no question of that.

As he ran, he remembered that he was also naked. Also un-armed, except for a pole that was shorter than it had been. Also much, much smaller than Tong . . .

He touched his tongue to the shard of jade, or rather to the flesh that had entirely healed over it, as though that little touch could somehow endow him with extra strength. And kept run-ning.

Where the lane met a stream and opened into a little garden, a grove of trees, a bridge more delicate than its use demanded, Tong stopped his lumbering run and waited for him.

HE LOOKED like rock in the moonlight, like a man of rock, vast and impregnable. Yu Shan faltered, wondering if Tong had actu-ally stopped to speak to him. He'd never heard the man put more than half a dozen words together, but he could hope. He slowed to a walk, came cautiously closer, waited.

Tong stooped, picked up a rock from a bed of flowers, and flung it at his head.

YU SHAN ducked and the rock flew above him, close enough to feel the hard wind of its passing; he felt a shudder in the earth under-foot as Tong followed the rock, a great shadow charging at him.

He had seen men set the butts of their spears in the ground and hold them at a jutting angle, to take the charge of a wild pig or a mountain cat. This bamboo was no spear, too short even before it was abbreviated. Still, he could improvise. Especially against the bull rush of a man who was barely looking, who must be half blind in this slippery, deceptive moonlight.

Yu Shan tucked the butt end of his staff into the cleft of a tree just at chest-height and swung the splintered end toward that shadow as it came, hoping to see the giant man impale himself on it; held it tight and felt the judder as flesh met bamboo and was pierced, yes.

Let it slide out of his grip as Tong straightened, roaring like a speared beast; meant to slide himself behind the tree for shelter but was too late, too slow. Never saw the swinging fist that felled him, only felt its sudden impact and went sprawling headlong into the grove, because the staff was and always had been too short to keep him safe.

Knocked dizzy, he clung to the earth as it reeled beneath him, as Tong belled and stamped behind him. Instinct or good sense set him crawling—sooner than he wanted to, while the ground still bucked and kicked like an earthquake—deeper into the shadows of the grove. Tong would come after, but slowly; and meantime Yu Shan could haul himself to his feet, try to shake the giddiness out of his head, reach up reluctantly to feel for damage where the side of his head pulsed with flame.

None to find, no soft or giving bone beneath his fingers. Good: it was only his brains that were bejangled. His mother always said it took no brains to fight.

Here came Tong, blundering between the trees, loud and clumsy and full of rage. Yu Shan was still learning how deeply the jade had its grip on him, blood and bone, how he was different from other men. He saw this moon-dark grove with a green cast to it, but he did see it, every trunk and branch and every hanging leaf. Tong could apparently not see it at all, but had to feel his way one-armed, while he held the other, blood-dark, hugged across his chest.

If Tong wouldn't run now, perhaps Yu Shan should. He was naked and alone and far from home; if he had a place in this city, it should be with his master Guangli. If he ran back now, Tong wouldn't try to follow. Guangli wouldn't blame him. Jiao would be relieved.

If he slipped away quietly, Tong wouldn't even know he'd gone . . .

But they were two men in a grove, alone in the dark; of course they had to fight.

And he had nothing to fight with now, and couldn't face Tong's simple strength empty-handed. One blow had taught him that. His head was still ringing, and his bare feet were unsteady on the ground. One more of those would finish him.

He needed a weapon, and was surrounded by trees.

He had stone in his bones, jade strength in his hands. He reached up to grip a branch, where it grew sturdily from the trunk of a young cypress; and set aside long years of disbelief and self-denial, everything he'd ever understood about the place and strength of a man; and heaved.

And tore that branch down, just ripped it from its mother-trunk.

And had no time to wonder at himself, or at its weight in his hands, so heavy and yet so easy. Of course Tong had heard the noise, and turned toward it. Perhaps his eyes were adjusting to this degree of shadow; here he came, charging between the trees. Yu Shan backed away fast, out of the grove and into the moonlight glare.

As he went, his hands were stripping twigs and leaves from the branch until he had a staff again, almost a long club that he could whirl around his head and flail at Tong when the man came bursting out from between the trees.

Tong saw it coming too late to duck, but he flung his arm up against it: the arm he'd been cradling, blood-soaked from his pierced shoulder. Branch and arm met with a fearsome cracking sound, and it wasn't the branch that had broken.

Tong screamed, but still he kept on coming, stumbling as he ran, all but doubled over; it was his barrel head that slammed into Yu Shan's chest, with a force that should have broken bones in its turn. It drove all the breath out of him, and knocked him to the ground again.

Then Tong fell on top of him, monstrously heavy and murderously inclined; but caught his arm in falling, and screamed again, and seemed suddenly to have no fighting strength.

His weight might almost have been enough. Would have been, surely, for any normal man. But Yu Shan had discovered himself to be almost unbreakable and stronger, so much stronger than he should be. A buck and a thrust rolled the agonized Tong off him.

It took him longer to catch his breath, longer yet to scramble to his feet. By then Tong too was getting up, slowly and painfully. For a moment they faced each other, each of them gasping, each a little bewildered.

Tong was no talker at the best of times. It needed to be Yu Shan who said, "Enough, let be. I don't want to hurt you anymore—"

And that was when Tong stooped and snatched up the fallen branch, and wielded it one-handed like a hero out of legend, and caught Yu Shan a dreadful blow in the ribs that sent him sprawling, falling one more time, only this time he fell into the river.

MOUNTAIN POOLS were colder but rarely so unexpected, except that time his clan-cousin had pushed him in for the laugh of it when they'd only been walking, talking.

He had no clothes to drag him down, but he had no breath to hold.

He fell into startling chill and was embraced by it, engulfed by it. Might have been kept by it, except that he kicked and struggled mightily and struck out frantically into air and snatched a desperate gasp before he went under again.

And came to the surface again and found himself under the bridge, just as there were heavy footsteps stumbling across it. Gazing as he was at the underside, he could see how it was made, how the pegged wooden beams all supported one another: how it would take only a tug here and a wrench there to pull the whole structure apart . . .

JUST TIME enough to see it, to understand it, to decide against. If he did that, then what? The bridge would fall, and there would be a chaos of heavy beams crashing down all around him; and among them all would be Tong, and perhaps they would fight, or perhaps Tong would drown, or perhaps they would both be borne under by the weight of falling timbers . . .

So Yu Shan clung to a beam and listened to the vast man's running, and he could hear Tong's pain in his footsteps and in his grunting moaning breaths, and was sorry. Even when he remembered the deaths and damage at the house, he was still sorry, a little.

He'd never seen treachery before, he'd never come across betrayal. It didn't happen in the mountains; your clan was your clan, and there was no shifting that. He'd heard stories, of course, but they were always from elsewhere, tales of emperors and mighty armies, politics and wealth and sorcery, nothing to do with Taishu.

Nothing till now, perhaps.

He pulled himself out of the water and walked home, slow and wet and disconsolate; and met Jiao halfway, who had dressed herself and armed herself and thought to bring a blade for him too, just not any trousers.

three

The ghost-woman had destroyed her own son, just to save his life.

Han couldn't stop thinking about it.

He'd spent days picking up bodies, and some had very obviously died before the soldiers reached them, and yes, he understood that. He could see absolutely why a mother would kill her children, sooner than see them violated and slaughtered by unloving hands.

This, though—this was something other. She had cut the boy's—the boy's *parts* away, apparently with her kitchen cleaver.

Han could hardly bear to think about it, except that he couldn't stop.

She had done that, and then she had dressed him as a girl and let the wound bleed into the clothes, so that the soldiers would think the child had been raped already.

Perhaps it was her own rape that had made such a ghost of her, but Han didn't really think so. He thought it was the knowledge of what she had done to her son.

It had cost them their voices, apparently, mother and son together.

The boy was mute from sickness and might recover, if he was lucky. If he was a boy still. Tien's uncle was reluctant to admit that; he called the child *it*, when he remembered.

Tien called him Bai, an assertion of the child's maleness as well as his newness, as though he were a whitened sheet ready to be written on again. It would do as a milk-name, but Han hoped for the day when the child would talk again. To Tien, at least, and her uncle Hsui. Han himself had duties otherwhere; if the boy took much longer to find a voice, he wasn't likely to be around.

"Pfui," Tien said, spitting such gloom aside. "Suo Lung, that idiot smith? He doesn't need you. You're no good at finding iron for him anyway, I do much better."

This was true, but irrelevant. Han said, "He's not an idiot. And I need him, not the other way around. He helps me keep the dragon under control. Without him, she'd be free."

Tien spat again, high and far, clear across the stream. They were sitting on the bank munching dried fruit stolen from her uncle's medicine jars. Perhaps she was only spitting stones, but he didn't think so. She said, "My uncle will help you more. There's nothing more Suo Lung can do, and he's done his little badly. Uncle Hsui's the man you need now."

That was likely true too. Unusually for a northerner, the doctor had heard tales of the dragon beneath the sea and the monks who kept her. He was quick to understand that these chains Han wore were a poor shadow of the spell-chains that had once bound Suo Lung and other smiths before him, crafted and renewed by masters over years and decades. Those were lost, but Master Hsui had sworn to rediscover the principles of their making and recreate what he could, in the interests of them all.

In the meantime, there were dry herbs to chew and foul teas to swallow, which the doctor said would strengthen Han, body and soul, against the dragon's assaults. Perhaps he was right, perhaps they would. Meantime they left Han feeling dizzy and detached, uncertain on his feet and uncertain of the world about him.

Which was why they were sitting here, Tien and he, chewing illicit sweetness in stolen time, misunderstanding each other so thoroughly.

It wasn't Han's duties as the smith's boy that would take him away from her; it wasn't his duties as the dragon's keeper. It would still be Suo Lung that he must go with, but the reason for it pierced his ear. He belonged not to the doctor and not to the dragon, not to the smith but to the *Shalla*.

Which was afloat, repaired, ready for sea again; and word had spread along the beach and through the army's camp, her former crew was recalled.

Han said, "I have to go to sea again."

"What, with your old pirates? What for?"

"Orders."

"Ignore them."

"I can't."

"We'll keep you here, stay with us."

"I *can't*."

"Why not? You're no use to them. You never were a proper pirate anyway, and you must be hopeless on a boat, with that hand and the chains too. What do they want you for?"

"It's Suo Lung they want."

"Fine. Let them have Suo Lung. I *told* you, you'll do much better with us. You're Uncle's patient now, you can't just go off in the middle of treatment. Give them Suo Lung, and you stay here."

He sighed. "They want Suo Lung, and won't go without him; he won't go without me."

"Oh, just tell him you're not going." Because the smith was slow, because he was illiterate, she thought him stupid; which meant, in her idea of the world, that he should yield to smarter minds. Which meant, necessarily, her own.

"I can't. He won't listen."

"I'll tell him, then."

"He still won't listen. You don't understand how this works, Tien," *you don't want to*. "Li Ton wants Suo Lung. Suo Lung doesn't have a choice about that, he has to go; but he wants me, and Li Ton won't argue. He won't see the point, except that he thinks I warm Suo Lung's blanket for him," the most roundabout way he could think to say it; on shipboard they used other expressions, or simply gestures, "but he'll take me anyway. However useless I am, I still belong to the *Shalla*. This says so," a touch to his ear.

Her hand snaked, to snatch at the iron ring; he jerked his head aside.

"Oh, you could take it out," he said, "but it would still say so."

"I could take it to your Suo Lung, and have him melt it."

She could be stubborn to the point of idiocy, and here it was. "You can't stop a thing, just by denying it. You can't change Suo Lung's mind, nor Li Ton's."

"I can talk to Uncle Hsui."

SHE DID, despite Han's protests; and the doctor was so fraught, so determined—"You cannot, you can *not* go off adventuring at this time!"—that he went storming out to find Li Ton and explain it to him.

And came back denied, repulsed, as Han had foreseen; but not chastened, and no less determined.

He was not exactly the only doctor in the army, far from the only man who claimed the skills of healing. Whenever anyone said "the doctor," though, it was Master Hsui they meant. Which meant he had reach, if not influence, he could ask for an interview with Tunghai Wang, the generalissimo.

He could be surprised—the second time Han had seen that—by a sudden irruption into his tent next morning. There were soldiers who chivvied his waiting patients out, who scared the ghost-woman away, her ailing son seized up and carried in her arms; there was Li Ton, and Suo Lung after him, nervous as the big smith always was in the presence of great men; there were greater men than these, men wearing fine robes and airs of importance, badges of achievement, scars and limps and such.

One stepped forward and said, "I am Tunghai Wang. I believe you want to talk with me."

"Yes. Yes, indeed I do . . ."

Han detached himself deliberately from Tien and went to Suo Lung, because somebody had to. The big man was trying to crowd himself into a corner, where he simply wouldn't fit. Han led him to a bench, sat him down, settled on the floor at his feet.

A minute later Tien came to sit the other side of him, so that he was pinned between the one who would take him away and the one who would have him stay. None of them mattered much in the debate; that went on between the great men, a few paces away.

". . . He is my patient, and not fit for travel. I want him here, general, under my eye. To take him voyaging would be both pointless and dangerous."

"He does not seem dangerous," the general said, after one swift glance in Han's direction. "Nor ill."

"His hand is crippled, his thumb hacked off by this same heedful captain. That wound needs my treatment. Furthermore, there is the matter of the chains."

"The chains that my own man Suo Lung put on him, when I gave the boy to him," Li Ton grated in response. "The boy is the man's, and the man is mine. Or say it another way, they both belong to the ship, and the ship is mine, and so are they. And the man will not come without the boy, and so I will take them both. General, you *ordered* this . . ."

"What exactly is it, general," the doctor asked, "that you have ordered?"

Tunghai Wang gazed at him, letting the question hang in the air between them. For that brief and lethal moment it was an accusation, a betrayal, a condemnation. But the general let it slip; he turned aside, looking from the doctor to the smith to the boy to the captain, and said, "Tell me about these chains. I see them, but they make no sense to me."

"General," Li Ton said, "they make no sense to any of us. They have no sense, they mean nothing except in Suo Lung's head."

"And yet they are written on, written all over . . ."

". . . and have been since the first day, the first shackle. Although the smith is illiterate," Master Hsui broke in. "There is more here than the chaining of a slave. Li Ton is wrong, those chains have a meaning; which I cannot grasp without having the whole at hand, the words and the chains and the boy too."

There it was, the necessary lie: they had agreed already, he and Master Hsui and Tien, that none of them would say a word about the dragon. If these northern lords knew the story at all, they knew it only as a tale to frighten children, a myth, a folly. The doctor lied to spare them the mockery of the great man—a *dragon?* beneath the *water?*

The slave-smith Suo Lung could have called him on it, and of course did not. That at least they could depend on.

But Li Ton also could have called the doctor on the lie, and did not; and that, Han did not understand. Li Ton knew about the dragon, Han had told him over and over. Why he wouldn't speak out now and so take what he wanted, at whatever cost to the doctor, was a mystery too deep to plumb. Han was only glad for his silence, and resentful that the captain should deserve even a hint of gratitude, and suspicious. Most of all, suspicious.

"And the smith will not leave the boy behind?"

"He will not, general." That was Li Ton telling simple truth, and here was Suo Lung proving it, laying one great hand on Han's shoulder.

"I suppose he cannot be, ah, compelled?"

They all looked at the massiveness of Suo Lung, and the stubbornness: *Here I am,* his body said, *and this is my boy, mine!*

"Not by threats, nor weapons," Li Ton said. "Not by whips. I suppose there are men enough to drag or carry him. At some cost, but men we can afford. The difficulty would be to make him work, if he had no reason."

"Yes. I see that. Take another smith, Li Ton."

Which was Li Ton's turn to show his stubbornness: "This is my man. He belongs to the *Shalla,* and to me. His work is good, and he lacks the wit to betray us, but those are secondary. He is my man, and I will have him."

"You will have him, and he will have the boy, and the doctor will not be parted from the boy because he sees some danger in this magic of chains and words that none of us can understand. Very well. Master Hsui, you will go too."

"General, I will not! I have patients . . ."

"And I have other men of medicine. No one will go untreated in your absence."

"Nevertheless, I will not go."

"But I say you will. The smith, perhaps, is too dull to be compelled, but you are not. You have a daughter, I think . . . ?"

"A niece," Tien said, her first words, the first from any of them at this bench.

"Very well, a niece. Threats and whips and weapons, I think the captain said. They will not work on the smith; so be it. I think they might work on you, Master Hsui. If they were used on your niece, I think they would work very well. Li Ton, you may bind her to your ship, to your service if you wish. Perhaps you should, to keep your men's hands from her . . ."

WHEN THE generals were gone and their soldiers with them, when the doctor's patients still didn't come back, Han said, "I'm sorry, I never thought . . ."

"Of course you didn't," Master Hsui said wearily, "why would you?"

"I should just have gone with Suo Lung, he's where I belong."

"No. I could not let you go. Without me," with a thin bitter smile against himself. "The generalissimo has the right of it: if you must go, then so must I. I will tell them I am willing after all, and at least they will lift the threat against Tien . . ."

"No," and this time it was his niece who spoke, more fierce than he could be. "If you go, I go." Perhaps she was truly speaking to her uncle, but her eyes were on Han.

"Tien, someone has to look after the tent, the practice . . ."

"I can't do that on my own. I don't have the skills or the respect. Tunghai Wang will put another man in here, and you can fight him for it when we get back. We'll all fight if we have to," meaning *We're all coming back*.

"Who will look after the ghost-woman and her child?" Han asked, siding with her uncle, not wanting to see her fight anyone.

"Bai, you mean, and his mother?" They could fight each other about anything, when there was something more important to avoid. "Where are they, anyway . . . ?"

"They went out the back, when the soldiers came in." Very quickly they had gone, one snatch and away. "She'll be down by the river."

The doctor went to look; Han said what was obvious, "We can't leave them here," among the very men who had raped her and would have killed her boy.

"No. She wouldn't trust another man."

"Where else, then?"

Where was there, that a distressed woman could go with a damaged child? In time of war, in an occupied city, where no one had counted the numbers of the ghosts?

"I would take her to a temple," Tien said, "but . . ."

But there were none surviving in Santung. The buildings still stood, mostly, and the figures of the holy still gazed down into prayer halls and courtyards. What they gazed down on, though, was mostly emptiness. The monks were dead, the nuns gone. Gone from the temples, at least. Like all the women of the city, some were dead, some scattered, some kept for women's duties in the soldiers' camp. The temples stood, yes, but they did not survive.

Han said, "There are temples outside Santung." All the living world was outside Santung now.

"Do you know where?"

No, he didn't; this was not his country. He had been a river rat, but not of this river. "I can find out," he said, "if they will give us time."

"It might take days," Tien objected, "there and back, to see her safe. I don't suppose we have days. The general and the captain both seemed . . . urgent."

"Well," Han said, "but if we are not here, they'll just have to wait for us, won't they?"

THEY MADE plans—hopeful, desperate, unlikely plans—to sneak the ghost-woman and her child out of the camp; and then they didn't need to. His men might not recognize the local gods, but

Tunghai Wang at least recognized the need for them. He gave orders that nuns seized in the city's rape were to be freed. The first of them meant to leave that day. They would journey to a sister temple, two days to the north; they would certainly not refuse the company of two more victims. Even the anxious ghost could travel with a parcel of women, not a soldier in sight . . .

Han and Tien shepherded the woman between them, while she carried the child. She was nervous at every step, but her child—or her child's need—seemed to give her courage; head up and staring forward, she bore her burden as she always would, Han thought, blind and unflinching and distressed.

When Han's small party reached the departure point, there was already a huddle of women crouched around a cistern, shaving one another's heads. Some had kept their dull brown robes; one or two had even kept them clean. Others were dressed like any of the camp women, in whatever clothing they could scavenge.

They should be safe enough, shaven-headed in a slow migration; everyone knew that nuns had nothing worth the stealing. From the look of these few defeated women, their bodies, their souls were as empty as their purses.

He said, "Go with these, they will see you safe. There is a temple they will take you to, where you can all look after one another. All of you can look after your son. You have the medicines, you know what he needs and when," and none of them knew what she needed, or how to deliver it. This was the best they could do. "Do you understand?"

It was the tenth, the twentieth time they had said this to her, one way or another. She had come with them unresisting, and she stood now as though she was ready to leave. They could have hopes for her and her child, he thought; that would have to be enough.

On the edge of going, then, just one last awkward linger—and there was a stir, another figure come to join the party. Another woman, not in nun's robes but with that soft stubble on her head that spoke of a shaved scalp growing out. The women around the

cistern made room for her. One perhaps lifted her razor in offering. None of them was ready for what she did.

She hoisted herself up by aid of one startled shoulder, stood on
the cistern's rim and gazed down on all her religious sisters. "You
know who I am. Some of you do. You, Sao Chai. You, Feng. And
you, though I don't know your name."

"I am called Chun Hua. And you are the mother of the old harbor temple."

"I am: devoted to the Li-goddess, as I have been all my life. As
you all are, whichever gods you served in other temples, other
lives. You are children of this city and these waters; you belong to
her, first and foremost. She will take care of you, if you come back
to her.

"Come back with me, now.

"Like you, I have been hurt and abused and appalled. Like you,
I have seen my city destroyed, my sisters slain, my goddess and her
temple desecrated. Like you I want to turn my back, to shun these
men and everything they've done, to shun this broken city too.
And yet, I am going back. To my city, to my temple, to my work.
To my *place*.

"Come with me, sisters.

"How often can we say it, that our goddess truly needs us? How
often is that true?

"Her house lies waiting for us, harmed but not beyond repair.
Defiled, but not beyond restitution. Empty of what it most desires,
which is its sisterhood, her devotees, its life.

"I go to see that life returned. Her house is destitute without us;
this city is destitute without its temples. Nothing will be whole
again until the goddess has her house again.

"Sisters, will you come?"

OF COURSE they would, if only because none of them quite had
the courage to say no, to be first to turn away.

And now they had a leader, and Han could in all honest con-
science hand the ghost-woman over to her, with the child too.

When he turned to take the woman forward, though, he found he
was too late. She had gone of her own accord, to the nun who had
the razor. Crudely, clumsily, she was hacking off her child's hair.
She cut it back to the scalp, in a ghost's approximation of a nun's
shaved head; then she did the same thing to her own thick locks.

four

Mei Feng had satisfaction for her daily meat, even if it was tempered by the hunger of her people.

Days in the palace, she could see how the generals, the councilors, even the dowager empress looked to her now as well as to her lord the emperor. They might despise and resent the upstart island girl, but they did have to acknowledge her influence.

She hid her smiles, her triumphs as a modest girl should, but she felt them keenly.

DAYS ON the road, she could watch from the carriage windows and see how the busy traffic crowded to the side-ditches to let them pass. That traffic was mostly men, and those men were mostly soldiers, and those soldiers were mostly headed for the site of the new palace. Every man on the road was one fewer to trouble her people at the coast: one mouth fewer to feed, one temper fewer to placate, one threat fewer to skirt around.

DAYS ON the site she loved for their own sake, for the traces they held of the life she used to know, wind and weather and far horizons.

The emperor laughed at her as she filled her lungs with air, spread her arms delightedly in soft rain, ran to the height of the hill to fill her eyes with distance.

"I swear," he said, loping after her, "you'd climb a tree just to see that little bit farther, if I'd let you."

"Oh, where," instantly looking around, "which tree?" She

hadn't swarmed a mast since he took her from Old Yen. She'd love the feel of a fat trunk, her arms wrapped around it and her legs likewise . . .

But life had changed since he took her from Old Yen, she had changed inside to match it; she was blushing already at the tumble of her own thoughts, before his hands settled on her waist and he said, "*If* I would let you. Which I will not. You would disgrace me before my army, and ruin your pretty clothes too. Stand quiet and be my perfect consort, and be satisfied with that. Until we're private."

"Yes, lord," she said, and smiled demurely up at him, and stepped away. Like the perfect consort, making no exhibition of herself or her master.

Satisfaction came with every glance around. In the beginning, Mei Feng had urged this project simply for its own sake, to occupy as many men as possible as far as possible from any of her own. Now she was learning to love the thing itself. They had a city-palace to build, she and her lord together; they had time and men and no limits beyond their own imaginations; how could she fail to love it?

Never mind that she knew almost nothing of cities, having only ever seen the two, Taishu-port and Santung, and really only the dockside streets of both. Her lord's was the voice of experience. He had grown up in the true Hidden City and then traveled all through the empire, seen city after city and an army on the march, which was a city on the move; he knew how people lived together, what they needed. All she knew was village life, boats and fishing.

And yet he let her speak, he listened. His mother and the council didn't care, if she only spoke about the city. It was his toy and so was she, that was understood; they could amuse each other, and so keep out of the way of wiser heads.

She might have been resentful on her own behalf; she might more easily have resented their treatment of him. Sometimes—in the palace, mewed up by rain and weary of the council's caution, the dowager's demands, their utter failure to understand that this

was a new world now—she could manage both. But never very
fiercely, and never for long. He would distract her with a word or
a touch, a kiss or a conversation; he might tug her shockingly to
his bed in the middle of the afternoon, for an hour's scandalous
play.

And then afterward he would pull out the plans for their magnificent new palace, he would take fresh paper and grind some
inkstone and look to her for new ideas. Were the towers on the
great gate high enough? Had they charted enough land for the
garden, if they meant to dam that stream to make a lake? What of
the barracks, should they be uniform or did she want to make
every separate building differently interesting . . . ?

And so on, until she had no resentment left. It was truly a fasci-
nating thing, to build a secret city. To bud an idea in her head and
then on paper, to talk it through with him, to see it modeled and
measured and finally marked out on the ground . . . It was a child's
game made manifest and a constant delight to her, and she cared
not a whit what her elders thought. They might believe it a toy, but
she knew better. They might believe the same of her, and she still
knew better.

THE SITE for the Autumn Palace had been her choice in the end.
Here in the foothills, with the mountains looming behind and the
wide plains stretched ahead, Taishu-port just a smudge on the far
horizon. Close to the Jade Road but not on it—so that the soldiers
would need to build a spur, more work, more men—they had
found a hill that rose alone, already a watchful presence over the
land.

"Here," she had said, "build here. Look, we can put a wall all
around the hill, then keep the soldiers and clerks to the lower
slopes and have a separate compound at the top for us. And another for your mother," and walls and guards between them, as
many barriers as she could invent.

Cities and palaces both must work that way, she thought, to
make access easy for some and impossible for others. She could
plan this one, to control who found their way swiftly to the em-

peror and who met one obstruction after another. Did the council think it ruled the empire, did his mother think Mei Feng was just a distraction? They might both learn better . . .

Much of the land had been cleared already; there were only trees she could threaten to climb because she and the emperor had stalked all over the hill marking those they wanted to keep. The rest had been hacked down, with all the brush and scrub. On dry days the air was thinly smoky; there were always fires burning, somewhere on the site.

At the base of the hill men were digging ditches, to make footings for the first rough wall. The men's own tents lay beyond that, an ever-increasing city in its own right. The emperor's accommodations were on the hill, of course, if not yet at the height. The oiled-silk tents they used first had been rapidly replaced with more solid and spacious structures, once it was clear that the Son of Heaven really would be spending days and nights here, week after week. His mother would be appalled, but to Mei Feng this was luxury enough.

Still, they did have to go back to Taishu-port, to the palace there, to the manipulations of the court. On the way, every time, she thought the palace walls enclosed him as much as they did her, long before the city was actually in sight; and yet he would still give up his horse and ride inside the carriage with her, simply because he knew how much she hated the return.

"When they have finished that first wall of palings," little more than a fence but she called it a wall, they both did, to make it higher in their minds and more defensible, "then no one could complain if we spent more time out there, days and days . . ."

"Mei Feng, one little wall—"

"—one little wall with half your army camped all around it—"

"—I was going to say, one little wall might serve to keep us safe, but not the empire, and not your precious island. I would love to, but if we waste our time—ouch!"

"Is it so very wasted? *Chien Hua?*"

"You can't hit me, I'm the emperor! If we *spend* our precious time doing what we want to do, lingering where we're happy, out of their eye, who knows what we might come back to? We barely fool them as it is. We trail bait and they bite at it, but they're none of them stupid. They need to see us, demurely building model palaces and drawing pretty pictures."

"I know, lord. I do know. And I'm sorry I hit you, but you're very annoying sometimes. When you're right."

AND so back to the flurry of the city, through the palace gates to her reluctant home. And the carriage jerking, creaking to a stop, and servants tumbling over themselves to bring steps to save his majesty the dreadful reach down, all that way; and more servants with cloths and carpets, to save his imperial foot from contact with the appalling bare gravel of the courtyard; and all those people bowing, kowtowing, crawling before him . . .

It was nothing but relief to be past them, inside the palace and their own particular wing, attended by their own particular servants for that little time before inevitably here came a summons from the dowager empress.

"Let her come to you," Mei Feng said, where she sat combing the dust of the road out of his hair. "You are emperor . . ."

". . . And she is my mother," he said equably. "When we have children, will you always be going to them?"

"I won't expect them always to be coming to me." But that quiet assumption earned him a little peace in return; she kissed the back of his neck and said, "Go, you. If you must."

"Come, you. If you want to."

She didn't particularly want to, but what would she do on her own? Bathe alone, and wait. It was better fun to bathe together. Besides, every time she let him go alone, she gifted the empress another opportunity to discount her.

So she bade him wait, still marveling that he would do that, that the emperor of the world would wait on her. The empress too: she made his mother wait while she took time to change his dress and hers, to put them beyond the censure of sour old eyes.

Then—hand in hand, because he reached for hers and took it— they walked out into the garden that divided their wing from hers.

Past shrubs and ponds, along a path that went directly, so that whoever was watching—and there was certain to be someone watching—could not say they meandered or dallied at all.

There were servants to open doors for them when they arrived, servants to bow them through; she would never be comfortable with this, but she was almost getting used to it.

And then there was the old dark room that was always smaller than she expected, no matter how many times she came here; and the old woman sitting in it, tea on the table and a servant to pour; and at least Mei Feng could take a cup quietly to a corner, watch her lord greet his mother, and neither one of them would expect her to have anything to say.

The empress asked about work on the site; he answered with honest enthusiasm, showing her what she most wanted to see, the child absorbed in his play.

Gratified, she offered him another gift: "There is a man," she said, "an islander, who came to see me. I would not, normally— but he is no normal man of Taishu."

Well, he couldn't be, if the empress would entertain him. She saw the provincial governor, at his regular audiences with the council; she might have seen him privately, once or twice; Mei Feng would be surprised if she had spoken with any other native of Taishu at all. Except herself, of course, and other servants.

The emperor was similarly impressed. "Who is he, mother?"

"A jademaster. Some say *the* jademaster. I believe this is his house that we are using." She wouldn't call it *living in,* she who was accustomed to a palace the size of a city; she was camped here, the most reluctant of guests.

"Then I must have spoken to him too." Less proud than his mother, more sensible of local power, the Man of Jade had spent an hour with the men of jade. And then another hour with Mei Feng in the bathhouse, *washing them away* he said.

"He says you have. That is one reason I have had him wait for you. Another is that you are emperor; the stone is yours, and so is the right to deal justice."

"What justice is that?"

"You will see. Go to the throne room; you will find him wait-ing."

Hand in hand again, they walked among the usual scurry of servants, through passages toward the public courtyard.

"Why isn't she coming too?" It was the emperor who asked, but he knew his mother so much better than she did: it wasn't a proper question, it was a test, to see if she had learned the lesson of it. He did this all the time.

"Because she knows what you will do, exactly. If there was any doubt, she would have dealt with it herself."

"I think so, yes. What can it be?"

That really was a question, and Mei Feng had no answer.

"She's subtle," he said. "Maybe she's already told the man what will happen, and she thinks I won't contradict her . . . ?"

He didn't really believe that, though. Nor did Mei Feng. The old woman was swift enough to see change when it came; other-wise she'd have stayed in the Hidden City, clinging to the invulner-able majesty of empire. The boy-emperor would have died there and then, and the rebels would have won in a month.

Instead of which he was here, in this last fragment of his rule, and he held Mei Feng by the hand and by the heart. By the hand even now, brushing past guards on their way to the throne room, to see the man who was perhaps the most powerful, certainly the richest on the island before the emperor came to displace him.

That rich man, that most powerful of men was on his knees be-fore the empty throne, a picture of supplication. At the sound of footsteps he kowtowed, on his own floor yet.

Mei Feng detached her hand firmly from her lord's and pushed him gently, discreetly to the throne, while she squatted on her modest little stool at his feet.

The emperor took his time to settle, shifting his weight and running his fingers over the carvings on the arms. She wondered if maybe they should get him a cushion—but it was not meant to be a comfortable place to sit, the Jade Throne. And he was happy to sit there for hours some days, with her in his lap, so let be . . .

"Rise," he said at last.

The jademaster sat back on his heels, kept his eyes low.

"Ban Hsu," the emperor said, and she felt a touch of prideful pleasure that he had remembered the man's name. "We are still mindful of your welcome, in giving us your house." Not *grateful,* and not *loaning*—if his mother was subtle, he had learned from her.

The jademaster Ban Hsu was a fat man, token of his good fortune. No one would ever say so, but the emperor carried the message of his own ill luck writ large on his own slender body. She loved that slimness, but it did him no good in the world.

Ban Hsu bowed low again, from his knees, and said, "Imperial majesty, whatever I have is yours."

Which was true, of course, in as many ways as she could count. The emperor was only being polite, acknowledging as a gift what in fact he had simply taken because he could, because it was his already. The world belongs to the Son of Heaven anyway, but the house of the jademaster, built on wealth derived from delivering the emperor's stone to him—how could that not be his own and his alone?

Politeness is one of the qualities of a prince. He said, "We are pleased to find ourselves honored, this far from the Hidden City. Loyalty will always be rewarded. In what way may the Jade Throne be of service to its friends?"

"Majesty, there is a jade-eater in this town."

He lifted his eyes to his emperor's, to show his sincerity. That was the only movement in the room. Mei Feng was seized by her lord's own sudden stillness and she thought, *Oh—this is why the empress was so sure of him . . .*

And why the old woman was right, of course. Stealing the emperor's stone—eating it yet, which was stealing in the worst way, making it lost to him forever—was a sin worse than treachery and worse than rebellion, because it was both of those and more. No emperor would be merciful to a jade-eater.

"Tell me," he said.

"Majesty, a man of mine who watches over one of the carvers I employ, this man came to tell me that the carver had a magnificent piece of jade that I had not sent to him. It had been brought from the mountains, by a boy from the mines. I sent men around to reclaim the piece on your imperial majesty's behalf, and to punish the thieves."

So far, so proper. This was why the jademasters were paid so handsomely, for the careful guard they kept.

"Yes," the emperor said. "And then?"

"The boy from the mountains fought my men, naked and unarmed, and they died. The one man ran and was chased and nearly died himself, though he is a mountain of a man and strong as stone. There can be no doubt of it, majesty. That boy is a jade-eater, and the carver no doubt has been feeding him."

The emperor grunted, and was silent. If Mei Feng had learned one thing at his feet, it was when to be quiet herself; she said nothing, tried not to move at all until he did.

Which he did with a sudden eruption, hurling himself up. "You will take me to them."

Mei Feng rejoiced secretly, because his mother had misunderstood him again; she most certainly would not have anticipated that.

Neither had the jademaster. Ban Hsu said, "Majesty, it would be more, more *fitting* for the guilty men to be brought here, where you may see them punished—"

"Fitting, would it be? Perhaps it would. But I don't want to see them punished"—he had lost all his imperial bearing, all his courtly manner of speech and distance; he was furious and curious, all boy—"until I have seen their crimes."

"They cannot deny them, majesty!"

"Perhaps not; but nor can I learn from them, at this distance. I am the Man of Jade and you are a, a purveyor, no more than that, and yet you know more of the stone than I do. I will go and see, and you will take me."

"It is not *safe*, majesty, this boy is deadly . . ."

"Well, and so am I deadly. So am I a jade-eater, Ban Hsu, although there has been little enough to eat this last year. But I am not a fool, either. We will take soldiers. You have your own men, but I suspect that mine are better. Come; we will go now."

And he began to walk the length of the shadowed hall, and he had not gone very far at all before Mei Feng was abruptly at his side. He wasn't ready; he hadn't expected this.

"No, Mei Feng; you are not coming."

She had his hand again, because this time she had taken it; she had her stubbornness; it was almost fun, to argue with her emperor. "Lord," she said, "I am." And then, because his name in her mouth always shook his resolution, "Chien Hua, I will not see you do this alone."

There was amusement in him somewhere, as there always was when she reared up like a hissing kitten against his inevitable majesty; it was almost lost, though, in the heat of his anger. That wasn't turned against her, but it might burn her regardless.

"Even my mother allowed me—no, she *sent* me to do this alone."

"Not this. If I prevented you, she'd thank me for it. She'd say it was madness to go down into the city, the emperor's own person. You know she would. She let you—no, she *sent* you to see the jademaster because she knew you'd be angry, as you are; and she thought you'd react as she would. She'd have these men brought here, it would never cross her mind to go to them. You *know* that."

"Do I? Well, perhaps I do. Do you think you can prevent me?"

"I don't want to, I think you're right—but you should not go alone."

"With the jademaster, and more soldiers than I want, and . . ."

". . . and you would still be alone. You need to take someone who loves you," which meant her.

"Do I? Why is that?"

"Because you are angry, and—"

"—and you think you can talk me out of my anger, because I love you? No, Mei Feng, that would be a reason not to take you; I am right to be angry—"

"—and I would not interfere with that anger for a little minute. These men have stolen from you something that belongs to the emperor alone; of course you must be angry. Of course you must do terrible things, to punish them. But if you do those things because you are a man among men, a commander in front of his soldiers, then it will all happen out of their fear and your pride, which is not good for you, nor for the throne. If I am there, then you will do these things because you are emperor and they are right to do."

She had made that up entire, on the wings of the moment, only because she didn't want to see him go through the gates on his own. She almost convinced herself; she thought she almost convinced him. For the last little distance he only had to convince himself.

Even so: "There will be deaths, Mei Feng."

"Yes, lord. Of course. If you brought them here, there would still be deaths."

"You wouldn't need to watch them."

"Someone would. Someone who loves you. Who else is there?" And when he paused, "I'm not afraid of death, lord."

"I know, you faced it daily in that dreadful boat of yours. It's not the same—"

"Oh, I have watched it too. I have seen men executed before this." She said it blithely, because it wasn't quite true. She had seen one man executed in her village, when there was murder done and so the traveling magistrate came on his donkey with his headsman trotting at his heel. She had been a young girl and had seen it all, and was sick with nightmares afterward for weeks. She had known the victim, of course, and the killer too, and it was all terrible. They would be strangers who died this time, and that ought to make a difference, and somehow did not. But she was still not letting him go off to do this thing alone. She had his hand, and she would hold it and simply not let go; and what could he do then, except humiliate himself under his soldiers' eyes, under the jademaster's . . . ?

He understood that; perhaps he read it from her sailor's grip.

He said, "We will go in the carriage, then. The street carriage." It was her victory, his surrender: not the first, but it might be the one that mattered most.

THERE WAS inevitably a delay while soldiers were summoned, while the carriage was fetched. Alone, he would simply have gone on foot with his soldiers running to catch up. Which would have been the wrong thing to do, all boy and not at all imperial. He didn't know that; you had to be a peasant, to understand properly how emperors should behave.

The carriage came, hand-drawn by soldiers, with enough spare men to make an escort. The jademaster had his own small carriage with his own small entourage, and would lead the way. Actually, Mei Feng thought, theirs too had been his own carriage, until the emperor took it as a gift. Imperial favor never had proved cheap.

Until imperial favor fell on her, she'd never left the dockside here in Taishu-port. Since then, she'd never left the palace except in her lord's wake. She knew the coastal waters, and now she knew the Jade Road very well; the city itself, between the docks and the palaces of the wealthy, she didn't know at all.

This was all new, then: broad streets and markets, open workshops, lanes where all the buildings were closed off and turned in on themselves. As the carriage drew to a halt, she turned to the emperor and found him stiff and silent, just as much closed off.

She touched his tense hand and said, "You've never ordered anyone's death before."

A sideways glance, a moment of drawing himself up within his pride—and then a sudden unburdening, the relief of confession, "No. No, of course not. When have I ever had the opportunity?" As though it were a rite of passage, something every boy had to look forward to. "There were deaths on the march here, when our own men mutinied or tried to run, or when others stole from us or denied us food or tried to bar our way, or . . ." Or a hundred other reasons, that he didn't like to list. "It was the generals who ordered those deaths. My mother said we were in the army's hands, until we came safe to shelter. Sometimes, there would be bodies by the roadside and I don't believe half those deaths were ordered. I think it was just soldiers, sergeants, taking their own decisions . . ."

Unwatched, unchallenged, an army in retreat. Yes. She looked at him, opened her mouth—and waited, gave him time to catch her up.

Which he did, nodding, saying, "It will not be like that anymore. This is my army now."

"The generals will not like it."

"They are my generals too. And can be replaced."

"Lord, do you trust them?"

"Mei Feng, I trust nobody. Except you, of course—and only you because you've had no time to grow treacherous."

"Yet," she said. Darkly. "I'm learning."

"I know you are. I'm watching."

They smiled at each other, momentarily content; then there was a slight knock against the carriage door as someone out there was careless with the steps, and his smile was lost.

She said, "Lord, if you don't want to . . ."

"It makes no difference. They have stolen from me. One of them has eaten jade, which is allowed only to the emperor. They have to die. Should I leave it to someone else, to see done? To my mother?"

His anger was stirring again, and he needed it; she stoked it deliberately. "Never, lord. It was you they stole from, it is yours to revenge; your mother would steal that too. She tried anyway, made it seem like her gift to you, which makes it seem like hers to give. That's theft, if you allow it. But you didn't, you came here to take it from the world, not from her hands. She would not have let you do this, lord, but it is done now," meaning *It is half done,* meaning *We can sit here all day and all night and no one will disturb us, no one will knock on the door and call for us, because you are emperor; but sooner or later you have to go out there and do this thing, or you will only ever be your mother's son.*

Which he knew. And he was determined, and certain, and angry with it; and oh, he looked so young . . .

And reaching out to knock on the carriage door, to have it opened for him; and stepping out into the lane, imperial feet in the common mud; and his guards closed in around him, but not quickly enough to close her out as she scuttled down at his back.

The gate to the house stood open. They went through to find Ban Hsu in the courtyard, with captives kowtowing in the gravel. She supposed they were captives. None of them was bound, but they really didn't need to be. The emperor's presence was a binding in itself. He could send all these soldiers away, she thought, and still no one would move a muscle without his order.

Even Ban Hsu was stooped over with his eyes on his feet, as though he'd really rather be down on the ground like a rain-rounded boulder with the rest of them.

Gazing down at the men—no, two men and a woman—before him, the emperor said, "These are the thieves, Ban Hsu?"

"Yes, imperial majesty."

"Is it known, is it *remembered* this far from court, what the penalties are for stealing jade?"

"Of course, majesty."

"And for eating the stone, that too?"

"Majesty, even the clans in the mountains, even the children who sweep up the chippings, they know. I ensure that they do."

"Well, then. Show me the carver."

Two men were kneeling by each of the prisoners. One pair reached forward an arm each, seized a shoulder each, drew their man up into the light.

For that first moment, she thought he looked like her grandfather.

A second look, a more thoughtful, fretful look confirmed it. Not to confuse one old man with another; only in that way that men can grow into what they are. Old enough to have fathered children who have children of their own, skilled enough to be a master of their craft, experienced enough to have some wisdom in the world: all that can show in the gray of a beard and the lines of a face, time's slow writing.

She saw him and thought of Old Yen, and didn't want to be there suddenly, wished she hadn't come.

And looked at the emperor, and was glad to be there however much she hated it. When this was done, the Son of Heaven would need someone to remind him that he was the son of his mother too. He looked—inhuman, almost: the Man of Jade, stone to the core. She thought there was even a greenish cast to his skin. That must just be the light. Sun reflecting off the water in the pond there . . .

The puddle of water, in the broken pond. She distracted herself by taking careful notice of how the courtyard had been brutalized: the pond spilled, plants uprooted, pots smashed. Gravel stained, she supposed with blood.

"Very well. Show me the jade-eater."

Even his voice sounded barely human suddenly.

The young man—no, not even that, the boy—dragged upright this time didn't even know to keep his eyes down. He stared back, seeming not so much defiant as bewildered.

Mei Feng let a gasp go, before she could bite it back.

His eyes were radiant in the late sun, the same brilliant green as the emperor's. She'd never seen it in anyone else: only in the Jade Throne, and her lord's rings, and all his other pieces. As though the stone had suffused his body, and shone out in his eyes.

The resemblance wasn't limited to that flashing gaze. The sense of vigor, of health, of strength beyond the normal in a man: the boy had that too. She thought it was his obedience that kept him on his knees, rather than the two men who held him. She thought he could stand up, shrug off his guards and walk away. With the emperor for companion, perhaps. She thought the two of them together could change the world.

But the emperor could change the world anyway, and was set to bring a swift and bloody end to the boy's experience of it.

"Very well," he said again. "And the woman you have there, who is she? Is she another of them? Show me."

The woman was no jade-eater, if eyes and strength and beauty were the measure. Even the carver had some glimmer of green to his eyes. The woman's were black pits, a scowl that needed no measuring. The clothes she wore were a loose and practical assemblage, a traveler's rig. If she'd been carrying weapons they were gone now, but even so she looked most like a bandit.

The emperor shrugged, dismissing her from his mind, though not from judgment. In stories, imperial law stretched a wide hand to embrace not only criminals but their families, their friends and neighbors. Given the emperor's mood, real life would not be so different. Anyone caught in this house was going to die.

Soon now, soon; it only waited on his word.

But he was looking about him, searchingly. If he were a dog, she'd have said he was sniffing the air for a scent he'd caught already, wanting to track it down.

He turned and headed across the ruins of the courtyard garden. Stumbling a little over the wreckage, because his eyes were absolutely not watching his feet.

There were half a dozen doors around the courtyard. He went directly to one and hurled it back, hard enough to break its hinges. It wasn't anger driving him now: something else, less easily discerned or named.

He broke the door and went inside, into shadow.

No one else seemed to be following him, so of course she did. How not?

IT WAS the jade carver's workshop. There were carved and half-carved pieces on shelves around the walls, there was a stack of untouched stone in a corner. There was a lathe to one side, that gripped a piece barely worked on.

In the center of the workshop was a bench, and on that bench stood what had drawn the emperor. Unseen, unsuspected, it had called him from the dark. Even now it had barely any light to work with, and that didn't matter, it almost shone on its own, as he did in its company.

It was a piece of jade; but her time in the palace, her little time among the imperial treasures had taught her just a little, and even she could see this was exceptional.

A great steep-sided wedge like a mountain cliff in miniature: it had black in its base and a streak of white at its height, but the black and the white together still carried that same hint of greenness that she'd seen in the emperor's skin and the boy's as well. And between the two lay all the shades of open green, from deep-sea colors to the pale streaks of a sky before dawn, by way of all the leaves that ever were.

It was a wonderful thing, even in its rawness. But there were tools on the bench, and a scatter of gleaming flakes to be seen around the stone and on the cloth beneath it; and the emperor had moved around to the farther side and was gazing, reaching, touching . . .

She followed, because nobody was trying to stop her.

As soon as she saw it, she too wanted to touch the work that had been done on the stone here, the first hint of its shaping. Jade belonged to the emperor; she didn't dare, until he glanced around for her, and found her, and beckoned her close.

That was all it took. Jade belonged to the emperor, but so did she.

She stood at his side, then, and reached to touch in her turn. Her fingers found sharp, and smooth, and rough; and, yes, raw, where the piece had been cut from its mother-stone and the carver's tools had not yet touched it. And everything he had done was crude and sketchy, only the first steps on a long journey, and even so . . .

Because she had to say something, because the silence was great and tender and terrible; and because she couldn't talk about the piece, because it was inherent in the silence, she talked about the man instead; she said, "How can he work in here with so little light?"

The sun was in the courtyard, which his workbench faced. The workshop was gloomy enough on its own account, but the face he'd been cutting was in utter shadow.

"Jade helps us see in the dark. How else would I know how beautiful you are at night?"

The gallantry was deliberate; it said *I don't know what to say either.* Also, it was generous. It meant she could say, "But he's not a, a jade-eater. The carver, I mean." Meaning, *He's not anything like you two, and you two are so much like each other.*

"No, but he's spent all his life with jade, touching it and cutting it and grinding it down. Splinters under his fingernails, dust in the air. He's breathed it, swallowed it, however careful he's been. Little by little, it's gotten into his blood. If he couldn't see in the dark—well, how could he see to make this, if he couldn't see the dragon in the stone?"

It was true. It was already obvious that she had always been there, only waiting to be cut free.

Mei Feng let her fingers slide one more time over the roughness of scale, the smooth flow of water, the first suggestion of flight. Her hand touched the emperor's; after a moment, his fingers closed over hers, like a distracted smile.

"Majesty?"

That was Ban Hsu in the doorway, curious and anxious too. How else should a jademaster feel, seeing the emperor lay personal, physical claim to the finest of his pieces?

"Yes. We are coming."

Was that *we* simply his imperial prerogative, or did it include her? His hand included her, which was an answer of sorts. His other hand, his finger trailed through jade dust on the bench and lifted it to his lips, to his tongue. She wondered vaguely what that was like, to eat stone undisguised in food or wine, how it would taste: gritty and dry, surely . . .

Nevertheless he sucked his finger as he tugged her out into the courtyard. He was still determined, resolute, but she thought something had changed in him, as though that cold fury had leached out into the stone, leaving him still imperial but no longer vicious with it.

Had any emperor before him ever delivered justice with his concubine at his side, hand in hand? There had been a lot of emperors, and some had been overfond of women, but she still thought it unlikely.

He said, "Carver."

"Majesty." The man spoke to the gravel, of course, but his voice was strong enough—just—to reach them.

"What is your name?" No man should die unknown. That was the law. Just as no man—or woman, or presumptuous girl—should ever find the emperor's name in his mouth. Hers.

"Guangli, majesty."

"Guangli." Probably no man would ever want to find his name unexpectedly in the emperor's mouth. Hers delighted her, when he spoke it; this man's, here and now, was a terrible thing. "What did you intend with that piece, when you had finished it?"

"Majesty, I would have brought it to you."

"Flattery is not your art, old man."

"No. My art is truth," and—doomed as he was, perhaps it couldn't matter?—he lifted his head to look the emperor full in the face as he said it. "It was brought to me for that purpose, to be a gift to you; and to bypass him," a contemptuous nod at Ban Hsu. "When your stone can come direct from the mines to me, and from me to you, what need him or his kind?"

"They act as wards," the emperor said neutrally, "to prevent thieves on the road."

"Prevent? Majesty, they are thieves. They steal from you, they steal from me."

"Perhaps, a little. Better the thief you watch, if he keeps other thieves away." That sounded as if it was frequently said: a wisdom of the palace, no doubt, whose dealings with the daily world must always be through agents, who would always take their share.

"Well. That is your majesty's choice, of course; but I did not steal this stone. It was meant for you."

"You smuggled it from the mountains," Ban Hsu said hissingly.

"No. It was brought to me; I had no notion of it, till it came."

"The boy is from the mountains; how would he know you?"

"I brought the boy." That was the woman, lifting her head in her turn, wirily resisting her guards' efforts to force her down again. "I found him, kept him, brought him here. Nothing is the boy's fault; he was bringing the stone to you."

See? We all wanted to give you gifts, no more than that, and they were all going to die for it. Inevitability was cold and hard, closing in around them like walls of jade. Around them all, the emperor included: he had no more choice than anyone. Less than Mei Feng, who might have turned and walked back to the carriage. He would probably have let her go.

She stayed. He said, "The boy is a jade-eater," and no one spoke; it was the ultimate accusation, and irrefutable. "I have seen the stone in there. I have *touched* it. I could lift it, yes; no other man here could shift it. Not Ban Hsu, who has handled jade all his life; not you, Guangli, who have worked it all your life. And yet the boy has *carried* it, all the way from the mines. You need only look at him to see he has more jade in him than I do."

No one stirred to contradict him.

"You owe me all a death," he said. "Any one of you condemns you all: for taking jade, and possessing it in secret, and concealing a jade-eater from the law. Your lives are mine, along with everything you own. I take that to be little enough; this house is not yours, Guangli, and the stone was mine to start with.

"But I want," he said, "I want," and for the first time there was a note of hesitation in his voice, a hint of self-doubt that he shrugged aside physically, a little shift of the shoulders, "I want that dragon revealed, and no other man could see her the way that you do, Guangli.

"That death you owe me, I will keep. Your life, that too; I will keep it. You will be entirely mine, imperial jade carver.

"You had best remain here; there is no space for you at the palace, that house is mad already with too many people. Until the Autumn Palace is ready for us, you can live and work as you were. With my own soldiers here to protect what is mine," he added, glancing around the ruined garden, more aware than he'd seemed.

"Majesty," the man Guangli said, "you are more generous than

I deserve; but may I plead also for my companions? Without them, there would be no dragon, after all . . ."

That wasn't good enough to win one pardon, let alone two. "The boy is a jade-eater," the emperor said, "and the woman I think is a bandit. What use are their lives to me?"

"They have become . . . necessary . . . to my work." He wasn't quite fool enough to say *Slay my friends and I will slay your dragon,* but it hung in the air between them, unspoken, unaddressed and deadly. "Besides, majesty, he is a jade-eater. If he dies, think how much you lose. Only train him, and he will be such a fighter for you . . ."

"I do not need another soldier." He had too many already, in Mei Feng's eyes: an army too many, eating more than jade, eating the whole island.

"A bodyguard, perhaps?" Guangli wasn't pleading at all, he was negotiating; so, she realized suddenly, was the emperor. Both of them were feeling for it, finding a way to let the woman and the boy both live. "Or just a study, majesty, to learn through his body what the stone will do to yours. He is ahead of you. It would be such a waste, to destroy him now . . ."

There was a silence, for a moment. Then the emperor stepped forward. "Stand up, boy."

Stone calls to stone. The two young men gazed at each other, eye to green and fierce eye; Mei Feng softly let out a breath she hadn't known herself to be holding.

No one even mentioned the woman, but this was a compact, truly. There would be no deaths in this garden, not today. Unless Ban Hsu was stupid; he had the look of it suddenly, twisting his fingers together, inwardly raging. Mei Feng caught his eye, though, and he did perhaps read her warning. Perhaps that was even a nod he gave her, before he dropped his eyes like a dutiful subject in the face of his emperor's judgment.

Breaking Free

one

Li Ton was not a talkative man, but he had talked with the doctor, a little, about why he sailed the strait at night to an enemy shore. Master Hsui passed it on to his own charges:

"The men we're carrying," a shipload of them, "they're an assassination squad. Hand-picked, the hardest in Tunghai's army."

Tien moved unhappily, where she was sitting close against Han's side in the well of the boat. "Who are they going to kill?"

"Tien. Think. These men have chased each other all across the world. Who do you imagine they're going to kill?"

"It's the emperor, of course," Han said, to spare her.

"But, but, he's the Son of Heaven! He can't *die* . . . !"

"Of course he can," Doctor Hsui said impatiently. "That's how he came to *be* emperor and Son of Heaven, because his father died who had those ranks before him."

"Yes, but he was an old man . . ."

"Indeed." A hundred and thirty-seven, by Han's own calculations. His late master the scribe had shown him dated documents; the arithmetic had been easy, though he'd had to check it three times. The notion of emperor was like the notion of dragon, something mythic and eternal, untouched by time. That an actual man could live such an actually astonishing number of years was something else entirely, to a cynical boy. "Nevertheless, the emperor is a mortal man and able to die."

"Not a boy, no, surely!"

"Able to be killed. At any age. When emperors don't live long, it's because they die in battle. Or are assassinated. This won't be the first time."

"What can we do?" Tien demanded.

"Do? Nothing. Why should we? This is the army we have followed—"

"—yes, to doctor them, not to support their war—"

"—and I'm no more interested in saving the boy-emperor than I am in helping Tunghai Wang steal his throne. Their petty war is nothing, Tien; let them fight it as they will. That's not why we're here."

"No, but—he's a *boy*, and the *emperor*, and, and, those men . . ."

Whether it was the emperor's age or his rank that mattered to her more, Han wasn't sure, but he knew how she felt about the men. He was just as uncomfortable, simply sharing the boat with them. There were a dozen clustered on the foredeck now, rolling bones raucously by lamplight. Every now and then a face would catch the light, but in the main they were dark, hunched figures and even the pirate crew stepped wary around them.

Emperor or not, no boy deserved to be given over to their untender hands. It was war, and death was commonplace; he had seen it, intimate and immediate, and even so he shuddered. "So why are we here, Doctor Hsui?"

"You know that, it's an absurd chain; one link drags all the others, in order. Suo Lung wouldn't come without you, I wouldn't let you go, Tien obliges me to follow." Tien wore the *Shalla*'s iron ring in her ear now, and fiddled with it unhappily, and tried gamely to be one of the crew but there was no real work for her nor any protection either, beyond Li Ton's order. She might be more frightened of the men on the foredeck, but only barely. For her sake, the doctor would do exactly as Li Ton demanded; so would Han, without hesitation.

"Yes," Han said, "but why was he so urgent to have Suo Lung at all? He doesn't need a smith on a night raid . . ."

"Suo Lung goes with the assassins. I think the emperor has run mad; they say he keeps his army in the island's heart, building a palace when it should be guarding the shore."

"Who says so?" Tien asked, oddly defensive of this unknown boy.

"Spies, niece. Did you think there was no traffic between his army and ours, across the strait? Every boat on Taishu will be constantly at sea, they must be desperate for food; small wonder if every now and then one exchanges men or news or rumors in the dark.

"It's said that Tunghai Wang even has a voice on the emperor's council, one of the generals in his pocket. Whether that's true, I don't know, but he certainly has spies on the island. They report this massive building work in the hills, using half the army and civilian labor besides. It's the emperor's pet project, he's there constantly; he even sleeps overnight in a cabin with a few guards, no more protection than that.

"These men we carry will join the civilian labor force, and be right there ready when the opportunity arises.

"But the emperor is not entirely foolish. There are no weapons allowed on the site; even the soldiers' blades are locked up in armories. It saves lives among the men if they have only fists and feet to fight with, and it saves the emperor's life too, or at least it's meant to.

"The tools they use for building with, those could be used to kill with, axes and picks and mattocks; but they're clumsy and the emperor's guards are well trained.

"Which is why the assassins want their own smith with them. They'll be searched going in, but not otherwise. Your Suo Lung has been making weapons out of scrap ever since you got here; it won't take him long to turn pick-blades into taos and spearheads. Fully armed, I'd back these against any number of palace guards."

"The emperor's men aren't just guards, they're proper fighting soldiers . . ."

"Yes, Tien, and these are the soldiers they've been fighting. The soldiers they've been running from, rather, and with good reason.

Let these within reach of the emperor with weapons in their hands, that'll be the end of him."

"And you're just going to let it happen? Uncle Hsui—"

"What can I do to stop it?"

"I don't know, but . . ."

"There is nothing I can or should do except what I came to do, which is to help Han here, work on his chains, give him what strength I can to keep the dragon down. Fail at that and it'll mean thousands of lives, not just one runaway boy. Thousands of lives and thousands of years, she won't be chained again. Let this go, Tien; it's not our business."

"Suo Lung will want Han with him, if he has to go with the assassins."

"Likely he will—but he can't have that. We'd all have to go, and how would that look? A chained cripple, a man of medicine, a girl—the men can pass as laborers, but we could not. All too obviously, we are part of some other story, and the most complacent of guards would feel obliged to inquire into it. If Suo Lung goes, he goes without us."

"He won't go, then," Han said, flatly.

"Perhaps not. In which case the assassins will find their task more difficult—but again, that is not our concern. Han, Tien, listen to me. We can*not* get involved in their war. If Suo Lung should want to take Han with him when he leaves the ship, we must forestall him if we can, slip away by ourselves. If not—well, I have a poison . . ."

"No!" It was Tien, of course, who cried out against it.

"Yes. He's done his work, and done it well enough. At least the dragon is chained again, although those chains are looser than I like. But there's nothing more that he can offer now. If we have to sacrifice him, we can."

She looked mulish, and helpless, and distressed. And wanted to argue, clearly, and had no words to do it with; and ripped herself away from Han's side, went stumbling across the deck to stare ostentatiously the other way.

Hsui sighed and looked at Han, and shook his head; and there was nothing Han could do but leave him and follow Tien, stand with her, hold her hand when she would let him. He wouldn't be drawn into a conspiracy with the older man.

"Look," he said, nodding at a shadow that loomed against the stars. "That's the Forge, where . . ."

His voice failed him, as that sentence did. Where could it go from there—*where this whole nightmare began for me?* But for her, he thought, it hadn't been a nightmare; not till now, and he had brought it with him. *Where I found Suo Lung, or he found me?* No . . .

"Look," she said swiftly, "there are lights on the water. Over there, see?"

"Fishermen from the island, I suppose." *Or spies, coming and going. Everyone sells what they have, what they can catch, fish or secrets. Or people.* "Should we tell the men up on the beak to put that lamp out? Or make sure Li Ton has seen the lights?"

"Neither," Tien said. "Why would you?"

"If we can see their lights, they can see ours. If they report a big ship passing through at night, the soldiers ashore will be alert, they may come looking . . ."

". . . and with any luck they'll find the *Shalla* before those men have gone off to kill the emperor, or at least in time for us to warn them."

"Tien. What your uncle said, remember?"

"Uncle isn't always right."

"Their fight isn't our fight." He laid his hand on the rail next to hers, where she could see the cuff and the hanging chains, to be reminded.

He'd used the wrong hand, a gift to her: she ran her fingers lightly over the tender scar where once he'd had a thumb, a reminder to him how little he owed the master of this ship.

She said, "If we were caught and taken to the emperor, he might help us. We might be safer on Taishu than the mainland. An island people, with the dragon just off their shore all this time, they must understand how important it is. They fed the monks on the Forge, didn't they? I'm sure they would help . . ."

"The monks are all dead, and the emperor and his people are from far away; nobody knows anything anymore. And we'd never be safe. If Tunghai Wang can land a squad of assassins now, he can land an army soon. When it comes to a battle—and it will, Tien—which side is the safer?"

"The islanders will fight for the emperor . . ."

"Perhaps. And they will lose, as the emperor will lose; why else has he been running all this time? And then when Tunghai Wang finds traitors at the court, people who had once been his, he will not be kind to them."

"If he can do that, if he can just land his army and win the war, why trouble to kill the emperor at all?"

It was a fair question; what was unfair was to ask it of him, when he'd had no more time than she had to think about these things.

The doctor was standing behind them. He had heard the question at least, if not what came before; he said, "Because it may pre-empt an invasion. Tunghai Wang is not profligate. If he can achieve the throne more cheaply, he will. Kill the emperor, and what happens?"

It was too monumental, they couldn't conceive it. Even the emperor-in-flight was still emperor; rebels were rebels, and would stay that way.

Doctor Hsui sighed, and spoke into their silence. "His generals will squabble among themselves, over which takes the throne. One will dominate, and crown himself; but he will always be weak on the island and nothing elsewhere, he will have no legitimacy in the empire. Tunghai Wang can go back to the Hidden City and proclaim his own ascendancy, in the place where emperors are always declared. Without the throne itself, without jade, that cannot last; which is why he has chased the emperor all this way, and why there must finally be an accounting. But it need not happen yet.

"With the emperor dead and his line extinguished, no one claim is better than any other. One has the throne, another has the empire, and likely the empire will tell in the end. Tunghai Wang will certainly think so. He will hold his army here, and wait; and in the end, perhaps he and the generals on Taishu will come to terms."

"You said he had his own voice, among the generals?" Tien murmured.

"I said that it was said so, yes."

"So perhaps it will be his own general who claims the throne?"

"Perhaps. In the short term, I expect that would suit him very well."

One death, and no one need fight. At least for a while. It did make a terrible kind of sense. And if they could—*if* they could sacrifice Suo Lung whom they knew and valued, then surely it should be easier to let a boy they'd never seen be sacrificed for so much benefit, so many fewer deaths?

Han was, just, wise enough not to say so. He looked out across dark waters with their scattered little lights, and wrapped his four fingers around Tien's hand, and wished for something to be different although he didn't quite know what—

—AND THERE was a sudden upheaval in his head that had him reeling, that had his free hand slamming down onto the rail to give himself an anchor, because the dragon was rising and all he could do was hold on;

—BUT TIEN was reeling too, staggering across the deck, and he still had her by the hand but his finger grip just wasn't good enough and she was suddenly gone, falling into her uncle and the two of them sliding together into the mess of barrels and timbers that filled the well-deck;

—AND THAT made no sense, because the dragon was in his head, he could feel her thrusting up through his thoughts, through his own self like a great rock bursting through soil;

—BUT HE heard screams all around him, and his head flung up and he saw the stars tipping and plunging across the sky, and that wasn't him and of course it wasn't the stars either, it was the junk swaying wildly as she was hurled across the churning face of the sea.

BECAUSE THE dragon wasn't only rising in his mind, trying to topple him from the throne of his own thoughts, to unseat his reason. She was rising in the sea too, straining against her chains. Trying to reach and break the *Shalla,* to sink Han alongside everyone who sailed with him, to let the chains he wore drag him down and down to her, and so let her rise free.

two

Old Yen didn't even think of himself as a fisherman anymore. A ferryman, yes, back and forth across the strait come fog or storm or any other weather; a night-ferryman, conveying men and supplies, news, occasionally weapons or wilder loads. Once he had a hold full of squealing pigs; once chests of unimaginable treasure, brought all the way from the Hidden City and somehow left behind in the chaos that was Santung, somehow recovered later.

That time he'd carried more than his regular squad of soldiers with him, there and back, their captain at his side throughout. He was trusted, yes—but sometimes he was trusted only because he could be watched all the way.

Tonight again he had a captain at his shoulder, men on deck. This time they were the cargo. Spies and saboteurs, Old Yen imagined, though no one was saying very much.

Mostly the men were slumped or sleeping. Their captain was the most alert, but even he was dog-tired and dirty as a hog in a wallow, almost as dirty as Old Yen's holds had been after the pigs. He asked no questions and gave them whatever they asked for, which was little enough.

Their captain watched the sky and the sea, almost like a sailor himself. Too long in enemy lands, alert for any danger, he had no way now to relax. He wasn't watching for weather or for rocks; it was rebels he looked for, stalking them on the wind, across the waves.

He said nothing, and neither did Old Yen. What was the use of muttered comforts? Anything the man might be told, he knew already; his problem lay in believing it.

Time passed, the stars turned above them, water shifted beneath the hull.

The captain spoke, or tried to. He made a scratched and hollow noise and scowled, took a drink of water, tried again.

"Those lights, there and there," pointing astern with a hand whose nails were either black or bloodied, "what are they?"

"Other boats, fishermen," *like myself* he almost said, and didn't. This was a scatter of the fishing fleet he used to lead; he knew them by the colors of their lamps and their heights above the water, their movements in the swell. He knew the boats' names and those who sailed them. That used to be enough. Now there would be at least a couple of soldiers on each boat. Crewing perhaps, learning to sail or fish perhaps; mostly they were there as guards, and mostly not to protect the boats.

Attacks had happened, rebel boats on pirate raids to seize men and fish and most especially vessels, adding to their invasion fleet and reducing Taishu's ability to feed itself, little by little. Mostly, though, the guards were there to watch the captains and their crews, to keep them from defecting or selling news to the rebels or simply disappearing. Desertion was as harmful as any kind of loss, and espionage was worse.

"Are they really following us?"

"Probably." If he knew them by their lights, so did they know him. At this time of night their bellies would be full of fish, they'd be turning for home; it was so much their habit to follow him, they'd likely do it without thinking.

"What's that, then, another fisherman?"

This time the captain was pointing ahead. Old Yen hadn't seen a light—but yes, he saw it now. Too low and steady to be a mast light, it must be a lamp on deck; but it was too high for any deck he knew except the jade ships, and those were all in harbor. His eyes made out the dark stiff roll of the silhouette against the silvered swell; he said, "No. That's a junk, a big one. I don't know her."

"Rebels?"

"She could be. She could well be."

The captain called a word down to his men; then, to Old Yen, "Can you keep this much distance between us?"

"Yes." The other boats in the forming fleet would stay behind him, because that was what they did.

"Can you follow?"

"If you want me to. She'll know." If her captain was any good, she'd know, even if they all put their lamps out. "And if she turns on us, she'll catch us." Not the whole fleet, because the others had the sense to scatter; but—again, if her captain was any good—she'd come for the largest boat here, which meant his. His bastard boat, the most awkward, the least maneuverable. If that were a junk full of pirates looking for another ship to raid, he'd be raided. Even a squad of soldiers might not be enough.

"Follow her for now, at least."

Old Yen grunted and leaned on his oar, whistled a note for the boy Pao, sent him scudding forward to tend the sheets.

THE THIRD time the captain pointed, Old Yen had no answer for him. They had barely begun to track the big junk—however good he was, her captain might not have noticed yet how the boat lights were tending to clump together, how they were tending to follow him—when the arm went up and the voice, far more hesitant this time, said, "There, do you see that? Lights under the water, what is that . . . ?"

Old Yen did see: a deep and murky glow, perhaps a doubled glow, rising and brightening even as he watched. No time for speculation; he felt the boat lurch beneath his feet and knew this, *knew* it.

"Hold on!" he yelled, broad across the deck. "Find something fixed, and hold hard! Wave coming . . . !"

Pao remembered, perhaps, how they had lost Kang. The boy was already wrapping his arm around a stay, pale face glancing back from the prow.

Which was lifting, uncomfortably high against the stars. At

least they met this surge bow-on; bastard though she was, his boat
should ride it out. So long as a surge was all that came. His eyes
kept straying forward toward those rising lights: and yes, definitely
there were two, and there was a great dark shadow around and behind them that showed in their own glimmer, not unlike the way
the vague shape of a hull would show in the light of its mast lamp
and against the shift of water; and he was a man of faith, always
had been, and his Li-goddess was not the only power known to
move in these waters, and—

—AND THEN the dragon breached, and he'd never imagined anything quite so marvelous and terrible and true.

She came slamming up like a spear, directly beneath the hull of
the junk ahead. Old Yen thought she even had her jaws open ready.
But so great was her bulk and so violent her rise, the water seemed
to mound above her and then to slide away; the junk went slipping
sideways down that slope, so that the dragon's head burst out of
the sea off her beam.

What she must be like in daylight, Old Yen couldn't imagine
and didn't want to learn. Even by the moon she had colors clinging to her, ghost-colors that shifted like iridescence, like oil on
water. Even her teeth, that moment before her great mouth closed,
even they seemed shaded, something other than iron-gray.

But her mouth did close, and she seemed to be . . . straining
against something, her head half out of the water, her shining
baleful eyes barely breaking the surface. It was as if she were still
chained, except that her chains had surely never been so loose, to
let her rise so far. Besides, the monks were dead and the Forge was
cold, and Old Yen had found chains struck off by the anvil. The
only wonder in him all this time was that she had not risen yet.

And now here she was, monumental and reverberant—but
sinking. Slowly, reluctantly, as though she fought every moment
against it. Her eyes, and then her snout, and the threatened bulk of
her was nothing but a fading shadow.

And all this time the boat had been pitching and tossing beneath him, and he'd been fighting it with the oar while Pao did the

best he could with the sails, and it was a wonder that the dragon hadn't caused another tsunami. She could have done that, she could have killed them all; but she'd been so focused on the junk, she'd cleaved the water spear-straight and made barely a ripple beneath the surface. And now she was caught, dragged down he thought by the weight of her chains, and exhausted beyond hope of fighting back.

He'd thought her free, no chains at all; he should be glad to be wrong. He was glad to be wrong. Only, he had not known her chains to be so loose . . .

The junk had been less fortunate than his own boat, broaching and almost turning turtle in the valley of that great water-mound. She must have been swamped when the dragon broke the surface. She was still afloat; the lamp was gone, of course, and it was hard to be sure of anything in moonlight, but Old Yen was sure she'd taken damage. She seemed lower and heavier in the water, wallowing awkwardly in the swell.

She still had masts, though, sails and crew. Even as he watched, it was harder to find her in the darkness.

The captain was at his side again, saying, "Gods, man, that was . . . That was . . ."

"The dragon. Yes. Did you not know there was a dragon in these waters?"

"Oh, I'd heard. I had heard. But, but not from anyone who had *seen*. I thought it was like ghosts, ghouls, the gods: endless stories, and nothing ever you could point at . . ."

"I could point at what my goddess does for me."

"No. No, never mind. If dragons, why not gods?" With an effort that was visible, the captain dragged his attention back to what was immediate, human, comprehensible. "The junk, it's moving on. Can you follow?"

"Yes, yes." One glance behind, to see the scattered fleet reassembling; one cry ahead to Pao, and he had the boat under way again. "You see to your men, be sure that no one's hurt or too much shaken. Leave the dragon to the sea where she belongs, the junk to me."

. . .

No more dragon. Only long hours hunting in the dark, tracking a vessel as dark as his, looking for how her sails occluded the starlight. Whatever her mission, the junk was heading south for Taishu. Heavy as she was, she'd be slow to respond to the tiller, so her master would want to stand off from shore at least until daylight; which meant the currents in the strait would bear her westerly . . .

He barely needed to give it so much thought. He made the one assumption, that the junk's master was as good a sailor as himself, but less familiar with the strait. Thereafter he followed his nose whenever he lost sight of the junk, and sooner or later—usually sooner—there she was again, a shadow against the stars.

At last, a smudge of gray to stern; they were still sailing into the dark, but dawn was coming.

Taishu too: the island made a rising shadow to the south.

The captain said, "Can you whistle up one of those boats, to take a message?"

"No, captain. The little boats can keep up, but they don't have wind or sail in reserve, to put on extra pace when I call for it. If you want to send one of them ashore, I'll have to heave to."

"Will you lose the junk?"

"Probably not," though he wouldn't promise. "Day is coming; either she sails on, or else she runs for shore. There aren't many deep-water creeks on this coast, and I know them all."

The captain nodded. "Do it, then. I need to alert the shore watch. One more sail on the horizon doesn't look like an invasion, and I want men ready to meet him."

"They'll need to be swift," Old Yen said, watching the sail ahead. "I think he's turning landward." With the first hint of light: of course he was. That's what Old Yen would do.

Idle on slow water, then, Old Yen lingered until the fishing fleet surrounded him. He picked the fastest of the little boats and bellowed for it, then waited with a patience the captain didn't share until Chusan had oared across for his instructions.

While that exchange was going on, Old Yen called to a few other boats that drifted close. He spoke to their masters, who listened and nodded and went to speak to more; and so word was spread through the fleet, that he thought the captain would be glad of in a while.

Chusan spread his sail and worked his oar and canted across their former course, headed for the closest harbor on Taishu. Old Yen yelled to Pao to set all the sail he could, and turned back to pursue the now vanished junk.

THROUGH THE murk of a gray dawn they chased, and could not find her. Working against the tide as he was, Old Yen was sure she could not have worked her own way faster, with her belly so wallow-full of water. Which meant for certain that she'd gone to ground, sneaking into one of the rare creeks that were too narrow and too steep-sided to make a harbor.

He turned back, with the fishing fleet around him, and saw a plume of black smoke rising from a headland; saw it mirrored, closer; turned his head to see a flare of light behind him, where the dawn was still half dusky. Beacons, all along the coast. Chusan had found the right man for his message, then.

Old Yen went nosing back along the coast, feeling the play of tide and current against his oar, watching the birds and sniffing the air, letting wind and water talk to him. At last he flung the oar decisively, turned the prow of the boat to land, came cleanly into one twisting waterway.

Around one bend, another, and there she was: the junk at anchor, by a slender paring of what might be called a beach below a cliff.

The captain said, "How did you know?"

Old Yen said, "Because this is not my coast; I sail from an eastward harbor. If I could find this creek, then so could she. And she needed it. I don't think this is where she meant to land, but she was dragging her belly and she may have other hurts. She needed harbor, so she felt it out. And so did I."

Need or not, the junk was hauling up her anchor at the sight of him. She was a significantly bigger vessel, and she had the river's current to ride on; she had oars and poles, she should be able to muscle by.

But here came the fishing fleet, working upcurrent at his stern: working up to lie beside him, in a long line from wall to lush green rocky wall. Tossing ropes from one to the next, binding themselves together, binding them all to him in a single wall of their own, a great boom of boats.

That was his gift to the captain, his word to the fleet. Elsewhere in the empire, there were cities that had boom-chains ordered from the Forge, that they could raise to blockade their entire harbor. Here he could forge a chain of the fleet entire, every boat a link, the whole together strong beyond the measure of its parts.

The junk's master might have crushed a boat or two, killed a man or two in trying to break through, but he could never have achieved it. He couldn't work up way enough to snap these ropes; nor was the junk light enough to mount the boom and slide over, with all that weight of water in her gut.

The junk lay still in the water, a shark at bay. The captain on Old Yen's boat sent his men to the bows, to show that it wasn't only fishermen aboard; the same happened all along the chain, every boat carrying its soldiers, every soldier standing in the bows.

And now here came men plunging down the cliff path, responding to the beacons. Armed men, hardened by the road as much as any pirate might be hardened by the sea: Old Yen knew, he had a boatload of them.

The junk might carry men enough to make a fight of it, by land or sea, but not to win a fight with such as these. Instead, there was sudden movement on her decks; men appeared both on the landward side and in the bows, where they were visible from both beach and boats. They started slinging weapons overboard, knives and swords and long pikes, a rain of steel in surrender.

When that rain stopped, when the junk was presumably disarmed, the captain had Old Yen call across, used as he was to bellowing over water.

"Send your men ashore! One boat at a time!"

That one boat plied obediently back and forth, once and then again, taking a dozen men ashore. It wasn't enough, surely: barely enough to sail such a vessel, certainly not a fighting crew. Old Yen said so, forcefully.

Still, there were only four figures left on the junk's deck. One would be her captain; the others were indecipherable at this distance in this murky light, but they were clearly not pirates.

The captain sent half a dozen of his men along the boom from boat to boat. The last they unhitched from its neighbor and rowed cautiously to the junk. Old Yen watched them swarm up her flank; one spoke to that little cluster of figures and conducted them to the side, to board the fishing boat while the other men disappeared belowdecks.

Those men came up again one by one, shaking their heads emphatically across the water, making signs to their captain that were easy enough to read: *No one else aboard, this ship is empty.* The fishing boat came directly back to Old Yen's bow, and the captain's men hauled its passengers aboard.

None too gently so; Old Yen snapped, "Tell them to have a care!"

The captain looked at him. "These are what we're fighting, old man."

"You don't know that, till you speak to them. For now they are guests on my boat, as you are. And one is a woman, see, and another—"

"Say a girl, rather than a woman," the captain interrupted; and indeed she did remind Old Yen painfully of his lost granddaughter. "And a boy to go with her, a slave I suppose, in all that chainwork; and the man must be his master, do you think?"

The second man, the junk's captain was not mysterious at all: easy to identify, easy to understand. There was a man whom Old Yen would far sooner see chained, but that was immaterial. What mattered now was the boy traveling with him, which made small sense, and apparently with these others, which put together made no sense at all.

Still, he might be master on his own vessel, but he was content to let the soldier-captain handle these newcomers: content already, even before the first man said, "Take me to the emperor. I have information for him, from the camp of Tunghai Wang. I have been there as a spy, and what I've learned brooks no delay."

"You chose a strange way to reach him," the captain observed mildly, "such a great junk to carry one man and two children . . ."

"These are my household," the man said, "the slave-boy and the girl. I couldn't leave them to face Tunghai Wang's judgment in my absence. I was his doctor; he will miss me soon enough, and he is a brutal man, betrayed. As for the junk, I thought she might be useful to the emperor, so I bought her and the crew together."

"The Son of Heaven is found at Taishu-port, not on this side of the island."

"We were a little lost in the darkness; and then the, the dragon rose, and we had to seek harbor . . ."

It was plausible, though for sure the man knew more about the dragon than his words suggested. He must do, with that boy in his train. He wasn't saying, though, and neither was Old Yen, yet.

Nor was the captain totally convinced. He sent a man ashore, to cast about for any traces of a landing party.

That man came back with nothing. The path down to the beach was steep and little-used, barely a path at all; it would have shown footmarks and torn undergrowth if anyone had climbed it. The shore guard had noticed none, coming down. And left plenty of their own, of course, so it was no use looking now.

The doctor—if he was a doctor: or the spy, the prisoner, the passenger, if he was any of those—was agitating to be away. The captain shrugged, and nodded to Old Yen. It wasn't for them to determine his truth or his value. They could bring him where he was demanding to go, and let him explain himself there.

SLOWLY, THEN, cautiously out to open water, men with poles to fend the boat away from the cliffs with their overhanging creepers that reached almost low enough to brush the deck. One man cried a warning, at a sudden rock in the water; it was not a rock at all but a vast corpse floating facedown, just a pale roundness in the shadows, all but the shoulders and back submerged. Old Yen spared a word for a blessing, for the Li-goddess to hear it if she would.

Then it was all sail up and be grateful to her for a friendly wind to take them easily around the island to Taishu-port.

Easy or not, it was half a day's sail. Old Yen would have been uncomfortable carrying both the pirate and the doctor, if he hadn't had a full squad of edgy men to watch them; men or no men, he was more than uncomfortable carrying the chained boy. He wanted to understand that boy, and did not. Did watch him, though, and saw how much more than exhausted he was: how unwell he seemed sometimes, slumping almost into unconsciousness or almost into a fever, and how frightened when he was more himself.

As they came under the shadow of the Forge, he saw the junk's captain—not exactly a prisoner, no, but sitting on the foredeck just where he'd been invited to sit, out of everyone's way and very thoroughly watched by several soldiers—lift his head and look.

Old Yen shuddered, remembering the monks, their bodies, their great failure; and watched the sea with a desperate anxiety, waiting to see the dragon breach again.

THE SEA was calm, the wind stayed kind, and not a dragon stirred. The army captain wanted to talk about her, but Old Yen would not; he shook his head and stood mute until they came to Taishu-port. At the mooring, the captain offered his passengers one last chance to explain themselves to him or his superiors. The doctor was stubborn, though. It had to be the emperor.

Old Yen left the boy Pao to swab down; he disembarked with the others, began the walk up through the city at the captain's side.

"You need not come with us, old man. I can tell the emperor what he needs to know, if he should choose to see us. If not, this fool doctor can hammer his hands bloody on the palace gates, unless my general decides to let him hammer them bloody on a cell door instead."

"You are wrong," Old Yen said. "You are from the north, like the doctor, like the Son of Heaven himself; I have things to tell the emperor that none of you know."

The captain frowned, as though that bordered on heresy. Perhaps it did. "What can you possibly have to tell the emperor, old man? And why would you ever think that he might listen? I am an officer in his army, bringing someone who claims to be his spy; you—"

"I have met him before," Old Yen said calmly. "Me he knows. My granddaughter is his preferred companion," it was still hard to say *concubine,* "and much of what I do is at his particular command." *Or hers.* "I think he will see me."

And then, because he was a kind man and not truly proud, he added, "I have to tell him about the dragon, and the boy."

"The boy . . . ?"

"Yes. You saw the dragon, but the boy is what matters now. If anyone is keeping that dragon under, it is the boy."

And yet the girl could barely keep the boy moving, at a slow and distracted shuffle. He was no stronghold, if he was all they had.

Together the party moved up from the dockside through the lower town, through the merchants' quarter to the exclusive broad avenues where the governor had his palace, where the jademasters had built theirs to outshine his: their houses more luxurious, their gardens greater, their trees more rare and wonderful. All he did was govern, by imperial license. They handled the stuff of empire, jade itself. They were the living link between the mountain and the throne, best beloved by the Man of Jade . . .

Old Yen had been here before, of course. The captain hadn't. Why would a simple soldier have cause to visit the Son of Heaven? He was entering a realm of uncertainty, and doing it filthy, exhausted, with dubious strangers in his charge.

Still, he bore it well. At every check he said, "I have men here from the mainland, with a tale to tell the emperor," and at every check they were passed through. His own rank took him some of the way, and that explanation took him farther: past the palace guard and past the palace gate, into the public courtyard. Old Yen was almost waiting for Mei Feng to conduct them to the imperial presence.

No Mei Feng, but an aide did come. He listened to the captain, looked at the whole party—the doctor, the boy in his chains and the girl half-supporting him, the pirate captain—and brought them eventually into the great hall where the Jade Throne stood.

Where it stood empty, while a man sat on a stool beside. Not the emperor.

The aide served as example to them all: walk so far across the hall floor, drop down, kowtow. This might not be the emperor, but kowtow anyway. Rise to your knees, shuffle forward, kowtow again.

Unexpectedly, wrongly, it was the girl Tien who spoke first: who lifted her head so sharply Old Yen had no time to reach out and push her down again. "His majesty—"

"—is not here," the man responded, almost kindly. "The Son of Heaven is elsewhere. I am General Ping Wen. Hush now," as her urgency almost overtook her again, "We will speak shortly. Yi, a word with you . . ."

He beckoned the aide forward, and had a murmured conversation. One by one the whole party lifted their heads, sat back on their heels; gazed about them in more or less wonder, watched the two by the throne with more or less anxiety.

At last, the general waved the aide aside. "Very well, I have it now. The guards may leave us. And you too, Yi."

"Excellency—"

"Yes, yes. Go, go." He chased the aide away with a flapping hand. "Now. This is an . . . unexpected end to my day. Which of you is the army captain? Very good. Tell me your tale, as neatly as you may."

"Excellence, this man asked to be brought to the emperor directly . . ."

"But the emperor is not here, and I sit as regent in his place. You may speak with certainty." And, when the captain hesitated one more time, "Swiftness would also be welcome. You and your men have been on the mainland . . . ?"

"Yes, excellency, securing a supply of rice for collection after the harvest and doing what we could to disrupt the rebels' comfort. Burning storehouses, attacking patrols. We were picked up by arrangement, by this man's boat—"

"Yes, the fisherman. We have met before, have we not?"

"We have, excellence. I brought news to the emperor before."

"I remember. Why are you here now? I hope not from presumption. A man may be received once and not a second time. Especially in his majesty's absence."

"Excellence, there is a dragon in the sea, and I may be the only man willing to tell you what she means," as the doctor and the boy had said nothing so far. The doctor threw him a glance he couldn't interpret; the boy seemed not to be listening, more slumped than obedient on his knees, half leaning against the girl.

"A dragon? Indeed? Yi said you were all here over an affair of spies?"

"We did see the dragon, excellence," the captain said. "I had not thought to mention her till now—"

"Because delivering your spy seemed more important. Quite so. Which one is the spy?"

The doctor raised his head. "That is what I told the captain, excellence."

"What you told him. Is this to say it was not true?"

"I have been Tunghai Wang's doctor, that much is true. My name is Hsui. I have . . . not been a spy for the emperor, before this. That was a tale we agreed with Li Ton, in order to achieve this interview."

The pirate captain's head jerked up at that, with a glare that could have been deadly; the general saw his face for the first time.

"Chu Lin."

"Ping Wen," the pirate said. "This is my time for meeting old friends, it seems; I have seen Ma in Santung. Captain Ma, as he was when I knew him."

"Ah, Ma. Yes. And now you work for him, do you? As a sea-captain?"

"Say I work for his master, Tunghai Wang, that brings you closer. Largely, I work against your own, and glad to have the chance."

"Against? Captain, I thought you brought these people here as our friends?"

"So did I, excellence . . ."

The general might not seem alarmed—amused, rather: leaning one arm on the side of the throne, surveying them with an ulti-mate of calm—but the captain genuinely was, rising to his feet, drawing his heavy tao, standing between them and the throne.

Again, it was Tien who spoke without an invitation: "So we are your friends! Well, we are, Uncle and me and Han. We're not friends of Tunghai Wang, anyway; we were only with him because an army needs a doctor. But, I wanted to *tell* you—you have to warn the emperor, there's a squad of assassins after him! They came over on the boat with us, dozens of them. They're going to the, the new palace, where the emperor is building it? They're going to join the workers there and kill him when they get a chance. They did have a smith, a friend of ours, they meant to take him with them only he wouldn't go, so they, they *killed* him . . ."

"Captain," the general said, still calm. "I understood that there were only these, on this man's junk?"

"When we found it, excellence, yes. And, yes, a body in the water. *He* said it was a crewman he had killed, for discipline. I could believe that of him. This? I don't know: there was no sign of a landing party, on the beach or on the path . . ."

"They didn't use the path," the girl said, almost frantic now. "They climbed the cliff, directly from the deck; there were these creepers hanging down, and he let the junk drift beneath them and they just went up like monkeys. Please, you have to believe me . . ."

"Oh, I do believe you," the general said. "I'm only trying to as-sess how disappointed I need to be in my captain. Why didn't you tell him the truth at the time? He might have sent soldiers after these assassins."

"Uncle said not to, that we could come here to warn the emperor in person, if we told a different tale first . . ."

The doctor said, "Forgive me, excellence, but protecting the emperor's life was not my first priority. At this time, young Han's here is the more important. It was crucial to bring him safe to port; and, as my niece has said, we expected to find the emperor here . . ."

"Mmm. Captain: step outside and send for paper. I will write a warning for his majesty; a messenger will fetch it to him shortly. When your assassins try to infiltrate the workforce, they will find our soldiers ready for them. Yes."

"Excellence," the captain said, "I would rather take the message myself. With a squad of my own men, for certainty."

"No doubt you would, captain, but you need a bath and rest before you go anywhere, I can see your exhaustion from here," which almost seemed to say *I can smell you from here.* "The new palace is like an ants' nest, soldiers everywhere; once they are alerted, there will be no danger to the Son of Heaven."

"Excellence, this man—" with a gesture toward the pirate captain,

"—is an old friend of mine, and will make no trouble for me. Go."

PAPER AND ink and brushes were brought by a man with a writing desk and a flustered anxiety. The general waved him away and wrote swiftly, folded the paper and sealed it with his chop. There was a messenger at the door, waiting; it was almost a ceremony, that they should all watch him take the paper and sprint away.

And then that they should all go back into the hall again: except that the general stopped the captain and said, "No, go you; you have done enough. Find your men. Wash, eat, sleep. Report to me at noon tomorrow, when I will have a task for you. For you all."

"Excellence, I can't leave you with him, quite unguarded . . . !"

"Captain, I told you, we have been friends."

"He is a traitor! I'd wager he has tattoos that declare it . . ."

"I know he does, I saw them made. I saw him . . . harmed and marked and sent away. Which is, of course, why I trust him. He owes us his death, twice over now: once for returning, once for whom he brought with him. And I stand in the shadow of the throne, and I am entirely safe from him. Go, captain. Enough debate."

And so back into the shadows of the hall, and, "Now," the general said, once he'd resumed his stool, "do try to explain to me why this boy's life is so much more important than the emperor's?"

The doctor did try. He spoke of the dragon, and the need to keep her chained, and the boy being the best that any of them could do, since the monks had been slaughtered.

And the general said, "Chu Lin."

"Excellence?"

"You know this island, which they call the Forge?"

"I do, excellence."

"Good. Fisherman," and Old Yen came very alert, "you have a boat in the harbor."

It was not a question, but he answered it anyway. "I do, excellence."

"Very good. Chu Lin, you have had care of this boy for some time, and seem not to have lost him yet. I want you to keep him awhile longer. Take these others too, take them all. Unless you want to tell me that their story is madness, and there was no dragon?"

"No, excellence. I did see the dragon; she nearly sank the *Shalla*."

"That was your junk? Well, she is ours now. Go with the fisherman here. You will land on the Forge, and climb to the peak. I understand that the works there are abandoned, but they should still furnish you with fuel. I want you to light a beacon, burn everything you can. I want a light bright enough to shine from here to the mainland, all night long."

Old Yen had known moments like the silence that followed, but very few.

Then the pirate captain said, "Excellence, are you sure? Do you know what a beacon means, in that place, at this time . . . ?"

"Oh yes, I know. Let it shine, Chu Lin. Let it shine. And keep an eye, by all means, open for your dragon. There and back again."

"Are we to come back?"

"Actually," and the general smiled, and made a gesture as though he played his own words between his hands like a silky scarf, "I really don't care where you go, when you have done as I bid. Go where you like."

three

Mei Feng stretched herself slowly, luxuriously, against the warm dense length of her sleeping lord—who grunted something unintelligible, reached a loose arm around her, and was clearly not quite so much sleeping after all.

"Lord?" she murmured quietly, probing.

"Mmph."

She smiled; that meant he was awake enough to be reluctant about it. In the palace she would strike a little bell to let the servants know, and by the time he could be troubled to rise there would be bathwater waiting. An hour's soaking and scrubbing, splashing and oiling and preening, he'd be almost entirely human again.

Here there was no bathhouse, and no little bell. Also no hurry in the world. They had license—no, better, his majesty was urged to spend an extra day, two days, however long he liked. They could linger in the bed here, she could tease him through the croaking incommunicado of his waking body and amuse herself—and him!—without benefit of talking . . .

She rolled onto her side and slid her hand up over his chest, over his cheek, into his hair. Sticky, sticky all the way: he really ought to bathe, she ought to find a way to bathe him. Perhaps a barrel, and water heated on a fire . . . ?

She snickered, to think of the emperor washing like a common soldier. If common soldiers ever washed. Doing it in full sight of any number of common soldiers . . .

He made another of his painful interrogative grunts, and his one visible eye cracked slightly open. She nuzzled his shoulder and he settled again, hitching her just a little closer. She supposed they would do what they could, as they usually did, with bowls of water brought in by the maids; but now she'd thought of it, all her skin did itch for a bath, and . . .

And there were voices beyond the wall, and not the familiar whispers of her maids. It took her a moment to understand who they were; she still didn't understand why they were allowed so close. It was the emperor's choice, of course. Even so, she wished that he'd discussed it with her first. In private, where she could speak her mind. He'd gone so swiftly from wanting to kill the thieves to wanting to keep them alive, and then to keep them at hand. The jade-eater, at least, he wanted that boy near enough to study; and somehow the woman just came with him, and now—

Well, now they lived under the emperor's eye, which meant under hers also. She didn't dislike either of them, exactly, but she hated the way they claimed so much of his attention, when they should have been quietly grateful for his mercy. Quietly grateful and somewhere else, for preference.

The woman Jiao particularly. She swaggered, with her mercenary airs and the sword that she was bizarrely allowed to keep, as though she were some kind of bodyguard. Mei Feng hated that, if only because it reminded her of a life she'd lost: a life of the body, of stretched muscles and salt-soaked skin in the storm's eye, the toss of waves, bare planking beneath bare feet, and . . .

And she had promised herself not to regret that, any of that, and she would not do it now. Let the woman pose with her bare arms, muscles on display. Jiao wasn't important to the emperor; she was tolerated, for the boy's sake. And the boy was quite sweet. He reminded Mei Feng of herself, a little, when she was first brought to the palace: wide-eyed, bewildered and amazed, afraid, too startled to be unhappy.

Yu Shan was very much the simple boy down from the mountains, knowing nothing. He didn't even seem to know how rare he was among men, how physically unmatched. Perhaps they were all like him, among the jade mines? She didn't believe that; he had to be the freak, the thief, the bad one who broke imperial law to take what he wasn't entitled to, strength and speed that should have been the emperor's alone.

No wonder the emperor was fascinated. Mei Feng was fascinated too, learning more about her own man through his study of this other. Even so, she'd still rather have more time with the original. This was typical: here they were, in the inviolable privacy of their bedchamber, and even here those two came breaking in, even if it was just their voices . . .

". . . What do we do today?" That was Yu Shan, always the one who waited to be told.

"Whatever they choose, of course. If we're not going back to the city." The woman was yawning as she spoke; if Mei Feng lifted her head to look, she was sure she'd see a lean shadow cast through the lacquered silk wall, stretching mightily.

"There's the river," the boy said.

"What about it?"

"We could swim, if they didn't want us. I'd like to swim." He sounded plaintive, a little boy missing a treat; she heard *I'd like to swim with you,* but wasn't really listening anymore. Her head was filled with images of water, running broad and clean and deep; her skin shivered with anticipation of it, the shock of entry and then the cool slide of it across her body, the clean bite and the warm work and the tingling pleasures after . . .

"Lord, are you awake . . . ?"

"Unh."

A kiss, to sweeten that difficult art of talking; and, "Were you listening?"

"Only to you." He sounded like a frog first thing, all croak. Sometimes he was like a great frog in other ways, all mouth and legs and slithering. Not this morning. This morning he could barely move. "You breathe all out of time with me. Little lungs."

"Great whale." Better, probably, not to call him *frog.* "But whales like to swim, I think? When they're not snoring?"

This whale shifted and groaned, and said, "Swimming. Who talked about swimming?"

"Yu Shan and Jiao." That should tempt him.

"Unh. Swimming sounds good. I can't remember the last time I swam. There must have been times, on the road . . . Mustn't there . . . ?"

"I expect your mother thought it was unsafe, if it wasn't in your own gardens."

"She probably still would. She's probably right. Is there a pond? I don't remember a pond. We're going to dam the stream to make a lake, but . . ."

"No, lord. No pond. There's the river, though."

She waited. After a moment, he snorted. "She would forbid it."

"Yes, lord. But she can't. No one can. You're emperor. Besides, we're here and they're not; and Ping Wen's letter said we should take what chances we could to enjoy the country. It might not be so easy to come again, if there are spies and assassins abroad; people will try to keep you locked up, where they know you're safe. Don't worry, if it's a *very* dangerous river, I won't let you swim in it."

He snorted, and his fingers drummed impatience on her ribs. "Shall we?"

"I think we should." Chillier than a bath but better too, so many ways better . . .

THEY WENT, of course, as a foursome. Which meant that they went, of course, with two dozen guards in train, and her maids, and a whole train of servants else. Which meant at least that they need not carry anything, because there were hands enough despite the extraordinary quantities of things necessary for a spontaneous imperial swim: towels and clothes and oils and combs, foods and drinks and tables, folding chairs and sunshades.

She would send them all out of sight, once they'd found a pretty spot with a good depth of clean water. And not too much current, because she didn't know how well he did swim, and she wouldn't want to see him swept away; his mother might be hard to reconcile . . .

"What are you grinning at?"

"Oh, nothing, lord. Just—this," with an expansive gesture that did not include the snaking line of guards and servants. "It's good to be out in the air, walking. I like to walk."

Jiao snorted. "Try walking the length of Taishu, before you say that so brightly."

"Or the length of the empire," she countered, "as his majesty has done," and never mind that he was carried most of the way in litters and wagons and carriages. She didn't think he'd worn out too many pairs of his soft padded boots. But it did flatter his vanity to speak of that long march as something heroic, rather than a desperate flight.

Desperate and possibly still unavailing: she didn't like the message Chung had brought, assassins discovered in Taishu-port, testing ways into the palace grounds. Where one group had failed, another might succeed. It had been hard on her, to see her island turned into a garrisoned fortress; it was harder now to see it as a fortress that failed, to see all the hunger and grief as wasted, his life precariously hung by a hair.

At least she didn't need to worry about it today. Or possibly tomorrow either; it might not be safe yet to think of going back. Ping Wen's letter had told them to stay.

THE RIVER came down from the mountains, of course. Yu Shan might have known it as a spring, a stream, a youthful bitter brook. Just here, where the force of its descent turned to a slow meander across the plain, it had chewed itself a basin. The main stream left a lot of water behind in a still, stony pool on the forest's edge,

where trees came down like cattle and stooped to drink, their
leaves trailing in slow currents.

It was ideal, everything she'd wished for. She could send the soldiers far enough that the trees would give them a screen of privacy;
the servants could set out their meal on the grass beyond. She was
happily babbling orders when she realized that the others—the
emperor, Yu Shan and Jiao too—were all quietly laughing at her.
She stopped mid-word, and listened back to herself; and her own
smile was pure confession as she bowed and said, "That is, of
course, if all this would please the Son of Heaven?"

"Everything you do pleases me, Mei Feng. You know that. And
this is lovely, this place that you have found."

He looked as though he wanted to extend the parkland of
his new palace to encompass it. Well, he could, of course, if
he wanted to; it would mean walls a mile long, but he was emperor.

He was emperor, and he was fumbling with the ties of his robe,
although she'd dressed him as simply as she could. She stilled his
fingers with her own, and made him wait until the servants were
busy out of sight and the soldiers had faded into the trees, even
until Yu Shan and Jiao had stripped off and plunged into the
water.

Then she helped him undress, and then she undressed herself;
and then, finding him still standing on the edge of the pool en-
chantingly waiting for her, she pushed him in.

AND DIVED in immediately after, because she still didn't know
how well he swam; and found that the answer was "very well indeed." The great whale might have bigger lungs than hers; she was
still surprised to find that he could stay under for longer. Indeed,
that he could grip her ankle and tug her down and hold her under
until the last of her air was gone. Just as her kicks were becoming
no longer playful, he wrapped himself around her flailing arms
and kissed her; and his used air was somehow enough for them
both, for that last little moment before they broke the surface and
she could gasp a real, desperate breath.

And then hammer her fists against his unheeding chest and growl curses against his grin. "I thought here might be one thing I could actually do better than you. Lord."

"Did you?" He was delighted, but that was no challenge; if there was one thing that delighted him more than she did, it was her telling him how remarkable he was.

Which was, again, no challenge. He astonished her, as he always had.

Her would-be cynical soul still said there would be other women, who would delight him anew; but it was hard to stay cynical when you were young and astonished, and the emperor of the world had twined his legs around yours and his arms about your shoulders and his magnificent body was drawing you down again into chill dark wonderful waters . . .

Yu Shan, as it turned out, swam as well as or possibly even better than the emperor. And lacked the grace to hide it, which delighted everyone, the emperor included. At length Mei Feng and Jiao both withdrew, to sit on the bank and rub themselves with towels and watch the boys still sporting.

She didn't invite it, but Jiao dried Mei Feng's back for her, so of course she had to do the same in return. And then of course they fell to talking of their two young men in terms of laughing disparagement, even though one of them was emperor of all the world; and then of other things, when those same young men still showed no signs of getting out of the water.

Vaguely dressed and rubbing at her hair, still grateful for the short crop that his mother so disparaged, Mei Feng had just taken a breath to ask a question when she was cut off by screaming.

It came from beyond the trees, where the servants were laying out the picnic.

Jiao moved while Mei Feng was still staring uselessly at the woodland, trying to see through it. The older woman snatched her tao from its scabbard and called sharply to Yu Shan. She waited long enough to roll her eyes at Mei Feng, "Why does trouble always come when he's naked? Get yours out of there, get him dressed and keep him here." Then she was gone, sliding rapidly between the trees.

As she looked back toward the water, Mei Feng noticed Jiao's boots, still sitting empty on the turf. Urgency had sent her away barefoot.

That was nothing. Yu Shan pulled himself out of the pool and padded after her with the water still running out of his hair: undressed, unarmed, unready. Naked entirely, except for the amulet he wore around his neck on a chain of beads. Jade beads, those were now: the emperor had had them changed, to keep the boy healthy, he said . . .

She stuffed her own feet firmly into her shoes, even as she snatched up a dry towel and went to intercept the emperor. Left to himself, he would clearly have followed Yu Shan, heedless, naked, vulnerable. She wouldn't let him do that. The Son of Heaven, running around butt-bare, exposed in every way? No. To prevent it, she was already working the towel on his hard body, knowing he would stand still to let her do it. He was too well trained, too complaisant, and she would exploit that as much as his mother ever had.

She talked, while she rubbed: "It was the maids who screamed. I expect one of them saw a snake. Or was bitten, maybe?" That was the worst she was prepared to allow.

He said, "No, I can hear weapons."

"Can you, lord?" His robe, his shoes; be grateful his clothes were so easy to manage this morning. "I can't, but you have such good hearing . . ."

Except that she could, suddenly: a distant muffled clatter, overridden by shouting and more screams. And loud voices, close and coming closer, those must be the soldiers drawing in from their perimeter, needing sight of the emperor and each other in this sudden confusion.

If they thought their emperor would wait patiently for their protection, they had misunderstood him badly; as badly as Jiao, who thought that Mei Feng could keep him close.

She had thought so herself, right up until he seized her wrist and said "Come on."

"Lord, you shouldn't . . ."

"What?" Apparently he could run and talk at the same time, and do both briskly. "I shouldn't see what danger threatens? I shouldn't expose myself to whatever is attacking my servants? I shouldn't care about my soldiers' lives, or my friends'?"

Yes, she thought, *all of those* . . . His mother, no doubt, would have said it. She would have liked to, and was quite glad to need all her breath for running, for keeping up with him.

Here was the tree line, here was the grassy ground beyond; there was the picnic upset and abandoned, thrown around. Among that spoil, people lay dead. Around it, men were fighting.

The imperial guards were a hand-picked mixture of veterans and youth, trained and devoted. They fought for their position, and fought to keep it. They were fighting now, as they had never fought before—and they were losing. She knew nothing of warfare, but she could see that. It wasn't hard. They fought, they fell.

The men who killed them, this sudden enemy looked like soldiers too: more roughly dressed but otherwise they might have traded places, except that all of these were veterans and few of them were dying.

Except where Jiao was wielding her blade with practiced skill, a warrior come to war, while Yu Shan fought beside her with another that he must have snatched from somewhere. He lacked Jiao's unexpected grace, her finesse with a weapon, but he was brutally quick and brutally strong. The men he fought could never quite find him with their blades, and whatever Yu Shan's found, it cleaved through.

Those two together were strikingly effective, but they were never going to be enough. The servants were mostly dead now, though a few were running. Being allowed to run. They didn't matter, she supposed. Neither did the soldiers matter, probably, except that they stood between the attackers and the emperor.

So would she, if she only had a weapon. She cast about for something, and realized that he was doing exactly the same; why would he carry a blade, to go swimming? With his guard packed about him?

His guard was tumbling out of the trees now, all around them and just in time. Those men who had stayed with the servants had held the enemy back, barely long enough, but their resistance was over. The attackers—rebels, she supposed they must be, soldiers from the mainland—pressed forward relentlessly, and even Jiao and Yu Shan were falling back now.

This new flux of guards ran on to meet the rebels, but they were outnumbered already; they would die as their comrades had, helpless and hopeless, in defense of a man they could not save.

Here came Jiao to say so, no doubt. Here came Yu Shan. The captain of the guard stood with the emperor, but his eyes were on the fighting and his blade was in his hand; he wanted to be out there with his men, and he might as well be, for all the good he was doing here. For all the good he would do, here or there.

Jiao was blood all over, but little enough of it seemed to be her own. She was breathing hard and grinning through a mask of blood, or at least baring her teeth; she said, "Majesty, come with us; you should not be showing yourself like this."

"*Showing* myself? Give me a weapon; I want to fight."

"No," she said bluntly, and it might have been the first time he'd heard the word, he seemed so startled. "That's what they want, too. We will not give you to them quite so easily."

"I will not leave my men to die!"

"Fool," the woman said, startling him again, though Mei Feng knew he'd heard that word before; she'd used it herself a few times, laughingly. "If you stay here, you condemn them to die. Leave now, and some of them perhaps will have the chance to live.

"Captain," she went on, "we will take the emperor. Not back to the palace site; there may be more of these expecting that, waiting on the road. In the forest, perhaps we can lose them. It will help if you can . . . detain them for a while."

The captain looked at his emperor, he looked at her; he nodded. No one said that with that nod, he had condemned himself and his men to death in any case. They all knew it. That was enough.

four

*B*ack on a boat again.

Sailing under Li Ton's command again—because he couldn't call him Chu Lin, though that might seem to be his name—and heading for the Forge, again.

Not knowing the real reason why. Again.

Bewildered and unhappy—again—Han sat in the bows of the old fisherman's boat and watched the water hissing by, and felt how the dragon fought below. She had tested them, tested *him,* with that sudden rise, trying to swallow the junk and him if she couldn't break the chains. She'd nearly won both ways, but the chains had held—if barely—and the junk had survived the flood, and so had he.

And had fought her down again, and now it wasn't the chains that she was fighting, it was him.

She squatted in his head, and he felt her contempt for that narrow cage; and he tried to pretend it was a victory, that he had caged her. That he was bait and jailer both, and the trap was sprung.

By contrast, she showed him glimpses—almost more than his mind could stand—of what she was: the power and majesty of her, the stretch, the breadth. The colors, roiling in the wind; the jewel edge, bright and glittering and lethal. The soar of height and the plunge of depth, the catastrophe of her fury and the wonder of her love.

Sick or stubborn or blind to his own defeat, he sat it out. He was what he was, a boy in chains in the prow of a boat; and she couldn't—quite—touch him and she could not, she could *not* quite break him, and he survived.

For what, he wasn't certain. It would never be any better than this. She would batter at him physically, emotionally, every way she could, until at the last he would fail. One way or another, she would defeat him and fly free.

Just, not today. He was determined on that. Not today.

A FIGURE came forward and dropped to the deck beside him. He didn't turn to see; she laid her hand on his shoulder, and he knew.

"Tien. How, how are you?"

"*I'm* all right," meaning *how are you?*—and not being at all surprised to be answered by a shrug and another question.

"What are the others doing?"

"Uncle Hsui is at the stern there, talking to the fisherman. Li Ton's with them, but he's not even listening, he doesn't care what they say. What's he doing this for?"

"I don't know, yet. I expect we'll find out." Even Han could hear the defeat in his own voice; it disgusted him. If he were Tien, he thought, it would disgust him—her—more. And yet she still came to talk to him. That was something.

"So why are we letting him do it," she said, "whatever it is? We outnumber him; we could, we could just throw him overboard . . ."

"Could we? He's armed, and we're not. If he wasn't—well, your uncle's a scholar, not a fighter. The old fisherman is . . . old; and you're young, and not a fighter. And me, I'm . . ."

"You're sick," she said, "you don't have to do anything. But there's the deck boy, Pao—"

"Who won't do anything unless he's told. It's Li Ton who does the telling, you know that. None of us can stand up to him, even though we know what he is."

"He's a traitor!"

"Yes, of course. His skin says so. A traitor to what?"

"To the empire, of course! And so's that, that general, Ping Wen. I don't know what he's sending us to do, but . . ."

"But it likely serves the interests of Tunghai Wang, back on the mainland. Who's the man you've been following all these months. Face it, Tien. We're all traitors here."

"Uncle says it doesn't matter who we follow, so long as we keep the dragon down . . ."

"But?"

"But I don't like Li Ton, and I don't like Ping Wen, and I don't trust anything they're hatching. Uncle says we're not devoted to the empire either, but even so . . ."

Even so: none of them really knew why they were here, or what Li Ton intended. They were all equally uncomfortable with it, and equally helpless to interfere.

THEY CAME closer and closer to the Forge, and Han was more and more oppressed by memories of the last time. The night he saw the dragon, through that other boy's eyes—what was his name? Yerli, yes. Strange dead Yerli, who went where he was most afraid to go, just to show Han something that they neither of them understood.

Han understood it now, too late.

Closer still, and the jetty was gone, that they'd tied up to before. Briefly he hoped that there'd be no way to land; but of course men must have landed before the jetty was built, or no one could have built the jetty. It was convenient, not crucial.

The fisherman said he had a way ashore. Was he old and wise, with these waters in his bones, or was he old and foolish, with water in his eyes and in his brain? Han found it hard to care. The Forge was the last place on earth that he wanted to set foot again; memories were hung all about it like the fog, like lights in fog, death and pain and cruelty and terror.

If the old man got it wrong, they'd never make it ashore. He thought he could almost welcome that. Almost. But then the boat would break apart and they would all slide down into the water, deep down to where the dragon waited far below. He would go first and fastest, under the weight of all these chains; she would welcome him most gladly, bright shining eyes like lights in fog to guide him through the murk. Bright eyes and open mouth.

NO FOG just now. In clear evening light they came to the Forge. Old Yen steered them past the ruined jetty and seemingly straight at the rocks. Tien's hand tightened on Han's; he took one glance back to see the old man working his oar hard, almost frenziedly against the surge and suck of the water. If the boat responded, it was only to leap on all the more swiftly. Han's eyes were drawn forward again, to see what doom looked like, rushing down upon him.

He thought the dragon was watching too, through his eyes. He was sure her thoughts, her senses pervaded the water—her waters, these, through right of long possession—so that she could feel the boat's hull in the surf, how fragile it was, and how very absolute the rocks. He could feel her eagerness, her anticipation. Her waiting mouth. She taunted him with it, lurking in his head like a lick and a swallow.

All the time, though, there was still one small whisper of himself that truly didn't believe it. The old fisherman wouldn't wreck his own boat.

Nor did he. Just as it seemed that calamity was inevitable, just when Han's daunted eyes could make out the molds and weeds that clung to the rocks that were going to break them, the old man let out a shout loud enough to carry over the roar of broken waters. At the same time, he flung his steering-oar over and braced it with all his bone-ridden body.

The boat answered, remarkably, impossibly: at that last moment it turned in its hectic progress, slid at an angle across the roll of a lifting wave and seemed to sniff out an unexpected passage, a break between two looming rocks like a gap in the dragon's teeth.

If the peace they found beyond the rocks was like the peace to be found within the dragon's mouth—well. They were safe enough, until she swallowed. Han thought that had always been true anyway, anywhere. Death was always only a moment away, a missed breath or a missed step, waiting on the dragon's swallow.

In fact the fisherman had brought them to a closeted little stretch of water, much like a tongue behind the teeth of rocks. The surf hissed and swirled between them, but all its force was broken into little eddies and waves that threatened weakly and meant nothing.

In that sudden stillness, voices still pitched for the sea carried farther than they were meant to. Han heard Li Ton say, "Well done," in a tone that measured surprise with respect. "And can you take her out again as neatly?"

"If we catch the tide right," the old man said. "High water, just as she turns: that'll lift us out over the jaw there and bear us away, sweet as a little girl's nutshell in a rain gutter."

"Good enough. We'll be all night anyway; high water won't come again till midday, but we can wait for that. Perhaps there'll be something to see. How do we get ashore?"

"Wetly," the old man said, without even the least hint of an apology.

WHAT THAT meant, for those who couldn't swim—which meant for Han, largely, though Tien and the doctor came with him, with Old Yen to work the pole—was an awkward slither down the side and into a sampan, then a punt across to the stone faces of the shore. Another graceless scramble over sharp and slippery rocks brought them at last to level ground nearly as wet as those who had swum it, Li Ton and the boat's boy Pao.

Old Yen returned to his boat, because this little gullet he had set her in was no secure anchorage and she couldn't be left unwatched. The rest of them were mustered under Li Ton's eye and marched uphill.

Again Han wondered why they all obeyed him so easily. He and Tien both wore heavy iron in their ears, to tie them to the *Shalla* and to him; they were committed already. Pao belonged to the boat and would do what the fisherman told him, which was clearly to follow Li Ton for his own health's sake. The doctor was perhaps not so easily dominated, but cooperated for his niece's sake as well as Han's, two imperatives.

THEY CAME to the monks' old settlement before they found the path that Han remembered. The settlement was twice a ruin now, gutted once by pirates' fires and then apparently raided for timbers to build a great pyre at its heart. A circle of rain-beaten ash still lingered, a heap of blackened bones that hadn't burned.

Han wanted to hurry by, so did Pao; Li Ton wouldn't let them. He led the search himself, scouring the ghost-huts in the last of the light for any wood that had been overlooked or only half burned through, anything that could hold or feed a flame.

What they found, they carried up the steep path to the summit, to the forge itself. Han could feel the dragon's awareness constantly behind his eyes, and something of her temper—like tempered steel, worked and reworked in the heat of her fury and the chill of the sea—as she looked at this place where her chains had been made and hammered home, renewed again and again on the bodies of determined men.

The forge was as it had been left, untouched. Now Li Ton said, "Tear it down."

They stared at him, perhaps. "That roof," the iron rain-cover, "I want that down. And I want all the wood heaped up there," in the heart of the furnace. "With charcoal from the bunkers; but pull the bunkers apart, I want that wood too. Build me a fire that can burn all night, and be seen all night."

IT WAS to be a beacon, then; a signal to Tunghai Wang and his forces onshore. Someone was being premature, perhaps, confident of an uncertain outcome. Or trying to subvert one plan with another.

Han could think of no reason to go to so much trouble, simply to say *We have landed*, or even *The emperor is dead*.

On the other hand, *come now, strike now, launch your invasion fleet*—that, yes. One blazing light to declare it, in the sight of every captain that the fleet could boast: that was an order worth the making.

five

Were they running, or were they being herded?

Yu Shan wasn't sure, but he didn't like either one. Help, hope was behind them, and falling farther; deliberately or otherwise, they were being driven away from the road and the palace site, away from all those soldiers. Deeper into the forest, higher into the hills.

Someone would realize soon enough that the emperor hadn't returned from swimming. A runner would be sent, and the bodies found. Then of course there would be panic, men streaming out in search; but it would take seasoned trackers to find and follow their trail, and seasoned trackers could never move at this pace. Yu Shan had seen deer run down by hunting dogs; this was like, in its relentlessness.

He could run and run. So, it seemed, could the emperor. Jiao and Mei Feng—well, they were both strong and used to work; one had the long road in her muscles, the other had the sea. But neither of them had jade in their bones, and the climbs were draining them.

The rebels at their backs weren't jade-eaters either. Together or separately, the two young men could have outrun them all; indeed, at one of the essential rest stops at the top of a slope, Mei Feng glared at them both and gasped, "You two, you're not even *breathing* hard! You go on, you," specifically to the emperor, "leave us. You're the one they want. Yu Shan'll look after you. They'll leave us alone . . ."

"Like they left the servants alone?" Yu Shan snarled, not entirely trusting the emperor to say what was needful. "They'd kill you for practice. For pleasure."

"Besides," Jiao grunted, trying hard not to look as though she needed this break as much as Mei Feng did, "are you seriously going to trust your man to Yu Shan's swordwork?"

"They won't need swordwork, without us to slow them down. Yu Shan knows the mountains; he can see my lord safe. Besides, my lord has very pretty swordwork of his own."

"Which doesn't matter," her lord himself replied, "because we're not leaving you. You'd be run down and slaughtered without a thought."

"And if you stay with us, we'll all be run down and slaughtered. You two can run forever, maybe, but we can't. *I* can't."

"You can run another mile." That was Jiao, coming easily to her feet now. "One mile at a time, girl. You're doing grand. And, look, downhill . . ."

"For now." Mei Feng peered over the ridge at their next slide down into shadow. "Uphill after. And then what?"

"We're coming into my country," Yu Shan said. If anything, the scent of the hills made him stronger; his legs welcomed steepness, as his eyes welcomed deep green shade. "Clan country. If they don't know that . . ."

"What?" It was the emperor who asked, and Yu Shan grinned at him reflexively.

"Well, if we can stay ahead of them long enough, they'll find out."

The emperor blinked, and then grinned back, a moment of young male conspiracy abbreviated by a sudden sharp thump on Yu Shan's shoulder, which was Jiao.

"Your people can't fight these! They're not all like you. Or are they . . . ?"

"No, they're not like me." His people followed the rules. Mostly. "But they'll fight anything. We grow up fighting each other. Come . . ."

· · ·

SOON ENOUGH, too soon, they were walking more than running; keep this up, and they'd be resting more than walking. Yu Shan didn't think the men behind them would be walking, or resting, or doing anything other than dog their trail. Night came swiftly, though, in the mountains—properly swift: he'd been baffled by the slow dusk of the plains—and not even these tireless rebels could track in the dark. They might ape dogs in their endurance, but they couldn't see by scent.

Yu Shan, on the other hand, could see quite well in the darkest night. The emperor too. They could take whatever rest the women needed, and still be miles ahead before dawn.

And meantime there were clean streams to drink from and fruit to pick to calm a roiling empty stomach, if you knew what was good to eat, which he did.

He kept them moving while the valleys filled with shadow, so long as there was any last trace of brightness in the sky. During that shifty time they found one more stream to cross, a hatchling river, slender but vigorous. Yu Shan waded out, and it came no higher than his hip. They'd dealt with worse before, but this time he heard a soft hesitance, a doubt behind him. Looking back, he saw Mei Feng anxious at the water's edge, peering blindly.

Yu Shan would have gone back for her, but there was no need; the emperor was there, stepping down into the water and offering his back, taking her legs and simply scooping her up when she dithered. She rode across the water like a child, clinging to him; Yu Shan thought she was almost sobbing with exhaustion. When they reached the farther bank, the emperor simply stepped up out of the river and went on walking, never showed a hint of setting her down.

Yu Shan grinned back at Jiao, his face an open invitation.

If she saw, she pretended not to in the gloom; but stepped into the water and waded slowly, sternly past him.

He followed, and watched her clamber out; and waited till she reached down a hand to help him, as he'd known she would. The clamp of strong fingers, the heave of a leanly muscled arm, an ex-

hausted flash of teeth in the gloom; they let him say it at last, because it was a conspiracy now. "I can carry you, you know. When
you're ready."

"I'll never be ready for that," she said, and dog-trotted determinedly after the others.

LATER, WHEN the sky was star-dark and the valleys utter black,
when only the emperor and Yu Shan could see at all, he led them
off the path and upslope. He found an earth-cave under an over-
hang of rock; in his own home valley, this would have been opened
up into a minework, a test shaft in search of mother-stone. Here in
the mountains' margin, where good stone was hard to find, he
supposed that no clan had found it worth the effort.

The women sank into its grateful shelter. At least, Mei Feng
sank. Jiao scowled at him and squatted in the mouth for a minute
before she edged deeper in, muttering something about checking
on the little one. When there was no sign of her coming out again,
Yu Shan called her name softly. And had no answer but a snore,
and settled his back comfortably against the wall with his legs
stretched out ahead of him.

And found himself mirroring the emperor, how he sat, how he
stretched, on the other side of the cavemouth. The Son of Heaven
said, "It's good to stop."

"Yes, majesty."

"I don't suppose you could call me by my name? Now that
we're running for our lives?"

Yu Shan thought about it. "No, majesty. I don't think I could.
I'm sorry . . ."

A wise young man stepped lightly around the gods. Even to the
point of saying no to them, apparently.

The emperor smiled, and shifted his shoulders against the rock
he leaned on. "It's good to stop—but I really didn't need to. I
could have gone on, I think. All night, I think, and through tomorrow too. Am I right?"

"I don't really know, emperor. I feel the same, but—well, you
can always take another drink from a water-skin until it's empty,

and then there's nothing. Maybe we'd have fallen over after another mile, or another minute. As you say, it is good to stop."

There was pleasure in being still: in the cool damp of the un-
moving earth, in slack muscles and slow breaths, the smell of
green and the fall of rain. But if he hadn't been frightened and always looking back, there would have been pleasure too in the simple act of running: the pumping of muscles and lungs, hard
ground and hot skin and effort rewarded, speed and stretch and
challenge. Why would he ever want that to end? Why would it ever
need to? He could run to the ends of the world, if he could only
cross the sea . . .

Before he could think about swimming, the emperor murmured, "Perhaps we shouldn't talk."

"We won't wake them. Sir. However loud we speak."

"Not them. The rebels. If they hear us, they can find us."

"Not in this valley. Listen."

They were silent, then, together, except for the noises that their
own bodies made, the unconsidered suss of breath and the lub-
dub and gurgle of blood in the heart.

Beyond and below them were the sounds of the valley: the vast
soft sounds of wind and rain on trees and rock and water, the
harder sounds of the nascent river in its stony bed, cries of occasional animals and the songs of nightbirds. The hiss, scrape, buzz
of insects.

"I don't hear anything."

"No. That's what I mean. If they came, we would hear them before they heard us."

And see them better in the dark too, see them first, however
good they were; but that meant fighting, and he didn't want to
think about that. If it came to fighting, he and his companions
would still lose. They weren't enough, to fight off so many. A hard
hot strength couldn't overcome cold numbers, however earnestly
he wished it.

Which was why they needed to stay ahead, until the numbers
stood on their side; which was why he had to lead them on before
the night was over. Especially if the men who chased them were

resting now, sleeping, waiting for the dawn. Before dawn, Yu Shan wanted another valley, another ridge between them. At least one more.

He wondered if it were possible to tell an emperor to go into the cave, to sleep with the women. He thought he might try, at least, but the emperor forestalled him.

"Do you still sleep, Yu Shan?"

"Yes, of course!" He was still human. He at least. The same stone might give the same gifts to two separate young men, but one of them would still be the Son of Heaven and the other would still be a thief.

"Do you need to?"

"I—don't know." He had endured nights of wakefulness at Master Guangli's. Those had been miserable, but for other reasons. He'd passed nights of wakefulness with his clan-cousin and with Jiao, which had been delightful but for other reasons. He hadn't tried doing without sleep for its own sake; he enjoyed it too much. In company especially, when one sleeper seemed to drag another with her, like a stone's weight pulling him underwater . . .

"If I told you to go into the cave there, join the women, sleep . . . ?"

"No. I can't leave you."

"Why not?"

"Because Jiao would be angry if I did. And Mei Feng too, I think."

A chuckle came back to him. "I think so too. Especially if I confessed."

"Confessed what?"

"That I'd sneaked off while you slept, slipped back along our tracks to find the rebels."

He was faster, stronger and he had better eyes in the dark, and better hearing too. He might not be a better swordsman, but that would matter less.

Yu Shan said, "They will have posted a watch."

"Yes. But we've been running from them all day; they won't expect to find us doubling back. And you know these forests better than anyone. You could bring us down on them undetected . . ."

Already he had shifted from *I* to *we,* he had made Yu Shan a conspirator. Certainly two of them together would be more than twice as deadly, and more than twice as safe. They could deal more handily with any watch there was, slay more of the sleepy before they had to slip away, guard each other's backs when they did . . .

"They'd be angry," the emperor said, "if you let me go alone. If you came with me . . . ?"

The women would—he knew, they both knew—be very angry indeed to find themselves abandoned in the night, while their men-folk crept off into danger. But they were asleep, and should be safe enough; what better way to protect them, indeed, than to do harm to the enemy right now, before morning, before the hunt could start again . . . ?

THERE NEEDED no more talking. They left silent good wishes for the sleepers—at least, Yu Shan did, and he saw the emperor slide a quick glance in at the cavemouth, with a thought surely attached to it—and padded away.

Yu Shan led, down to the loud little river and through the chill of it. A great crashing, splashing noise startled him almost into shrieking, but that was just a munjun deer that he'd startled him-self, diving out of cover and hurling itself away upstream. The em-peror almost folded up right there in the water, with his struggle to laugh in silence; Yu Shan almost resisted the urge to splash him. Almost.

"And you're the one who has to call me 'majesty'?"

"I suppose you could pretend I was calling you *munjun.*"

That was a breathy little exchange as they hauled themselves out, wet and cold and excited. Then there was the more cautious sneaking up to the ridge, which was narrow and rocky, overhung with trees. Yu Shan and the emperor crouched there side by side, peering down into the woods of the next valley: remembering what they could of that ground, seeing what they could by dim starlight enhanced by the gift of jade, listening intently for any sound that rose up from the bowl below.

WHAT STRUCK Yu Shan came from the side, a brute blow that sent him sprawling backwards, sliding down the slope again until he caught on some tree roots. Pain flamed in his skull, and giddy lights swam before his eyes. Blinded and dizzy, all he could do was lie still and listen, grasping weakly for words that swelled and faded and hardly touched him, rolled over him like thunder, like the rain . . .

"What have you done?"

"Don't move, or you get the same."

"Who *are* you? You're not—"

"Who are *you*, more like. What clan? This is our valley now, we don't welcome—"

"Clan? You think we are mountain folk? Yu Shan is, yes—"

"Was. That one's dead. You can be too, if you don't talk straight. You don't talk like one of us, but you don't look like a plainsman either. What are you, then? And what are you doing in our valley? Going back to fetch your friends, down the gorge there? We've got an eye on them too."

"Not our friends, no. We have been running from them; they're assassins, sent from the mainland."

"Assassins?"

"Yes. They've been chasing us all day."

"Oh, who'd send assassins after two boys?"

"And why bother with so many, when boys are so easy to kill?"

"After us. Just us, not Yu Shan. They come from Tunghai Wang."

"Who's he?"

"The rebel generalissimo. Is Yu Shan really dead?"

"A slingstone on the temple, from so close? He's dead. So will you be, soon, if you don't tell us—"

"If he's dead, why is he moving?"

"He can't be."

He was, though. Apparently, not being dead, he was struggling to get up.

It had all been so easy, before this. Now he had to haul himself up a tree trunk because there was no steadiness in the world, and his jade eyes couldn't help. He thought the night-dark was leaching in through a hole in his skull. He thought there had to be a hole, it hurt so fiercely. If he lifted a hand to touch, he'd find it, wet and raw and broken-edged. Only he needed both hands to cling to the tree just now, so there was no touching: only the hurt of it, and the peering through flicker and shadow that only made it hurt more, trying to see.

There was the emperor, yes. He didn't have his tao in his hand. Yu Shan couldn't see whether they'd taken it from him.

There were two, no, three of them, standing on the high ridge there. Staring down at him, and he could feel the weight of their wonder. Not dead, and standing: he could wonder at himself. He'd seen a bull antelope die in a moment, its skull cracked open by a slingstone.

Here came one of them plunging down with a blade in his hand, looking to finish: *Not dead yet, but you will be.* Perhaps he even thought it was a kindness: a boy with a hole in his head, he couldn't possibly want to *live,* now could he . . . ?

Even broken-headed, Yu Shan didn't want to die like that. Perhaps he drew strength from the tree's solidity. For sure it wasn't fear or fury that drove him; he felt strangely distant, cut off somewhere behind the pain in his head. But his arms dragged him up the tree, branch to branch, before the man could reach him; then he swung his body so that his heel-hard feet caught the man full in the chest, a jarring double blow that must have broken bones.

The man fell, sprawling. Yu Shan jumped down, staggered, lifted himself anyway to go to the emperor's aid—and saw that he didn't need to. One man lay on the path, sick with some unseen hurt; the other had the emperor's hand clamped around his throat and his heels swinging helpless in the air.

"Don't kill him, majesty."

"Why not? He would have killed us. They tried to kill you. Why aren't you dead?"

Because I'm a jade-eater, like you; we have stone in our bones. And in their blood, their muscles, perhaps their minds and souls. He didn't think the emperor really meant to strangle the man to death; assuming not, he said, "Because I am your servant, majesty. You had not released me." Let the man ponder that, as he dangled.

Despite himself, his fingers had found their way to his scalp. There was flinching soreness there; there was stickiness, as though the skin had broken but more or less decided not to bleed. He seldom did bleed much, these days. Nor, apparently, were his bones keen to break. He took pain, but not damage. He supposed he could live with that.

He said, "Majesty, if you kill him, if we kill any of these, we have their clan at our backs, as well as the rebels. If we take them back alive, we earn the clan's welcome," or at least they could walk boldly into the serpent's mouth and hope not to feel its teeth.

"The emperor does not need to earn—"

"No, majesty," interrupting the emperor seemed to be a growing habit, "but their gratitude will not hurt us," in the way that their hunting spears might, those minutes it might take them to understand that they had the Son of Heaven in their midst. Once they did understand it—well, the people of the mountains might feel little bond to the empire, but they would give their allegiance to the Man of Jade. He thought they would.

Slowly, with a seeming reluctance, the emperor set the choking man on his feet again. And held him—by the shoulder, firm but not unfriendly—until he could stand securely on his own, until his ratchet breath had eased.

The man stared, took one more painful draw of air and said, "Are you, are you truly emperor?"

"Do you doubt us?"

"No! No, majesty"—he looked almost inclined to kowtow, except that it wasn't a gesture that came naturally in the mountains;

maybe he only wanted to drop to his knees and breathe awhile—
"but . . ."

"But no one will be looking to see your majesty here, and un-escorted," Yu Shan said, an interruption boosted by his own un-certain legs, his vicious head, his sudden yearning to get back to the women. "It would be easier if we were all together, and away from here." If the rebels were camped just in the gorge below, an alert guard might hear muttered voices coming down to him.

"There are more of you?"

"There are," he said. "Come."

One of that bewildered man's companions had surely-broken ribs, the other a visibly dislocated shoulder, where the emperor must have wrenched it out of its joint. It was a difficult and painful walk for them, down from the ridge-height and across the valley. Yu Shan was unsteady himself, on the downslope. One more wade through the river all but undid him, except that when he lost his footing altogether the emperor was there to seize his arm.

Out of the water, he led them up to the cavemouth. Which these men hadn't found or known about, seemingly: they must be new to the valley, for all that they laid claim to it.

The emperor went in, to wake the women. Yu Shan stayed outside with the clansmen, but his attention was in there, in the dark, with Mei Feng's sleepy confusion and Jiao's sharper in-quiries. What men, who were they? Where and how had they been found? And why was the emperor's clothing wet?

His majesty managed to avoid the most awkward of those ques-tions, by dint of backing out of the cave and leaving the women to follow.

Which they did soon enough, making the clansmen blink.

"These are—?"

"Yes," Yu Shan said. "We are all the companions his majesty needs."

One man swallowed, another flinched. Given what they had seen and felt already—an impossible survival, unnatural strength, the savage impact of simple blows—they must imagine that every one of the emperor's companions was a jade-eater. Let them think it; let their own fears work against them for this little time, to keep everyone safe.

IT WAS an easy illusion to maintain. Yu Shan and the emperor could see quite clearly—jadelight, he wanted to call it, this cast of green across the world—and the women weren't slow to catch on, walking easily between their two men, asking no more help than that.

On the way back down to the river, Jiao said—loudly— "What's wrong with those two, then? The ones who are walking like jungle crabs, all sideways?"

"Uh, we hurt them, the emperor and I . . ." Despite his own hurt, he was almost embarrassed to admit it.

"Hurt them how?"

"I think one has broken ribs, the other's arm is out of place . . ."

"Nothing I can do for ribs, but a displaced shoulder I can mend. Bring him to me."

The man was in easy hearing, of course, and came of his own accord: wary but hopeful, wild-eyed and in extraordinary pain. One look at the great lumpen swelling under his skin and she grunted, "Yes. Give him something to bite on."

It was the young man himself who objected. "I don't need that. Put the shoulder back as it should be, I can take the pain."

"You'll have to. But I don't want you screaming all down the valley, there are people out there who mean to kill us."

Yu Shan might have interceded, but the emperor was there before him: "He didn't cry out when I did this to him, Jiao."

"Did he not?" Her voice acquired an air of grudging respect. "Maybe I'll trust him, then. Take his arm, though, his other arm. I don't want him flailing at me."

It was the emperor himself who gripped the young man's good arm, wrist and elbow. As though he too felt there were amends to make.

Jiao held the bad arm in much the same way, wrist and elbow. She lifted it and pulled a little, twisted, testing; then jerked it straight and hammered the heel of one hand into the shoulder, right on the nub of protruding bone.

Yu Shan wanted to scream, just from watching. He saw a sudden agony of sweat on the young man's distorted face, a measure of how very much effort it took, not to scream.

He heard the dreadful click, as the bone slipped back into its proper place; he saw the sudden relief from pain, that transmuted almost into tears except that if he didn't scream, the man wasn't going to weep either. Obviously not.

There was a little pause, a stillness all around, and then nods of gratitude, touches of support. The party moved on together, its balance subtly altered now.

The running river brought them eventually to the head of the valley, and the traditional settlement. The wood of the buildings was raw and unweathered, and there were stumps still in the ground where trees had been freshly felled. Traditionally Yu Shan would have been looking for a family group, but these were young people, men and women all together, one clan but surely not one family.

It wasn't even clear who led them, not clear among themselves. They all came out, sleep-sodden and edgy from their rough new huts, lighting lamps and muttering, looking for someone else to take charge.

It couldn't be the emperor. Yu Shan didn't want it, Mei Feng wouldn't touch it; Jiao straightened her shoulders and said, "Don't you children have a headman?"

It wasn't tactful, and it brought some graceless snarls, sent a murmur of fierce indignation through the throng; but it won her what she wanted, someone to talk to. One of the young women called back, "We don't need one. We can keep thieves out of our territory by ourselves. Doshun, why bring them here and wake us all up with it? Why not just kill them and leave their heads on the ridge?"

Doshun was the one not hurt, except for his sore neck. Not hurt yet. He eyed Jiao a little askance, where she was fingering her blade quite prominently. "They are not thieves. Not what you think. This, this is the emperor. He *is* the Man of Jade. I have seen . . ."

If the emperor had expected the whole gathering to kowtow at once, or at all, he was disappointed. If he had expected instant acceptance, he must be disappointed again; what he faced instead was incredulous laughter.

"I know. I *know*," Doshun shouted, above the ruckus. Shouting must have hurt; he lifted a hand to his throat, and let it fall again. If anybody could see bruises in this difficult light, they were still only bruises, no proof of anything. "It sounds crazy, but it's true. I think it's true. Everything the stories say about the emperor, he has it all . . ."

All except the long parade of pomp: the guards, the servants, the yellow carriages. The jade. If jade-eating was any guarantee, then Yu Shan should be emperor himself.

He didn't say so. He didn't say anything. He thought he might make a gesture, kowtow himself, only to make the point; but if the emperor was a fraud, then so was he.

Jiao spoke to the woman who had challenged Doshun. "It is true, but never mind it. This is true too, that your friends attacked mine, and two of yours are hurt. Here, take them," the one with his arm bound up in his sleeve, and the one whom only time could help, "and give them rest and tea. They will tell you what they know. What I know is this, that there is a team of killers in pursuit of us, and come daylight they will be here. They slaughtered the emperor's servants, and his guards: all but us. Which is why you see him like this, all but alone, all but unprotected," though she made clear how strong that unprotection still was, with a glance at the wounded as their friends took them away.

"It is true," Doshun insisted again. "There are soldiers in the gully beyond the north ridge. We saw their camp . . ."

"How many?" That young woman again, assuming an authority she might not own. Perhaps she saw a chance to rise.

"We weren't sure, in the dark. Two dozen at least. We were coming back to warn, but then we saw these . . ."

And had tried to kill Yu Shan, on the instant, without warning.

It might have been shocking, to anyone not raised in the mountains. Here it was common practice, clan manners. Nevertheless, if these youngsters tried to see off the rebels face to face, hand to hand, he thought most of them would die. This wasn't clan warfare, it wasn't anything they'd ever met. Clan war was all about territory, seizing or defending land. This was simply about lives, and those soldiers had been killing for years. They must live and eat and sleep with death as their companion.

Jiao said, "It's too late now, to organize an attack on their camp—"

"We wouldn't do that," the woman cut in. "There's nothing in the gully that we want."

Which was exactly what Yu Shan expected, and why these youngsters would die. Jiao was exasperated: "Don't you understand yet? They'll come here and kill you. That's all. It's not about land or jade. You still have time to run, I suppose; if they don't confuse your trail with ours, they should just keep coming after us, but—"

"They won't drive us out of our valley."

Again that was inevitable, a stubbornness born of mountain imperatives, where the only value lay in possession, in holding on. A fisherman's wealth is in his boat, a trader's in his goods, a herder's in his flock, all movables; a miner's wealth is in the ground he holds.

"Well then," Jiao said, "we need to be ready to meet them when they come."

THE YOUNG woman's name was Tantan. She might not be prepared to believe in the emperor, but no blame to her for that; it was an absurdity, the master of the world vagrant in the hills with a handful of unlikely companions. It might be true, but it was still absurd.

Tantan was happy to accept Jiao for what she so obviously was, a competent and organized fighter. The two of them put their heads together and started issuing orders. Yu Shan was so relieved, he barely noticed that this included orders to the emperor—who listened, nodded and obeyed. Jiao had lived all her life at the blade's edge, and it showed. What she said made sense, what she demanded seemed possible. Yu Shan still thought they would need to be lucky, but it was an achievable kind of luck.

WAITING FOR the dawn, he found himself side by side with Doshun.

"Tell me who you are," Yu Shan murmured in the darkness. "You're Clan Chao, I know that," it was there to be seen in their clothing and how they wore it, how they decorated their bodies, how they braided their hair, "but this isn't Chao territory." It wasn't good territory for any clan, too marginal and leading nowhere. He didn't need to say that. He could feel how thinly jade lay within the rock, just a faint and fading whisper.

"No." The proper answer would have been *it is now,* but Doshun shifted awkwardly. "We . . . are not Clan Chao anymore."

If that was true, their fingers didn't know it yet. But, *"Exiled?"* The thought was brutally shocking. He was familiar with the concept, of course, there were tales told: great mythic tragedies, lessons to be learned. He'd never heard of its actually happening.

"No, we left. We chose to leave."

Something else he'd never heard of. He had left himself, of course, but only because his family sent him. He thought that was ironic. Except that now he was unexpectedly back, and bringing something better than the emperor's favor: bringing the emperor himself. If they could survive the morning.

There was still time to pass, before the morning. He said, "Tell me."

"The clan lands are exhausted, almost; the seams we mine are failing, and we can't find more. And there are too many of us, almost more than we can feed."

Yu Shan nodded. That was how he'd always heard it, that when a valley's mines were on the way to being worked out, the families of that valley would have more children, to make a fighting force to find and claim more land. Not like this, though, independently and far from home. He said, "Why come here?"

"Because Clan Chao is penned in, with other clans on every side and only the peaks above. There is no jade there. Our elders wouldn't sanction a war, to take territory from another clan; they want only to cling to what they have, and leave starvation for another generation. For us. We couldn't wait for that. We might have deposed them, but . . ."

But there was only one thing worse than clan war, and that was rebellion, uprising against your own chiefs, son fighting father. That was understood.

"So we left," Doshun said. "This is . . . what we came to. What we could find and hold." Bad land, but better than none at all; better yet, there was no one fighting for it, no one to fight. Thin jade, but at least there would be jade. For a generation, for a while.

Privately, Yu Shan thought that they would be fighting soon enough, among themselves. Without family lore and authority to give them place and purpose, why would they not fight for what their neighbor had? Cousin against clan-cousin . . .

DAWN BRIGHTENED the sky long before there was any sign of sun above the valley's eastern rim.

It was in those long shadows that the assassins came.

They came slipping through the gloom like half-remembered ghosts, some following the easy trail along the river's bank while others paced them, deeper in the woods. They kept to the one bank where the trail was, not to divide their forces; they kept in touch by brisk little whistles. They came at trackers' pace, but swift enough; those they tracked had left marks in plenty, especially with three hurt and not walking heedfully.

It was some little time before one man on the river path noticed that he had heard nothing from the rearguard for some time: no stray sounds, no deliberate whistles.

He glanced back, and found that to all intents and purposes he was the rearguard; there were no rebels in sight behind him.

A call brought those ahead to a halt. That man and one more went doubling back along the trail, to see what had happened to their missing.

They didn't run far or fast, not fast enough. Still in sight of the men ahead, they crumpled and fell, one on the path and one into the hurried water.

One of the watchers shouted, "Slingstones! Quick, into the trees—!"

The air was suddenly deadly around them all, furious little missiles fizzing across the river. They could glimpse the figures with the slings, even, moving among tree trunks, unreachable on the far bank.

Safe in the trees they gathered all together, forerunners and flank; regrouped, reorganized, went on again. Not following the trail now, knowing they faced some other enemy. They kept within the shelter of the forest and meant to cross the water higher up, double back and find the slingers. Some, they thought, had been girls; it would make no difference, unless perhaps they took any of them alive.

Girls, they must have been thinking, *boys, shooting stones across the water: afraid of close quarters, afraid of a real fight . . .*

They still weren't looking behind them. Soldiers don't, as a rule. They know where the enemy is: forward, the way they're pointed.

Again it took a man to glance back, looking for a comrade where he felt a sudden absence, to understand that the enemy wasn't only on the other side of the river.

No slingshots in this density of undergrowth, but broken sightlines and deep shadows made it possible for someone light of foot to slip up behind even a wary soldier, take him with a swift and silent blade, lower the body and slide away.

Someone, for example, who had spent all her adult life and half her childhood before that with a blade in her hand and a lethal caution in her head; or else someone who might have been eating jade awhile, who saw the darkest shadow as noon-lit, who could step leaf-light and use a blade with a savage finality . . .

NOT YU SHAN. Jiao and Mei Feng both had taken a look at his head and told him what he knew already, that he was uncannily lucky to be alive and in no condition for this work.

He was there, though, he watched it happen. His head still throbbed with a dull and distant thunder, but he wouldn't let two others do this on their own. He and Doshun watched each other's backs but more particularly Jiao's and the emperor's as those two melted in and out of shadow, each of them using different skills and training to do the same work, to kill in secret and in silence.

As before, it couldn't last; someone would and did have to look back and see missing faces, absent bodies.

If that had been all he saw, so much the better. It wasn't: he saw Jiao's tall slenderness fade behind a tree and yelled accordingly, which yell brought two of his comrades back to join him in a sudden lethal chase.

The one still not wholly steady on his feet, the other throat-sore and intrigued: this at least they were fit for. The rebels came running, blades drawn, in pursuit of one lone and ducking woman; they ran into a clearing and found that woman no longer ducking, ready for them and flanked by two men.

One-on-one they fought, then, skilled soldiers against a circus of mercenary, miner and—well, whatever Yu Shan was now, he who had been a miner, and was now something else, jade-eater and companion of emperors.

He was facing a man better trained and more practiced, and he didn't care. His head still hurt and he didn't trust his legs, and he didn't care about that either. He had a blade in his hand and his arm was strong and fast, his sight was sharp, Jiao was at his side.

At his side and hard-pressed; she might need his help. He didn't have time to linger over this one. Arm and blade together, swing and strike: it was all he knew.

The man he faced knew more, and was just as urgent. The dark glimmer of his tao in the shadows was like a fish in water, spearing toward Yu Shan. Who swung more like a peasant clearing reeds, and clattered the blade aside; and then tried to catch its owner on the backswing, but the man had already jumped out of reach. He had strength and speed, as well as skill and lethal intent. Together, those must always have been enough, till now. He was scarred, of course, he'd taken wounds, but he was a survivor.

Till now.

Now Yu Shan needed him dead, and quickly. He couldn't afford hard, focused fighting; the longer they stood blade to blade, the more chance the other man had. Skill and experience would tell in the end, if blind luck didn't play a hand.

Yu Shan stepped forward, ignorant and eager, the tao hanging in his hand. The rebel saw his chance and thrust again, neat and clean and straight for the chest.

Yu Shan brought his tao up from below, just in the moment that he needed to, to catch the blade and deflect it upward. He felt the rebel's tip snag his shirt, so close it was; but the blade was already flying over his shoulder and the rebel was unbalanced, toppling forward, and Yu Shan's blade was right there, one dreadful stroke that opened his chest and spilled his body out.

And Yu Shan was already turning away, before the man had properly fallen, perhaps before he properly understood that he was dead; turning to find that Jiao did not after all need his help, and that her man could have no doubt at all about his condition, because his head was tumbling some distance from his body.

Jiao dashed the blood-spray from her face and grinned brightly at Yu Shan, and then looked past him for Dushon, just as Yu Shan heard a grunt and the sound of a body falling.

One more time he turned to look for bad news, and was surprised: happily relieved to see the young miner bleeding and breathless but still on his feet, while his opponent lay before him with his face cleaved.

Jiao shook her head a little, and said, "Yu Shan, how did I ever take you so easily, when I found you in the forest?"

"My hands were tied, remember?"

"Yes, and you had a leash around your neck, and you let me lead you about for days. I think you could have broken those ropes in a moment. But you let those clumsy fool bandits take you in the first place, and then you let me keep you, and . . ."

And her hands said *All that time, you and your people can fight like this.* He shook his head at her and said, "Where's the emperor?"

Doshun gasped, and was gone in search. Jiao's eyes rolled a little, but she took off after, with Yu Shan just a deliberate moment behind her. Anyone who tried to surprise Jiao would find himself surprised in his turn; Yu Shan had her back.

His own could look after itself.

So, APPARENTLY, could the emperor. They found him by following a short trail of bodies, none of them his. He had a tao in each hand, and there was blood on both.

"I broke my own blade," he said, a little ruefully.

"You should have fallen back, found us . . ."

"It was quicker just to take theirs, and wait for you."

Yu Shan wanted to tell him that he wasn't immortal, and ought not to be stupid either. That could wait; Mei Feng would do it better, with more passion and more conviction.

THE REBELS were still moving forward, but more watchfully. Where the valley started to rise, where the clansfolk had cleared land to build their settlement, they paused inside the last fringe of forest. Necessarily, the four who followed them paused too; even now, they were too few to challenge the group. The rebels knew they were there, but not in what numbers; all they could know was that every man of the rearguard was lost. No wonder, then, that they weren't inclined to come back.

They must imagine that the emperor had gone ahead, leaving these miners to delay them. Yu Shan still thought he should have done exactly that. No clan in the mountains would willingly let a squad of armed men pass through their territory; the rebels would have been attacked again and again, whittled down to nothing in the end.

Whether the emperor would have been let pass, ahead of them—well, that was another question, and didn't need answering now. The emperor was here, and behind them. And now, at last, they were moving out from cover, into the cleared ground before the settlement.

They went fast, against the danger of slingstones; but the

slingers were all on the far side of the river, and the settlement was built on a rising slope away from the water, almost out of range. A few stones did fall among the rebels, but with no more than stinging force. They did no more than a whip would, to urge the men on faster.

IF THEY needed urging. They had death in their hands, on their blades, many deaths; they had death on their minds, at their backs, deaths of their own, unexpected and unwelcome. They had death in their eyes, on their breath, in their fingers: a promised death to everyone who stalked them, anyone who waited for them now beyond the compound wall.

Death called them, death sang to them; they ran to it, as men will.

six

Mei Feng was up a tree, armed with knives and nerves.

It was the tallest tree in the compound; indeed, it was the only proper tree in the compound, left standing perhaps for its own sake, because it was young and hopeful and determined, like those who built the compound, claimed the valley and would defend it now.

She wasn't meant to be any part of that defense. The emperor had tried to send her across the river with the slingshots, but she'd refused to go. She had tried to go with him into the woods, to ambush those who chased them, but he'd refused to take her. Each blocked by the other's stubbornness, neither had been satisfied; she was here in the settlement, neither safe nor useful, frustrated and afraid.

Climbing the tree had been the best she could think of: not from fear like a tree'd bear, but for oversight, the command of a good view.

The illusion of command. She'd said she could call down what the enemy did, how their friends were doing, where help was needed most; but that was only for her comfort. In truth, she knew, no one would be listening.

She'd only climbed two-thirds the height; it was tall but slender and already the trunk had a whip in it, like the masthead in a wind. If she didn't keep still, it swayed like the masthead in a storm.

This was plenty high enough. The tree was just inside the settlement's palisade, and gave her a wide view over the cleared ground between here and the river. The forest's margin was a clear line, trees and undergrowth that gave quickly into shadow.

When shadows moved behind that line, she called down the news of it in one clear cry that went apparently unheeded in the stillness of the compound. Duty done, she went back to looking and worrying. The emperor was somewhere in that forest. He must by now have made contact with the rebels, blade to blade. He had others with him, but not enough: three fighters, how could they swear to his safety? He wasn't used to personal danger, he would forget; his fury and his arrogance together would carry him into a fight he couldn't win, and he'd be lost. Maybe he already was lost, just one more body in the woods . . .

She didn't know, she couldn't see.

What she did see, she saw the rebels come.

They came in a hurry, in a tight wedge, barely troubled by the light hail of stones from the youngsters across the river. Those were out in the open now, whirling and hurling, but to little avail: one man stumbled and recovered, a couple more would carry hard dark bruises for a while, no more harm than that.

Packed close under the sting of those stones, the solid phalanx charged toward the fence of timbers that circled the settlement.

Toward the gap in the fence, rather: as broad as two men lying head to head, where surely there ought to be a gate but somehow wasn't.

Impelled by rage and blood-hunger, stung on by stones, the sprinting rebels would have no time to wonder about that.

She hoped they'd have no time to wonder. When men run together, so hard, who will be the one to falter, to raise a question? And how can he make his companions listen?

Some will always be faster; there were three or four men leading the pack when they came to that alluring gap and plunged through.

Others were pressing close behind them. So close and so quick, they couldn't stop themselves in time when they saw the men ahead literally plunge through.

Through the ground they were trying to run on, that open and deceptive space that had looked so like a foolish welcome in . . .

WHERE THE miners had spent the last hours before dawn digging; where they had dug a pit and prepared it, and then spread bamboo splits across and covered those with leaves and soil to make it look entirely like the ground around.

Where the assassins were breaking the splits and falling through into the pit, and onto the sharpened bamboo spikes set like a miniature forest in the floor of it, so that their feet and hands and torsos were pierced as they fell. And as those who followed piled in on top of them, tumbling and stamping, crushing them down . . .

MEI FENG watched it happen from her eyrie. She saw the chaos and confusion, she saw the deaths and the terrible injuries; she saw the main body of rebels check at the pit's edge and mill uncertainly, stalled like cattle.

They might turn to track the palisade north or south, they might choose to force a way in right there, across the bodies of their brothers if they had to. Mei Feng was all ready to call it out across the compound, what they chose. People would know, but she would sing it out anyway, just to be involved . . .

Except that the fool emperor and his idiot companions came running hot on the rebels' trail, to offer them another choice. This was no part of any plan she'd heard, that a dozen stalled men could turn and see four people, just four of them, coming out of the trees.

Coming out and being seen and not faltering, not being sensible, not going back into cover . . .

MEI FENG screamed in her tree, but it was futile. Futile twice, because she screamed twice: once at the emperor, who presumably couldn't hear her because he paid no attention, just kept running straight at the rebels even as they ran to meet him; and once again at the miners, who didn't need to hear her.

They could see what was happening from their spy-holes, they were doing the only thing they could: cutting the bindings that held the palisade apparently together, north and south of the gateway where they had laid their two ambushes, where they had been waiting to intercept the rebels either way.

Palings fell from the fence, crashing down like unhinged gates as they were meant to. Men and women poured out, blades in their hands, as they were meant to. But they were meant to be confronting the rebels, and in fact they were chasing; it was all turned around, and they couldn't hope to catch up in time.

The rebels had come here to Taishu, here to the mountains, to kill the emperor; and the emperor was coming to give them their chance.

At a guess, he was just tired of running away. He had run for a year, at his mother's insistence; these last days he had been running again, running personally and physically from men he knew that he could beat. One to one, in an honest bout of blades, he could beat any of them. Any one. One by one, perhaps he could beat them all. He had seemed tireless in the forest; perhaps he truly was. She didn't know.

But this was no honest bout he was running to. There were a dozen men all wanting to kill him, and they would try it all at once; and she didn't think it would matter then how strong he was, how fast. With a blade in each hand, he still couldn't hope to block every blow.

He was not quite alone, of course, but only Yu Shan was keeping up. Yu Shan was only a fighter by courtesy of the jade in his blood; he had no skills. It would be folly to depend on him. Jiao and the other, Doshun, they were coming too, but more slowly. Too slowly, like the miners from the compound. Four blades against a dozen, that might almost have been fair odds, when it was those four who held them; but the emperor ran as though this were a race, and as though he meant to win it. Mei Feng was cursing him heedlessly as she stood on her branch and stretched to see better, as she swayed in her agitation, as the branch and the whole slim tree swayed with her.

She saw the moment when man met man, when her man met his; a moment later—because the gods delay all news—she heard the clash of it, blade on blade.

The rebels had chased all year across the world to achieve this. The emperor had fled an empire to avoid it. It was meant to be a great war, not this petty clash on uncertain ground. If she let go the trunk, she could cover the whole skirmish with one hand. Then she wouldn't have to watch . . .

If she climbed higher, perhaps she could see better. She saw the emperor meet the first man and at last—too late!—stop running; she saw the rebels gather around, a second man, a third . . .

She climbed with the distant sounds of steel and men like a blade under her own skin, working. It was good to climb, to focus on the immediacy of fingers and feet, grip and effort; but that was cowardice and she wanted to be better than that, and it was her man out there. The tree bent and kicked beneath her slight weight, but she had to look; she couldn't come this high and turn her face away.

She saw her emperor still on his feet, which was a blessing; still fighting, which was a wonder, he seemed to do it so well. He and the men who fought him spun and twisted and thrust while their blades flashed and blocked and went to strike. Yu Shan was there too now, and so were Jiao and Dushon, though they all lacked his grace. Her eyes came back to him and her heart steadied almost to a normal pulse, because he was magnificent and the others were reliable and the bodies on the ground were all rebels, and the miners from the compound would be there any moment now, and then surely she could swallow this choking lump of anxiety and simply admire her man in his strength, in his achievement, surrounded by all the gory corpses of his enemies . . .

BUT JUST then was when the sweet fleeting vision foundered, because he was careless or heedless or simply thought himself immortal, as the peasants were supposed to do.

There was a blade he did not block, a blow he didn't see or couldn't reach or thought would be stopped some other way, by someone else or some god's intervention because he was emperor and the Son of Heaven and so invulnerable to common mortal blades.

She didn't see the stroke herself. What she saw, of course, was him: him suddenly still, and then doubling over, falling amid the stamping feet and clashing blades of those who were still fighting.

His fall did little good to the man who must have struck him, because it opened up a space and Yu Shan stepped into it, hewing. She saw that stroke and what it did, how it hacked the rebel almost in two. That didn't matter, it was meaningless. What mattered was the emperor, one among that sprawl of bodies; she could barely see him through the shock and rally of his people, how they crowded around him.

She couldn't stay here, tree'd like a frightened animal; she wouldn't take the time to shin down before she could even start to run to where she had to be.

Instead, she climbed. The higher she went, the more the tree bent beneath her, until she was hanging from it upside-down, arms and legs both wrapped around the trunk as she determinedly worked her way upward. It swayed too, wildly now, worse than any masthead; Old Yen would never have let her climb in any storm this fierce.

But she climbed until she wasn't climbing anymore, until the tree had bent so far that its top was hanging toward the ground, so that she was actually letting herself down lower.

Then she hung by her arms and bounced, to get more action into the creaking wood. The tree's head dipped and sprang back, and tried to fling her off and couldn't do it and so dipped again, lower yet.

Dipped over the fence, and she let go just a moment before it would have sprung again. The tree whipped away from her in a battering of leaves and twigs, while she fell down through that and into soft wet mud where the miners were starting to dig a paddy.

Fell and rolled, and rose up smeared and foul, and no matter.

Rose up and ran heedless and barefoot to the fight.

· · ·

AND IT didn't matter, because the fight was over when at last she reached it. The last of the rebels lay dead, and she could overleap their bodies and shoulder her way through the crush of sweating, bleeding, slightly bewildered young people suddenly uncertain what to do with themselves. She could squeeze through to where her own people sat or knelt or lay on the ground. There was Doshun, crouched on his heels, awkwardly between his people and hers; there was Jiao, sitting cross-legged and quite calm in the midst of slaughter, examining a cut on her arm; there was Yu Shan, on his knees beside . . .

Beside the emperor, who lay broken on this broken ground, his robe ripped above the heart and sodden with blood.

She hurled herself down to lie full-sprawl at his side, nowhere quite touching him, because she couldn't bear that yet; and the worst of it was that he wasn't dead, that he turned his head to meet her eye to eye.

Stone-green eyes: she had seen them deep as undersea currents, dark as a cavemouth, flat with anger, always that immeasurable color.

Now, unaccountably, they were sunlight-shining, and she thought he was laughing at her.

It was an expression she was familiar with. His mouth wasn't really up to it, but there was a twitch in the corners that gave him away entirely.

She was almost outraged, except that she still had the blade in her own heart that must have cut so savagely at his. If he was taking these last moments to die, if perhaps he had lived this long to give her just the time she needed to reach him, that was heroic and epic and wonderful but he was still going to die. It was extraordinary that he was not dead already; his heart should have been half cut out by such a blow.

And if he really did choose to spend his final breaths in teasing her—well, that was his to do and hers to love him for. No place for outrage, though he was emperor of the world and it was unthinkable that he should die like this, outside some dirty scrub of a settlement in the elbow of a lost mountain valley, under the blade of a dead and meaningless assassin . . .

No place for tears either, if he was smiling. She wouldn't be mocked, not now. She swallowed down that rush of grief that was almost a terror in her mouth, a bitter dread of the world. Swallowed that and tried to smile back, or at the very least to scowl, as she often did when he mocked her—

—AND SAW him struggling to lever himself up onto one elbow, and cried out in protest, "Chien *Hua*!"—

—WHICH WAS no struggle at all to say his name, which drew out that feeble flicker of a smile again and didn't discourage him in the least.

So then there was nothing she could do but scramble onto her knees and take his head in her lap, to spare him the effort of supporting it. That put him oddly upside down but still smiling, getting better at it; and that hand of his was trying to guide itself to her cheek, not doing a very convincing job but close enough for her to snare it between both of hers, nest herself into the palm of it, struggle again not to cry until finally she did manage to listen to what Yu Shan was saying, at what was evidently his third or fourth attempt to make her hear.

"Mei *Feng*! He will be fine!"

"No," she said, shaking her head vigorously, "no, don't lie to him. Or me, don't lie to me. We're not blind, nor stupid," assertively, speaking for the emperor because he clearly had no breath to speak for himself.

"Look," Yu Shan said, and lifted back both sides of that terrible rent in the emperor's robe; ripped it farther, indeed, his hands clenching in the blood-soaked silk and tearing it like paper. Showing her that chest she knew so well, all swaddled in blood; and then wiping the torn silk across the great slashing open wound, to clear the wet dark blood away and let her see deeper.

She should have been seeing clear through to the literal heart of him, she should have been seeing that heart torn in its turn; but there was the rent flesh, and there was the pallid glimpse of bone below—but those were only rib bones, and they looked set and solid, as though simple bone had defied sharp steel.

She watched that trench in his chest darken again with blood, but it didn't seem even to be bleeding as freely as such a tearing wound demanded.

Watching seemed to be an impertinence, but she couldn't help it. She watched as the blood settled and clotted, as it sealed the wound, as it knitted edge to slashed edge of the emperor's flesh and skin. She had seen wounds enough aboard her grandfather's boat and others, among the villagers who sailed on other boats and came home hurt. She knew that no hurt behaved like this, healing itself as you watched.

Yu Shan smiled at her, self-satisfied.

She ignored him, as he deserved. And turned back to the emperor, whose smile had that mischief to it though it was still a weak and fugitive thing; and he tried to speak but she hushed him, her fingers covering that bewitching, bewildering mouth. And she scowled at Yu Shan—good, could still manage the scowl, then— and said, "How . . . ?"

Yu Shan lifted a hand to his own head, where a slingstone had caught him full-force on the temple. "The blade . . . slid off his bones, is all. He'll have a grand seam of a scar, maybe. But . . ."

"But it should have opened him up like a fish on the quay, and it didn't."

"Yes."

The emperor's lips moved, against her skin. She couldn't smile yet, but she did lift her hand away; except then it seemed that wasn't what he wanted. His frail scowl drew her fingers back to his lips again, where he kissed them lightly.

And closed his eyes and lay quiet, which was so unlike him; she said, "Why's he so weak?"

"He's lost a lot of blood. You can see . . ." She could; he lay in a swamp of it, though she didn't think it was all his. They were moving the bodies away now from around him. "Lucky he's got enough left to let him heal. He'll need rest, and food. Lots of food."

"And jade in it, I suppose?" There was an odd acidity in her voice that surprised her as much as it did Yu Shan. "It must be the jade in his bones that kept him alive. Like you, you too." Two Men of Jade in the world and somehow both of them here on this wretched patch of bloody mud, and listening to her. "And I suppose it's the jade in his blood that lets him heal while I, while I *watch,* but we'd better make sure he eats plenty more, if he's lost so much. You can, oh, you can dig it up for him, as we're here, and . . ."

And she didn't really know what she was saying, or why she was so upset, but it took the emperor to silence her: the slight shift of his head—impatient suddenly at his own weakness, and that was more like him, more like her man, the Son of Heaven, yes—and the voice that was barely recognizable, like the scrape of a blade against porcelain, the finest possible of scratchings: "Don't be angry with me, fishergirl. I didn't know. I broke my arm before," *before I was emperor,* he must mean, *before they started feeding me jade,* "and it just broke. Blame Yu Shan, he never told me I was invulnerable now . . ."

Yu Shan was shaking his head at everything. "You're not. Don't think it. That blade could have gone between your ribs, and then nothing would have saved you. And, well, I know I don't bleed much, and I've never broken anything, but I'm sure I could if I was careless . . ."

"And if you're thinking," another voice said drily, unexpectedly, "that you might just chop Yu Shan up into little pieces to see, the way you've been testing him in other ways, you really might want to think again, majesty. That boy's mine."

And Jiao drew a slow stone along the blade's edge of her tao, and eyed the emperor's ribs with a lurid speculation.

And the emperor—to whom they all belonged, to whom Yu Shan's life particularly was and always would be forfeit—smiled privately, inwardly, and didn't argue; and then rolled his eyes back to find Mei Feng's, and said, "Do you think you could find a run-ner here, who would know the way to the Autumn Palace?"

"I'm sure of it, lord."

"Good. Send a couple, then, to be sure. People will be frantic. They are to say that I am safe and in the hills, visiting the jade mines. They are not to say that I am hurt; only that I will spend some time here, and return when I am ready.

"Then tell them to find that pet messenger of yours, have him take them to the city and give the same news to General Ping Wen. Only, they can tell the general something else as well. Tell him, I think I may have found a new imperial guard, to replace those who were slaughtered where we bathed . . ."

seven

The beacon fire had blazed all night. Li Ton's sparse crew had sweated all night, to ensure that it did. The captain had sweated too, helping to haul fuel up from the ruined settlement or else to ax and trim fresh timber from the slopes, but that was small consolation.

For Han, no consolation at all. There was none, in Li Ton or in the world. Only in Tien, and watching her labor at his side did nothing to heal his soul; watching her flinch in sympathy with him did nothing to heal his hand, which was agony too soon and abiding all night long.

Even Tien couldn't see into his head, to know how he struggled there to keep the dragon quenched. Great effort, small results. Exhaustion and pain together might have been excuse enough for his dry sobbing desperation, but in truth it was the madness that battered at his mind. Or the fear of madness as the dragon battered at him, relentless, merciless.

He saw her face in the fire, as he fed it; he felt her yearning for the winds, for the sea's freedom, for light and dance and destruction, the power and authority that were long since stolen from her. He was all that stood in her way, and even chained as she was, crushed by centuries of sea-burial, she was mighty; she was a mountain, where he was a grain of sand. She showed him that, and reached to roll over, to crush him, to lose him utterly beneath her bulk . . .

"Han . . . ?"

He grunted; he didn't seem to have words anymore. She didn't deal in words. Her mind roiled inside his like a boil of water, blistering, flooding him with her heat of images, sensations, feelings. Her long-pent fury, his weary fear.

"Han, stop." Tien's two hands wrapped around his one, the good one, below the cuff of his chains. All her slight weight hauled at him, until he was still. "We can rest now. See, it's dawn already? They won't see the fire now, there's no point . . ."

There had been no point for the last long time; if they hadn't seen it yet, they weren't at all looking. Li Ton had kept them working for the celebration of his rage, his joy at being able to strike a blow against empire, even empire so weak it had retreated to one tiny island. Empire so weak that its last downfall would come from betrayal, from within. Li Ton could initiate that betrayal, set the final blow in motion, and he exulted in it; this beacon wasn't only the signal to launch the invasion, it was his own furious rejoicing blazed out to the stars.

Even now, he wasn't finished. Han heard his voice, somewhere in the shadows behind: "Yes, rest now. Watch the sun come up. Then help me gather the trimmings," all the greenery, the leaves and branches they'd cut from fresh-felled timber, "and throw those on the fire. If no one will see flame now, we will send them smoke . . ."

So when they had rested, they raised a pillar of white smoke instead, and sent it creeping cautiously higher and higher in the still air. Han could barely see it. His world was pain on the outside, in the clumsy case that was his body, and terror within; his eyes that should have joined the two together were a broken gate.

Tien pleaded with Li Ton to let them stop now, surely they were done; he said, "You, yes. You can sit and watch to the north, and cry out what you see. The boy, though, I want him. Over here."

He was sitting on the forge's great anvil, which stood close enough to the beacon fire that it was warm to the touch even on the side that didn't face the heat. Li Ton had one of the smithy's old chisels in his hand, and was sharpening the edge of it on a stone. Han went, because Tien took him over; he sat on the ground because Tien nudged him to it, with his back to that warmth and his face turned to the sea.

Then Tien was gone. He hadn't closed his eyes, but he might as well have; unless it was right in front of him, nothing in the outer world could reach past the dragon.

He heard Li Ton's breathing, he felt the man's movements, he knew when one big hand reached over his shoulder to heft the weight of chains where they hung from his neck. It was all removed, though, all distanced, as though it were a story someone told him once, about a boy in trouble. What was immediate, what was real was the struggle in his head.

It was only the dragon who was struggling now, reaching for her freedom; he was too dulled by exhaustion to try to quell her anymore. She could do no harm in his head, except to him, and he didn't believe she could kill him. Which meant—which should mean—that these chains would hold. Weakly, unreliably, but he thought that they would hold.

Why fight, then? When all it did was drain him further? Let her rave, let her surge, let her storm and peak; she would subside at last, she'd have to.

He thought.

Li Ton said, "Raise your dragon again, boy. Do it for me. Have her rise in this sea, just here, where I can see her do it."

"What? No . . . !"

The sting of Li Ton's hand across his ear, a sharp little pain that helped to clear his head, just a little, to pull him a short way back into the world. The great throbbing hurt in his maimed hand was something else, more inclined to push him away.

"You're forgetting, boy, you belong to me. You do what I tell you."

No. No, he didn't. Not this. Astonishingly, he found a way to say so: "I belong to the *Shalla*, not to you."

"And the *Shalla* belongs to me," and his hand struck again, almost welcome, "and so therefore do you. Must I explain this again?"

"Does she so?" Han asked, almost astonished by his willingness to argue with the captain, absolutely astonished by his ability to do so while the dragon surged in his skull. "I heard she was taken into the emperor's fleet; the general gave you charge of the fisherman's boat instead. I don't think I belong to you. I think I belong to the emperor now."

"That's what you think, is it?"

This time, when Li Ton's hand lifted, it had that chisel in it.

Even so, Han faced him with a curious certainty. "You won't hurt me. My life isn't yours anymore, to be commanded."

"Most of the men I've killed have not been my own men, boy, and they have died regardless."

"I'm sure." He had seen, indeed: on this island, right here in front of the Forge, he had seen men die at Li Ton's whim. "But I crewed for you and worked for you, and I don't believe you'll kill me now. What would be the point? There's no shipful of men to impress or discipline. And if I'm dead, you lose any hope of the dragon."

Or the other thing, perhaps, he earned a great certainty of the dragon: but not under his control, which was all that interested him.

"Well, perhaps I can find another way to . . . persuade you. Tien! Over here!"

Han wanted to say *No, don't, run away . . . !* But of course she came, wary and suspicious and tired to the bone, but she came; and all her watchful nervousness did her no good at all, because Li Ton simply reached out a long arm and seized her by the hair. And held his chisel to her throat instead of Han's, and said, "Now, boy? Call up your dragon!"

Still, Han didn't move; nor did he surrender. He said, "Tien is not yours to kill, any more than I am. She belongs to the *Shalla* too."

"Which means, you say, to the emperor. Whose enemy I am, and whose people I will not hesitate to destroy. But I say that's nonsense anyway, the *Shalla* is mine and so are you and she, and I will have your obedience or she will die for it. You two think you belong to each other. It isn't true, but I can use it nonetheless. I want to see that dragon rise, out there beyond the rocks."

Han could see how the weight of the blade pressed into Tien's soft skin, just above the slender vessels of her throat; he could see how the edge of it was chipped but lethally sharp; he could see how desperately still she held herself, and what little difference that made.

He could see the defeat in her eyes, as she stared mutely into his. She knew as surely as he did, what he would do next. What he would try to do.

If he failed, if there was a penalty for failure—well, even he didn't know what he would do then.

He said, "I don't know if I can raise her. Everything we've done, everything the doctor's taught me and Suo Lung before him," *before the assassins killed him, because he wouldn't leave me: before they hewed his throat and threw him over the side, to no purpose, while you watched,* "it's all been about keeping her suppressed. When she rises, it's because she's attacking me, trying to break free. I don't know how to rouse her; I don't know if I can."

"I suggest you learn," Li Ton said, his hand moving no more than Tien did, the chisel rock-steady at her throat. "I suggest you try, and keep trying, and hope to succeed. Soon."

THERE WAS that space in his head where she lurked, the darkness she struck from when she rose. The place where her voice was a mocking whisper when she spoke. When she chose to speak.

He had never chosen to speak to her, never thought to poke her into stirring. He thought this was madness. Whether it was his madness or Li Ton's might be debatable, but he would be the one to suffer from it. Tien would be the one to suffer otherwise, so there was truly no alternative.

Another boy—one who didn't understand Li Ton, or care about Tien—might have tried to pretend. Not Han: he wouldn't, couldn't be that stupid with someone else's life.

He reached inside himself, sent his awareness to that dark place in his mind and tried to peer into it.

Thought he'd failed from the outset, because he didn't see her in there peering back at him, great vicious eyes that shone against the dark.

Called out to her anyway, to show willing if only to himself, to be sure that he was genuinely trying:

—*Are you there? Will you come?*

—*I am always here. I am chained.*

Her response was like a whip of hot iron across his mind, searing and scarring; and yet it came from far away, far down.

He said to her:

—*Come up.*

—*Come down,* she said.

And he felt her tug at him, as though he could topple all the way into his own mind, into this crevice that was somehow a connection to her. Topple and fall, plunge all that way like poor doomed Yerli, knowing all the fall that she would be waiting at the bottom . . .

He hung on, he teetered back from that dangerous edge, he would not go to her.

—*Come up.*

—*Little thing, you have been struggling against me all this time, trying to keep me down here when I would rise. Are you so eager to see me now?*

Eager, not; terrified would be a better way to say it. Urgent, though, yes.

—*Come up. Will you come?*

—*In my time, little thing. I promise you, in my own time I will come.*

—*Now, though. Now, will you come? Please?*

—*To please you?* Her laugh was acid, burning in his skull. *You might as well say, to obey you. Little thing, you do not understand. Yet. Wait till you are a little broken thing, and we will practice obedience, you and I.*

And then she did rise, but only in his head: a sudden uprushing that he felt like a ravening wind, that ripped at his thoughts until he had none, until they were all frayed into rags and nothing, until he opened his eyes and was staring at rock so close he couldn't focus on it, and there were noises that were outside his head and not her, not come from her . . .

His sense of self came back to him, and found him lying on his side; and those noises were voices, Tien babbling breathlessly and entirely overborne by Li Ton saying, "Aye, go to him, girl, if you must. Pick him up, give him water, calm him down. Then we will do this again. He knows what he has to fear now; he'll try it and try it, and we'll see if he can. If he can't—well. He knows what he has to fear. So do you."

And so those hands on his body lifting him, setting his back against the warmth of the anvil again, they were Tien's hands; and if he turned his head, if he concentrated, he could see them, anxious and clinging. Or he could turn his head the other way, and see her face.

Focus on that, and try to speak, and fail: words were too complex, he couldn't remember how to shape them in his mouth or how to work the air to make them sound.

Just sit, then, and look at her until he heard Li Ton's voice again, they both did, summoning:

"Here, see this: this is what you've worked for all the night . . ."

Tien's hands on his shoulders said *Stay there,* as she pushed herself up on her feet to go and see for both of them. They were pretty feet, he thought, dirty though they were; but once they were out of his field of vision, he didn't have any reason to go on sitting there. He'd rather be where she was, and look at her some more.

Standing up was an exercise in ruthless rediscovery: working his legs, his arms, finding a balance, finding his way.

Toward Tien, that was his way: who was standing by Li Ton and looking out across the long glitter of the sea.

Han didn't go far, just a pace or two. From here by the anvil he could see both Tien and the waters beyond; that was good enough.

Li Ton's voice came back to him, though it was pitched for Tien: "Here it comes, see: doom for the emperor, that army he's been fleeing all this time."

There were dots, specks on the water, countless little shadows that were not in Han's head or a blur in his eyes, and not actually so little at all. Every one of those flecks was a boat, and presumably crammed with soldiers, and they would flood over all Taishu and slaughter the emperor and all his men.

And Han didn't really care about one army fighting another, and he didn't really care who won. But Li Ton did; and Li Ton might well believe that this coming army would be enough, and he might well be right, but he certainly thought that the coming army with a dragon too would be invincible. And he was certainly right about that, and he would certainly do whatever he could to make it happen.

Which meant that he would drive Han back to the chasm in his head, time and again, to try to raise the dragon. And he might have left the chisel on the anvil for now, but Tien's life still hung against the edge of it whether or not it pressed against her jugular.

Li Ton was accustomed to keeping his promises, carrying out his threats. Han couldn't control the dragon for him; he couldn't even raise her. Li Ton would never believe that, though. Which meant that sooner or later, when he lost patience, Tien would die.

Unless Han could show him, *prove* to him that he had no control over the dragon, that there was no controlling her . . .

Han didn't care about the armies, or the emperor, or the war. He didn't, he couldn't care about people he had never met, or courts he had never imagined.

What he cared about had always been limited, and was growing tighter, narrower by the day. Right now he thought there was nothing within its bounds except himself and Tien, and perhaps her uncle too.

Her uncle would be upset whatever he did, and so might Tien, but he couldn't let her die. That was all, it was absolute.

When it was clear that the dragon had no cause to listen to Han, perhaps Tien would be let live.

Perhaps.

It was all he had.

MANY OF the smithy tools were still here, spilled onto the ground now that the racks they'd hung from had been fed into the beacon fire.

Han picked up a lump hammer and carried it back to the anvil.

He laid the slack of his chains across the iron, set the chisel's edge against a link, hefted the hammer and brought it down.

Cut the link.

Broke the chain.

Set the dragon free.

eight

This time, she was ready.

Drenched under spells of sleep and simple weight of water, she had been too slow before, when she felt the chain part: slow to wake and slower to understand, far too slow to move. Her awkwardness had left them time enough to chain her again. Not well—it was hard, they had found, to chain a dragon in her rage—but enough to hold her, more or less. In the strait and under the water, on the bed of her long prison.

They hadn't contrived to soothe her, to lull her into sleepfulness, however much they tried to load that word upon her. She was alert, and scheming. She had fought in her own body, and heaved it in its chains as far as the sea's surface and breathed air just for a moment; she had fought the boy—the weak, stupid, confused, and frightened *boy* they'd chosen to bear the shadow of her chains, which was an insult and would be repaid—in his own body, and had him close to breaking.

And then, now, he broke the chains himself, deliberately. Which she had not anticipated, had not been working for and could not credit; but she watched it happen from inside his head, she felt her sudden freedom and seized it in that moment.

THE DRAGON ROSE.

NOT AS before, struggling against chains every fathom of the deep. She struck upward to the light and felt no weight and no resistance, had nothing to fight; she carried nothing with her but herself, this body. This sinuous, stretching, exulting body that twisted and writhed through the water, that relished the flow of it across scales and skin, that rejoiced in her own power as she thrust water aside, as she broke into air, as she spread the wings of her will and soared as easily as she had swum.

Exultation, rejoicing, she had those; and she had her perpetual anger still, which was not assuaged.

Humans had done this to her, puny humans had chained her and left her chained. In the centuries she'd lain below, she'd been dimly, distantly aware of constant traffic above her head, boats always on the water—*her* water!—as though she could be utterly disregarded, as though she mattered not at all.

Well, she mattered now.

All her waters were newly clear to her, as they had not been for so very long; she felt the tides, the currents like her own extended breath, she felt the ridges and caverns of the seabed like her own skin. And the surface too, that too was her own, every ruffled wave, every cast of spume where it broke on rocks; and every boat that broke it, she felt those, every one, like a sea-thorn against her skin, scratching.

She felt a great many of them, those intrusive boats, right here where she had breached.

She was free now, and she need not tolerate it. She would not tolerate it. She would assert her freedom, reclaim her waters, show the world who was the master here . . .

SHE TUMBLED in the air and swooped down low, and came to the first of those very many boats, and didn't bother even to open her long mouth.

She struck the boat abeam—though they would call it a ship, probably, these petty mortals, they had crowded so many of themselves aboard it—and felt its planking splinter beneath the impact.

One snapped mast fell across her head, and the sail draped itself over her eye, but that was nothing; she flung herself into a loop and it fell away, to let her see how many men were clinging to the shattered wreckage, how many already in the water.

. . .

ANOTHER BOAT, and she did this one the grace of opening her jaws to seize it, to lift it from the water, to shake the clinging, screaming men from its decks and rigging before she closed her mouth again and crushed it.

AND SPAT it out and took the next one in her claws, for variety. And snapped it in two and dropped the broken halves of it, and found one fool man still gripped to her claw; and bent her head and took him in her teeth and swallowed him, and turned back to the water.

AND DID not leave that little stretch of water until there was not a single boat left floating in it, but only the ruin of boats. And those men who could still swim, and some of those who could not, floating now in their deaths. Others she had fed on. Some lucky few, she supposed, might survive if they found wreck enough to cling to, if the sharks didn't find them before they could kick their way to shore.

THEY COULD keep their luck. She didn't care; she meant to fly the bounds of her territory, all the stretch of the strait, to let the disbelieving see that she was free and home again.

THERE WAS one human more to deal with, but he could wait.

SHE KNEW where to find him, after all. He was in her head.

IN HER *head* . . . !

acknowledgments

Nothing in this book would have happened without the Taipei City Government, who originally took me to Taiwan. I am abidingly grateful to them, and to Stanley Yen of the Ritz Landis hotel; also to Olivia Chen who held my hand both then and later on, and Amelia Hong who invited me back to Taiwan and offered me a floor to sleep on, and I do hope she meant it, because I did most certainly go.

about the author

DANIEL FOX is a British writer who first went to Taiwan at the millennium and became obsessed, to the point of learning Mandarin and writing about the country in three different genres. Before this he had published a couple of dozen books and many hundreds of short stories, under a clutch of other names. He has also written poetry and plays. Some of this work has won awards.